STRANGE
FORTUNE

STRANGE FORTUNE

JOSH LANYON

Blind Eye Books
blindeyebooks.com

Strange Fortune
by Josh Lanyon
Published by:
Blind Eye Books
1141 Grant Street
Bellingham, WA 98225
blindeyebooks.com

Edited by Nicole Kimberling
Cover art by Dawn Kimberling

This book is a work of fiction and as such all characters and situations are fictitious. Any resemblance to actual people, places or events is coincidental.

First edition December 2009
Copyright 2009 Josh lanyon   12-1-09
Printed in the United States of America.

ISBN 978-1-935560-00-5

Library of Congress Control Number: 2009937003

Dedication

To Jessica K., a brave spirit and a generous heart.
Thank you for many hours of delightful discourse.

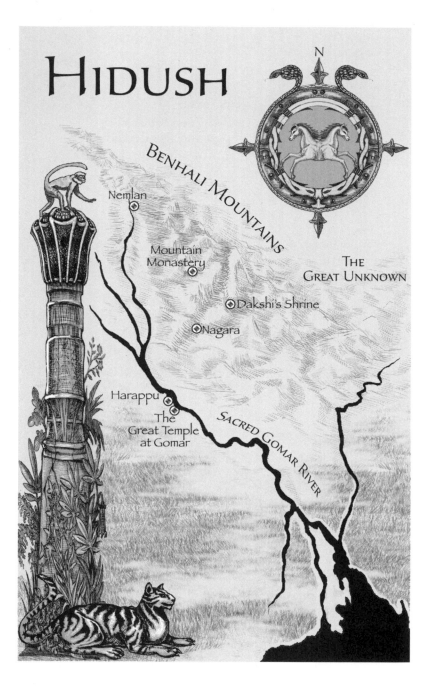

HIDUSH

N

BENHALI MOUNTAINS

THE GREAT UNKNOWN

Nemlan

Mountain Monastery

Dakshi's Shrine

Nagara

Harappu

The Great Temple at Gomar

SACRED GOMAR RIVER

Contents

CHAPTER ONE

The bite of spade on stone rang hollowly in the excavation site.

This was followed by an equally ringing silence—and then shouts of dismay. From what Major Valentine Strange, late of the Emperor of Alba's 21st Regiment of Benhali Lancers, discerned, a nest of baby cobras had been discovered in the bowels of the ancient temple. Just one of any number of unpleasant surprises that had been laid bare as the bones of the old building were picked clean.

The Great Temple was less than an hour's ride from the noise and bustle of the great capital city of Harappu to the eerie green silence of the jungle where the ruins of the ancient tombs had lain buried for centuries. Unsettling really, were Strange a fanciful man, to note how fast the jungle moved in to reclaim its own once life had departed.

Sometimes before life had departed.

In the great open pit below, Strange could see the excavated walls and courtyards where native laborers, the marl— worker caste—were running around like ants in a downpour. Typical. No discipline. No organization. The only surprise was that the Holy Orders could find anyone at all to work the site. A lot of unsavory legends about these ruins.

Untroubled, Strange continued on his way down the rickety wooden stairway. Sultry early autumn heat shimmered from the torn, wet earth. Behind the veil of humidity, the crooked towers and broken statuary gleamed with the eerie pale blue light that proclaimed this a place of Power. Which, in Strange's opinion, was good enough reason to steer clear, but he had an appointment here today—and the promise of a job.

Strange needed a job. Rather urgently. His luck at the tables had not been the best lately, nor had he been able to recoup his losses on the polo fields. In any case, he was growing bored again. Bored with civilian life, bored with the rules and rituals of polite Harappun society. He was beginning to reminsce fondly of his good old days in the cavalry. That was always a bad sign.

Insects droned in the heavy air. Something skittered away through the golden ferns on the hillside. Strange glanced its way, but did not slow his brisk progress down the stairway built into the hillside by the excavators though he was glad of his tall riding boots. Many unhealthy things, both natural and magical, lurked in this place. The disinterring had halted during the Inborn Mutiny, but now the temple was the focus of much national interest as the Alban colonial rulers tried to legitimise their century-long reign by allying themselves with conquered Hidush's mystical past.

After nineteen years spent protecting the frontier border from the menace of outlaws and outcaste—not to mention suppressing manifestations of that same mystical past —Strange found this turn of events grimly amusing, but then he'd been told he had a black sense of humor. He'd killed the man who told him so in a duel, although that had happened a few years later. Nothing to do with the bloke's boorish sense of humor and everything to do with the honor of their regiment. Or so Strange had believed at the time. He had been much younger then.

He was thirty-six now. He felt a good deal older.

Reaching the bottom of the staircase, he crossed the cracked and missing colored paving stones of an enormous courtyard. He could see that once the interlocking pieces had formed the austere face of the moon, but now one eye and several pieces of mouth were missing, giving the image a half-blind and toothless look. Wild flowers and herbs grew in clumps between the bricks.

Strange spoke briefly to one of the Natal guards at the temple door, showing her the indigo-edged card he had received. Blunt features impassive, her green eyes studied the card closely before she handed it back with a nod.

Strange continued down a winding, steep stairway lit by primitive wall torches. The flames cast odd shadows against the irregular stone walls. Beyond the hiss of the torches he caught the whisper of voices from down below. Two voices in quiet argument augmented by the weird accustics of the ancient architecture.

"I tell you, it's not a matter of being afraid. There is something here."

"Of course there's something here! This is a temple. Purya's own temple. A place of great and awesome power."

"You're not listening to me. That chamber has nothing to do with Purya. It's much older."

The second voice hissed, "*Older than Purya?* Beware, Grimshaw. You risk heresy."

"Oh for the sake of...why won't you listen to me? I tell you, something ancient has awakened here. It's watching us. Learning us."

"Nonsense."

At the bottom of the stairway, an arched doorway lead into a cavernous chamber. Daylight dappled the floor and leaves drifted gently through the great holes in the ceiling. In the center of the chamber was a huge green marble edged pool fed by an underground spring. In the center of the pool was a very large golden statue, the features of which were obscured by moss. Beside the pool stood two men. One was tall and thin and fair in the way of Alban true bloods. The other was the most beautiful man Strange had ever seen.

The beautiful man, who wore the rich blue-purple garb of a priest, beckoned to Strange. "Ah! Major Strange, is it not?" He smiled, and for a moment Strange forgot anyone else was in the room. "I'm Brahman Ehimay Warrick. I sent for you."

"Holiness," Strange said, shaking hands.

Warrick was shorter than himself. He had the creamy complexion and the wide, tawny gaze of the half-blood. His hair was dark as a raven's wing. Taken individually, the parts of him were nothing distinctive, and yet the sum was extraordinary.

"I'm delighted you've come."

"I was intrigued by your invitation," Strange admitted. "It's not often I find my services required by the Holy Orders." Although if anyone could afford to pay for them, it was certainly the church.

As though reading his mind, the priest chuckled. His ears and hands were adorned by the saphhires and gold of his station, and though he was quite young— several years younger than Strange—he had the assurance of a church elder. He turned. "And this is Master Aleister Grimshaw."

Master. A witch then. Valentine Strange was not fond of witches. In fact, he probably disliked witches more than magicians, which was saying something. At least you knew where you were with the paid practitioners of magic. Not that witches didn't have their uses, though they were mostly scholars and academics these days. The Church certainly put them to good use—native borns anyway. Not quite so much demand for the true bloods since the Inborn Mutiny when the witches of Alban descent had joined with the insurgents.

"Major Strange," Grimshaw murmured, offering a perfunctory hand. His lashes veiled his eyes. His eyebrows were dark and delicately winged. He had a bony, intelligent face, neither attractive nor unattractive. His skin was honey-colored and his hair was ash blonde. He was probably about the age of

Brahman Warrick. A small gold earring pierced his left earlobe, indicating the witch strain was on the maternal side.

"Master Grimshaw," Strange said, and the younger man flicked him a quick uncertain look at something he heard—or didn't hear—in Strange's tone. His eyes were gray, not the expected blue of the true blood.

"Have we met?" Grimshaw asked warily.

"Not to my knowledge."

Braham Warrick said, "You'll soon know each other very well indeed. That is—if you'll hear me out?"

Strange suddenly realized something that had been secretly bothering him since he had entered the excavation pit. There were no monkeys. Despite the leafy bowers provided by the towering trees lining the excavation site, Strange had not heard the chatter of a single monkey since his arrival.

Odd. Very odd indeed.

"That's why I'm here, Holiness," Strange replied.

Grimshaw said nothing—although he looked as though he wished to.

"You won't mind my speaking as we walk," the priest said. "Much of the excavation of the temple is my responsibility. I'd like to show you something." He rested a light hand on Strange's sleeve, and then turned leading the way from the main chamber.

Grimshaw followed behind, and Strange found himself oddly aware of that tall, silent presence as Brahman Warrick paused to light a brass lantern.

"I've heard that you're a man who gets things done, Major Strange. That you have experience and discretion as well as courage—and that you know the Benhali Mountains as much as any Alban can know them." He didn't wait for an answer. "You've heard of the Diadem of Purya?"

"I can't say that I have," Strange admitted. He thought, but was not sure that the witch gave a little snort from behind them.

Brahman Warrick was unphazed. "Long ago, when the world was threatened by fire and demons, Our Lady Purya went into battle and defeated the monsters and destroyers, and from the dying flames and the gouged-out eyes of demons, she forged a diadem to be worn by her successor the next time the world was in great peril."

News to Strange, but he was not much interested in the Hidush dieties. In fact, he didn't put much stock in any deity, although like most colonial soldiers he wore the likeness of Brigantia on a small silver medallion. After a century of occupation Purya had been largely amalgamated with the Alban goddess. Strange had heard rumors of a movement to bring back the old faith, but there were always such rumors in a land of religious fanatics.

He drawled, "One does like to face such things appropriately kitted out."

Brahman Warrick laughed, but there was an edge in his voice as he said, "That was something else I'd heard about you. That you take few things seriously and lack reverence."

As a matter of fact Strange took a number of things seriously. These included, but were not restricted to, the meticulous care of his weapons, the health and welfare of his polo ponies, and gambling debts. He also put high value on fine brandy and a cheroot after an evening meal shared with good friends—of which he had many. All of whom would have earnestly advised him against getting involved in anything to do with the church.

"I'm not much for old legends," Strange stated. He could see where Warrick was headed. In these days of civil unrest, the church—or rather the emperor—needed some symbol of unity and Power, which was why they were revisiting the abandoned excavation at Gomar.

"But Major Strange, one man's legend is another man's crusade." Warrick sounded unexpectedly cheerful. The witch made no comment.

They were halfway down a long winding stairway. The smell of damp and incense made Strange's nostrils twitch in distaste. Something dashed between his boots, and he nearly stumbled, reaching out to the slimy wall. He saw a white rat racing down the steps ahead. It vanished into the murky darkness below. The shadows from Warrick's lantern swung across the glistening walls, briefly illuminating the enigmatic moons and shooting stars carved into the stones.

"You seem to have made remarkable progress on the excavation of late. I remember when the only sign of this temple was the tip of the tallest tower poking through the earth that buried it."

"We've made progress," the priest agreed. "Not as much as we would wish, but then so much of our work was undone during the late uprising—"

Strange could feel the stark silence emanating from Grimshaw like a field of energy. *Grimshaw...yes. He remembered that name now. One of the oldest true blood families. Reformers and do-gooders who had sided with the Inborn rebels—and faced the same fate. This would be the son and grandson—too young to have taken part in the Mutiny. His dam must have been well-connected indeed, since he was not only practicing The Craft, he was employed by the Holy Orders.*

They had reached the bottom level now. Wet and mud lay on the floor, and the smell of burned out torches and forgotten sepulchers permeated the air. A dead snake lay a few feet from the staircase.

"This way," Brahman Warrick said, squleching ahead.

Strange glanced back at Grimshaw who held his gaze without expression.

A short hallway lead to a small room with an alcove at the far end. Once the walls had been painted, but only ghostly streaks remained beneath the mold and damp. There were shelves for books and scrolls, but the shelves were empty. In the alcove stood a battered statue. The youth depicted in marble must have been beautiful, but at some point he'd fallen on his chisled face and smashed his nose and pouty mouth. He still looked amazingly confident for all that. In one hand he held a sword, in the other, a small red glass globe. His breastplate was emblazoned with a cobra.

"Behold the goddess Purya," Brahman Warrick said. "She's not merely an old legend, you see."

Goddess?

Strange approached the statue slowly. It was a beautiful piece of workmanship that could make cold marble look warm and lithe and supple. Impressive. Not that the existence of the statue of a minor diety and proof the diety had been worshipped indicated the diety had actually *lived*; priests had trouble with those kinds of distinctions. This individual had likely been a young sorcerer of some kind—with excellent press.

"Look at her face," the priest ordered.

Her face? Mildly, Strange said, "Rather a…robust little thing, isn't she?" Leave it to a priest to get it wrong, but this happened to be one of Strange's fields of expertise—if he did say so himself.

"Indeed." Warrick's tone was quelling, understanding perfectly.

Well, if it made him happy to believe this lissome youth was his goddess, it was nothing to Strange, was it? As though reading his thoughts, the priest said with unexpected archness, "I suppose people often see what they wish to in the beauty of others."

Vaguely entertained though he was by the implication that "people" were something Warrick had only viewed at a safe distance, Strange was less amused—and he did not think he imagined it—by the suggestion that he would wish a goddess into a god. Not that the love of men carried the same stigma for colonials that it did for native born, but it had been many a year since he'd given into the temptation of "soldier's affection."

He said neutrally, "I've not stayed alive this long by seeing only what I wished to see."

"Perhaps not. Turn your gaze then to this and tell me what you see."

Strange followed the graceful gesture, and his gaze narrowed.

There was a smooth, slightly indented band around the statue's curly marble crown—just about the width of a diadem? He threw a look at Brahman Warrick who was watching him with a suggestion of smug knowingness.

"So you see," Warrick said. "What we wish you to retrieve is Purya's own diadem. And we will pay you two hundred thousand rupees to do it."

Two hundred thousand…!

After the first astonished flash of understanding, he felt a dizzy rush of shocked jubiliation. Two…hundred… thousand…

Had he misheard? But no. Warrick was standing there, smiling, looking pleased with himself, looking intent and…eager.

Half his problems solved in one instant. Just like that…his difficulties halved as though by the fall of an axe.

He was very careful not to give himself away.

"And you'll pay me that whether I succeed or not?"

The witch made sound. Not a laugh exactly. Not a cough. Something in between. Surprisingly cynical for such a small sound.

The priest's face changed. The pretty mouth turned down. Strange regretted having to disappoint such a beautiful young man. "We'll advance you half, certainly, if you agree to go. But it's a great deal of money and we're paying for results. That's why we're hiring you. You're a man who gets results."

Oh yes. He was a man who got results. That was one thing that had not changed.

Still, he had to try his hand. He needed the money too badly not to make the attempt. For all he knew, his…creditors might not let him leave this city without more on account.

And the truth was, as much as he needed the money—and he needed it desperately—the sheer mad adventure of it appealed. Appealed strongly. Reminded him of the old days. The good old days.

Cooly, Strange tipped his head to the side, studying the statue. "I don't deny the idea intrigues me. But if I'm to spend how many months of my life searching for this trinket—"

"Oh! But that's just it." Warrick brightened at this promising sign that they might reach a compromise. "We know exactly where the diadem is. It's in a monastery somewhere in the Benhali Mountains. For years we've heard rumors of it. Now we know that the stories must be true."

"Why must they be true?"

Warrick blinked. "Er…it's difficult to explain. However, in case it *is* a trick, Master Grimshaw will go with you. He's an expert in such antiquities."

"I'll *what*?" Master Grimshaw said, coming suddenly to life.

"You'll travel with Major Strange into the Benhali Mountains," Warrick said. The gazes of the two younger men locked and held. It was the witch who looked away first. His profile was stonier than the statue's as he stared at nothing.

Warrick threw Grimshaw an exasperated look, and then turned the full battery of his smile onto Strange. "We have it on good authority that the priests there are willing to sell the diadem. What we mostly need here is someone to negotiate for us and bring the relic safely back through the mountains. From everything we've discovered there is no man in Harappu better equipped for such a challenge than you, Major Strange. Will you take on this quest for us?"

"If you pay me the two hundred thousand rupees up front, yes." As the priest opened his mouth, Strange continued dispassionately, "I know the White Mountains well. Too well to discount the difficulty of the task you ask. There are no guarantees, and if I don't come back I should still like to know my debts have been honorably discharged."

Warrick's gold-brown eyes met his own. He seemed to be weighing unpleasant alternatives. His gaze shifted to the tense, mute figure of the witch.

"Very well," he said reluctantly at last. "You shall have the money upfront. And if you fail—well, you must *not* fail, Major Strange."

It was all Strange could do to preserve an appropriately grave expression. He asked blandly, "When do I leave?"

Chapter Two

Fool that he was, Aleister rushed into speech the moment the sound of Major Strange's bootheels had died away.

"What are you doing? I can't leave now."

And Ehimay—now (and forever more) Brahman Warrick to Master Grimshaw—had given him that long, equable stare and then the faintly distasteful smile that never failed to raise the hair on the back of Aleister's neck.

"Walk with me, Master Grimshaw," he ordered gently, and they had left the inner chamber of the earlier shrine—the shrine the Holy Orders erroneously insisted was part of Purya's much later temple—to walk in the ruined courtyard where no one might overhear.

"I had hoped that by lightening your workload we might avoid this conversation." Warrick sighed. "I suppose that was unrealistic. You've never been particularly…"

Tactful? Cooperative? Smart? Probably all three in Ehimay's view. And perhaps he was right for Aleister couldn't help replying. "We both know why you want to send me off on this fool's errand."

"We both certainly know why you *imagine* I want to send you away," Warrick said with asperity.

"You can't honestly believe that…that rogue is going to manage to find, let alone deliver, a priceless mystical artifact into your hands."

"He doesn't have to find it. He merely has to deliver it. And he's a rather charming rogue, don't you think? I thought that might appeal to you given your…appetites."

They were both silent as a miniature dust devil spun and bounced across the broken stones of the courtyard like a top and dissipated in the hot, humid air.

"You had a taste for it once yourself, as I recall," Aleister said a little bitterly.

Warrick's tawny gaze met his own levelly. "But I outgrew it, as one should."

"And entered the priesthood."

It still hurt sometimes, remembering. Silly, really. Ehimay had always known what he wanted and had been straightforward about it.

"Yes." Warrick said. "I joined the Holy Orders, and it is the wish of the Holy Orders that you accompany Major Strange on this quest."

"*Why?* You could send anyone on such an endeavor. Why send me unless you're deliberately—"

"Of course it's deliberate!" Warrick snapped into Aleister's astonished silence. More calmly, even kindly, he said, "The Bishop is concerned that we've demanded too much of you—and for too long. He fears—and I concur—that the balance of your mind has once more been affected."

Aleister stiffened. "That's nonsense!"

"It's not nonsense. I suppose it's not even surprising given the unfortunate circumstances of the first dig here. But if you could only hear yourself, Aleister. Babbling of ancient mysteries and hostile spirits." For a moment the old warmth, the old caring was back in his voice, in his eyes. It undermined Aleister's anger.

"I never said—"

"If you'd only consent to place yourself once more under the care of our church healers. They could help you now as they did before."

"I'd *have* to be mad to agree to go through that again."

"Oh, Ali!" Warrick sighed. "That's what I thought you'd say. Well, we can't force you. So for your own sake we're sending you away from this place."

"And what of my duties?"

"Master Scrivener will assume your duties."

"*Scrivener*? You must be joking. That queachy, lugsome, mutton-headed pen-pusher?"

Warrick's face turned a lovely rose color. "That'll do, Master Grimshaw. Believe it or not, the Holy Orders employ any number of capable practitioners of the Craft besides yourself. Master Scrivener is a highly respected master witch with training equal to if not surpassing your own…"

And so it went. Had Aleister paused long enough to consider, he could have predicted the outcome of his conversation with Brahman Warrick. Too impatient, that was his problem, according to his old preceptor. *Too keen.* But postponing such a discussion would have made no difference. It was now clear to him that from the moment he had been foolish enough to argue with Warrick about the identity of the statue in the original shrine, a lengthy trip out of the city had been in his immediate future.

Pointless to continue debating his case, though he did for longer than was strictly wise. Perhaps because it was the only attention he got from Warrick these days, and there was still a part of him that missed—well, no point to such thoughts. It was a relief at last to escape back to his duties, to lose himself once more in the dissection of Hidush's far off past —and a greater relief when the day's work was finished and he could escape the eyes that watched and judged.

It was nearly sundown when Aleister reached the relative solitude of his bungalow in the in the oldest part of the Alban cantonment at Harappu. Most of the surrounding mansions in this antiquated section of the settlement were derelict or destroyed, but this was a comfortable old place, a sprawling white villa, well-concealed within the lush garden of the walled compound. Petals like blue snow were scattered across the tiled pitched roof from the flowering jacaranda high above.

When he was a small child, his family had wintered here every year. He remembered playing Pachisi on the polished wooden floors, moving stick puppets against the white washed walls, and waking in the sunny room where the doves nested outside his latticed window. He remembered the parties, music and laughter ringing from the high ceilings, the jewels and shiny satins and furs of Harappun society sparkling in the mellow candlelight. He remembered listening to his father and grandfather on the verandah, smoking their pipes and speaking sedition late into the night.

The youngest son of one of Alba's thirty-four noble houses, Aleister's great grandfather had thrown his lot in with two other cronies and founded the Hidush Trading Company. The Grimshaws and Alba had prospered greatly, but by the second generation the Grimshaws were getting a name as reformers and zealots. And by the third generation...

Perhaps it was the cost of losing two sons in the White Spice Wars. That was what the shocked colonists had whispered when the truth came out about the role old Archimedes Grimshaw had played in the Inborn Mutiny. Many true blood witches had supported the mutiny, the Grimshaws were not the first or only people of Power to openly question the morality of how the Hidush Trading company and others deliberately undermined the authority of the native nobility for monetary gain—nor to protest the brutality of the White Spice Wars, fought mainly by hapless Hidushi conscripts to fill the coffers of Alban landowners. But the Grimshaws had been an institution, one of the three founding families. That their political and social ideals should have lead them beyond revisionism to outright revolution shocked and horrified both nations. Well, one and a half, for the weapons of Power used in the White Spice Wars had left the island of Alba a razed and dying land. What had once been the most alien of an empire's outposts, Hidush, became the new capital of Alba, melding the two countries and cultures forever. Now any threat to Alban supremacy met with the harshest of responses.

Aleister's father and grandfather had died for their ideals.

Knowing they had no home to return to, the Albans who remained in Hidush seized lands and conscripted soldiers as never before in a bid to consolidate power. Yet even now whispers of another Mutiny circulated through the tea houses of Harappu.

Aleister closed his ears to it and devoted his attention to the artifacts and antiquities of the ancient Hidush past. He found comfort in measuring, weighing, and cataloging these cool beautiful relics of a violent and magical history.

As the son of a convicted—and executed—mutineer he was not allowed to own property; so, technically the secluded bungalow belonged to his mother, Lady Styrling. Over a decade earlier she had retreated, with the ladies of her coven, to establish a cloister in the peaceful south, and to all intent and purposes, the villa and garden had become Aleister's. He was happy here. Happy, he believed, as he would be anywhere. It was quiet and private, and these were the main things he required now days.

Arriving home on that airless and muggy evening, he let his elderly manservant divest him of jacket, breeches, and boots, and help him into his silk robe. He did not need, nor want, this help as a matter of fact, but to decline Jishu's services would have been the equivilent of striking the old man to the ground, so Aleister gritted his jaw and graciously put up with twenty minutes of assistance for something that should have taken two.

When Jishu had finished his daily regimen of complaining about Priti, the other remaining ancient family retainer, Aleister made his escape to the garden where he settled on his yoga mat and attempted to meditate himself into a state of serenity.

The balance of your mind has been affected once more… He forced the unpleasant encounter with Warrick from his mind, closed his ears to the memory of the cruel, foolish words— surely said as a diversion? Surely Warrick didn't believe he was slipping? Granted, he was not a man of much imagination. It seemed to be true of a lot of those who chose the church now days, but then the church was a very different thing even from when Aleister and Warrick had been boys.

Anyway…silly to be rattled. He wasn't…he was all right.

Aleister closed his eyes to the memory of Warrick—and then to the unexpected, intrusive thought of the swaggering, handsome Major Strange. Where had *that* come from? He focused inward, rejecting all earthly aspects of his being.

He relinquished control of his thinking, active self to the inward—

There. The cool white silence. He was without form. Without thought. He simply *was*.

The chimes swayed in the breeze, a single low tone humming through the garden, reverberating off the black echo stones and dissipating into the cool night air.

He became aware of other sounds: the lap of water, the rustle of leaves, the soft batting of the death-head moths against the window screens—sounds from within the bungalow too. The chink of china and crystal (the rituals must still be preserved), the amiable bickering of Priti and Jishnu. He noticed the spicy scent of dinner cooking in the kitchen. His stomach growled.

Aleister opened his eyes, his meditation broken.

Briefly, his eyes were dazzled by the cozy gleam of lamps from behind screens, and then the shadows of the garden took solid form once again. Black velvet elephant leaves flapped in a gentle breeze that tasted queerly, abruptly, of faraway snow…

Although he continued to practice faithfully, Aleister was not particularly good at meditation. Too restless, too keen again, unfortunately. The meditation was supposed to balance that, of course, and if there was ever an evening for the calming influence of meditation, it was tonight.

Journey to the Benhali Mountains? *He?* But better not to worry about the future—let alone brood on the the conversation that had taken place after Major Strange's departure. It was difficult though. The mere memory of the impatient pity in Warrick's eyes heated his face with angry humiliation. His own bloody fault. He should have waited. Should have bided his time. He knew Ehimay. Knew that that had not been the time to push him, but he had been rattled by the news that he was to be sent off to the edge of civilisation with that soldier of fortune—sent on a fetch and carry mission that any still-damp-with-wolfsbane-oil initiate could carry out.

And Strange...Aleister knew the type. Well, had encountered it before. Men who resisted the evidence of their eyes, believed magic was something that belonged to the superstitions of the past—or believed, like the church, that it should be strictly regulated and controled. A stubborn, ignorant, violent man, no doubt. And Aleister would have to travel weeks into the wilderness with such a companion?

Ehimay had been right about one thing, though. Still, better not to think of that.

He tried very hard not to think of that. Though sometimes the hunger to touch and be touched became too much for him. For such reasons were the whorehouses of Harappu built.

Aleister rolled onto his heels, rose from his crosslegged position on the mat and went to the triangular pool in the center of the garden. Starlight shone on the still water, and white and silver stones sparkled beneath. Aleister knelt beside the pool, scooped a hand in and anointed his forehead, lips, and the place over his heart.

Leaning over the pool, he gazed into the shimmering depths and pictured the one he wished to see. A large lean man with the unconsciously graceful carriage of the cavalry officer. Curly black hair, bright blue eyes, and a dimple in what appeared to be a very stubborn chin indeed.

"Valentine Strange," he murmured. Perhaps Aleister was not much good at meditation, but he was very good at other things—scrying being one of them.

As he gazed, an image began to surface as though floating up from the silvery bottom.

A room. A sumptuous room filled with fine old Alban furniture. Carved chests, claret brocade-covered chairs, and golden globe lamps...one of the old palaces near the river, he thought. The windows were covered by finely carved sandalwood screens and there were several painted portraits of Hidushi nobles. A tiger skin lay across the back of a long brocade sofa. Major Strange sat on the sofa kissing a beautiful woman with dark, coiled hair.

"Master Aleister?"

Aleister's eyes refocused slowly on the wrinkled face of Priti. He blinked at her. The light from the bungalow behind her seemed blazingly bright.

He made an effort. "What?"

"Will the master sup now?"

*Will the...*slowly his brain caught up with his hearing.

Oddsblood, how many times had he asked her—told her—she must not interrupt him? But it was useless scolding Priti. Not that he would dare. She had been his childhood nurse—the day before yesterday, as far as she was concerned.

"Later," he said. "Soon."

"Now." Priti spoke softly. Stubborn as an old goat, she was. "You've been out here stargazing all the evening. The food was cold hours ago."

He said, equally soft—and even more stubborn, "Then the food will have to be reheated, will it not? In the meantime, I'll work." As she opened her mouth, he added coaxingly, "I'll be in shortly, *ayah.*"

Her face softened, seemingly against her will, and she returned to the bungalow.

Aleister looked down at the pool once more, but the waters had gone dark.

⌒

The lamplighters were busy with lantern and ladder when Major Strange climbed out of the rickshaw in front of the Golden Ram. A hot gust of wind sent the street lights guttering and flaring, casting shapeshifting shadows across the pavement as Strange went into the gambling house.

Inside, a nubile young woman in a black cheongsam took his hat and lightweight coat and smiled demure welcome. And well she might. Strange had lost a packet between these four walls.

"Is he in?"

"To you, always, Major."

He went swiftly up the staircase ignoring the gaming rooms with their faro and mahjong tables. Beneath the scent of tobacco and incense was a hint of white spice, although its use was illegal within the city limits.

Upstairs a very young girl was coaxing a very drunk grenadier into one of the reserved bed chambers. The grenadier giggled even more loudly than the whore, but perhaps that was not so odd.

A short, stalwart bald man stood outside Lamb's office. When he spotted Strange, he straightened abruptly, loosening his shoulders.

Strange laughed. "He'll want to see me. I've brought his money."

"Lucky for you," growled the bodyguard, and Strange laughed again.

The man thumped on the door behind him and a raspy voice called, "Come!"

Strange opened the door and stepped into a room furnished in a style which would do any whoremaster and gamer proud.

Everything that could have been gilded, encrusted with semi-precious stones or upholstered with exotic animal skins had been. Military weapons and sporting prints hung on the wall, though Lamb had never served and did not play games.

There was an old legend that at the dawn of time, outcastes had interbred with man-sized lizards. What might have happened to these mansized lizards was anyone's guess, but Lamb seemed living proof there was no boundary to the bad taste and foolishness of some females.

"Major Strange. I wondered when you might deign to pay my humble abode a visit."

Strange dropped his money belt on the desk.

"Ah!" Brightening, Lamb reached for the belt, unzipping it and emptying its contents. He looked up, pencil thin brows drawing together. "But where is the rest of it?" His yellow gaze fixed suspiciously on Strange's face. "A hundred thousand rupees is hardly more than half of what you owe, Major Strange."

"I have other debts and other debtors," Strange replied.

Lamb swallowed his smile. "Lady Isabella Hyde." He had a way of hissing his S's that was most unappealing.

"That's right." Strange wasn't pleased at Lamb's knowledge of his private affairs, but he wasn't surprised either. Such news had a way of spreading.

"That's *wrong*," Lamb snarled, and Strange narrowed his eyes. "What do I care of your debts to someone else? I only care what you owe *me*, and this is a debt of honor long outstanding."

The debt was, in fact, two weeks old. It was unquestionably an embarrassment. The fact that Strange was convinced the dealing boxes at Lamb's faro tables were rigged was beside the point. He had suspected so before he ever sat down in one of Sittappan Lamb's gaming rooms. Suspicion hadn't kept him from wagering heavily, though. He was, after all, a gambler.

"I'll get you your money. Keep your shirt on."

"How? How will you get me my money? You gave my money to Lady Hyde. You could have cleared the debt to me, but you chose to pay your light o' love first."

That was true. Partly because Strange owed Isabella less and could completely clear the debt to her with something left over to share out amongst his other creditors. Partly because he had plans for Isabella which necessitated him appearing to be a better matrimonial prospect than he currently was.

In the meantime…his fist shot out and bunched in Lamb's silk shirtfront, dragging the much smaller man half across his marble-top desk.

"Mind your tongue when you're speaking of a lady in my presence, Lamb. That lady in particular."

Lamb's long red tongue licked nervously at his pale mouth. "My apologies, Major. No disrespect to the lady was intended."

Strange let him go, and Lamb fell back into his chair. His hand went to his collar and adjusted it. He said hoarsely, "Very well. How will you get me the rest of the money you owe?"

"Leave me to worry about how. As for when… three days."

Another gamble but if push came to shove, Strange could shove harder than most.

"But it is my worry too, Major. I cannot be perceived to allow debts to go unpaid." Lamb tapped a long fingernail against his tooth and said slowly, guilessly, "However…were you to sign over your polo ponies as a marker I could extend your credit."

Yellow eyes met blue.

Lamb said softly, "I should hate to be forced to make an example of such an excellent customer."

"You could always try."

Lamb grimaced. Then his face cleared. Strange liked that expression less than the first. "Perhaps, as you've proven yourself a so good investment, you might convince Lady Hyde to advance you back the necessary sum?"

Strange eyed the gamester levelly. Tempting though it was to shove his pointy teeth down his throat, it wasn't even a temporary solution. True, in less than a week he would be out of the city and unreachable, but eventually he would have to return and he preferred that it not be to Dun territory.

And...Isabella *was* rather fond of him. And very wealthy.

He didn't like the idea. Only a cad borrowed the ready from a woman, but...she'd insisted the last time. After all, he was headed out on a dangerous mission traveling into the wilds of the Benhali Mountains. She might never see him again. Women tended to be sentimental about that sort of thing—and Strange would prefer not to spend the upcoming week of preparation watching over his shoulder for Lamb's thugs.

Perhaps it wouldn't hurt to drop a few hints her way.

Lamb was watching him closely, a bit warily. He blinked as Strange's mouth slowly widened into a smile.

CHAPTER THREE

Strange did his best to keep preparations for his expedition quiet. He hired just three marl-caste bearers, a couple of pack ponies and brought his favorite horse, Balestra, instead of the caravan of men and supplies and arms that Brahman Warrick would have been happy to finance. That kind of expedition would have attracted attention—and most of it from the wrong quarters. If they made good time—and were lucky—they'd be in and out of the Benhali Mountains and back to civilization before most of Harappun society knew they'd left.

But they had been followed from Harappu. Strange had been sure of it, though the pursuit was mostly invisible in the jungle that surrounded the city. Soldier's instinct—or maybe just a talent for trouble. Once their party had left the jungles for the poppy-covered plains, their pursuers were easy to spot—a chain of horsemen following at a cautious distance.

The question was, who was following them? Isabella had come up to snuff like the grand girl she was, and Strange had been able to appease Lamb. Not that he was overjoyed to find himself in debt to Isabella again, but perhaps matters were moving to resolve themselves in that direction in any case. After all, a man had to settle down eventually, didn't he? And he could do far worse than the lovely Lady Hyde. Very nice set up she had there in that palace by the river, and she was about as easy to rub along with as any female he'd known...

Of course he had other creditors; though it was hard to picture his tailor sending cutthroats after him.

Strange was still making his mind up what to do about the horsemen shadowing them when he called the midday halt. When he did, Master Grimshaw stalked out to the edge of their camp, scooped up a handful of sand, groused some words no one could understand, and hurled the sand into the furnace of still air they sat sweltering in.

The sand blew along propelled by…well, that was the mystery…and as the grains flew they picked up other grains and velocity until a wall of sand descended on the watching riders. The chain broke and the horsemen scattered in the dusty maelstrom.

In the wake of the sandstorm Strange scanned the scrubby desert hills and crevices for the riders with his spyglass but saw no sign of them.

Grimshaw joined him on the hillock, bony khaki-clad shoulder brushing his own. "They're still out there."

"You think so?"

"Yes. And so do you."

Strange compressed the sliding lens protector on the telescope, avoiding looking directly at the other man. Magic made him uncomfortable. Not a logical reaction, but there it was. Where he came from only primitives used magic.

Anyway, there was a note in Grimshaw's voice Strange didn't care for. He turned to eye him for a long moment. Grimshaw eyed him right back with that pale, unblinking gaze. He was right, of course. Strange did think the riders were still out there. But did Grimshaw know that because of something he read in Strange's face or because of some more arcane reason?

"I'm not expecting trouble."

Grimshaw mouth twitched into a sly smile. "You're *always* expecting trouble, Major Strange."

Well, he wasn't entirely wrong there. So long as the trouble wasn't of Master Grimshaw's devising.

The day passed and the next. They made good time. Occasionally they passed a pilgrim—once they passed a gipsy with a trained yellow bear on a lead. The scarred and shaggy bear elicited the first sincere reaction from Master Grimshaw that Strange had yet seen. The witch reined up and let loose a stream of native invective that had the gipsy shaking in his yak boots and pleading for mercy while the bear rose on its hind legs, swaying and seeming to dance with claws outstretched.

Grimshaw raised an impatient hand.

The gipsy, still crying about his livelihood, reluctantly freed the bewildered animal. For a moment Strange thought he'd have to shoot the damn bear and beggar both, but Grimshaw spoke a few soft words in the witch tongue—Parlance, they called it—and the bear lumbered away through the poppies. They left the gipsy wailing in the bronze dust.

It was a perplexing situation. Strange had never worked directly for the Holy Orders before. Technically, the command of this expedition was his. But somehow the witch fell outside his bailiwick. Strange was in charge of all practical matters and Grimshaw of all spiritual, but the decision as to what was practical and what was spiritual was apparently Master Grimshaw's and included the welfare of itinerant dancing bears. Fortunately for Master Grimshaw's own health and welfare, he showed scant interest in interfering in any matters, practical *or* spiritual. His sole concern seemed to be getting back to Harappu as soon as possible. This should have endeared him to Strange, but something about the younger man continued to play on his nerves.

Maybe it was the things he had learned before they left the city. Strange liked to know who he was traveling with and he'd done some checking on Master Grimshaw in the days spent putting their expedition together. Difficult, unpredictable, that was the consensus. Not that there was a lot of information available. Grimshaw had been twelve years old at the time of the Inborn Mutiny. He'd had to witness the executions of his father and grandfather for treason. Tough luck. Strange had been nineteen, and in his considered opinion, he'd seen many, many more terrible things in those eleven months of uprising than two relatively clean executions—and all of it thanks to people like Grimshaw's sire and grandsire.

Shortly after the incident with the bear, Strange decided to simply ask about it. "The day we met at the temple ruins you had the wind up about something. What was it?"

At first he thought Grimshaw hadn't heard him. He continued to stare out between his horse's ears. Then he asked colorlessly, "What did you overhear?"

"That you think there's something not right about the ruins."

"I do believe that, yes." Grimshaw looked at him then; there seemed a hint of defiance in his gaze.

"Such as?"

He saw Grimshaw consider and discard possible answers. He said, "You saw it yourself. That was no statue of Purya, Brahman Warrick showed us."

"Could have been," Strange said indifferently. "Art's a funny thing."

Grimshaw snorted.

"And that's it? You think Brahman Warrick has his icons wrong?"

Grimshaw slanted him a look and said nothing.

"And they—the priests—don't believe you?"

"I don't know if he—they—believe me or not." His mouth curled. "Since you've asked, I suspect one reason I was given this assignment was to remove me from the excavation site."

"Why's that? Trouble-maker are you?" Strange brushed aside a large red bloodfly that had landed on Balestra's neck. The black tossed his head, chewing his bit.

Grimshaw offered only an austere profile. "I don't know."

"You don't know if you're a trouble-maker or you don't know why your employers might want to get you out of the way?"

Grimshaw cast him a look of dislike.

"You said to Warrick something old was waking and watching. What was that about?"

Grimshaw gave a curt shake of his head.

Strange could see why Master Sticks and Stones' employers had lost patience with him. "Normal thing for temples and shrines, isn't it? Places of Power. Wouldn't be unexpected to find some sort of…spirit awake and keeping on eye on things, would it? Gratifying, in fact." He was deliberately goading, and Grimshaw fell right into it.

"You've no notion what you're talking about. The thing in the temple…the spirit as you call it…it isn't some benevolent guardian."

Beneath the irritation was something else. Something that surprised Strange, made him uneasy, though he didn't comment. But Grimshaw must have seen the recognition in his face. He said shortly, "Yes, I *am* afraid. It wasn't only watching us, it was studying us—all of us. Learning us. It knows my name."

This was why Strange preferred to work without the help of witches and magicians. He said politely, "I expect it heard someone address you."

Grimshaw stared at him in disbelief. He bit out, "Unfortunately, I'm unable to find the matter as amusing as you, Major Strange." Digging his heels into his horse's flanks, he cantered a few yards ahead of the train of men and ponies.

In truth, Strange had not been joking. But apparently to witches there was more to this naming business than he'd realized.

⌒

Grimshaw had forgotten how it was out here on the plains. How hot it was—even when it was raining—and how the wind blew. He hated the wind. Hated the voice he heard whispering and whistling within the steady, constant sough. It reminded him of the things it was safer not to remember. Maybe that was the reason he felt as he did. Uneasy. As though he were being watched again.

Though he *was* being watched, true enough.

The marl watched him. The handsome, dismissive Major Strange watched him. And the riders who had followed their small caravan from the city watched him. The latter had been easily dealt with. A handful of sand and a few words in Parlance. Any neophyte magician could manage that much. And surely there would be no call for The Craft. No call for the skill and training—and tools—of a witch. Lucky thing, for he was rusty on all three scores. Lucky that he need only let the brave major lead him to this monastary in the mountains, take a look at this trinket supposedly belonging to a newly reinstated, government-approved goddess, pronounce it genuine.

Goddess.

Warrick must think he was stupid as well as mad. Interesting, though. Even Strange had caught it. Not quite as foolish as he looked, this soldier of fortune. Not that he looked stupid, precisely, just far too handsome to be of much practical value. Aleister was surprised—but no. Not really. The major needed money, that had been obvious enough from the way he'd jumped at this fool's errand. And clearly he was not above bending a few rules to lay hands on it.

No reason then for that prickle at the nape of Grimshaw's neck, that crawling feeling at the base of his spine. They would ride into the hills, into the Benhali Mountains—the White Mountains in the native tongue—and they would find this diadem and bring it back to Warrick, and perhaps then he would leave Aleister in peace to study and meditate, which was all he wanted.

All he had wanted for a very long time.

A week out of Harappu – the latticed steel towers of the windmills and the white sea of poppies a distant shimmering haze behind them—the whispers began in earnest. The three bearers—men recommend to Strange by his old friend Captain Desmond, V.C.—grumbled to each other in their native dialect and watched the witch with narrowed black eyes. They did not like him. They did not trust him. Magicians could be dangerous creatures, but you knew where you stood with them. Witches... only a fool trusted a witch.

Strange's own feelings toward the witch remained neutral. Grimshaw had been unhappy about this assignment from the instant Warrick had tapped him for it. Had he no choice in the matter? Strange had no idea how the Holy Orders arranged such things, but temple witch was a highly coveted position. Presumably he hadn't been conscripted. Still, he plainly harbored resentment. Or maybe he just hated camping.

While clearly out of his element, Grimshaw was an excellent horseman—the chestnut gelding he rode was fine piece of horseflesh—and where all else was concerned, Grimshaw knew enough to keep his mouth shut and obey orders. Dancing bears aside.

In fact, he kept to himself, answering politely—mostly—when addressed, and otherwise ignoring them all. In the evening he retreated to his tent and shortly thereafter the pale blue light signifying the use of Power would illuminate the drab canvas. Casting the runes or fooling with that small crystal ball he always carried in the pocket of his breeches. Alban magic. Whatever he discerned with his buttons and twigs and baubles, he kept to himself.

Mostly.

But despite his personal feeling—or lack of feeling—for the witch, the man was Strange's responsibility and he made it a point to know the men under his command. Anyway, he was interesting to talk to—good company being something of a premium out here.

Strange reined Balestra into step beside the witch's chestnut gelding, observing man and horse critically.

"Stap me, you ride like a cavalry man, Master Grimshaw."

Grimshaw gave him a sour smile. "The highest of compliments!"

"The real question is, can you shoot worth a damn?"

"I'll leave the killing to you, Major Strange."

"Ah." One of those.

Grimshaw was still watching him. "In answer to your question, yes. I can shoot."

"But can you hit anything?"

"It depends how hungry I am." Grimshaw added, "Or irritated."

Strange laughed, genuinely amused. "Good enough."

He'd brought his own guns, so Strange would take him at his word. He'd supposedly spent several years on the Frontier, which was generally conducive to great familiarity with side arms. No military service, though. Naturally not. Not with his family pedigree. The offspring of mutineers were not welcome in the armed forces. Nor anywhere, in fact.

After a week Strange wasn't entirely sold on the three bearers recommended by Captain Desmond. Like Grimshaw, neither Tej, Rashid, nor Nanak had seen any military service; the difference being Strange had a suspicion *they'd* funk under fire. Grimshaw was too stubborn to give way to mere bullets. "Though I don't expect it will come to that."

"We're just out for a jolly little picnic, are we?"

Strange shrugged. "Well, I've had better food and the accommodations aren't the finest, but…"

Grimshaw slanted one of those derisive little smiles. "But I imagine you find the change of scenery welcome."

There was something in his tone Strange didn't like, but most probably he meant the obvious: that an ex-soldier would find Harappun society dull.

"Speaking of change of scenery, there were tiger tracks not far from last night's camp. Keep your eyes peeled."

"Tiger tracks?" Grimshaw was not smiling now.

"That's right." It was Strange's turn to smile—albeit maliciously. "Not afraid of cats are you? Thought witches were supposed to be fond of them."

"I'm not afraid of cats." Grimshaw said, then added, "But I've no experience of tigers."

At last. Something Master Grimshaw admitted he had no experience of. Strange said, "I've experience enough for both of us. I've bagged my share of big cats and will bag this one too if he makes a nuisance of himself."

Grimshaw raised his brows pretending to be greatly impressed.

They did not speak again and the day's ride stretched long and hot and dusty. As the poppies gave way to plains, so the plains gave way to foothills terraced with tea bushes.

The sun sank behind the gold-tinged hills and they made camp for the evening. Rashid and Tej staked tents while Nanak prepared salted pork, bread and mung bean soup. Master Grimshaw did not—for once—immediately retire to his tent following the meal. In fact, he seemed in an uncharacteristically sociable mood and lingered at the campfire while Strange enjoyed his coffee and cheroot.

Strange was not sure he wouldn't have preferred his own company and the stars. Feeling that light, curious gaze upon him, he asked, "Do you play cards, Master Grimshaw? Would you like to while away the evening on a hand or two of whist perhaps?"

"Whist? No." Grimshaw offered with one of those sly smiles. "I could tell your fortune, if you like,"

"I'll make my fortune as I go."

"Ah." Grimshaw tossed a small match box back and forth, his eyes glinting colorless in the firelight. "You're from Marikelan, Major Strange?"

"That's right." It was always a tiny jolt when someone accurately pegged him for Outborn. He'd left the north colonies for Alba when he was seventeen—couldn't wait to strike out for adventure, and the Alban government had needed soldiers more than ever back then. Back before the White Spice Wars had put an end to Alban conquest once and for all. Pretty much put an end to Alba as well. But when Strange had enlisted, the focus had been on suppressing the various uprisings in Hidush, and he had shipped out less than a month after his arrival in Alba. He'd arrived in Hidush ten weeks later and never yet left it. Maybe there was still a trace of Marikelan in his vowels, but most people took him for Inborn, an Alban true blood, an impression he did nothing to discourage.

His brief response seemed to confirm Grimshaw's thoughts. He smiled—the first natural, open smile Strange had seen out of him. "You must have been very young. I'd have taken you for an Alban Inborn."

Not true blood—Strange didn't miss that distinction.

"'s right." Damned if that betraying Marikelan slur hadn't suddenly cropped up.

"Did you arrive on these shores expecting to find lost cities and armies of giants and flying monkeys?" Grimshaw was still smiling, teasing, but he happened to touch a nerve. Strange *had* arrived believing all those wild legends of the distant western lands. A regular *goo obo gudgeon,* as they called 'em over here.

"I didn't come expecting mutiny from the colonists we were supposed to be protecting," he said harshly.

The smile faded from Grimshaw's face, his gaze dropped to the fire. At once he looked very young—and very old. "No. I suppose not."

Neither of them said anything for a second or two. Then Grimshaw rose in a quick, lithe movement. "Well, Nanak will be brewing the morning swill soon enough. Good night, Major Strange." He tossed the box of matches to Strange who caught them with a snap of his wrist.

He grunted goodnight, slightly put out with his own churlishness. Hardly Grimshaw's fault he'd been born into a house of dissension and revolution. He watched the younger man walk across to his tent, pull back the flap of his tent, and disappear inside. A short while later the pale blue glow illumined the canvas from within.

One of the bearers, Tej, had been playing a small flute. The sound went abruptly dead, and the men began to grumble back and forth.

Strange spoke to them, reassured them that Grimshaw was on the errand of priests. They listened to him in stolid silence while the blue light grew brighter in the tent and a faint humming that did not come from any human voice whispered across the clearing.

Magic was less and less trusted these days. And witches—those who commanded the Power through blood as well as training—were least trusted of all. Even when the church was ostensibly directing them.

That night Strange slept lightly, one hand on his service pistol.

Chapter Four

The following afternoon, eight days out of Harappu, they came upon an old fakir.

He seemed to materialize out of the sea of wild tea bushes that carpeted the foothills. A bundle of dirty rags suddenly standing up on two filthy legs, purple and yellow streaked beard and matted hair, eyes squinting against the blazing sun.

Hard to guess how old he was—anywhere from thirty to seventy. His toenails were blackened spirals necessitating walking on his deformed heels. His emaciated body was powdered and smeared with ashes and dust and covered in open sores, which were kept fresh by the swarm of insects that infested him. His loin-cloth was rotting.

It was as though a corpse suddenly jumped up out of the earth.

So sudden it was, Strange nearly rode him down. Balestra shied and sidestepped, Strange swayed easily in the seat, reaching for his pistol. He was chagrined to have been caught off guard, preoccupied as he was with thoughts of the set of tiger tracks he had spotted again that morning. It appeared they were being stalked. He had seen it happen once or twice. Usually tigers weren't man-eaters, but once they got a taste for such easy prey, they began to actively hunt humans. He was thinking that they would need to be extra vigilant that night, but that telling the bearers exactly *why* might not be the best idea.

The old man pointed a claw-like hand at Grimshaw.

"Don't shoot," Grimshaw told Strange, and Strange lowered his pistol as the old clothes bag began to speak. A hill dialect, Strange thought, although it was not familiar to him.

Grimshaw sat like a statue, saying nothing while the old man babbled, his blackened tongue flicking in and out between the long streams of words.

Strange regarded both men. Grimshaw looked pale but he often looked pale toward the end of the day's ride. He did not seem alarmed or Strange would have intervened. The bearers began to mutter to each other.

Then in the impenetrable mumbling a name stood out. *Grimshaw.*

It was obvious from the ripple of shock that went through the Hidushis that the old fakir's arcane knowledge of Grimshaw's name had not escaped them.

The witch answered in a stilted version of the fakir's own dialect. Whatever he said seemed to anger the old man who vigorously scratched his head with both hands dislodging purple sand or perhaps tiny beads at Grimshaw.

The chestnut danced sideways. Grimshaw flicked his hand. "Avert."

Strange's gaze veered to him, and because of that one distracted instant he did not see what happened to the old man. Certainly he did not see him actually disappear, but the bearers saw…something…and began to object loudly.

Strange ordered them to silence. "What have you done?" he snapped at the witch. It was an unfortunate choice of words, and he regretted it even as he stood in the saddle, searching the waves of greenery for any trace of the old fakir.

Grimshaw's face tightened. He said flatly, "I've done nothing."

And Strange *saw* nothing. Nothing but billowing white clouds and ruffled green tea bushes—and the razored alabaster peaks of the highest and most distant of the Benhali Mountains.

The bearers were still murmuring discontent. Strange barked at them again. Sullenly they stared back at him, black eyes hostile. Ignoring them, Strange focused his attention on Grimshaw.

"What, by the dust from the four corners, was *that* about?"

Grimshaw pulled up his skittish mount, said evenly, "The old one believes we're ill advised to continue."

"Why?"

The wide gray eyes met his—their expression ironic. "I can't imagine."

"Let's not fence, Grimshaw. Has he cast a spell on us?"

Grimshaw glanced back at the angry bearers. "'Us?' No.. The curse was for me alone."

"He *cursed* you?"

"Not exactly. It amounts to the same thing."

But yet wasn't the same thing? Could the man never speak in anything but riddles? "Why? Why you?"

Grimshaw shook his head.

"You don't know or you decline to answer me?"

"I don't decline to answer you, Major." He raised an indifferent shoulder. Or was it defensive? Strange considered himself an expert at reading men, but he could not read Grimshaw at all. Maybe the other rumor he had heard was true as well: that Grimshaw was not entirely... sane.

"But who was that? Why should he object to you coming on this expedition? You didn't even want to come." And what was the source of this otherworldly objection? This was why Strange hated any and all such manifestations of Power. It didn't operate in a logical manner. A reasonable manner. Or at least not to Strange's way of thinking.

Grimshaw removed his helmet and wiped the sweat from his face. "No. I didn't." He replaced his helmet. "I bloody well wish I hadn't."

No one moved or spoke. The bearers watched with unblinking intent. The tails of the ponies swished leisurely at flies. "Why?"

"Because it's a fool's quest."

"Your Brahman Warrick doesn't seem to think so."

A slight, rather bitter, smile. "No. So he says."

"Do you doubt his word?"

"No."

Strange scrutinized Grimshaw's face, but he could find no sign that the witch lied. He nodded over his shoulder at the men who had begun muttering again.

He said, "The marl sure as the devil think this is an ill omen."

"Perhaps."

Strange straightened in the saddle, searching again for any sign of the fakir in the tea bushes growing wild, but the creature was long gone. He turned back to Grimshaw. "Are we likely to have any …?"

"Any?" Aleister's smile was sardonic. "Any trouble? Not from that old one."

"Then who from?" Strange heard the question and winced inwardly. He was asking *Grimshaw* if there would be trouble? Next he'd be asking him to cut cards and reveal his future.

Aside from demented mystics, there was the all too real possibility of bad weather and man-eating tigers. There were the riders sent to track them and the threat of ordinary, run-of-the-mill bandits. And they were nearing Phansigar territory where the gruesome murder of travelers was not merely an occupation, it was a religious duty. Trouble? Only as much as the day was long.

Grimshaw nudged his horse forward, and said over his shoulder, in that same mocking tone, "Nothing you can't handle, Major Strange."

Strange gritted his jaw against his automatic retort.

They rode on until the sun began its long, slow slide out of the red sky. The tea bushes had given way to the ragged beginning of forest. Their long, ink-stroke silhouettes flashed against the green wall of trees and grass until at last Strange called the day's halt and ordered them to make camp.

They dismounted wearily, pulling saddles from the horses and staking them to graze. Strange was driving them hard and they continued to make good time. Yes, they were fatigued at the end of the day, and that was exactly the way Strange wanted it. The horses were holding up well and their provisions were supplemented by his hunting. They were in good shape all around, despite the unasked for opinions of wandering holy men.

For the next half hour the bearers were busy setting up the two tents, lighting the fire, and fetching water.

Grimshaw retired to his tent as soon as it was pitched and soon after the pale blue light glimmered. He did not come out for his meal and the men grew more restive. There was no cheerful talk or the playing of the wooden flute.

Strange ate his supper, drank his coffee and smoked his cheroot studying the map by firelight.

The headman, Nanak, approached him. "What does the witch do?"

Strange said easily, "Whatever witches do to amuse themselves on long dull evenings."

The man stared at him with dark unsmiling eyes. He returned to his fellows and there was more undervoiced talk.

Strange waited till they had quieted again and then went to the tent.

"Grimshaw?"

There was no answer although he could see the man's motionless silhouette outlined clearly. He suspected before he opened the flap what he would see, and sure enough there was merely the shadow of the witch thrown against the canvas wall and no sign of the man himself. There was a small blue enamel bowl with shiny silver and black pebbles at the bottom of it. The glow from the stones threw enough light to illuminate the tent; so much so that Strange had mistakenly thought Grimshaw was burning a lantern.

Quickly, he closed the flap once more against the men smoking and talking quietly by the fire, and sat down inside to wait. He studied the silhouette outline of the witch. Head bent demurely, Grimshaw's shade knelt there like a lifesized shadow puppet.

"What are you up to?" Strange wondered aloud.

The silhouette remained motionless, unwavering. Having worked with witch scouts in the cavalry, Strange knew Grimshaw must be projecting himself far away. But where and to what end? Grimshaw was playing a lone hand and Strange didn't like it.

An hour ticked slowly past on Strange's pocket watch before the blue light dimmed and the witch knelt across from Strange, head bowed. The pale hair curtained his face, the thin hands resting on his thighs. Then spontaneously scratches and shallow cuts began to open on his hands. One after another they appeared as though Grimshaw was crawling through thick underbrush or a over a rocky slope.

Strange moved, starting to speak, and Grimshaw jumped and then relaxed. His eyes glinted in the uncertain light.

"Valentine…Strange." His voice was thick…his mouth curved oddly.

"Where've you been?" Strange hadn't intended his own voice to come out so sharply.

After a moment or two Grimshaw blinked. He said slowly, "The tomb."

"What tomb? What are you talking about?"

Grimshaw did not seem to understand the question.

"Why are your hands torn up?"

"I was…trying to get out."

"Get out of what?"

"I…" Grimshaw scrubbed awkwardly at his eyes like a drowsy child. "Sorry?"

"You're making the lads nervous." Strange had not meant to say that either. Let alone have it come out sounding like an accusation. Witches…witched. That was why Grimshaw was on this expedition, after all. But this talk of tombs…

Grimshaw's mouth twisted in that smile that was not a smile. Without answering, he scooped the shiny stones from the bowl of water and dropped them one by one into a small leather pouch. They clicked musically against each other as they fell.

Reluctantly, Strange tried again, "What did your scrying tell you?"

It seemed to take a few seconds before Grimshaw appeared to hear him. His voice seemed to drag with weariness. "It's not…clear."

Strange snorted. Magic was conveniently unclear when it suited the practitioner. "Do your stones tell you the future?"

"The…future?" Grimshaw sounded as though it were a foreign concept. "No. Not as you mean it."

"Then what?"

Grimshaw was blinking at him in that puzzled, almost sleepy way.

It irritated Strange. "So far, Master Grimshaw, you've not proved to be a great deal of help on this mission. Quite the contrary. You've got the men spooked and you seem to be a lodestone for bad mojo."

Grimshaw's eyes widened. "Bad what?"

"Bad magic."

Awake at last, Grimshaw stared at him in offended surprise. "What do you know that I don't?"

Grimshaw made that little sound that was not quite a laugh. Strange resisted the temptation to paste one in his arrogant, bony nose.

He said through his teeth, "What do you know that you're not telling me?"

Irritably, Grimshaw said, "You haven't asked me to tell you anything, Major Strange. I assumed you knew all that you wished—or needed—to."

"Did Brahman Warrick explain to you why these mountain priests should hand over what is clearly a valuable diadem—assuming the bloody thing even exists?"

"No."

"*Does* it exist?"

Grimshaw hesitated. "Yes. Apparently."

Strange relaxed a fraction. He'd begun to wonder. Not that he could see why the Holy Orders would pay him to journey into the Benhali Mountains if they weren't fairly convinced of this diadem's existence, but early in his career he had learned not to trust to appearances. He said—throwing the idea out to see what Grimshaw made of it, "Well then. Perhaps these priests need to be rid of it."

Grimshaw seemed to give the idea due consideration. "Perhaps. I can't imagine what those circumstances would be. Such a holy relic would be valuable beyond price."

"Everything has its price."

Grimshaw looked interested. "Including you?"

Strange grinned. "Only the young or the very naïve would ask that question, Master Sticks and Stones. Or a priest, perhaps. But you're no priest, are you?"

Grimshaw stared back at him for what felt like a very long time, and then he smiled. Strange blinked at the deliberate and considerable allure of that smile. The bones and hollows of Grimshaw's thin face appeared to rearrange themselves into elegant—almost beautiful—lines. It was really quite a charming face in an odd way. His eyes appeared almost silver in this light...

His gaze held by Grimshaw's bold one, Strange found himself wondering if the stories about the glamour of witches—and their carnal appetites—could possibly be true. There was something suddenly...well, bewitching...about Master Grimshaw....

He broke the spell—if spell it was—by turning squarely away, and yanking open the tent flap.

"You'd do well to leave off with the water and stones. The men are already nervous, and nervous men are dangerous."

"Are they?" As though Grimshaw only too easily read Strange's own discomfort.

He didn't have to look at Grimshaw to know he was smiling that annoying smile again.

Chapter Five

The next morning Rashid tried to kill him.

Aleister had no warning. It happened very quickly. The big man had been near the horses—but was well clear before Aleister mounted Caspar. The gelding let out a near human shriek and began to pitch and buck like a demented thing. Half in the saddle, Grimshaw hung on for a few seconds trying to get his other leg over, but there was no time. No time for witchcraft or horsecraft. He lost his grip and went flying, hitting the grass hard in a rolling fall—narrowly missing landing on an outcropping of rocks.

He was not seriously hurt although he laid there for a few stunned seconds blinking up at the cloudless blue sky through the waving tree fronds. He was mostly astonished, unable to remember the last time he'd been thrown. Then he absorbed the anger and fear of the bearers taking form and substance like a were-creature. He could also feel Caspar's outrage and pain as Nanak and Tej ran to catch his reins.

"Are you injured, Grimshaw?" Strange asked from the back of his own mount. He sounded more curious than concerned, and Aleister scrambled to his feet.

The bearers dropped Caspar's reins and moved back. The horse stood still, shaking, his ears flicking nervously, sweating hide twitching as Aleister approached him, hands out, murmuring Parlance. Caspar tossed his head and blew out nervously, but stood motionless and allowed himself to be soothed.

Aleister ran gentle hands over the cinnamon withers and flanks, projecting the quieting force of his will over the horse's panic. It was not one of his talents—his own mind was too restless—but he could usually control an animal. And Caspar knew him. The horse shook his head, his mane crackling.

"What the devil happened?" Strange was asking. Aleister ignored him.

"You know me. I would never harm you, my friend," he spoke to the horse in the old language.

Caspar tossed his head again, nostrils quivering. His eyes rolled back as he tried to watch the bearers.

The Tej and Nanak moved further away as Aleister felt under the saddle flap and removed the large thorn, spike bloodied. He held it up to Strange. The major's expression barely changed, but he was off his horse in an instant, grabbing Rashid who had stayed well to the background during the commotion.

The bearer cried out, insisting he was innocent of any wrong doing, but the faces of his comrades gave him away. They knew. Aleister felt an odd fascination as he recognized the hatred and fear they felt for him. What did they imagine he might do? It wasn't the first time he'd run into this kind of thing but it still took him aback. It wasn't as though he had created magic, he simply wielded it.

Strange shook Rashid like a rat—he was big enough, powerful enough to lift even a man as large as Rashid off his feet. Strange threw the bearer to the ground and kicked him. Hard. Rashid screamed for mercy from where he sprawled in the rocks and mud.

"Shut the fuck up," Strange told him. He bent down, yanked Rashid to his feet and then threw him doubled and groaning on his pony, which staggered and nearly went down. "Try that again and I'll shoot you where you stand."

Rashid insisted it was all a ghastly mistake, begged for mercy, and swore it would never happen again—all in one long shrill breath.

Strange directed a blazing look his way and Rashid hitched a sobbing breath and fell silent. Strange turned again to Aleister. "Are you able to ride?"

"I'm fine." And he was. Grass-stained and muddy, but otherwise unhurt. That was the advantage of the yogic sutras he faithfully practiced. He might not be as strong or large as the major, but he was almost certainly faster and more agile.

Strange nodded curtly. There was a line of white around his mouth and his eyes looked almost black. It wasn't concern for *him*. Aleister was well aware the major didn't like or trust him anymore than the marl. It must be ire that the bearers had dared to challenge his authority by this attack. Major Strange wouldn't tolerate such a flouting of his command.

"Mount up," Strange told him, and Aleister wordlessly swung back into the saddle.

Strange fired crisp orders to the other two bearers who jumped to obey. He picked Aleister's helmet off the ground and brought it over to him, saying undervoiced, "Stay close to me today and try not to spook them more than you've already done."

Aleister nodded curtly. He took the helmet. He understood why Strange didn't want to appear to be in conference with him, and he continued stroking and soothing his jittery mount as Strange moved away. The implied criticism stung, but he was angry with himself. Angry for the carelessness of dismissing the marl's hated and fear. He had dismissed it as Strange's problem—as a trivial nuisance. Like…gnats on a summer's evening. That had been more than careless. It had been foolish. Arrogant. He had no wish to die. Especially out here where his soul would be left to wander lost and unconsecrated. He'd have to—that was the problem of course. He had no idea how to deal with…people.

It was a difficult day's ride. Strange drove them all hard. Harder than ever. No doubt wishing to keep the marl too busy and tired to think of making mischief. And possibly Aleister as well.

"Any sign of your tiger last night?" Aleister asked during the brief stint Strange rode along side him.

"No. I expect he found easier prey. This isn't really tiger country."

He could feel Strange's gaze, but when he turned, Strange was staring ahead. Aleister tried to think of a topic that might hold Strange's interest, but nothing came to mind—he was useless at such things—and a few seconds later Strange cantered on ahead and Aleister was left with his own thoughts. They were not pleasant for he had realized that he was lonely. Strange's company was better than nothing, though "company" was hardly the description for the needling catechism with which Strange typically whiled away their brief encounters.

Midmorning they came across a pilgrim, a young man—younger than Aleister, at least—dressed in the white robes of a novice priest. He asked to join their caravan fearing to travel further on his own in Phansigar country.

Strange considered him gravely, then said, "Sorry, Holiness, but you wouldn't be able to keep up on foot."

"We could shift the packs around," Aleister suggested.

"No."

"But kind sirs," the young priest protested, beginning to sweat with more than the rising heat of the day. "I'm willing to do whatever you wish. Only...don't leave me out here!"

He was an attractive youth. Slim, brown-eyed, gentle-faced. It would have been pleasant to have his company for a time.

"Sorry, no," Strange said, and he would not be moved. The marl didn't like it, and neither did Aleister, but they left the young priest in the kingfisher green shade of the trees.

When they stopped for the midday halt Grimshaw took himself off to a shady place and meditated in full view of all, like any good priest-trained witch. It was a sincere effort, but the bearers were not impressed.

Nanak sidled up to Strange as he was finishing his afternoon meal.

"The major-sir is my master and I obey."

Strange gave him a level look.

"But the other sir. The witch." Nanak made a point of not looking toward Aleister who sat cool and crosslegged, turned up palms resting on his knees, his eyes peacefully closed.

"Well?"

"My fellows are simple men. Superstitious men. They have grown up half believing the fairytales and legends of their childhood." Nanak's wizened face contorted at the idea of such foolery.

"Master Grimshaw is in the employ of your own Holy Orders."

Nanak nodded. "You need not explain this to *me*, major-sir. I understand that witches have their uses. Even Alban witches."

Strange had always thought it ironic, if just, that despite their role in the Inborn Mutiny, Alban witches were so feared and distrusted by Hidushi natives.

"What's the problem then?"

Nanak made a broad gesture. "This one. There are stories of him. Of the dig at the Gomar River."

Strange didn't so much as blink. More curtly than before he asked, "And?"

"But you must have heard major-sir, for you were in the army then."

Oh, he'd heard all right. Who hadn't heard the stories? The excavation of a 1st Dynasty temple had gone very wrong. Some kind of accident had occurred and nearly all those sent to unbury the past had been buried in its stead, twelve fresh graves on the banks of the river. Even to this day rumors of a curse persisted, though it appeared the Holy Orders had found marl willing to step foot on sacred ground, as evidenced by the frantic industry he'd seen during his visit with Baraman Warrick.

Nearly twenty years had passed since then. Grimshaw would have been, what? Ten years old. A child. Strange said calmly, "If that's true then being inside a collapsing ruin would have been a bloody frightful experience for a boy."

"You think it cannot be the same man," Nanak said shrewdly. "But this is the very one, though he was but a *paiyan* at the time."

Rather impatiently—for he was uneasy—Strange snapped, "Well, what if it is the same man? I never heard any suggestion that those who survived were to blame for what happened. Are you suggesting Master Grimshaw was somehow at fault? A small boy?"

Not that he was very clear on what had happened. No one was. And The Lancers had not been one of the regiments sent to the rescue.

"Only three survived, major-sir. A woman who went mad and later threw herself in the river, the boy, and the grandfather of the boy."

"Which grandfather?" Strange asked unwillingly.

"The paternal grandsire. The mutineer." Nanak was gazing modestly at Strange's boots. "These Grimshaws are powerful witches. And bad luck."

Unease slithered down Strange's spine. He said shortly, "Mostly to themselves, it sounds to me. Enough of this nonsense. Tell the others it's time to ride."

Nanak bowed deeply and withdrew.

Strange rose and crossed over to the patch of scrubby shade where Grimshaw sat in meditation. As his shadow fell across the younger man, Grimshaw's lashes lifted immediately. So much for deep meditation.

He studied Strange with his light, lucid gaze and waited.

Strange said, "Tomorrow we leave the foothills and start the climb into the mountains. They'll have no time for wives tales."

"You think not?"

"I'll make damn sure not." Strange nodded at Grimshaw's crosslegged pose. "Thanks for this, anyway."

"It won't do any good. They know I'm no temple witch."

"Aren't you? You appear to be employed by the Holy Orders."

"True." He gave Strange a funny smile. "I don't like trouble."

Meaning the son of a convicted traitor might have difficulty practicing The Craft if he wasn't under the protective geis of the church?

Aleister said, "Speaking of priests, why did you do that today? Leave that boy to be murdered in Phansigar territory?"

"Is that what you think I did?" As Grimshaw seemed more puzzled than upset, Strange said, "If he's really a priest, why should the Phansigars harm him? He has nothing they want."

"The Phansigars are religious madmen."

"All religions seem mad to men of other religions."

"I'd no idea you were a philosopher," Grimshaw said dryly.

"I've seen enough to form an opinion or two. The boy should be all right. You're probably in greater danger than he is."

Grimshaw rose in one of those effortless moves. "So true, but I've you to protect me, Major Strange."

"That's right."

To Strange' surprise Grimshaw grinned, and an odd feeling swept through him. Partly it was... to do with the way Grimshaw's cheek creased when he smiled that mocking smile, the way his lashes lowered and then flicked up, the peculiar color of his eyes that was neither gray nor blue...

He pulled his thoughts up short. Yes, perhaps there was truth to those legends about witches—although Grimshaw did not appear to be making much effort to beguile. Far from it, irritating little sod.

They mounted up again and Strange kept them at a brisk pace despite the intense moist heat that glistened on the great green leaves of the ancient trees and plants. Snakes dangled from trees, large amber-eyed creatures slunk silently through the undergrowth. Monkeys chattered overhead.

"Here are your winged monkeys, Major Strange," Grimshaw remarked pointing at two strange creatures sailing gracefully from tree top to tree top. The "monkeys" had clawed feet, giant eyes, and a membrane of coppery skin stretching from the long tail to the forelimbs.

"Those aren't winged monkeys, Master Grimshaw. Nor bats. Nor any creatures familiar to witches."

"They are good to eat, major-sir," volunteered Nanak from behind them, and Strange laughed at Grimshaw's expression.

He kept them moving late into the afternoon and it wasn't until his own back and arse were protesting that he at last called a halt within the enormous carved stone gates of what had once been a great city between the feet of the Benhali Mountains. They dismounted within sight of the ruins of the old outdoor theater, and hobbled the horses. The bearers made camp ostentatiously avoiding each other.

"Where are we?" Grimshaw asked, staring up at the scarred green-marble face of a monolithic man.

Strange showed him the map and the compass. "These are the ruins of Nagara."

"Nagara?" Grimshaw looked up from the map, gazing about himself with interest. "The lost city?"

"One lost city." Strange added wryly, "Probably the least lost of the lost cities."

"I've examined artifacts from here. Dragon wine vessels and a bronze ceremonial axe used in ritual sacrifice."

"Ah, the good old days," Strange drawled.

A true academic, Grimshaw didn't even register this. His face was alight with the most enthusiasm he'd shown yet. "But this is excellent. I've always wanted to see the Lost City of Nagara."

"And to think you believed this was a wasted trip, Grimshaw!"

Grimshaw did catch the raillery that time. He said seriously, "Such historical landmarks as Nagara are important to us all. If we don't learn from the past how can we avoid repeating its mistakes?"

"We can't. Do you truly believe that people learn from the mistakes of others?"

Grimshaw slanted him one of those odd looks. "You're a cynical man, Major Strange."

"All soldiers are cynical. We see the worst of humankind."

"The best too, surely?"

It was Strange's turn to be taken aback. "How do you figure that, Master Sticks and Stones?"

"Loyalty, courage, sacrifice, faith. Don't you see these things in battle?" And when Strange made no immediate reply, "Love of comrade for comrade?"

Strange threw him a sharp look, though he didn't suppose Grimshaw meant it the way it sounded.

"Perhaps," he said grudgingly, and changed the subject.

While the evening meal cooked, he looked over the map, calculating the following day's ride. By tomorrow they would be well and truly into the mountains. While he charted the next stage of their journey, Grimshaw explored. Strange looked up once to see him climbing the red granite staircase to the overgrown foundation of a now roofless and wall-less structure. Strange didn't begrudge him his intellectual amusements, but he had the uneasy feeling that when Grimshaw's attention was fully engaged he forgot to be cautious.

"Grimshaw, stay close," he called. "These ruins are home to many wild things."

Natural and unnatural. Already an old city when the world was young, Nagara was believed to have been a seat of great wealth and power. Strange had seen the occasional ghost of Nagara's nobles—tall, elegant, and yellowed by time—in the broken pottery and mosaics of Harappu's museums. Nagara's overconfident citizens had grown increasingly indifferent to the world outside their gates—and that world was changing. There were many stories about the decadence and corruption of the old ones, but there would be. Stories about cities like Nagara served as cautionary tales when the colonies started protesting the cost of keeping a standing army. The cultured lords and ladies of Nagara had devoted their days to the pursuit of pleasure and beauty. And one afternoon a well-armed and well-organized army of barbarians had showed up at those tall stone gates. Legend diverged as to whether a demon prince was leading the army or just the ordinary run-of-the-mill barbarian chief. On one point all were agreed: Nagara had fallen, never to rise again. And now only the grandchildren of the elephants remembered when this had been a great city.

Grimshaw waved acknowledgment from the harlequin green shade. He returned a short time later, sitting down across from Strange. The firelight threw his face in knife-edged angles as red-gold light flared against the composed faces of stone in the pillars and crumbled walls around them.

"Enjoying yourself?" Strange inquired dryly.

"Yes." Grimshaw smiled and the brightness of it made Strange blink. A trick of bone structure and coloring and character, no doubt, but occasionally Grimshaw was a good place to rest one's eyes.

"Find anything interesting?"

"I did, yes."

"What?"

"The remnants of a storm-water cistern. It's full of catfish."

"You've a unique definition of the word interesting."

Grimshaw chuckled. "What are you expecting? Treasure? A hard-carved piece of white jade or a gold figurine?" He shook his head. "It's an interesting place, that's all. I'd like to come back someday and study it in earnest."

"I suppose that could happen."

"No. Now days no one wishes to finance such expeditions. All funds are diverted to establishing Alban authority and reinventing history."

"Be careful, Grimshaw," Strange said holding the younger man's gaze with his own.

Grimshaw's blinked, and then looked stricken. His stare fell. "I...spoke out of turn."

Strange shook his head and returned to reading his map. But he was not thinking of Grimshaw's careless words of treason; he was thinking about the story Nanak had told him about the excavation at the Gomar River.

He was absently aware that Grimshaw ate his supper with unusual appetite, dipping coarse bread in the rice soup, eyes shining with his thoughts. Strange found it mildly amusing, and left him to it.

The bearers were quiet—tired. Well, they were all tired. Strange had driven them hard and intended to do the same tomorrow. And every day that followed.

Grimshaw turned in first. As he said his goodnight, Strange sent him a long, warning look. Grimshaw nodded. Though still preoccupied with his earlier explorations, he clearly understood what Strange meant. Perhaps the morning's attempt on his life had knocked a little sense in him. Probably not.

After he disappeared inside his tent, Strange sat by the fire smoking, watching the moonlight shifting through the branches overhead. The white peaks loomed in the distance like spectral pyramids. He listened to the bearers bickering as to who would take first watch. Tej lost the dice toss. The other two settled down for the night and the jungle sounds filled the darkness. Tej smoked and watched Strange.

Predators took wing overhead. Something large moved stealthily through the undergrowth.

It was late when Strange turned in. All was quiet but he slept uneasily that night, waking several times to phantom movement and soft rustles. The open flap of his tent offered an unobstructed view of Grimshaw's a few feet away. Once he thought he saw a faint blue light in the other tent. As he stared, it vanished.

Another time he raised his head to spy what at first startled glance appeared to be the silhouette of a tiger in the orange glow of the campfire embers. But the next second the shadow of a fern swayed against the stone wall and he knew that his eyes were playing tricks on him.

CHAPTER SIX

There was a hint of tobacco smoke in the moist autumn air and a bulbul was singing, sweet and pure, when Strange stepped out of his tent just after daybreak. A spatter of dark earth kicked up beside the toe of his boot. A fraction of a second later the tent pole cracked behind him.

Strange dropped, groping for his rifle. "What the —?"

Tucked neatly behind one of the broken, vine covered pillars near the edge of their camp, calmly smoking his pipe, Nanak remarked, "I try to warn the major-sir."

Strange threw a quick glance at Grimshaw's tent which was still closed against the dawn. He looked at the place where his other bearers had slept, and his jaw tightened. There was no sign of either Rashid or Tej. "They've gone?"

"They are going, major-sir."

Overhead, monkeys chattered outrage and a flock of birds rose in whirring panic as another bullet chipped a bit off the ear of the squat stone idol to the left of Strange. As he'd expected, the bearers couldn't shoot for shit. No real familiarity with weapons.

"They are indeed going," he said. On the trail he kept a cartridge chambered in the rifle. He rose, slipping out and taking cover behind another pillar.

Two more shots rang out, each missing its mark by comfortable margins.

"What do you know about this, Nanak? You'd bloody well better not lie to me."

Nanak's voice floated placidly from his hiding place. "I did not think they would actually mutiny, major-sir." Which really wasn't much of an answer, though about what Strange had expected.

"What did they take with them?" He cast a quick look at the stores piled in the deep gloom on the far side of the evening's burnt-out fire.

Nanak replied, "Two horses, two guns, major-sir. This they must have to survive."

Purya's fucking knuckles. And along with the horses, Warrick's gold—well-concealed with the extra ammunition. He'd outsmarted himself this time.

Strange swore, his gaze raking the overgrown stone forest of broken columns and walls. *Should have taken the gear and kept going, lads.* He was surprised they hadn't. Were they afraid that he'd turn Grimshaw loose on them? Very likely.

Patiently, indifferent to the off-key song of bullets in the air, Strange scanned for muzzle flash in the shadowy greenery. Within a few minutes he had pinpointed them both: one had concealed himself in a crumbling tower overlooking their camp-site, the other was moving swiftly between the jagged teeth of the furthest tier of marble seats in the ampitheater. There was no sign of the missing horses. They must be hidden in the timber beyond the outside perimeter walls of the city. Strange brought the rifle up, and fired at the man ducking and running along the far gallery of the theater. The crack rolled around the hills above them bouncing off the shattered stones.

An instant later the ashes of the fire gusted in cheeky reply from the man in the tower.

Nanak chuckled. "They are well concealed."

"Not well concealed enough, I think they'll find."

The flap of Grimshaw's tent twitched open. From inside he called quietly, "Are we under attack?"

Trust a scholar to want corroborating evidence.

Strange called back calmly, "We appear to have a small rebellion on our hands. You said you could shoot?"

Grimshaw disappeared. Strange wasn't sure if that was his answer or not. But he reappeared a moment after with carbine in hand. Immediately shots rang out, one bullet tearing through the canvas of the tent, the other gouging the loam beside his boot.

"Stay low," Strange snapped even as the younger man dodged back into his tent. "The tent's not bullet-proof, you know. Keep your head down. Even one of those two misbegotten sons of jackals might eventually make a lucky shot." He fired off a quick retort, but didn't hit anything. He reloaded.

"The witch is climbing out from underneath the tent," Nanak informed him.

Sure enough a few seconds later Grimshaw, carbine in hand, was crouching behind the pillar across from Strange. "Shall I try to circle around?" His face was bleak, but he sounded calm and businesslike, which pleased Strange who had enough to worry about without someone losing his head and firing off rounds of unpredictable magical spells. Not that judicial use of The Craft might not be handy now.

"No. Stay put. I think you might be their target. Otherwise they'd be long gone by now."

Grimshaw cocked his head, considering this. "They could have killed me as I slept if that were true."

"They'd never risk whatever magical wards you guard yourself with."

Another couple of ricochets zinged by. Grimshaw inquired politely, "Magical wards? Like what? Pieces of pink coral? Chili-lime garlands?"

"You know what I mean." Strange risked another look around the pillar and then glanced at Grimshaw. "Let's discuss it later, shall we?"

"As you wish."

Strange asked reluctantly, "I don't suppose you have a spell or special charm for this kind of occasion?"

"Do I look like a magician?"

Strange opened his mouth, but Grimshaw said thoughtfully, "I suppose I might knock that tower down. I can't guarantee where all the boulders will land. Or I could try a flash flood, but again, we're standing awfully close to the epicenter."

Useless in other words. Strange said curtly, "Another time, then."

"It's your party, major-sir."

Strange threw him a quick look and Grimshaw offered a crooked smile. Well, if he could still joke he was probably steady enough.

"All right. Stay put and give me what cover you can."

Grimshaw nodded.

Without further adieu, Strange darted from the shelter of the pillar to an arched doorway.

Carefully, he moved from cover to cover, traveling swiftly across the overgrown ruins of foundations and streets. The firing was occasional but persistent—centered mostly on the camp behind him where, from the sound of things, Grimshaw was offering enough glimpses of himself to keep Rashid and Tej entertained. Now and again, his carbine responded to the shots from the tower and theater. This would be followed by shots from their former bearers. They were getting faster at working the rifles' lever action, but their preoccupation allowed Strange to slip unnoticed closer and closer to their positions.

Picking his way through the remains of what was once a narrow alley, Strange paused, spotting a deep indentation in the soft earth between the cracked paving stones. He made out the distinct outline of a footprint beneath those made by Tej and Rashid. Five digits and the faint indication of claws. Tiger prints. A smallish tiger, probably a young cat, and almost certainly the same animal that had been tracking them since the plains.

He flattened himself against a freestanding wall as the bark of twin rifles reverberated through the trees and empty roofless shells of buildings. The clang rang off the red granite floors and marble statuary. This time the carbine answered almost absent-mindedly. Perhaps Grimshaw had noticed some pottery shards and was losing interest in the battle.

After a quick reconnoiter Strange shifted position again, running across the old pleasure garden with its fractured fountains and splintered mosaics. Now and then a bullet tore through the greenery near him as he zigzagged from concealment to concealment.

Reaching the end of the garden, he raced across the uneven pavers of a small courtyard and began working his way up the tiers of the outdoor theater, making toward higher ground.

The morning air was warm and moist and scented with the sweet intoxicating scent of the sal trees. Insects hummed busily around him and a hairy jumping spider scuttled out of the way of his boot as Strange climbed. All the while his eyes raked the rows of white marble, white as bleached bones against the green backdrop of jungle.

He paused behind an enormous armless idol listing drunkenly to the side, and listened. The rifles in the ruins seemed to hesitate as well. The sun was higher now and the play of green and gold light flared like the crackling heart of a jade lantern.

The camp below was silent. Strange meditated on this for a moment. Nanak would keep himself well protected. Grimshaw...all bets were off as to what Grimshaw might do.

A bullet stung past. Lead flattened against the breast of the idol he leaned against. The echo seemed to ring off the marble seats and the towering mountains beyond.

Dropping behind the row of benches, he waited. When no shots followed, he began to travel again, keeping low, sticking to cover as much as possible. He made it up to the top gallery only to find it abandoned.

He risked a look over the edge of the final row of seats. From this strategic position he could see the two pack horses and Tej, who was apparently about to make his escape and leave Rashid to find his own way home. Strange brought his rifle up, fitted it to his shoulder and took aim.

A bullet hit the top of the marble seat next to him spattering him with dust and bits of stone. Rashid's aim was improving.

Strange fired.

Tej yelled and toppled from his horse. Strange observed him in the wavering sunlight filtering through the treetops high above. To be sure, he put another bullet in the downed man.

He dropped down, flattening himself to the leaf-strewn tiles as Rashid fired again. And then again. Yes, he was getting much faster at reloading. Fast enough that he was starting to make a genuine nuisance of himself. Bullets peppered the stones around Strange, occasionally deflecting with wild but deadly force.

Reloading, he weighed his options as Rashid continued to waste ammunition at a brisk pace. He was pinned down, but Rashid was not in proper position to hit him, although there was always the danger of a lucky ricochet.

Strange wondered at the prolonged silence from the camp. Assuming Grimshaw had not been careless enough to walk into a bullet, what exactly was he doing? Well, besides conserving ammo—which, granted—Strange appreciated. On reflection, he hoped Grimshaw was doing nothing. He was not unduly worried about his own situation. It was annoying, but he had been in tighter spots than this on many an occasion. Any minute now Rashid would run out of ammo or lose what patience he possessed and do something stupid—more stupid—and Strange would have him. But it was galling to lose the morning to this nonsense.

Abruptly, through the whistle of bullets cutting the air over his head and ringing off the stones around him, he heard the crack of Grimshaw's carbine. One shot and a scream. Strange lifted his head in time to see Rashid tumble out through the window of his tower vantage point.

The body hit the side of the tower and landed like a broken doll on the bushes below. And all at once it was very silent.

Strange traveled quickly down the tiers of the theater. He reached the base of the tower at the same time Grimshaw came from around the back.

The younger man looked, at second glance, rather white beneath his tan and it occurred to Strange that it was likely the first time he had killed a man. He looked down at the motionless bundle of rags, formerly Rashid, now lying face down in the brambles and bushes. There was a neat hole in the center of the marl's back.

"A clean shot," Strange said.

Grimshaw's eyes jerked to his face. He swallowed. "Was it?"

Strange started to add that it had also been unnecessary, but it occurred to him that it had taken considerable nerve for Grimshaw to brave that tower on his own. If Rashid had heard him coming, he'd have turned the rifle, and Grimshaw would have died on the stairs. Considerable nerve or considerable lack of commonsense.

He said instead, "It was. Nasty business. No way to start the morning."

Grimshaw was staring at Rashid's corpse again, his profile very angular. He said evenly enough, "Could they have been bought off? Perhaps they always meant to rob you and only chose this morning to chance their hand."

"I don't think they knew about the gold." The idea had genuinely not occurred to Strange. It was possible, of course, but his instinct said no, and he was a man who trusted his instinct. The bearers' antipathy and distrust for Grimshaw had been growing steadily as each day's journey took them farther and farther from civilization and the material world to an unknown land.

"You think it's because of me."

Strange did, and he did not generally pull his punches, but he heard himself say, "Who knows. Perhaps it's simply the loneliness of the hills." He let it go at that. There was enough truth in it. The echoing emptiness of this dead city could do things to men raised in the narrow crowded canyons of Harappu. Strange didn't think that was the case here, but he didn't want to give voice to what he really thought: *because they feared you more than death in these ancient hills.*

The hum of insects seemed loud in the close heat.

Grimshaw wiped his wet forehead with his sleeve. "What now?"

"Now? We'll bury them and leave them to sleep within Nagara's walls." He studied Grimshaw's face—all bones and hollows and dark eyes. "Send Nanak to me. I can handle this."

But Grimshaw looked startled and shook his head. "Naturally, I'll help you. I'll need to invoke the prayer for the dead, in any case."

That courtesy alone ought to keep the spirits of Rashid and Tej howling through the rubble for the next decade or so. But Strange curbed his tongue again and said briefly, "As you choose."

He did not expect Grimshaw to be of much use, but in fact the witch helped him lug the bodies to the soft earth of the pleasure garden, dig the shallow graves, and cover them well with rocks and broken statuary.

When they were done, Grimshaw drew Suri, goddess of the Underworld's, sigil at the foot of each grave and said the briefest of the prayers for the dead—*The truth is known now and shall not be disputed by the living. Judgment comes in accordance to our acts in life and the mercy of the She and the He*—then he startled Strange by spreading his hands and reciting the Alban incantation to prevent ghosts from pursuing the living.

As Strange stared, a pale blue light seemed to surround Grimshaw. The witch spoke softly in Parlance, but Strange knew the words. He'd heard them translated more than once during his years in the Lancers.

"You stand behind the gate of time. Your heart is still, your hand is stayed, your tongue is mute. All those that you hate are forgotten. All those you love. You cannot cross the threshold. You cannot find your way back. That which was your life is but a dream now. You are banished from the realm of the living."

He pointed at first one grave and then the other, it seemed to Strange that the sigils he had drawn in the soft ground at the foot of each grave blazed into white light. They glowed for a few seconds and then pinched out. All was silent but for the rude calls of parrots overhead. So much for sending Rashid and Tej off on their final spiritual journey; Grimshaw's interest seemed to be in keeping them from coming back.

Grimshaw lowered his hands and bowed his head. The blue glow around him faded and died. At last he raised his head and met Strange's gaze.

"I'm not afraid of ghosts," Strange said.

Grimshaw's pale mouth curved into a bitter smile. "No, you wouldn't be."

Perhaps his nerves were more frayed than he realized because all at once Strange was finished with these sarcastic jabs. He opened his mouth to challenge the younger man. It would be easy enough to corner him into flagrant insult and then punish accordingly. Nor would he have to seriously injure Grimshaw, just hurt him a bit in pride and body. Teach him a much-deserved lesson. But after a long, cold assessment of Grimshaw's colorless and pinched face...he lost the stomach for it.

Shouldering his spade, he turned away.

When they returned to camp the second time Nanak had started cooking breakfast over the campfire, and the aroma of frying catfish reached them. Nanak offered a wide smile.

"What are you so happy about?" Strange growled.

"It is a good morning to be alive. Any fool can see that the major-sir would not be prey to fools and robbers."

Again Nanak smiled at Strange, but would not look at Grimshaw.

CHAPTER SEVEN

Despite the late and violent start to their morning, they made good time that day. Strange did indeed seem to know the Benhali Mountains as well as he had boasted. Or perhaps he just had a very good map. In either case, the tall forests of pines and firs and birches were soon a green carpet far below them and the air was much cooler, for which Aleister was grateful. He did not do well in heat, and the humidity of the jungle made him feel like he was suffocating.

It didn't appear to bother Nanak or Major Strange—but then Nanak was being well paid and nothing appeared to much bother Major Strange.

They passed into a valley called Purya's Bower, known for its many waterfalls, which were supposed to represent the unbound hair of the goddess. Silver water tumbled down the lush green hillsides, rising sparkling in the bright sunlight. Giant scarlet and white orchids and yellow rhododendrons lined the rocky trail.

Aleister rode slightly ahead, pretending not to listen as Strange questioned Nanak.

"If I had but known what these two miserable dogs would do, major-sir!" Nanak protested as he had several times throughout the morning.

Aleister grimaced, but kept his face forward. He didn't think Strange was convinced either, although the major kept his voice too low for Aleister to hear his words.

"There was no plan, major-sir. Those two fools were not men to plan and plot. Nor men that other such men trust. They were fearful, that is all. They feared the witch and feared that major-sir could not see the danger."

"What danger?" That time Strange's voice came through loud and clear. Not a particularly patient chap, the major, and Aleister's mouth quirked in private amusement. "You don't mean that old rag bag's malediction?"

"Major-sir should not speak lightly of curses," Nanak said. "Or fakirs."

Indeed he should not. But that wouldn't stop him. Aleister suspected very little could stop Strange once he built up speed. He was like a juggernaut propelling them all toward disaster.

Or triumph.

It was difficult to see that far ahead.

There was silence but for the thud of the horses hooves on the dirt trail, the creak of saddle and jingle of bit.

Aleister wondered if Strange would call a halt soon. He had not eaten breakfast, unable to face anything more than tea and he was beginning to feel lightheaded. The weight of the morning's deaths pressed on him. He needed to do a purification ceremony. He wondered if he could bring himself to ask Major Strange for a halt and decided he would rather drop dead out of the saddle than admit to such weakness.

"What danger did Tej and Rashid think I couldn't see?" Strange repeated. One thing about the major. He didn't give up easily.

Reluctantly, Nanak said, "Tej, the fool, said that the witch had turned the evil eye upon him. Rashid, the greater fool, said that the witch was beguiling *you*, major-sir."

"He *what*?"

"He has bewitched you major-sir and that is why you agreed to take him into the White Mountains."

Strange bit out, "I agreed to take Master Grimshaw into the Benhali Mountains because I'm being paid by your Holy Orders to do so—as Master Grimshaw is also being paid."

Not exactly. But close enough for government work.

Nanak said cheerfully, "So I told them, major-sir. But these were greedy men. And it is a great deal of gold that you carry."

"How would you know?" Despite the evenness of Strange's tone, Aleister could hear the warning.

"It must be. You took great pains to remake the packs and now your saddlebag is heavy with something that clinks and chimes like a great many coins. And if it is true that the priests have sent you, then they have sent you to buy something for them. The priests are buying many things these days."

"Of course it's true. Where would I get that kind of gold? Where would Master Grimshaw?"

Whatever reply Nanak made to this, Aleister missed. Caspar balked, standing still in the middle of the trail, ears twitching nervously. As Aleister spoke to him, urging him forward, there was a clack of stones overhead. A shower of small rocks rained down and Caspar shied and then tried to back up on the narrow trail.

"Get your bloody mount under control, Grimshaw!" snapped Major Strange.

Aleister looked up in time to see a tiger singling its way down the hillside above them.

Caspar whinnied his fear as the other horses began to shy and buck on the narrow trail.

The tiger, well out of its element, seemed to lose its footing, half-sliding, half-slipping down the rock slope. Caspar backed into Balestra, and it was only Major Strange's horsemanship that saved them from going over. Swearing, he pulled his rifle from the scabbard, drawing bead on the tiger, which, having regained its balance, was leaping in great bounds across the face of the hillside, a flash of gold and black stripes.

It happened so quickly there was no time for fear. Caspar reared up as Strange fired, and—his hands full with keeping his horse from plunging off the mountain side—Aleister didn't see what happened next, but he heard Strange's "Got 'im!"

The tiger screamed and tumbled down into the denser forest, out of sight.

As the other two men struggled with the panicked pack animals, Caspar suddenly charged forward. Aleister gave him his head, concentrating on staying in the saddle and preventing the frightened horse from losing its footing on the narrow trail. They made it across the next narrow bit of trail with a clatter of hooves, and came to a halt in a small clearing with a waterfall. Aleister jumped down and set about calming Caspar.

It was several seconds before he heard the scrabble of hooves on loose stones. Strange, on the black followed by Nanak and the frightened pack horses, trotted into the clearing.

Aleister walked up to meet them. "A tiger!" Nanak was babbling. "It was stalking us all the while."

"Stalking three adults?"

"It won't be stalking us any longer," Strange said.

Aleister met his gaze. "It will be more dangerous if you only wounded it."

"Thought you didn't know anything about tigers?"

"I've heard stories enough."

"I didn't just wound it. It was a clean hit and it went down the mountainside."

"All the while it was following us," Nanak protested. "Watching and waiting for a chance to eat poor Nanak. Who would cook your curry stew then, major-sir?"

Strange ignored this. "We'll have our midday meal here." He studied the shady clearing. A thin, cascade of water uncoiled like a silver chain, winding through the rocks and splashing into a deep, clear pool at the bottom of the mountainside. The horses were already calming, beginning to graze on the tender grass and flowers. Nanak, still grumbling, set about starting the fire and unpacking the cooking utensils.

Aleister pulled off his helmet, running a hand through his hair so that it stood up in damp spikes. The mountain breeze felt cool on his temples. He strode to the pool at the bottom of the waterfall. Golden fish darted in the clear green water. Strange joined him, his bare muscular forearm brushing Aleister's.

"I don't know about you, but I feel like a swim." Strange was undoing the buttons on his tunic even as he spoke. He cast a sideways glance at Aleister.

Aleister's mouth twitched into a response. As a matter of fact, it sounded like the best idea of the day, if not this entire bloody expedition.

In a few minutes they were splashing and swimming in the chill green water. The silver fall of water from above kept the surface churning, and a silvery mist rose in the air.

Despite the bronze of Major Strange's face and arms, the rest of his body was marble white. Smooth and muscular and perfectly proportioned, he could have passed for one of those finely crafted statues at the base of the Great Temple. Aleister found it difficult not to stare. It seemed to him that Major Strange should have a greater assortment of scars on his hide. Either he had been a very good soldier—or a very bad one. Aleister tended to believe Strange had been a very bad one, but there was no real reason to believe this other than the fact that he disliked inordinately handsome men.

And Strange *was* far too handsome. His teeth were very white in his sun-browned face, and his eyes were very blue. His wet black hair curled romantically over his brow and his perfectly straight nose seemed to beg for someone to take a swipe at it. No doubt many had tried. The dimple in his chin seemed pronounced as he grinned at Aleister.

"This is more like it, eh?"

Aleister couldn't help smiling. Strange rollicked through the water like an overgrown boy. The small silver medallion of Brigantia—the soldier's goddess—gleamed in the dark hair of his chest.

"You seem mightily pleased with yourself, Major Strange."

"As Nanak says, it's good to be alive, Master Grimshaw." He shook his hair and silver beads of water dotted Aleister's face. He wiped his face with his wet hand.

"Ah yes, you killed two men and bagged your tiger—and all before a hearty breakfast." It was the wrong thing to say—and in the wrong tone—but when had that ever stopped him?

The sky-blue eyes met his. "It was only a small tiger." Strange's smile was sardonic. "And one of those men died by your hand, Master Grimshaw."

Aleister swallowed. "Yes."

Strange's smile twisted. "Feeling guilty? It's a waste of emotion. Those two cutthroats would have slain you without a moment's regret and left your corpse for the kites. And well you know it." He added as though in afterthought, "And myself as well. In fact, I don't believe I ever thanked you for blowing Rashid out of the tower."

Aleister was unable to manage more than a choked sound of acknowledgement. He did not regret killing Rashid—it had been Rashid or Strange—but he had not enjoyed it. In fact, he felt sick at the thought. If he closed his eyes, he could feel again the sweating panic of climbing that dark, moss-slick staircase in the tower, see again the dirty blue, very broad—and unsuspecting—back of Rashid in the window for the seconds before he blew a hole in it.

"Not what you signed on for, was it? But then you never signed on." Strange swam close alongside him and stood in the waist-high water. His skin glistened like polished stone in the sunlight. Aleister could not seem to look away from the other man's curious eyes. Strange, too, seemed caught in the uncomfortable tangle of their gazes.

"Why d'you suppose they feared you so?" he murmured. "You seem ordinary enough to me... Except for this." His wet hand brushed lightly down Aleister's back, and casual though the touch was, Aleister felt it tingling inside his skin.

He glanced over his shoulder, though he knew Strange was referring to the two narrow blue columns of tattoo running down his left shoulder.

"Blessing and protection," he said, which was near enough the truth.

"This line is older." Strange's finger traced the longest column and Aleister shivered. It had been a very long time since anyone touched him like this. And he knew that although Strange didn't like him, he wanted him. No glamour necessary. Strange was similar to Aleister in that respect. What did they call it in the military? Soldier's affections?

Yes, Aleister had seen that about Strange the first day in the temple—when Strange had looked at Brahman Warrick.

Well, Aleister couldn't fault him there.

Strange brushed another light finger down the line of tattooed letters. Aleister's breath seemed heavy in his chest. Other things were growing heavy too, despite the coldness of the water. He said, "Those are the marks of my first initiation. I was ten. The second column marks my second initiation when I was twenty."

"So every ten years?"

"Yes."

"Is that an Alban nobility thing or a witch thing?"

Aleister turned to face him, water swirling gently about their bodies. "A witch thing."

"And what is this?"

Strange's hand moved under the water and touched the tiny gold ring in Aleister's navel.

"That's...an Alban nobility thing." There was no hiding his body's response now, cock standing quite erect. Strange's own cock was also proudly flying the colors, but that was likely a semi-permanent state of affairs for the ex-soldier of fortune. Nothing like a little bloodletting to whet a man's appetites—and it had been a bloody morning indeed for the major.

Strange's hand moved to Grimshaw's face, tracing the line of his jaw to his earlobe. "You bear the name Grimshaw but you wear your earring on your dam's side."

"If I wish to officially practice The Craft, it has to be through my mother's line. As you've pointed out, I'm the son of a traitor."

"Why didn't you change your name then?"

"I am who I am. I won't deny my birthright."

Strange's blue gaze held his unwaveringly—what long, sooty lashes the man had. "You've more pride than sense," Strange said softly.

He knew what Strange would do next, and he closed his eyes as Strange delicately touched the tiny gold ring in Aleister's right nipple. Goosebumps that had nothing to do with cold water rose over his back and shoulders.

Strange said softly, "Is this a witch thing or an Alban nobility thing?"

Aleister replied faintly, "That...is something...else."

"Yes, I thought it might be." Strange's tugged lightly on the ring and Aleister caught his breath and pushed forward into Strange's large hand. He didn't wish to; it was as though he had fallen under one of his own spells. His nipple stiffened under the twisting pressure. Dizzily, he wished Strange would bend his head and take both ring and nipple in his mouth—touch them with his tongue.

Two things saved him. The small sound of amusement Strange made and the drifting scent of firewood and the smoky flavor of the cooking food. Aleister pulled away, ignoring the tug as Strange reluctantly loosed him.

He struck out for the far side of the pool. When he had his emotions under control, he turned and saw that Strange was out of the water and dressing again. Aleister continued to swim until the meal was ready. Neither he nor Strange spoke again until they were on the trail once more.

They continued to make excellent progress, the horses weaving their way up the rocky trails and narrow paths of the mountain while Nanak regaled them with cautionary tales about various relatives of his who had been eaten or mauled by wild animals. The air grew cooler. They crossed a long grassy meadow where mist rose from a boiling thermal spring and horned red gazelles stood and watched unafraid. Winding still higher past a glacial lake and dense woods, they crossed a narrow divide where large stones were carved with prayers and painted bright yellow and red.

By late afternoon they were looking for a good place to make camp when they crested the top of a rise and saw ahead of them the gilded minarets of a monastery.

CHAPTER EIGHT

Strange signaled for the others to wait and rode ahead to the monastery, finding a winding cobbled road down through terraced gardens of fruit trees.

White prayer sheets along the path whipped in the wind, the black characters rippling in silent incantation. Strange wheeled his mount around, retracing his way back to where Grimshaw waited with Nanak and the pack animals.

"This looks like the place."

Grimshaw nodded. Strange gave Nanak his orders and left him with the pack horses, all three well concealed in the thick foliage. He and Grimshaw rode unchallenged down the hillside.

They entered the monastery courtyard through graceful stone pillars carved with odd lettering and lotus entwined with snakes. The atrium itself was unevenly paved in a checkerboard of black and blood-red stones, and ringed with a high wall behind brambles and wild berries. An old and barren place. Even the chimes ringing faintly on the breeze, had a dusty sound to them.

No surprise if the only residents were ghosts, but Strange felt unseen gazes watching them. He glanced at Grimshaw, who tilted his head in acknowledgement.

Highly unlikely any kind of trained resistance would meet their arrival, odds definitely in their favor. All the same, Strange didn't like it. They could be boxed in and cut off in this courtyard far too easily. He unbuttoned his holster, aware that Grimshaw followed his lead.

The gameboard squares led them to double gates with bronze rings that curved through the mouths of smiling demons with pointed ears and more pointed teeth. Strange dismounted, tossed Balestra's reins to Grimshaw, and went to the giant doors, banging on them.

Nothing happened.

"Perhaps they're out for the day," Grimshaw suggested.

Strange raised an eyebrow and pounded again.

At long last wood grated on stone and the door pushed slowly, slowly open.

A stooped and elderly figure wearing a mask of carved ebony and garbed in a scarlet robe trimmed with black feathers shuffled out. With an accent as archaic as the cracked paving stones he inquired what they wished.

Strange said he was there at the behest of the Harappun Holy Orders asked for the abbot. There were times when it was better to be frank and straightforward, and Strange was of the opinion that this was one of them. Grimshaw had volunteered no opinion on the matter. He sat on his horse surveying the courtyard with the detached interest of a true scholar.

The elderly monk retreated without comment and the massive doors swung shut again. Strange looked at Grimshaw who grimaced.

"It's possible he didn't understand me."

"It is, indeed, possible," agreed Grimshaw. "I've never heard an accent quite like yours."

Strange offered him the soldier's salute—the other soldier's salute, that would be—and the door grated open once more. He turned as several more monks, all quite elderly by their posture and gait, wearing the featureless black masks and scarlet robes filed out to join them in the courtyard.

Painstakingly Strange spelled out their quest. Either his accent was deteriorating with the architecture or they did not wish to understand him. The monks seemed more surprised than pleased to learn of his quest. So much for Warrick's assertion that they desired to sell their diadem. He wondered if they'd ever even heard of Brahman Warrick. Or the Holy Orders. He wondered if they were aware of anything beyond their tall gates and the sheltering mountains.

"What need of gold have we?" asked he who seemed to be the abbot—or at least the designated speaker. He seemed to be the youngest and most vigorous of the order. Strange put him at a spry sixty or so. He was tall and very thin. The sleeves of his robes hung like bedraggled wings. He reminded Strange of a stork. Stork said, "In these mountains we are sufficient unto ourselves."

He had a point. Contact, let alone trade, with the outside world, must be limited, yet never had Strange come across anyone who did not value gold for its own sake. Perhaps it was some odd opening gambit to their bartering.

More odd was the way their interest and attention seemed focused on Master Grimshaw, shiny black masks turned in his direction like the black hearts of red poppies facing the sun.

Perhaps they had simply never seen a true blood in this remote place. Or perhaps it was something else. Whatever it was, Strange didn't like it.

He made his way over to Grimshaw's horse while the monks went into a huddle.

"Do you think they have the diadem or not?"

Grimshaw, without looking toward him, said calmly, "It's here."

Strange started to question this, but Stork seemed ready to parley again. Strange returned to the bargaining table, as it were, and reiterated his honorable intentions, finishing with, "We are willing to pay a fair price for this item."

The man spread his hands as though he had no idea what item Strange could be referring to, but the light brown eyes in the holes of his mask were cool and knowing.

Strange looked his inquiry to Grimshaw, but Grimshaw was staring past him.

The clutch of monks parted and a tiny and very elderly figure in a much more ornate blackwood mask hobbled toward them—the abbot at last? The others waited patiently and attentively for him.

Reaching them, he looked Strange over with disconcertingly amber eyes and then spoke directly to Grimshaw.

"What brings thee here, wizard?"

Grimshaw replied politely, "I am no wizard, grandmother. I am no paid practitioner of magic."

Grandmother? Not a monastery after all? Granted, concealed behind the mask, the shapeless robe, and extreme age she was as sexless as a stick.

"Thou art no priest," the old crone said.

"We are on the errand of priests."

"Witch, then."

Grimshaw did not look his way but Strange felt his inquiry. Felt his uncertainty. Grimshaw seemed no happier than himself with the way in which matters were developing, and yet…there was no hint of threat to them. A handful of unarmed and elderly monks – or nuns? Did the temple even have guards? This old holy ruin? But large. Surprisingly large. Large enough to hide a few over-fed sentinels perhaps. The gleaming tips of the minarets winked and blinked like heliographs in the sunlight.

Once again Strange took the lead, delicately broaching the matter of the diadem and was met with blank astonishment.

"Where did thee hear this fable?"

"From a priest. I saw the broken statue in the great temple at Gomar."

"The great temple at Gomar is long gone."

"It's being re-excavated and brought back to life."

"That is not possible."

Strange looked at Grimshaw, waiting on him to jump in there somewhere. But Grimshaw seemed to have nothing more to add to the dialog. What did he imagine he was along for? To take notes on the bloody architecture?

"It's true enough, I assure you," Strange said. "The temple is being rebuilt even as we speak."

There was a long silence.

At last the abbess said quite genially, "Even if such a thing as this diadem existed, only one descended from a god could wear it."

But which god, that was the question. Or maybe the descendant of any old god would do. Grimshaw looked noncommittal. The monks continued to eye him, their black masks bobbing as they tilted their heads and commented to each other, a rustling of words behind fixed ebony mouths.

No. Surely not. It had to be merely that these rustics had never seen a true blood. Still, the outlandish notion of Harappu's most notorious upper-crust lunatic being somehow divine tickled Strange's dark sense of humor. He was going to dine off this story for months when he returned to the bosom Harappun society.

"What is thy name?" the abbess woman said to Grimshaw.

He answered.

She considered and then seemed to lose interest, turning back to Strange. "Tis a great pity ye have come so far for no good reason. We do not have that which ye seek."

Astonished, he opened his mouth to protest, but she was wishing him a safe journey and already turning away, unsteady with age. The monks hastened to support her, although she waved them off. Slowly she retreated back up the stairs and through the immense doors. The monks filed in behind her and the doors closed behind her with great finality. The bronze demon faces grinned cheerfully in the glinting light.

Grimshaw looked at Strange. Even he appeared taken aback. He said slowly, "I suppose it could be a bargaining ploy?"

"Possibly. Generally the bartering begins with the mention of a price." Strange studied him. "What did that mean 'only one descended from a god'? What god?"

Grimshaw slowly shook his head.

"Purya's knuckles, man. You must have some idea." He tried to conceal his frustration, but he saw by the way Grimshaw's eyes narrowed that he was not entirely successful. "Right. Well, can't you use The Craft?"

Grimshaw appeared all innocent interest. "To what purpose?"

Not for the first time Strange considered the possibly beneficial effects of drawing Master Grimshaw's cork with a swift punch to that supercilious nose. "To *read* them. To interpret them. To enter the temple—monastery—whatever it is, and listen to them. See if the diadem is really there."

"There are wards to prevent me from scrying inside the monastery," he said regretfully. "In any case, we already know it's there."

"Really? You're certain? Our information has been faulty so far." Irritably—Strange was liking his options less with each passing minute—he said, "Could you try at least?"

"What d'you imagine I've been doing these past nights?"

"Well now, that's been the question on everyone's mind, hasn't it?"

Grimshaw's lips tightened. "The diadem is here."

"Would you stake your life on it?"

Grimshaw watched him warily.

Strange leaned in close. "Because if they won't sell the bloody thing, we need to find a way into the monastery to take it."

Oh ho. At last he had Master Grimshaw's full attention.

He half-stuttered, "Y-you want to rob this monastery?"

"Keep your voice down." Strange threw a glance at the formidable doors. "What I want is immaterial. The Holy Orders want the diadem, and they're authorized by the Emperor himself." Strange concluded, "We can't go back empty handed."

"Yes we can," Grimshaw said. "We can if we have to. We're not—we can't—we aren't here to incite a religious war or another rebellion."

"We can't return empty handed and expect to still be paid."

Grimshaw stared at him. The open disbelief on his face gave way to something unpleasantly like scorn.

It was an expression that irked Strange more than it should have. "Or perhaps you've a plan of your own?"

"No." Reluctantly.

"Or perhaps you're looking forward to explaining to Brahman Warrick why we chose to give up and go home at the first obstacle."

Grimshaw's face grew tighter still.

"I thought not." Strange threw another glance at the doors that showed no indication of ever opening again. "One thing's certain, we're not going to solve anything standing here hissing like a pair of old maids." He swung into the saddle and reined his horse toward the hills where Nanak waited.

Grimshaw followed in silence.

At the camp, they ate a silent supper and, meal finished, smoked and drank their coffee. The stars rose high in the ultramarine sky.

No plan came immediately to Strange's mind. He expected—half-wished—that Grimshaw would go to his tent and scry after the meal was finished, but Grimshaw showed no signs of retiring to his quarters. They preserved an uneasy quiet.

Strange pulled out his rifle and began to clean it. "All right then. What about this god these people worship? It's not Purya, I take it."

Aleister said, "No, I think they worship—venerate at least—Dakshi."

There was a sudden clatter as Nanak, scrubbing the pots with sand, suddenly dropped one. Grimshaw stared at Nanak who was once more scouring the pots as though they needed to pass military inspection.

"Well?" Strange demanded. "You two both seem to know about this. Is it supposed to be a secret?"

Grimshaw continued to stare at the marl. Feeling their gaze, Nanak looked up and hastily looked down again. "No secret, major-sir. Just an old folk tale. A wives' tale. A tale to scare small children."

"Go on."

"It is not wise not to speak of these things."

"I said *go on.*"

Nanak made an uncharacteristic sound—almost exasperated—before saying, "The one you name was a magician, major-sir, long ago. The greatest of the magicians and best friend of a great king. So it fell to him to stop the madness when the great king—"

The pans rattled against each other as a long shadow fell across the sand. Nanak jumped to his feet. Strange dropped the unloaded rifle and drew his revolver. He leveled it at the figure on the edge of the campfire, but the shape was indefinite as though the smoke were trying and failing to take form.

At first it looked like an old man stood there, then his form seemed to change to something much larger—shiny black and tusked. Would bullets penetrate that hide? Even as Strange was trying to decide, the smoke seemed to vacillate, and now a bent old man stood before them, and a wavering voice spoke.

"The Crux asks that you return to the temple tomorrow when the sun is directly overhead." The words were directed at Grimshaw; the other two might not have been there for all the attention the shadowy form paid them—even though Strange was poised, pistol in hand.

"Why?" Grimshaw inquired.

"What do you mean 'why'?" Strange threw him a look. "We'll be there," he told the now formless shadow.

He was ignored. The wavering voice spoke. "It is you, witch, the Crux wishes to speak with."

"She wasn't in any hurry this afternoon," Grimshaw pointed out.

"That was before the Crux read the entrails."

"Ah."

One single and sardonic syllable. Strange said, "He'll be there. We thank her—the Crux—for this audience."

The figure did not move. Grimshaw said wearily, "We are honored to obey the summons." He couldn't have sounded less honored if he'd tried, in Strange's opinion, but it didn't matter. The figure seemed to slowly, slowly melt back into the shadows. Or perhaps he merely drifted away like smoke on the breeze.

"What the devil was that?" Strange demanded, keeping his voice low in case someone else was lurking outside the ring of their campfire.

"A hearth herald."

"I've seen hearth heralds before. I never saw one with tusks or hide like a rhinoceros."

Grimshaw said indifferently, "It depends on who casts the spell, I suppose."

Strange holstered his pistol. "Speaking of spells and sup-posedly magical relics, I suppose you recall why we're on this pleasure jaunt?"

"I recall." The wide eyes glinted colorless in the mutable firelight.

"Then what the devil's got into you?"

"I'll tell you what's got into me. I don't like this sudden change of heart. I don't trust it."

Strange considered him. Grimshaw was not particularly fearful, so he was forced to give this sudden uncooperativeness his close attention. "What is it you think might happen?"

Grimshaw made an impatient movement. "I've no idea. I can't see into that wretched monastery at all. That alone worries me. Why are there so many wards? Why so *many* protective spells? Centuries' worth of them. Spell upon spell. Why? And something else. Why didn't they at least offer us shelter for the night? It would have been the hospitable thing to do, the normal thing."

Strange laughed. "Would you offer me shelter if I came hunting a valuable artifact you wanted to hide?"

Meeting his gaze, Grimshaw smiled reluctantly. "Perhaps not."

Nanak said, "I would take my chances with a dozen tigers before chancing the hospitality of such as those."

"Why?" Strange asked. "You weren't even at the monastery today."

"I do not need to see the poison in the cup for the poison to kill me."

Strange reflected it might be best if he made the morning's coffee himself. "You two've got the jumps, that's all. It's what we thought before. They turned us away in order to raise the price."

"Possibly."

Nanak said nothing, but began to rub his pots with renewed fervor.

CHAPTER NINE

The hand on his shoulder woke him.

Aleister opened his eyes and Strange said grimly, "Nanak's gone. He's taken one of the ponies and half our provisions."

"*Half?*" He wouldn't have thought old Nanak had it in him. Maybe he didn't think they'd be needing provisions where they were going. Sitting up, raking the hair out of his eyes, Aleister asked, "The gold?"

Strange's face, in the gloomy light of dawn, was grim indeed although his words were reassuring enough. "Safe in my tent."

"Are you planning to go after him?" *Let him go*, he thought. Another death over this bloody artifact? He'd only just completed the last purification rite.

"No time."

Aleister relaxed a fraction. "I expect we can live on hardtack for a few days. Or perhaps the monks will offer us luncheon?"

"There's a thought. How do you suppose they eat in those masks?" Strange was backing out of the tent.

Aleister rose and dressed. The comforting smell of hot coffee and spicy curry reached him as he shaved. He joined Strange at the campfire, studying the businesslike arrangement of boiling coffee and simmering stew.

"Don't look so surprised," Strange said in answer to whatever he read in Aleister's face.

"I suppose you learned this in the army."

Strange chuckled at that, although Aleister failed to see the joke. "D'you think I was an army cook?"

Other than killing, Aleister had no idea what skills men learned in the services. Cooking, at least, would be useful in civilian life. He said a little defensively, "I know you were in the Benhali Lancers."

"The White Lancers. That's right. Nearly twenty years with the Lancers. Twenty years spent fighting to protect this country from the enemies on her border." Strange dipped a long spoon in the pot, and glanced up, adding, "And within."

Of course it always came back to this with Strange. Just once it would be nice if…but it was useless thinking that way. As far as Strange was concerned, Aleister was the spawn of traitors. Nor could Aleister entirely blame him. He still remembered the terror of those long days, the long months of the Inborn Mutiny. The monstrous violence, the atrocities against complete innocents. He recalled too well the horror his father and grandfather had felt upon seeing what they'd unleashed on their adopted country. Helped to unleash. It didn't matter that they were right, that the Alban overlords were raping and pillaging Hidush and that something needed to happen. What had happened was a tidal wave of violence and madness that had swept across the entire land. Strange would have been a very young soldier then, and he would have seen things that turned much older, harder men sick and faint.

No, Aleister didn't blame Strange. And Strange was right about Aleister too. He *did* believe that some kind of revolution needed to take place—peaceful revolution—that the balance of power in Hidush needed to be…balanced. Truly balanced. But he was not foolish enough to voice these thoughts.

So he ignored Strange's comment, and said mildly, "Then where *did* you learn to cook?"

Strange seemed caught off guard by this deliberate change of topic, but then, to Aleister's relief, answered neutrally enough. "In Nawrlong. Do you know where that is?"

"A great city in the south of Marikelan."

"Thass right." For a second the Outborn accent was back. "Famous for its food and music and beautiful women—fine enough to rival anything in old Alba. I grew up on the docks." He hooked a thumb at his chest. "Wharf rat."

Aleister was impressed despite himself. A dockland wharf rat growing up to be a major in the prestigious Benhali Lancers? Either Strange had made influential friends along the way or he was one tough—and lucky—soldier.

"And you learned to cook in the dockland?"

"Mostly. My grandmother was chef for Lord Byland."

Aleister had no idea who Lord Byland was—he could barely keep the old former Alban ruling families straight—but apparently this was a source of pride for Strange. Fair enough. Chef to a great house would be an achievement for someone from the docks—from anywhere, really. He nodded encouragingly.

"She thought I should become a chef too." Strange's lip curled derisively, but there was a trace of affection in his smile. "Funny old girl, she was. Tough old bird. And I suppose it wouldn't have been a bad life. I had a knack for it, according to her. But I wanted adventure, action, excitement. And by Purya's knuckles, I got it."

No question there. Aleister asked, "So you joined the army? But how did you win a commission to the Lancers?"

"In a lucky hand of vingt-et-un."

"You won a commission to the Lancers in a card game?"

Strange was grinning reminiscently.

"What were you betting?" Aleister couldn't help his curiosity.

Strange's smile widened still further and grew wicked. "Nothing I hadn't lost before."

Aleister was still blinking over that as Strange rose to pack their supplies.

The monks were already gathered in the courtyard when they arrived. The black masks gleamed in the harsh sunlight, the blank faces frozen in that perennial expression of mild surprise. Funny thing, that. With all the expressions this clergy could have chosen to represent them, they'd picked perplexity.

No sign of the head lady—the Crux—as far as Strange could tell. He leaned toward Grimshaw. "What do you think?"

"I think the price of the diadem has risen appreciably."

Strange suspected he was right. He dismounted and went to check with Stork.

"As you see, we're here. Are we going to bargain in the courtyard like peddlers?"

The light brown eyes studied him. "Bargain?"

"That's why we're here. To discuss the sale of the artifact. Purya's diadem."

"There is no such artifact." Stork spoke with flat and utter conviction.

"Then what are we doing back here?"

"The Crux wishes to question the witch."

"About what?"

Stork spread his hands in a sort of *who can know?* gesture.

Strange controlled his mounting irritation and returned to Grimshaw. "He still insists there's no such artifact as the diadem. Says they wanted us here so the old crone could talk to you. What do you read?"

Grimshaw removed his helmet, wiped his forehead, and replaced it. "Nothing. I told you. The spells and wards securing this place leave me completely shut out."

"Then how are you so sure the diadem is here?"

"I know."

"Don't give me any mumbo jumbo. *How* do you know?"

Grimshaw said tersely, "Because Warrick would never risk losing that much gold if he wasn't absolutely certain."

He probably had a point about that. "Know him that well, do you?"

"Very well," Grimshaw bit out.

Well, well. Strange opened his mouth but at that instant the great doors swung slowly open with a geriatric groan of aged hinges.

There seemed to be a long pause before the elderly abbess at last appeared, framed in the massive doorway. She tottered slowly, slowly down the long steps.

Behind her came a small figure, a child or a dwarf bearing a satin pillow and on the cushion a twisted circlet of gold and darker metal. Rubies and topaz stones blinked in the blinding sunlight.

Strange turned to Stork. "No such artifact?"

"This diadem does not belong to Purya," Stork returned stolidly.

The Crux approached them, speaking in a rapid, clicking tongue unlike any Strange had heard before. Now and then Strange could hear what sounded like "Grimshaw."

The witch sat motionless through the long speech, listening without expression, just as he had when the fakir had stopped them on the road.

The cluster of monks watched and murmured to each other, nodding and shifting as though trying to get a still better view of Grimshaw. Uneasily it occurred to Strange for the first time what he might have to trade for the diadem. He wondered if Brahman Warrick had known it before he sent them on this quest. He wondered if this unpleasant notion had yet dawned on Grimshaw.

When the old woman finished speaking, Grimshaw answered her in the same rapid, clicking tongue. Apparently whatever he said did not go down well. Murmurs of dismay rippled through the assembly.

"What does she want?" Strange demanded.

"They've asked me to perform a feat of magic."

"So? Perform one."

Grimshaw looked pained. "It's not that simple."

Why shouldn't it be? Witches were so much more temperamental about these things. A good magician simply did as he was asked. Say the word and they'd have a mechanical man or a winged dog or a fire lizard standing in the courtyard with them. Witches always had some complicated rule about why they couldn't do something that needed doing.

The old woman began to speak again. When she finished, she gestured impatiently to the dwarf figure who stepped forward with the diadem.

Grimshaw shook his head.

"What are you doing?" Strange demanded, moving forward.

He was grabbed roughly by the masked monks and dragged back. He could have broken free—it would be like snapping a handful of twigs, but Grimshaw called out angrily and Strange was released—though with obvious reluctance. Trying to move forward, he found his way barred again. Grimshaw spoke harshly, but although heads were ducked in presumed obedience, no one moved out of Strange's path.

Slowly but steadily the courtyard was filling with people. Villagers? But from what hamlet? And what manner of folk were these? Strange thought he knew all the tribes of the Benhali Mountains but the crowd joining the pool of black masks surrounding himself and Grimshaw, widening the gulf between them, were unlike any he had seen before. They were very tall, striking looking, with hazel eyes and bronze hair and skin that was just...unless it was a trick of light? No. Their skin was the palest, most delicate shade of...green.

Green.

Something in their diet, no doubt.

But...indisputably green.

Much like the stories told about the ancient ones of Nagara. He'd never believed those stories although he'd seen a few green looking citizens on ancient murals and serving platters. Always figured it for artistic license.

Grimshaw's horse moved restively and kicked out at the bodies beginning to hem him in. Monks and peasants hastily moved clear, and Strange was able to reach Grimshaw's side, putting his hand on Caspar's bridle, quieting him.

"Why are they so interested in you?"

"She's suggested I might be the incarnation of her god."

"You *what*?"

Grimshaw didn't answer, and following his gaze Strange saw that a small cadre of burly men dressed in the black livery of monastery guards had appeared at the top of the stairs. Arms folded, they seemed prepared to resist any onslaught against the monastery. What kind of monastery even kept a house guard?

"Does this god of hers answer to the name of Dakshi when he's at home?"

There were exclamations from those standing near at the mention of Nanak's magician.

Grimshaw sounded distracted. "I don't know. Dakshi's not a god. Not technically. But maybe they think…"

What?"

Very softly, Grimshaw said, "I don't believe she's telling the truth. She knows I'm no god. But for some reason she seems to want me to think that's what she believes. She suggests that I enter the monastery so we can converse in privacy."

"No." Strange spoke automatically, but then questioned his own reaction. He didn't like it—it felt unlucky, unsafe— but there was no practical reason not to comply, was there? Beyond the fact that there was something going on here that he didn't follow.

Grimshaw said quietly, "It might be the only way. She wants me to put on the diadem, but only inside."

Strange shook his head, his eyes holding the gaze of the tall monk he'd dubbed Stork. "I don't trust that one. Make them bring it to you."

In fact, he didn't trust any of them. He looked around but did not see the elderly Crux anywhere.

Grimshaw tossed his helmet to Strange and thrust out an imperious hand toward the monks. "Bring me the diadem."

But now the monks seemed unsure. There was a hasty withdrawal and conference which lasted several minutes before at last the diminutive figure came forward again, proffering a small silken pillow faded with age. Strange stared at the intertwined metals of workmanship from a bygone age. One of the largest stones was missing but it was still a strange and twisted amazement of gold and red gems.

The tall monk clicked and chattered at Grimshaw.

Grimshaw did not speak, did not move.

Never taking his eyes from the winking, blinking jewels Strange asked, "Have they mentioned how the thing came to be here?"

"It's a little vague."

"Or why they pretended they didn't know what we were talking about?"

The crowd had fallen silent, waiting. The dwarfish figure nearly overbalanced in an effort to raise the pillow to Grimshaw's outstretched hand. Fingers closing around the diadem, Grimshaw placed it gingerly on his forehead.

There were a great many gasps and ducking heads as light caught the glitter of jewels. The crowd fell back. The monks began clicking furiously to each other. The elegant green folk, too, were talking in weird little trills that reminded Strange of birds. He heard the whisper start and blaze through the crowd like fire through dry grass.

"What are they saying?"

"Apparently, only Dakshi can wear his own diadem and live." Grimshaw added. *"Now* they tell me."

Strange bit back a fierce grin. Hand on his revolver, he was waiting for something—anything. Matters had already moved far beyond their control. They were badly outnumbered, surrounded. They might still triumph—the fact that Grimshaw was still sitting there alive and unharmed wearing the diadem of a god was greatly in their favor. The crowd, still reeling with shock and awe, were beginning to drop down on their knees, touching foreheads to stone.

Grimshaw jerked his head, and following his nod, Strange saw that the monks were in conference again—the Crux had reappeared at the top of the monastery stairs, apart from the others watching them with her odd gold-brown eyes. He turned sharply back to Grimshaw as the younger man caught his breath as though in pain.

"Alright?"

"Oddsblood...," Grimshaw swore softly as though he had just made an astonishing discovery. Eyes closed, hand at his forehead, his fingers pressed against the diadem.

"Grimshaw?"

Grimshaw didn't reply.

Strange wasted no more time, stepping over the bodies and going to his horse, grabbing the bag of gold he'd brought. He pushed his way back to the monastery steps and tossed the bag down. It spilled open, gold coins flashing in the sun. The monks drew back as though it were poison. More clicking and clacking of tongues.

"Time to go," he told Grimshaw.

Grimshaw opened his eyes. He looked dazed.

In three steps Strange was to Balestra and mounted. He threw a look back to see Grimshaw wheeling his mount, a hand going to the diadem to steady it.

A shout of protest went up from the monks, and the temple guards rushed forward even as the previously prone worshippers were on their feet, hands grabbing at Grimshaw's stirrups and bridle. The mob closed in about him dragging horse and rider back in a relentless surge toward the great carved doors standing wide and waiting. Not trained to be a warhorse, Caspar allowed this, balking only slightly.

Strange spurred Balestra forward, trying in vain to intercept Grimshaw. The younger man was kicking at those hanging to the chestnut's bridle. He planted a boot in one chest, knocking the man down—but another was there to take his place. Ahead of them, Strange glimpsed painted swinging lanterns, and walls carved with the faces of demons and monstrous beasts.

The clamor was deafening as his own bridle was caught and he was dragged in the opposite direction. Balestra landed a hard bite on the monk leading him and shook his head free. Strange reached for his pistol but hesitated. So far they were unharmed. If he tipped the balance toward violence, Grimshaw might be the first to pay the price. He spurred Balestra forward again, trying to ride through the crush of bodies, but there was no room to maneuver as the screaming, chanting crowd swept Grimshaw along, hauling witch and horse up the steps and into the great hall.

The heavy doors swung shut behind.

Chapter Ten

Time stopped.

He was buried again in the collapsed tombs at Gomar. Back with the dead. The ancient dead and the still torn and bleeding. Back again in the scarlet-tinged darkness, clawing at the walls, screaming, screaming while the thing lurking in the pitchy blackness drew closer, whispering, reaching for him.

The whispers rose louder than the chanting voices, and the echo of the long ago was louder than the reverberation of the monks' prayers down the long hallway of the monastery. Aleister struggled to keep the past from fusing with the present, forced his eyes to *see*. Torches blazed around him, uneven light trembling across the carved face of the demons—and he felt himself slip, begin to slide, tipped slowly but remorselessly toward the edge, toward the gaping jaws of madness —

Help came from an unexpected quarter—the faraway cries of Major Valentine Strange. A tiny voice, like a death-head moth beating, beating against his consciousness, and what the voice said was, *"Open this fucking door or I'll knock it down!"*

And, abruptly, the past drew back and the present snapped into focus. Somehow, despite the pandemonium around him, Aleister could still hear Strange's voice, still hear the pound of his fist upon the heavy doors, and he knew that Strange would not leave him to the mercy of that which waited for him in the tombs.

No. That was wrong. The tombs were in the past. This was the monastery in the mountains. And he was not a child and Valentine Strange would not leave him to die here.

A gong was booming down the long hall and the sound rebounded off the teeth and eyes of the demons and gods cut in the shining red stone of the walls. All around him was a sea of expressionless black faces, a wave of silent black mouths turned up to him and behind the masks, the monks were chanting.

Welcome home to he who is born again, he who lives again...

A prayer for a birth—no, for a rebirth. He knew—had known since he slipped the diadem on—and he bit down hard on the hysterical laughter welling inside his chest. Ehimay would be so worried for him. Here was real madness.

Caspar was not happy about any of this, but there was nothing he could do—nothing either of them could do—dozens of hands clutched at bridle, reins, mane, stirrup, even the flesh of the horse. No one touched Aleister, and for that he was grateful.

They reached the central chamber and more monks joined the crowd, these carrying large silver quaiches that looked very old and of unknown design. He wondered about that, wondered at foreign relics here in the heart of the Benhali Mountains, and then he caught the first whiff of the rising smoke.

White spice.

All at once the air seemed thick with it and Caspar seemed to shudder beneath him. No option but to breathe it in although instinctively Aleister tried not to. Tried to hold his breath. And then he wondered why because it was...bliss. A rare and ethereal fragrance like the scent of moonlight or laughter or music. Until this moment he had not realized those things carried a scent but now it was in his nostrils and making him dizzy with happiness. He had never felt quite so happy or free.

Curiously, he watched as a bleating ram was dragged out from between the pillars. Two temple guards held it still and the ancient abbess, the Crux, took a great curving dagger and slit the ram's throat. Blood gushed onto the stone floor.

Tiny woman to hold such a great knife...and so much blood...

The chanting voices lengthened and slurred into a humming sound, like a swarm of bees growing closer and closer. The very monastery seemed to shake with the rising hum.

He could feel the vibration in his chest. Rather soothing, really...

Someone was raising a cup to him. A goblet. Aleister stared down at the watchful eyes behind the black mask. The goblet was silver, also of unknown design. Earlier than First Dynasty? Not possible was it? A lot of lovely silver work done in the First Dynasty, though none of it was not designed for church use. Funny to think of a time before the church. Before *any* church....

He reached for the goblet.

⌒

The gold was gone.

Someone had had the presence of mind to grab it in that great surge into the monastery, and Strange found that bleakly amusing. He needed a laugh about then.

It had taken him a full hour to accept what he had discovered in the first fifteen minutes—there was no other viable entrance into the monastery. It was built right into the side of the mountain; its small, walled courtyards overlooked a bottomless chasm. Geography as much as engineering was responsible for the construction of a monastery as secure as any fort or prison. Unless you were a bird or a mountain goat, there was no getting in or out except through the massive front doors. And to break through those would require a battering ram—or witchcraft.

Which didn't mean Strange wasn't tempted to give into fury and open fire at that wall of stone and wood and metal.

But as Aleister had pointed out—was it only the day before?—they hadn't been sent there to start a war. For centuries the monastery had withstood any and all attempts at invasion and was unlikely to fall to the desperation of one man and a revolver. He could shout—and had done so in the first long minutes after Grimshaw vanished inside—but it was unlikely those within could hear him any more than he could hear them. Given the deafening peal of the bells overhead and the unbridled revelry of the atrium, Strange doubted the monks would notice if he dynamited the front doors.

Granted, if he'd had dynamite, he'd have given it a good try.

As it was, there was nothing to do but wait. He had neither the diadem nor the witch. He told himself it was the loss of the diadem worrying at him, but his thoughts kept returning uneasily to Grimshaw.

Well, assuming those lunatics weren't feeding him to their god, whatever and whoever that might be, Grimshaw was probably all right. He had not panicked. Strange's last sight of him had shown Grimshaw startled, but not unduly terrified as he'd been dragged into the monastery. Probably a dream come true for a scholar-witch.

Once again Strange rose and went to the towering doors, pounding his fist and demanding entrance. But no one came to answer his summons, and he could hear nothing on the other side. Even if the entrance had not been impregnable, he'd have been unable to hear over the hysterical rejoicing going on around him. It seemed that the mountain monastery had been short a deity too long and Grimshaw's appearance—and abduction—was cause for great celebration.

The tall, elegant green folk continued trilling to each other—like demented nightingales—as the wondrous news spread, and more and more people arrived from villages and hamlets hidden through the mountains. Soma and smokeweed were being passed around the packed courtyard, and musicians were playing cymbals and flutes and little drums. Inexplicably, no one paid any attention to Strange at all. He might have been invisible.

That suited him fine because he had no intention of leaving. Not without what he'd come there for. Perhaps later, when things had calmed down a little, he might be able to bribe one of the locals into getting him inside. In the meantime he would wait and he would trust that Grimshaw kept his head—literally and figuratively. He had his revolver and presumably the weapons of his Craft. He was intelligent and resourceful. He would be all right. Strange reassured himself with this thought.

Given what a sarcastic, moody sod Grimshaw was, maybe the monks would chuck him back out after an hour or two.

But they did not. The monastery doors did not open again. All that afternoon Strange waited outside while the bronze grinning demon faces moved from bright sunlight to deep shadow. He waited all the long day—and all the long night.

The courtyard festivities continued in full swing. Shut out from whatever was happening inside the monastery, the mob celebrated with more soma and smokeweed. As yellow sunset fell, the torches were lit and the chanting and dancing began. Menacing shadows moved against the courtyard walls to the rhythm of the drums and bagpipes, and yet the crowd seemed harmless and even good natured. No fights broke out. There was singing and more drinking and more smoking.

Strange continued to be ignored. He ate jerky and hard tack, drank water from the fountain. He wound his watch, checked his weapons. Waited.

Toward dawn the celebrants began to drop into exhausted and drugged stupor, littering the courtyard and monastery steps like fallen leaves. Strange stepped over them to feed and water Balestra and the pack pony. He returned to his place at the monastery steps.

The sun was gilding the berries and thorn bushes in a golden glow when at last there was the screech of bolts. Strange was on his feet, pistol in hand as the doors swung open.

Two doddering masked monks came out leading Grimshaw's gelding which seemed to weave and stumble as though drugged. The monks seemed none too steady on their feet themselves and were obviously surprised to see Strange—and further confused by his demand to be taken to Grimshaw.

When he finally made it clear what he wanted, he was told the reincarnation of the god was sleeping. They tried to stop him but Strange scattered them like skittles, striding down the great empty hall with walls carved with the giant faces of demons and naked youths. Perhaps Strange hadn't much familiarity with monasteries, but he had enough experience to know *this* was not usual.

The place reeked of woodsmoke and white spice and death. Dread rose, nearly choking him.

Strange stopped in his tracks when he saw the pool of blood like a black lake at the end of the hallway. It took his eyes a few seconds to make out the motionless forms of two white rams, lying with throats cut and bellies split so that their entrails might be read.

Grim sight though it was, it came as a relief.

He turned away, shouting again for Grimshaw, but hearing nothing but the echo of his own voice and the protests of the monks.

He caught motion out of the corner of one eye. An overweight captain of the temple guards was attempting to steal up on him—like an ox trying to tiptoe. He turned, caught the man in a headlock, and tumbled him to his knees. Relieving him of his sword, Strange advanced on one of the gabbling monks. He grabbed the monk, raising the guard's sword in crude threat. Again he demanded Grimshaw.

Stork appeared before him making conciliatory gestures and indicating that Strange should follow. He did, keeping tight hold on his luckless prisoner, as he strode unseeing past macabre smoke-dulled paintings of a beautiful youth doing battle with all manner of fantastic creatures. He kept a wary eye on the monks and guards scuttling after him, ignoring the bawling of the man he dragged along the rabbit warren of corridors.

They came at to the doorway of an inner chamber. Stork stood to one side and gestured for Strange to enter. The bland black mask gave nothing away. Still holding tight to his hostage, Strange went through the crystal beads glittering like rainfall across the doorway.

He found himself in a large room lavishly furnished and hung with fine silks and rugs. Silken punkahs hung from chains wafting gently back and forward. The air was heavy with white spice despite the carven lattice open to the pink and flaxen dawn.

Grimshaw was sprawled unconscious on the floor beside a dais. He was naked. Sumptuous robes of scarlet and saffron spilled from the divan on the dais and pooled beneath his body.

Strange shoved his captive away. The monk staggered a few steps and leaned against the wall, mask askew, hand to his throat, Strange knelt beside the witch, touching his shoulder.

"Grimshaw? Aleister?"

Grimshaw felt warm, his skin smooth and unmarked by any sign of violence. The gold rings in his ear, nipple, and naval glinted—untouched—in the muted light. He didn't move, didn't stir as Strange swiftly examined him. Aside from a few old bruises and assorted scratches that might as easily have occurred during the past few days, he seemed unhurt. Unconscious, yes, but that might be due to any number of things including simple exhaustion or shock.

Strange spared a quick look at the doorway where the monks huddled watching him. He raised Grimshaw in his arms. The witch's head lolled drunkenly, his breathing fast and shallow.

Strange called his name softly, urgently. Grimshaw's hands were clammy, his temples warm. Shifting the younger man in his arms, Strange raised an eyelid. The pupils of Grimshaw's eyes were enormous and velvety-black with the drug.

What very long eyelashes Grimshaw had. Something Strange had not noticed before. They gave him an unreasonably vulnerable appearance.

To his relief the man in his arms stirred and groaned, turning his head away.

"Grimshaw? Can you hear me?"

His head rolled against Strange's chest. He opened heavy eyelids.

"Grimshaw? Are you all right? Say something."

The witch licked his lips. "You are...very good to look at."

Strange felt a flash of relieved humor. "Something besides that."

Grimshaw blinked at him in a grave owlish way.

"Wish...you'd kiss me."

"Eh...?" Strange spared a glance for the monks still watching from the doorway. "Do you know me, Grimshaw?"

Grimshaw seemed to consider it. He mumbled, "Prefer you to call me Aleister, ac...tu...ally."

"Aleister, then."

"Like your name. Too. Suits."

Strange snorted.

"Not *Strange*," Aleister told him seriously, blinking those ridiculous lashes. "Valentine. Like that."

"You're doped to the gills."

Aleister nodded very slowly. He seemed pleased that Strange had noticed.

Strange shot another look at the monks crowded at the doorway, trying to peer inside the chamber. Then Aleister was pushing at him. Strange let him go as Aleister sat up.

He put an uncertain hand to his head. "Oddsblood...I feel...don't feel quite..."

"Do you remember what happened?"

"When?" Aleister's voice was muffled.

"When —" Strange gave that up. "Are you hurt? You don't seem to be."

Aleister laughed unsteadily and moved onto his hands and knees before trying to stand. Strange rose with him, and when Aleister reeled, he caught him.

"Steady. Take your time."

Aleister leaned into him, panting softly into his neck. It was...oddly arousing. Possibly due to the face that Aleister was warm and naked and Strange had been without release for sometime. Or, possibly, for another reason...

For a few moments they stood there. Strange noted that, preoccupied as he had been with Aleister, he had allowed his hostage to slip away.

He looked over the bowed blond head resting on his shoulder. The monks in the doorway had been replaced with blunt-faced men with glinting swords. Overfed and out of practice they might be, but there were enough of them to present a problem.

"We've got trouble."

"D'you think so?" Aleister muttered. He raised his head, stared at the men in the doorway. He commanded them to leave, speaking in the broken hill dialect the monks had used when they first arrived.

Hard-faced and suspicious, the guards did not move.

On the bright side, they did not approach any further.

Aleister bristled, reiterating his orders. He was indeed to the manor born; that particular tone raised the hair on the back of Strange's neck. The guards withdrew slowly, reluctantly, muttering among themselves and making obsience. The sparkling beads fell back into place behind them.

Strange aided Aleister to the dais—he had some trouble with the step up—and then to the long divan scattered with silken cushions.

"Where are your clothes?"

"Hmm?" Aleister scrubbed his face with his hands and leaned forward, nearly toppling off the divan. "No notion." Strange caught him back and tried not to react as Aleister turned to him, wrapping an arm around his shoulders and leaning into him once more. He could feel eyelashes flickering against his skin and the softness of lips as Aleister mouthed, "Think I'm supposed to wear that." He inclined his heavy head at the robe on the floor without opening his eyes.

"Didn't the style suit?"

"None of this suits."

"Try to wake up, won't you?"

Aleister nodded sleepily and kept nodding. Strange let him go, stepping down from the dais, and Aleister stretched out on his side showing every indication of falling back asleep. Strange picked up the robes, shaking one out. They were the kind of things that court magicians wore. Magicians with wealthy patrons. Not the kind of thing one expected to find in a mountain monastery.

Returning to the dais, he shook awake his drowsy colleague and helped his uncoordinated efforts to don the robe.

"Very…theatrical," He remarked, guiding one arm through a wide fluttering sleeve.

"Mm." Aleister pushed the sleeve back and peered blearily down at himself. "First Dynasty, I think. Probably quite… valuable."

"It's your color." Strange stood back, pretending to admire, and Aleister stopped rubbing his face and spluttered a half-laugh before resting his head in his hands again. The robe slid off one wide, bony shoulder.

"You need fresh air. Stand up." Strange hauled him to his feet and guided him off the dais and across the floor to the window.

The silk rustled distractingly against Aleister's nakedness as he leaned against the casement breathing in the fresh air. It was tempting to continue to hold him close, but Strange resisted. Hardly the time to be thinking of such things.

Gradually color returned to Aleister's face as he breathed deeply. Gaze more alert, he glanced sideways at Strange and then away. He cleared his throat. "Er..."

"Think nothing of it."

"No. I-I shan't. I mean, it's—it was the white spice talking."

"I didn't doubt it."

Aleister's winged brows drew together. "Are you...laughing at me?"

"There's not a tremendous lot to laugh at so far. Where's the diadem?"

Aleister shook his head—and winced. "Last thing I remember, I was wearing it. They gave me something to drink. Soma then some native brew. And then the white spice too."

"The places stinks of it." Strange was conscious of their shoulders brushing, conscious of the sleepy, warm scent of Aleister edged with sweat and the drugs, but still himself...and appetizing for all that.

"I don't remember much of anything after the white spice."

"Probably just as well. You being convent reared and all."

Aleister gave another of those spluttery laughs.

Strange stared at him for a long moment, hard pressed to put a name to his own instant response to that husky laugh. Relief, perhaps? After all, it could be worse. A good deal worse. They were both unharmed, together. Now all they had to do was find the diadem and get out of this alive...

CHAPTER ELEVEN

After a few minutes more of fresh air, Aleister professed himself recovered and they returned to the dais and the divan where they quietly discussed their options, conscious of the fact that the chamber might well be riddled with listening stations or spy holes.

"What do they want of you? That's the first question."

Aleister shook his head—and winced again.

"But they believe you're a god? Or the reincarnation of a god?"

Aleister's forehead creased. "I don't know. Some of them, perhaps. Some of the more ignorant folk."

At a tangent, Strange asked, "Did you notice the people in the monastery courtyard were green?"

Aleister squinted as though he were trying to see Strange from a long way away. "But that makes sense, doesn't it? The people of Nagara couldn't simply disappear, could they?"

"You think these green villagers are descendants of Nagara?"

"Why not? They look like them. Like they look in the mosaics and murals. Tall and thin and..." Aleister broke off yawning widely.

"The color of green tea." Strange said grimly, "But the legend is that Nagara was wiped out by barbarians."

"I heard demons. Either way *someone* would survive. Someone always survives."

Very true. In fact, a philosophy Strange was committed to.

Aleister's eyelashes drifted closed. "Not *her*, though. I think she knows well enough what I am. But..."

Strange tried to follow this. He joggled Aleister's shoulder. "But?"

Heavy lids raised. "It suits their purpose to pretend."

"*Their*? Who is *their*?"

"The Crux. Her and...and the tall one." He snickered. "Stork. He does look like a stork, you're right." He offered this as an earnest confidence and Strange controlled his exasperation.

"Have you found out who this god you're supposed to be is?"

"Dakshi." Aleister seemed surprised as thought it should be self-evident. "I told you."

"You said Dakshi wasn't technically a god. But now you're saying this is his temple?"

Aleister seemed to consider this from an academic distance. "It's no one's temple. I mean, it's not even really a temple. Not a place of worship. It's a kind of monastery now but I suspect it used to be a fortress. This might be Dakshi's palace or hunting lodge at one time. I think there is a battle for power between those two."

"Between Dakshi's palace and hunting lodge?"

Aleister squinted at Strange. "Between the Crux and Stork."

"Ah." Strange considered this. "A power play? That could work in our favor."

Aleister nodded wisely, but then he kept nodding as though about to drift off.

"How does this Dakshi tie in with Purya?"

"He doesn't. Purya is a third dynasty goddess. Dakshi is pre-first."

"But the statue of him was found in Purya's temple."

"*Under* Purya's temple." Aleister's eyes opened. His voice took on the tone of a preceptor, only slightly impaired by the effect of white spice. "Any fledgling archeologist will tell you buildings get built on top of each other all the time and they're hardly ever related. The diadem belongs—belonged—to Dakshi. When I wore it I felt —"

When he didn't continue, Strange probed, "What?"

Aleister gave him another bleary look.

"What exactly did you feel when you wore the diadem?"

It was difficult to tell in the uncertain light, but he thought Aleister might have lost color. "I didn't. At least…I'm not sure." And then before Strange could question him, "The monks here have had the diadem in their safe keeping for twenty years. Since around the time of the accident at Gomar."

"You're saying they had something to do with—?"

"No. At least…no."

"Very convincing."

Aleister said tersely, "How should I know? Like that answer better?"

"Not particularly. But you do know—you're absolutely convinced that this diadem has nothing to do with the Goddess Purya?"

"Yes. Any fool can see that."

Strange ignored the unconscious haughtiness that crept into Grimshaw's tone. "Then Warrick deliberately lied to us."

Aleister hastily backtracked. "No. Ehimay doesn't lie. At least…"

"Everyone lies, Grim-Aleister."

"Not Ehimay."

Ehimay. And not for the first time either. A bit of knowledge that might come in useful at some point. Strange said briskly, "Then he was wrong. He didn't know what it was he sent us to look for."

Aleister's expression grew shuttered. "Perhaps."

Neither of them had much to say after that, each lost in thought. Strange was considering and discarding various strategies. They could fight their way out of the monastery; he was reasonably certain of that, but getting out without the diadem was a last resort. Somehow they must find out where the artifact was kept.

Aleister finally curled up on the divan with a muttered apology and, to Strange's astonishment, rested his head in Strange's lap, closing his eyes.

Strange stared grimly down at the colorless profile resting against his khaki-clad thigh. Odd to see Grimshaw stripped of all his natural arrogance and hauteur. That was the white spice. It could take two days to leave a man's system.

Absently, Strange touched the soft, pale hair.

"It's not only the drug, you know," Aleister said drowsily. "I've been wanting you to kiss me since the desert."

A moment later his chest was rising and falling in peaceful sleep.

Strange let him sleep while he mentally reconnoitered. Now and then he forgot and stroked Grimshaw's hair.

The sun moved slowly across the room, picking out corners and chasing away shadows. The scent of roses growing outside the bullet-shaped window grew stronger. It seemed quiet enough; the celebration was over and now the monks were left with the problem of what to do with this living breathing incarnation of the god who was not—according to the living incarnation himself—a god. Dakshi. No wonder it was quiet.

Equally exhausted—and curiously relaxed by the presence of Aleister—Strange permitted himself to doze, still sitting up.

A small disturbance outside the flimsy door woke him at what Strange estimated to be around eleven in the morning. Two temple guards appeared, flanking the gnomish figure of the Crux.

Strange squeezed Aleister's shoulder and he opened his eyes at once.

"Company."

Aleister sat up, pulling the robe up over his shoulder. Side by side, they eyed the Crux.

She clicked her tongue at Aleister and he clicked back. Strange looked from one to the other of them. The guards moved forward pulling one of the peacock backed chairs forward for her to sit. She settled herself and began to speak.

Aleister listened politely then responded. She seemed to draw back affronted.

"What did you say?" Strange asked, uneasily watching that yellow basilisk gaze behind the black mask.

"I told her it wearies me to use the ancient tongue and that she must use the common language so that you can understand and speak for me. I said that on this earthly plane you are my interpreter and voice." He glanced at Strange. "It's safer for both of us that way—gives a good reason for you to stick close to me—but she's not pleased."

"I can see that. You said she doesn't believe you're the god?"

"She's not committed herself. She says there is some confusion—a division of opinion—as to whether I am Dakshi reincarnated or another spirit. Stork believes I am Dakshi, the Crux is unconvinced."

At each passing reference to the god's name, the monastery guards seemed to flinch.

"Ah."

"Exactly." Aleister sounded grimly satisfied.

One eye on the motionless figure in the chair, Strange said quietly, "How do we work this to our advantage?"

Aleister shook his head.

Recovering from her ire, the Crux began to cluck at him again. Aleister stared off into space with the expression of one thinking lofty thoughts.

She fell silent. After a moment she said to Strange in rusty hill dialect, "If thy lord is indeed son to the One, brother of the stars and flame of the fire, then as promised in holy scrit he has returned to us in our time of need."

Strange tried to look noncommittal as befitted the traveling companion of a reincarnated god. He said, "What do you want of my…er…lord? He has undertaken the mission of the emperor of all Hidush."

The Crux said flatly, "What is the emperor of Hidush to a god? If he will undertake the bidding of an emperor, why will he not assume the commission of his loyal priests and subjects? Who in Hidush remembers the name of Dakshi save those who serve here in his monastery? Why does he consent to give them his own diadem?"

Utterly adrift, but shamming for all he was worth, Strange said, "There is some truth to your words, but my lord must first fulfill his obligation…" Did gods have obligations to mortals? Aleister's profile gave nothing away although Strange could feel him listening critically to each word, "his *promise* to all the people of Hidush."

The black mask bobbed curtly. "But your lord has not yet heard what boon his devoted retainers wish of him. Perhaps he will determine that his interests lie with our own." Safe to say one did not get to be abbess—or Crux—by sitting meekly by.

"All things are known to the gods," Strange said repressively. "My lord has no earthly interests." He stopped aware that Aleister was now staring meaningfully—though what precise meaning he wished to convey was uncertain—at him. Strange added diplomatically, "I'll speak to my lord. In the meantime, he must eat to support the human form he has taken."

She seemed to consider this. Or perhaps she was simply too nettled to speak. The mask made it difficult to read the silences. At last she rose.

"Food and drink will be sent to the god and his servant."

Strange rose too. "I and no other may prepare my lord's food and drink. There are rituals that must be preserved."

No one spoke for what felt like several very long seconds. The two monastery guards were uneasily stroking the hilts of their swords. Finally the Crux's voice issued from behind the unmoving mask. "It shall be as thy lord wishes," she said tersely and departed.

"She's a witch," Aleister said when the sound of their guest's footsteps had faded.

"Thou art right about that."

"No. I mean she's a witch. Born to the Power and trained to the Alban Craft. Some training anyway. She's definitely born to the Power. But she's hid it well and for so long, I nearly missed it."

"She can't be."

Aleister raised one of those winged eyebrows.

"She'd have had to conceal that particular complexion long enough to be trained. How's that possible?"

Aleister continued to eye him in that maddening way. But Strange was growing accustomed to his little tricks and that supercilious eyebrow no longer made him feel like he'd fallen off a Nawrlong banana boat.

Aleister said, "It's unusual for anyone but an Alban to be trained in the Craft, true enough, and most certainly not encouraged, but there's no real reason she couldn't be both witch and monk devoted to Dakshi. I assure you she is. Perhaps back when she was a novice it wasn't frowned on the way it is now."

"What, back in the day of Uruk's Flood?"

"She *is* very old," agreed Aleister. "Not sure she *wasn't* a mate of old Uruk's."

"Speaking of legendary warriors, I suppose there couldn't be any truth to this idea of your reincarnation?"

Aleister was studying him head cocked to one side. He suddenly grinned. "You're not serious?"

"No." He knew the defensive note in his voice was a giveaway. "*I* don't think you are, but I wondered if *you* imagined you were."

Aleister was still giggling—the aftereffect of the white spice—when Stork entered, flanked by two more of his frail brethren and another pair of beefy monastery guards.

Mostly decorative, Strange decided, sizing up the large, impassive men. Their oiled hides were free of the dents and scars that would have indicated much experience with weapons and warfare. How many guards altogether? How many monks? More than one would expect in such a remote retreat, yet it was a large monastery and felt curiously empty.

Stork preferred to stand to address the god. He used the hill language without being asked, and his grasp of the common tongue was much better than the old woman's.

Once again Aleister gave his speech about being wearied by his travel to the mortal plane and relying on Strange to interpret and communicate for him.

Stork nodded affably. "All shall be as the god wishes."

That seemed too easy, although it was a small enough concession. Strange was tempted to push it, to request the diadem and announce their departure, but he was quite sure what the answer would be, and it would be a strategic mistake to change the dynamic—the pretense that they were honored guests rather than prisoners.

He wondered why Stork was paying them his own visit, and he decided that Aleister was correct about that too. There was a struggle for power here. They would need to decide how to use it in their own interests. The alliance of the reincarnation of the god Dakshi was bound to be a valuable bargaining chip. The question was, with whom was it in their best interests to ally? The Crux was an opponent in the game they now played; Strange had no feelings for her one way or the other. This one…he didn't trust him and he liked him even less. He studied Stork, taking note of the precise words, the long narrow hands tucked neatly in the feathered sleeves, the cold watchful eyes behind the ebony mask. No, he did not trust Stork.

Unlike the Crux, Stork had no requests. No pleas, no soliciting favors like a character in a folktale. There was a smile in his voice as he formally welcomed the god and spoke of the great honor to the humble monastery in the White Mountains. He promised that any request for the god's comfort and convenience would be met if humanly possible. He asked only that he be kept informed of anything that would make the god's stay in his new home more comfortable.

Typically, Aleister asked after his horse and Stork assured him Caspar was being well tended, along with the black stallion and the pony. Strange thanked him on the living incarnation's behalf.

Both he and Stork waited to see what Aleister might have to say next, but Aleister did his impersonation of one whose thoughts resided on a higher plane than mortal men could possibly know. With the aplomb and timing of one of the waiters at the Star of Hidush Hotel, Stork excused himself. His retinue shuffled out behind him.

Only when the beads had fallen back into place and the whisper of slippers and boots had died away, did Strange risk another look at Aleister.

Meeting his gaze, Aleister said calmly, "He means to kill me."

CHAPTER TWELVE

The first day passed slowly, and then the next—and nothing happened.

In his role as the living incarnation of Dakshi, Aleister proclaimed himself pleased with his new earthly headquarters and explored every corridor and chamber with his faithful servant and interpreter—always beneath the watchful gaze of the monastery guards. It did not take long to ascertain the truth of what Strange had already told him. The only way in or out of the monastery was through the great doors leading to the atrium.

Unless one could fly—in which case one might jump from the stone walls of the courtyard gardens which overlooked the red rock chasm below, and swoop off to the distant snowy peaks.

He could not fly.

They pretended to give into their captivity with good grace. It wasn't as though they had any choice in the matter. Aleister would have been happy to grab the first opportunity to escape, but Strange was not leaving without the diadem. That was clear. And while Aleister believed he could get back to Harappu on his own, it would not be easy. Nor would it be wise to try.

Nor did he have any intention of leaving Valentine Strange.

So they remained as they were, waiting. Strange prepared their food and drink himself—taking precautions that nothing was tampered with—and making up his own "magical" rituals which apparently kept the kitchen staff mightily entertained.

At night they took turns sleeping. Not only was no attempt made against them, they were, for the most part, ignored.

Or so it seemed.

They rapidly figured out that while Strange was free to come and go from the monastery—and, in fact, was given every chance to escape—Aleister was watched at all times.

Just what exactly their hosts wished to do now that they had their very own god was not clear. Perhaps they could not decide.

On the third day Aleister was summoned—though the summons was phrased in flowery and flattering terms—to the innermost sanctum of the monastery where the likeness of the god was kept. Strange's insistence that he accompany the living incarnation was politely but inexorably refused. Only monks and the god himself could be permitted in the Chamber of Reverie.

Aleister pretended a diplomacy he did not feel, and assured his interpreter that he would be all right on his own for a brief time. Strange's blue gaze held his in grim inquiry, and Aleister was slightly reassured. If asked, Strange was ready to draw sword or pistol. He did not ask, although it was tempting. While he could not remember what had befallen him once he'd placed the diadem on his head and the monastery doors had closed on him, he remembered that terrifyingly familiar sense that his grasp on the present—on reality—had started to slip. It was not something he could confide to Strange. Even if Strange could help him—and he could not—he couldn't admit to this weakness. Not to anyone, but particularly not to Valentine Strange.

The closest he came to speaking of it was the first night. Strange had settled down facing the doorway to take the first watch. Aleister had been lying on the divan watching the faint wash of stars outside the window.

He said unemotionally, "Promise you won't leave me here."

Strange had answered without hesitation, his brusque voice cutting the darkness between them, "I won't leave you."

"No matter what. It would be kinder to kill me."

"I won't leave you. You have my word."

That was all. And that was enough. Aleister was putting his trust in Major Strange, but there were things here that Strange had no knowledge of. Things that even Major Valentine Strange would not be able to deal with.

For one, there was the thing in the Chamber of Reverie.

Afterwards Aleister remembered very little. He remembered following the slow, hobbling figure of the Crux down a long hallway and up two flights of stairs to an open pavilion with gold columns and a large gold star mosaic. All the while he was conscious of the four guards who followed him with heavy, measured footsteps.

They came to another short staircase and then a round door painted with a gold star. The Crux opened the door and indicated that Aleister should crawl inside the chamber. He could smell the heavy scent of white spice and he could see candles burning behind amber glass.

"What is it that you wish from me, grandmother?" he asked.

She answered him in the old tongue. "I wish thou to see for me, my lord."

Despite the courteous reply, it was not a request. Still, Aleister considered refusal. He didn't want to go inside the little chamber with the smell of white spice and old candles and dusty velvet. It reminded him of Gomar, and his heart began to pound so hard he could feel it shaking his frame.

He said, "I need the tools of my Craft. My scrying bowl, my —"

She said impassively, "Your diadem lays within, my lord. All other Craft tools are as the toys of children beside that."

She was correct. He had felt the truth of that the first time he wore the diadem, and he was filled with a mix of dread and longing. To feel that power again...yes, impossible not to be tempted. But he was only too conscious of his own failings. He was not certain he could control it, and to lose control meant to lose himself. Perhaps to madness. Perhaps forever.

In the end it was the thought of facing Strange, admitting that he had retreated from even seeing the diadem again, that sent him crawling through the childsized door into the dark room beyond.

One thing Strange was not good at was waiting. He could do it, he understood the value of patience, but it was not his nature to stand by idly and wait. He paced the chamber after the Crux took Aleister with her. He did not believe they would harm the reincarnation of their god, but he was uneasy. More uneasy because he knew Aleister had been uneasy too.

Suppose they decided to test Aleister's divinity? But if Aleister was correct, they already knew he wasn't divine, and no purpose would be served demonstrating that fact. No purpose that Strange could see, at least, and so he continued to pace.

Two hours after they took him for whatever it was they wanted, Aleister was escorted back to their chamber asleep on his feet and reeking of white spice.

"Know where the diadem is kept," he slurred as Strange went to him, helping him to the dais.

"You damned fool. I should have been with you."

Aleister was shaking his head. "Didn't want to take a chance...they would refuse me. Bad precedent..."

He crawled right into Strange's arms and slept. Even sleeping, Strange could feel the hard beat of the vein beneath Aleister's arm thudding against his own arm. He felt a general and unfocused anger and would dearly have loved to punch someone or something. Aleister was his responsibility and he could not—would not—allow him to be harmed.

But gradually his anger cooled. What did a few whiffs of white spice matter? Aleister was uninjured and he had found the diadem. That was excellent. Now they could begin to plan their escape.

"Good work," he told Aleister softly.

Unhearing, uncaring, the witch slept deeply, exhaustedly, and Strange wondered vaguely what had befallen him during those two long hours.

When at last Aleister opened his eyes, he said, "She will betray you."

Strange's hand, passing unconsciously over Aleister's hair, stilled. "What are you talking about?"

"The woman."

"What woman?"

His eyes, huge and black with the drug, gazed up at Strange, but it was obvious he saw someone else. Perhaps he was still dreaming.

Later, when he was somewhat recovered, he described being taken up a series of outside staircases to a small square and windowless room. The painted walls depicted the life of the young sorcerer Dakshi.

"In the center of the room there's a plinth where the statue of the…Dakshi perches. And at the base of the statue sits a little faded silk cushion and the diadem."

"So? Was this Dakshi god or man?" Strange asked.

"Man…" Aleister said slowly.

"But they worship him as a god."

"I know but…the story Warrick told of Purya saving the world from demons using the diadem…did you ever hear that story?"

Strange shook his head. Granted, he'd never paid much attention to Hidushi religions—let alone mythology.

"Nor I. There is no such story. Purya was not a warrior goddess."

Strange absently fingered the fine silver chain around his neck. "She's associated with Brigantia."

"Only in recent times. Traditionally Purya was the goddess of home and hearth. She was no demon-slayer."

"So?"

"Dakshi is the demon-slayer. You've seen the carvings and the paintings in this place. The Crux had me wear his diadem and see for them."

A dozen questions occurred to Strange. He settled for, "Why would you need the diadem to see?"

"I don't....except..."

"Except?"

"It seems to act as a kind of focus stone. I can see into the past when I wear the diadem."

"What's the point of looking at the past? Wouldn't it make more sense to look at the future?"

Aleister gave him a strange look.

"Right. Well, what did you see?"

Aleister shook his head.

"What is it they want you to see?"

Another shake.

"You don't remember? Or you won't say?"

"I don't remember." Aleister sounded defensive.

"How can you not remember?"

"I tell you I can't. At least…sometimes…I recall fragments. Images. As in dreams." His hands were knotted together, knuckles white.

Strange couldn't decide if Aleister didn't want to say or he truly didn't recall. The important thing was that they now knew where the diadem was kept. The rest of it, their escape included, Aleister could leave to him.

This was the pattern of the next few days. For Aleister there were meetings with the monks and many trances—none of which he remembered. Or so he claimed. Otherwise they were left alone.

As long as he was on his own, Strange was allowed the run of the monastery which underlined both how confident their captors were that he would not discover a way to get Aleister out—and how dearly they wished Strange to leave without him.

Tentative broaching of the subject of leave taking was met with blank incomprehension.

Undiscouraged, Strange continued to investigate their prison—and to befriend their jailers. He took to gambling with the guards in the evenings when the monks were occupied spying on Aleister as he induced himself to visions in the Chamber of Reverie.

The guards favored a game called Three Sparrows. Strange recognized it almost immediately as Soldier's Brag, but pretended ignorance to the delight of his new-found companions. He did not have a great deal to gamble but he lost and regained his pocket watch numerous times before he began to slowly raise the stakes.

He was obliged to wager—and temporarily lose—Aleister's horse before he finally, inexorably, maneuvered Cholai, the big, slow captain of the guard, into staking a peek at the inside of the Chamber of Reverie. By then he had won everything but the wings off that particular pigeon, but in Cholai he had found a man who liked to gamble even more than himself—and had never learned to be truly cautious.

When Aleister was returned to their chamber one evening, Strange said, "I believe I've the beginning of a plan for our escape."

Aleister's wide gaze—soft with the effect of white spice—wandered to his. "Soon?"

"Soon enough. It'll take a little planning."

"Soon would be best. Else they'll continue feeding me white spice until I don't want to escape. Until I'm happy to spend the rest of my days smoking and dreaming."

Oddly enough, Strange liked this about Aleister. Liked that he could see the danger to himself, see his own weakness, and speak of it coolly, plainly—address it like another soldier debating a point of strategy.

"That's another thing. Can you convince them to let you go into the chamber without the white spice?"

Aleister shook his head.

"Why not? Feign illness. Tell them it's the white spice."

But Aleister was continuing to shake his head. "You don't understand. I can't face the chamber without the white spice to calm me. Without it…"

Strange's brows drew together. "Without it what?"

"It doesn't matter." He swallowed hard.

Something here Strange didn't understand. Well, that was generally the case with Grimshaw. Strange said, "Right then. What about casting a spell on them? Something to blind them, to make us invisible to them? Something like that?"

"I've told you. Not within the monastery walls, no. No more than you can shoot or slash your way out of here."

Strange wasn't sure he saw the correlation. They could probably fight their way out of the monastery—would probably have to eventually if they were to take the diadem, which was certainly his intent. The real trouble would begin once they fled the monastery. The monks would not only send the monastery guards after them but summon help from the villages below. And that would alert every bandit in a fifty mile radius. They would be hopelessly outnumbered as they tried to fight their way down the mountain pass.

Strange decided to postpone any immediate decision. They would hold fast and see what the next few days brought.

The next few days brought more of the same. On the seventh day while Aleister sat in the womb of the monastery babbling whatever he saw in his smoke dreams, Stork respectfully invited the servant of the god to walk in the twilight garden.

Strange was interested to see that they had the long courtyard to themselves. Previously, Stork's rare visits to the incarnation of the god had been accompanied by the same two of his elderly brethren. Not that night. With no one to disturb them, they walked along the wall overlooking the white canyon below.

Stork was talking too much. Strange kept quiet, his gaze fastened on the white peacocks, tail feathers dragging along the ground. The scent of lemons and cloves perfumed the cool mountain air. The fountain splashed pleasantly covering the sound of their voices—or, rather, Stork's voice.

In the way of priests and politicians, he took his time coming to his point. He spoke of old legends and myths, of the days when gods took mortal women to bed. Strange continued to listen patiently, nodding occasionally when Stork seemed to expect it.

At last Stork came to the subject of Dakshi who was said to love both women and men.

Strange was careful not to give anything away by word or expression. He had no idea where this was going, but he already didn't like it.

Stork droned on about the complexities of life in the monastery. He had lived within its walls since his twenties. A challenge for a man of intellect and faith to find a way between the blasphemies of the present and the superstitions of the past.

Strange gave another of those noncommittal nods. Stork was ambitious, that much was clear.

Sure enough, a few meandering sentences later the monk described himself as a man on the rise, a man of the future. He grew a little heated on the point. But the other—the Crux— was lost in the fantasy of the past. No vision of the future. No understanding of what was needed in this new age. She would keep drugging the living incarnation of the god and insisting that he look into the past and tell her what was already known by anyone with eyes and a mind.

Here we go, Strange thought. He said, "The gods take no side in the affairs of men."

The beady eyes scrutinized him from behind the black mask.

"Nonsense," retorted Stork, and though he still wore the wooden mask, Strange had the impression that he was seeing the bare face of the man. "The holy texts are full of gods taking sides when it suits them."

"My lord makes it a policy not to take sides."

Stork spoke right over this. "Not to mention the times when the gods openly and actively interfere in the business of mankind."

"My lord is different." An understatement if there ever was one.

Stork didn't actually reply this was short-sighted on the part of the living incarnation, but he did suggest that She Whose Days Were Numbered might ultimately, even if inadvertently, lure the god into making a mistake. A mistake that might prove...unlucky.

Strange listened without comment, but perhaps his face gave him away because Stork hastened to add that no harm could befall a god or even the living incarnation of a god. Everyone knew this and rejoiced that it should be so.

Strange smiled although he didn't suppose it was a very convincing effort. He decided to cut to the chase.

"By odd coincidence my lord, the living incarnation of Dakshi, grows weary of this earthly realm. He's lonely for his own kind. In fact, he was saying only...er... yester'een how much he wishes to return to his home."

He thought it sounded pretty good, but apparently it was the wrong tack. Stork turned away and walked up and down in some agitation. Strange watched curiously.

Stork returned to face him, and his breathing made a funny sound through the mask. "No, no. The living incarnation cannot consider leaving while he is still needed here in the earthly realm! As for loneliness...this is my very point.

If the living incarnation were to take a consort two problems would be solved at once."

"Beg pardon?" Strange got out.

"An alliance," the muffled voice reiterated. "A strategic alliance advantageous to the living incarnation and to his… unworthy and devoted followers."

Hell of all hells, thought Strange. Had they found a little green mountain-raised and white spice-fed virgin to tie Aleister to the monastery? It certainly sounded that way.

"It is a wise and generous thought," he said gravely. "But in this particular incarnation my lord prefers the company and bodies of men."

Stork's long, skeletal hands clapped in pleasure. "It is as I and my brethren thought. We have observed the way the living incarnation watches his unworthy servant and it is clear that his romantic desires are for men."

Strange, who had been trying to absorb the bit about the living incarnation's clear romantic desires for his unworthy servant nearly missed mention that Stork and his mates had been consulting various divining methods in order to find the perfect suitable consort. He snapped out of his abstraction in time to hear the last bit.

He asked blankly, "Who?"

From behind the unmoving mask came a faint tittering. "You?"

The head tilted in amusement, the long fingers spread in modest acknowledgment.

"But you're a monk."

Stork seemed to find that even more amusing.

Strange took his leave shortly after, unsure of whether it was Aleister he should feel concern for—or Stork.

Chapter Thirteen

When he opened his eyes again he was back in his chambers, lying on the divan, and Valentine was gazing down at him with a peculiar expression on his handsome face.

Aleister smiled dreamily up at him. "I traveled afar this evening. I think it upset them. But I saw your giants, far to the north. An army of them standing still as stone. Waiting." He frowned, trying to remember. "Perhaps they *were* stone…"

"I thought you weren't going to travel like that. If they think you can leave any time, they'll watch you all the closer."

"But I can't really leave. Not physically."

"They don't know that." He took the hand Aleister stretched toward him, and his grip was warm and reassuringly solid. "Do they?"

"Maybe not." Aleister chuckled. "I gave them bad news."

"Then it's bad news all around. I've been speaking to your future bridegroom."

Aleister heard that distantly, lost in contemplation of the purple shadows through the lattice work.

"Grimshaw." Valentine shook his arm. "Are you listening to me at all?"

Aleister made an effort. It was not easy. He was very tired and it was more and more difficult to shake off the effect of the white spice. He noticed that Valentine was still holding his hand, and he squeezed it encouragingly.

Valentine said grimly, "I'm afraid I've been too smart for my own good—and yours. In an effort to sidestep a tangled bit of priestly intrigue, I've played right into their hands."

He related his conversation with Stork. Aleister heard him out in silence, and by the end of it felt considerably more alert. He sat up, scrubbing his face. Glancing up he caught Valentine's expression and smiled wryly.

"How were you to know? It's part of the legend that Dakshi was a lover of men. Don't blame yourself."

Strange said slowly, "And are you...a lover of men?"

Aleister stared out the open window at the shadowy white peaks in the lavender distance. He thought of Ehimay. A boy's first attachment, that had been. Fierce and foolish. Odd that it should have become the yardstick by which he measured all other friendships. Not that there had been other friendships. The encounters at the whore houses of Harappu where he sometimes went when the longing for touch was more than he could bear could hardly be considered "friendships."

Constrained, he said, "I have loved a man."

"What happened?" Valentine did not sound particularly surprised.

Aleister considered it from the safe distance of time and experience. "For him it was only the passing affections of boyhood. Too, he was ambitious. And, I was..."

"You were what?"

Afflicted. But he couldn't admit this. Not to Valentine. He said instead—and there was certainly truth to it, "I was a Grimshaw and as you've no doubt noticed, my family pedigree is not one conducive to social success." He managed to say lightly, "Anyway, I suppose it's preferable that Brother Stork wants to fuck rather than kill me."

"The two things are not mutually exclusive."

Aleister grinned. "Speaking from personal experience?"

But Valentine didn't smile. "What bad news did you give them tonight?"

Aleister's smile faded. "I..." His voice trailed as he remembered the jarring overlapping of past and present that had occurred in the Chamber of Reverie...the glimpse he'd had of buildings on fire and horses running bridle-less in the streets of Harappu, of soldiers firing at crowds of civilians...

Valentine's hand closed hard on his shoulder. "Aleister? What did you see?"

"The Extinguisher of Light is coming," he whispered.

Valentine's free hand gripped his other shoulder, and Aleister raised his head, his eyes refocusing on the other man's frowning face.

"Smoke dreams," Valentine said.

"Yes."

Valentine made a disgusted sound. "You know what's happening to you. Why do you do it?"

Because he could not face the Chamber of Reverie or the visions of the diadem without the numbing effect of the white spice. Because if they closed him in that warm, dark room with the starry blue floor like the night sky—closed him in with the thing that waited for him—he would be screaming and clawing the door before they turned the lock. But he could not tell Valentine that. Could not tell him he feared his grasp of sanity was so tenuous...

"A white spice addict," Strange said scornfully. "Is this how you plan to end your days?"

Was it? It began to feel more and more likely. Inevitable. And wasn't it better to end a brain-addled addict—his burgeoning cravings meticulously fed by his caretakers—than a downright raving lunatic?

"It's most remarkable," Aleister told him pensively. "I know that the white spice is robbing me of my direction and will, but when the smoke rises from the brazier my fear leaves me. I feel completely relaxed, calm and mellow. There's a special vibrancy, a sparkle to things. The things I see, the things I feel. And yet I feel dreamy and...gentle."

"Gentle!"

"The taste of it too... as I exhale, a delicate flowery perfume fills my mouth and nostrils... There's nothing quite like it, I promise you."

Valentine kept his voice low, but the anger carried, "Purya's knuckles, man. You need to keep your wits about you. If you can't be relied on —" He changed that. "You never needed the white spice before. Tell them you'll trance without it."

"No. They want me addicted. They know..." Aleister stared at Strange's face and read the truth. Strange was beginning to weigh whether it would be best to leave him behind when he left the monastery. So much for dicers' oaths. The only surprise was that this truth came as a jolt.

A vast and utter weariness filled him. A weariness too deep for sadness. For any emotion at all. He said simply, honestly, "Already it would be difficult for me to make such a request. No wonder what's left of Alba is buried beneath its ashes."

"Aleister..."

He stretched out on the divan once more. He only wanted to sleep now. To sleep and forget. His lids fluttered, lowering, raising. "I've always understood this. Understood the danger. And yet, I feel like I understood nothing." His lashes stilled. He slurred, "It has found me."

From down a long and dark tunnel he heard Valentine swear softly.

And then he was sleeping.

⁀

The next day Strange sought an audience with the Crux.

He had not spoken directly with her since the first morning he had forced his way into the monastery. When she required the services of the living incarnation of the god, she sent her emissaries to fetch him. Strange was fully prepared to have his request rebuffed—and had already worked out how he would phrase his insistence—so he was surprised when within the hour of his request he was escorted to a small, secluded patio on the far side of the monastery.

Strange sat on a flat silk cushion while the Crux bathed her hands in a small stone basin the dwarf monk held for her. The small man then carried the basin to Strange who splashed his hands in the cold water as he had seen the Crux do.

The dwarf removed the basin and then returned to help the elderly woman lower to the white silk cushion on the black and red tiles. When she was seated, she nodded, and the dwarf brought a short darkwood table and positioned it with great care between Strange and his hostess.

Strange opened his mouth to speak, but the Crux held up her hand.

The dwarf reappeared and placed a tray on the table. On the tray were two bowls and a small plate. Apparently they were having lunch.

In fact, *he* was having lunch. The Crux sat and watched while—obeying her adjurations—Strange contained his impatience and drank first the salty golden broth, then bit into the soft white bread slathered with honey and rose petals and almonds. He finished with small squares of tangy cheese and button mushrooms and sun-dried dates and apricots and apples.

The meal was followed by spicy tea, and this the old woman did partake of, managing to siphon through her mask as neatly as if she'd had a funnel.

Through the eating and tea drinking not a word was spoken. Strange was beginning to think he had merely been fobbed off with a meal fit for birds when the Crux finally set her tea cup aside and spoke.

"Thou hast met with the Adjunct. What hast been said between ye?"

Strange met the shrewd amber eyes behind the hardwood mask. The Adjunct was clearly Stork, which must make him second-in-command? That was certainly Strange's impression. His other impression was that the Crux was suspicious of this meeting with the Adjunct.

Suspicious? Perhaps more than that. Disturbed?

Soldier and man of action he might be, but Strange had been around enough to understand the ways of diplomats and courtiers even if he generally had no patience for that kind of thing. It was clear to him that the Crux had formerly enjoyed a position of near unassailable power but that this was now changing and that the vehicle of change was Aleister. Aleister had become a pawn in monastery intrigue. Never good for one's popularity and one more reason for them to be on their way as soon as possible.

"The Adjunct was concerned for my lord's health."

She didn't move a muscle. He'd have hated to try his luck at Three Sparrows sitting across the table from her. At last she said, "Aye. He ails. What else did the Adjunct say?"

Strange had been caught off guard by the confirmation that Aleister was ailing. Was he? Was something wrong with him beyond too much white spice and not enough sleep? Surely not?

He tried again the approach that had failed with Stork. The living incarnation was wearying of his earthly existence and longing for his own kind. Strange phrased it as carefully as possible; he didn't want Aleister murdered in a helpful effort to hurry him back to his unearthly existence.

Given the vast and bleak stillness of his listener, he suspected the idea had already occurred.

He doggedly pursued his point. The living incarnation tired of the childish plots surrounding him, moreover the living incarnation refused to be a party to the intrigues and machinations of mortal men, loving all his worshippers exactly the same.

That ungodly attitude toward caste was allowed to pass unquestioned as the Crux had picked up what he was getting at, her gaze hard as agates.

The living incarnation had neither the patience nor the inclination to continue in his current role of celestial mouthpiece. Had *she* not once been the sole and infallible arbiter of the god's word?

Her jet-tipped fingernail tapped an abstracted tattoo on the small table. She said at last, "When I was but thirteen years of age they brought me to this monastery from my home on the other side of the mountains. Even then I had the gift of prophesy."

What was on the other side of these mountains? Strange had always wondered. Legends abounded. He was momentarily distracted by the thought as he remembered what Aleister had said about her being born to Power and trained in the Craft.

A brief girlhood she would have had if she was brought to this mausoleum when she was only thirteen. Imagine spending the next sixty or so years in this living tomb with those old scarecrows for companionship? Small wonder if she wasn't utterly mad by now.

No proof that she wasn't.

He smiled his most charming smile. "But now that the living incarnation is here...what use is there for you?"

She was so still he wasn't sure she was still breathing.

Strange continued, "Even if the living incarnation was not, in fact, the living incarnation—and therefore unassailable—two soothsayers in one temple is one soothsayer too many. And being out of favor in such circumstances might not be a healthy thing."

Nothing. She might have been turned to wood like the mask hiding her expression from him.

"And the living incarnation—like all celestial beings isn't used to guarding his tongue. He has a habit of...er...speaking the truth. His unworthy servant and humble slave can testify to that. This business about the Extinguisher of Light —"

She was on her feet and Strange had the unpleasant sensation that he made a serious miscalculation. He could see her bony chest rising and falling rapidly beneath the scarlet robe. One of her hands was clenched in a tight fist. He waited for her to…he wasn't sure. Cast a spell on him? Summon the guards?

What exactly had Aleister seen the previous evening?

When she did not speak, he said, trying to keep his tone calming, "Fortunately for all —" in case she'd missed the point earlier "the living incarnation pines for his own kind, and his unworthy servant and humble slave is willing—nay, eager—to take him home…if the way might be found."

If…

Hard to tell behind the molded expression of permanent puzzlement but Strange sensed fear. Anger too, certainly, but definitely fear. She said nothing, however, merely pointing for him to leave her private garden.

↬

That evening the living incarnation created a minor sensation by professing himself unwilling to prophecy.

Aleister had been restless and irritable all day—well, they both knew what that was about—still, the refusal to go into the Chamber of Reverie seemed to be something more. When Strange taxed him with it, he was terse.

"I'm not a bloody court magician. I can't perform to order."

"Why not? You've been doing it for nearly two weeks."

"Because I don't want to!"

"Well, that's different, then." Strange studied him. "Is it something to do with the Extinguisher of Light?"

Aleister went so white Strange thought he might faint dead away. "Where did you hear that name?"

"You spoke it last night when you came back from using the diadem. Why?"

"The Extinguisher of Light is the other name for—for Venavir."

The name was hazily familiar, but Strange couldn't quite place it. He hazarded a guess. "Another Hidushi god, is he?"

But Aleister was pacing restlessly around the room. "I don't know what to do. This doesn't make sense. Oh, if only my mind was clearer!"

"Well, don't strain yourself." He meant it literally. Aleister was beginning to make him actively uneasy. He had developed that edgy irritability some soldiers exhibited in states of siege. The kind of thing that made for liabilities rather than allies.

Aleister put both hands to his temples as though feeling the presence of the diadem. He said distractedly, "I have to think what this means."

Whatever it meant, he continued distracted and short-tempered—and he did not relent about entering the Chamber of Reverie.

Later, over their late supper of kedgeree—one of Strange's specialties and fast becoming a monastery favorite—Strange caught Aleister watching him.

"What's the look for?"

"You could get away, you know." He seemed deadly serious. "You might even manage to escape with the diadem. You know where it's kept now. I know you've considered it."

"I told you. We'll go together when the time comes."

"Perhaps the time won't come."

"It'll come. Believe it."

Aleister said with a glimmer of his old mockery, "Do you never lose, Major Strange? Nothing? Not even your confidence?"

"Everyone loses on occasion, Master Grimshaw. One may lose a battle or two and still win the war."

Aleister stared at him. He opened his mouth...then closed it.

"Don't lose courage," Strange told him.

Aleister's face twisted. He pushed his chair back, rising and crossing to the window to stare out at the faraway white-capped peaks.

Chapter Fourteen

They had locked a bear in the tomb with him. He could feel its hot breath—the stink of fur and fish and blood—and the pain as its claws ripped into him. He drew his dagger and tried to plunge it into the beast's heart, but a young priest cried out to him to stop. The bear's tiny, wicked eyes turned on the priest. Aleister tried to speak the words of Parlance, but he couldn't remember them. He could only grab at the coarse fur, tug fruitlessly as the white robes of the novice turned scarlet with gore.

He became aware that one of the shroud-wrapped corpses in the tomb was speaking to him, saying his name over and over again. *Venavir...*

"Aleister!"

He sat up and opened his eyes.

He could smell burning oil and the acrid scent of his own sweat as Valentine Strange drew hastily back, the small brass lamp he held casting crazy, crooked shadows all across the bed chamber. Strange hissed, "Purya's knuckles! You'll have the whole monastery down on us."

"Sorry," he gasped. His heart thundered in his chest. He could still hear the growls of the bear and the screams of the dying priest—even as he remembered that he had forced the gipsy to turn the bear loose on the plains, and Strange had insisted they leave the young priest at the foot of the Benhali Mountains. Neither were following him, neither were a threat to him. Indeed, the greatest threat to him came from...himself.

"What did you dream?" Valentine's eyes looked black in the trembling light.

Queer that he never dreamed of Valentine. He would have greatly preferred that.

"I was back in the tomb on the Gomar River..."

"And?"

He looked away. "I don't remember."

"What happened in the temple?"

He tried to make sense of that. "The...temple?" Did Valentine mean the Chamber of Reverie?

"On the Gomar River."

He could hear the pound of his pulse in his ears as the words fell between them. He said at last, "But you see, it wasn't a temple. It was a tomb."

A tomb. And then later—centuries later—a magnificent temple had been built on the ruins of those great catacombs.

Valentine was waiting for him to say more. But what more was there to say? Gomar had been his first dig—and nearly his last. His grandfather had led the expedition to explore and excavate the ancient tombs. One by one the team had died and only his grandfather's skilled use of The Craft had saved the two of them. And the woman. Lady... Oriel. That was it. He hadn't thought of her in years. She'd given him hard candies. Peppermint sweeties. But his grandfather hadn't been able to save her. Not really. She had drowned herself in the Gomar River, driven mad by the voices. The same voices that had then come to haunt him.

"I don't remember. It was—I was a child." He was sure the lie was there to read on his face.

Valentine seemed to stare at him for a long time. "You're shivering," he said at last, abruptly. "Mountain nights are cold. Lie down."

Aleister obeyed and the silk sheets and tapestry quilt were tucked warmly round him.

"Go back to sleep. I'm a few feet away from you. Nothing can harm you." Valentine lingered a second or two before moving away.

Aleister wished he had the courage to ask him to stay, ask him to share his bed. He craved the warmth of another body, the cradle of another's arms. Sometimes he thought he longed for that simple pleasure even above sex—and he longed for sex very much.

Instead he pulled the bedding closer about himself and closed his eyes.

⌒

Originally they had shared the night watch, but as white spice and long hours of spent in visions took its toll on Aleister, Strange had taken to sleeping across the threshold of their quarters, pistol beneath his pillow. That night as he returned to his makeshift bed he found Cholai, Captain of the Guard waiting for him.

After Aleister's screams the only surprise was that the entire guard wasn't there—along with every monk and servant in the temple.

"Supper did not agree with my lord," he said crisply.

Captain Cholai nodded politely and informed Strange that *She* wished a word.

Strange glanced back and Aleister was sitting up on the divan, watching, his eyes a silver glitter in the lamplight. Strange signaled that he was going with Cholai. Aleister tipped his head in acknowledgement, but Strange could feel his unease. Night nerves. They did not spend every daylight moment in each other's sight, but something about being separated at night felt like a perilous thing.

Another guard stepped out of the darkness and Cholai assured Strange that the quarters of the living incarnation would be well guarded in his absence. He didn't like it, but what was the choice?

With a final glance at Aleister he followed Cholai down the hallway. The big man went straight to the carved frieze and tugged on the extended hand of one of the dying demons depicted there. A panel slid open revealing a passageway.

The passageway was painted in long murals of more battles, but these seemed older and more primitive in style. Cholai moved swiftly down the passageway without speaking. Aleister would have found it fascinating, no doubt.

Strange followed, his hand going to his holster, which he unbuttoned as he silently counted down their steps and turns in the hidden corridor.

Two left turns and one hundred and thirty-two steps brought them to a halt. Cholai tapped on the wall and a panel slid to the side. Strange had the impression of a room where many mirrors reflected the light of glowing lanterns and candles arranged in a calculated attempt to confuse the eye. In that first glimpse it was impossible to be sure what was real and what was reflection, but out of the corner of his eye Strange caught sight of a slight, stooped figure in a dove gray robe. This was followed by fleeting impressions from every angle of bare feet, white hair in a long braid, and a liver-spotted hand snatching up a black mask.

He realized with a shock that these must be the personal quarters of the Crux.

The prism-reflections hastily donned the mask and turned to face him.

"Holiness," Strange said warily.

The mirrored Crux gestured sharply and Cholai crossed the chamber and went out into the hallway.

When they were alone, the she spoke in her creaky hill tongue, "I have been considering thy words most carefully, Major Strange."

It was the first time she had used his name and title. Strange said automatically, "You honor me."

She made a faint sound behind the mask that might have been a muffled laugh.

"Your witch has indeed become a problem for me."

Witch. Not god. So perhaps the masks were coming off after all. Strange opened his mouth to say that Aleister was not his witch, but…it occurred to him that the words would be false.

Before he had a chance to examine this thought, the Crux continued, "At first I was decided on the most expedient course of action, and I dwelt carefully on how best to bring about thine deaths." She paused to see how Strange took this.

He waited.

"But in the end I decided that this might cause more problems than it resolved. And there is the danger of that which followed him, and which might remain if he sheds his mortal skin."

Strange had no idea what she was talking about. He was mostly relieved that he did not, apparently, have to kill her. He was not a squeamish man, but the idea of slaying a woman, an elderly woman at that, was not a notion that appealed. He'd have done it if it had proved the only way of saving Aleister and himself, but he was glad she'd rethought her strategy.

Pleasantly unaware that in deciding to spare their lives she had saved her own, the Crux continued, "It came to me that there was another way, an easier way. If the witch were to simply vanish…in the way of the old gods and ancient monsters…without a trace…"

"That could be arranged."

"So I thought thou would say." The dozen images pointed and Strange turned first one way and then the other until he spotted a red lacquer chest in the corner. Aleister's boots stood in front of the chest and his clothes were neatly folded atop it: breaches, shirt, tunic, pistol and the leather bag with the tools of his Craft.

"We'd need our horses. And supplies," Strange said. "It wouldn't be possible to make it down the pass without horses and supplies. Not this time of year."

"All is provided. Thine horses and supplies await thee outside the temple. But thee must leave now."

Strange scooped up Aleister's clothes and weapons. "And the diadem."

Silence.

Strange said, "The living incarnation came for the diadem. No one will have forgotten that. No one will believe he left without it."

Unblinking silence.

"Were it to remain behind it would be reminder perhaps. A reminder of that which you might wish forgot."

The bright eyes watched him from behind the mask.

"After all," Strange coaxed, taking a gamble, "did you not send word of the diadem to the priests at the great temple in Harappu? You must have had some purpose?"

The Crux said flatly, "There was a purpose and a plan. There was a prophecy. All that has changed now."

"Why?"

He could feel her hesitation, then, "The Holy Orders are corrupted. I cannot give it to them."

The Holy Orders *corrupted*? Not that Strange entirely disagreed, but to hear such a thing spoken aloud was tantamount to treason. And to hear it in such a place and at such a time?

Yet he said only, "If we return without the diadem, the Holy Orders will simply send others to get it."

"Perhaps. That will be as Fate wills it." She clapped her hands and Cholai reappeared.

He went past Strange and the wall panel slid soundlessly open. Strange threw one final look at the reflected Cruxes before stepping into the passageway after Cholai. The lights in the room behind him went out as though a blanket had been thrown over them.

The Crux's voice said softly in his ear, "Kill him before you reach Harappu, Major Strange."

Strange froze, the hair rising on the nape of his neck.

He could feel her whisper against the side of his face. "If you wait, he will be too strong to stop. For the sake of all…you must not fail. Kill the witch before you reach the city."

He reached out but there was nothing there. The panel slid closed and Cholai—apparently deaf to the exchange—was already leading the way down the passage, his lantern swinging.

Strange followed slowly, turning the Crux's words over and over. What by the dust of the four corners could the old madwoman mean? Kill…Aleister? Was it—surely it was—more of her own political maneuvering? Ensuring that Aleister did not return to claim the diadem?

Thought of the diadem jarred his thoughts back into some kind of order. He caught Cholai in a couple of steps. The big man turned, suspicious.

Strange smiled. "Looks like this is your last chance to make good on your promise, my friend."

"Promise?" Cholai said, although it was clear from his expression that that he remembered only too well what Strange meant.

"Promised me a sight of that room, didn't you? The dreaming chamber where my lord and master spends his evenings scrying for your monks."

"No time now, soldier." Cholai started to turn. Strange caught his arm. As the big man glared at him, Strange lifted his hand away with exaggerated care.

"Ah. I suppose it's different out here in the wilderness. You probably don't know any better, but where I come from a gambling debt is a debt of honor."

Even in the poor light Strange could see the other man's stony features darken. "I'm a man of my word. Why's it so important to you to see it?"

"Gives me an edge, doesn't it?" Strange replied easily. "Dealing with the living incarnation of a god, day in day out, I need an edge. You can understand that. You've got your hands full with that lot, I know." He nodded over his shoulder in the general direction of the Crux's chamber.

Cholai stood irresolute. "You want to steal the head band, I know."

Strange laughed. "What would I do with a head band? Especially the head band of a god? I've got my hands full with the god himself. His living incarnation anyway."

Cholai was shaking his head.

Strange shrugged. "As you like. You can figure out how you'll make it up to me when I'm back in the spring with the priests from Harappu."

That finally got through. "You're coming back?"

"Of course. The old woman is sending for help from the Holy Orders. Got to do something about Stork doesn't she?" Strange started to move past.

"Wait!"

Strange waited.

Reluctantly, Cholai said, "If we're quick you can see inside the dreaming chamber. Not that there's much to see. But, by the immortal herbs, you *can't* tell anyone that you've seen inside."

"I know that. Given you my word, haven't I?"

"I know, I know. I shouldn't never have agreed…well, never mind. Come on then. And be quiet or we're both finished."

Strange sped after Cholai who marched him quick-time down the passage and then up the long staircases to the outside pavilion. At the foot of the small staircase leading to the womb chamber, Cholai reached for his keys.

"Someone's coming!" Strange hissed urgently.

As expected, the big man nearly dropped the ring, looking away from Strange for an instant. Strange whipped his pistol out and slammed Cholai over the head. Cholai's eyes rolled up in his head, his knees buckled, and he went down, slumping onto his face.

Strange bent, grabbed the ring of keys, selecting the one Cholai had separated from the others before being distracted.

He shoved the key in the lock, turned it, and the door swung open. Strange had to stoop down to enter the room. It was dark and windowless and yet a faint and fuzzy blue glow allowed him to just make out that both the floor and ceiling were painted a star-spangled blue like the midnight sky. It was curiously disorienting—and the strong smell of white spice wouldn't help anyone's focus.

The walls were painted in elaborate murals depicting the life of the god Dakshi. It looked...eventful. In the center of the chamber was a raised platform and in the center of the platform was another—smaller—version of the statue Strange had seen in the great temple at Harappu. Dakshi held a cobra in one hand and a globe in the other. At the base of the statue was a faded and tasseled cushion, and on the cushion was the diadem.

Strange snatched it up, shoved it inside his shirt, and left the chamber.

He hesitated over Cholai's still unconscious body. He'd hit him hard but there was no guarantee he wouldn't wake before they were out of the temple. Easiest—best—to finish him now. He was the only one of this lot with any actual fighting experience.

But in the end Strange spared him, shaking his head at himself. Getting soft in his old age. He sprinted across the pavilion, raced down the stairs, taking them two and three at a time, and then walked sedately down the long central hallway.

No one challenged him. Either the sentries had grown used to his prowling after hours or the Crux had arranged for their escape to go unnoticed. Strange suspected the latter.

He told the man guarding the chamber door that Cholai was on his way but in the meantime had given orders he was to guard the front entrance for them, and the man nodded and slipped off.

Aleister was on the other side of the waterfall of beads, pacing up and down as he waited. Strange shoved the beads aside and tossed him his clothes.

"Get dressed."

"What's up?" Aleister caught his clothes automatically.

"We're doing a bunk."

Aleister began to undress. "What's happened?"

Strange's gaze lingered on the long legs, wide shoulders, thinly muscled arms as Aleister shed the magician robes, tossing them aside. In the weird light he looked smooth and warm and golden. Weirdly beautiful. Granted, they'd been a long time traveling. "You're becoming a political embarrassment, I think."

Aleister raised an eyebrow, dressing quickly in his own khakis. Strange threw him his bag of Craft tools and he let out a small exclamation of relief. "Where did you find these?"

"The Crux gave them to me. She wants you out of here. Tonight. Now."

Aleister dropped down on the dais to tug his boots on. "What about the diadem?"

He glanced up and Strange nodded in answer to his look. Aleister whistled softly. The next moment he was on his feet.

Strange handed him his pistol and Aleister shoved it in the holster at his waist.

"Take a good look around you," Strange said. "We won't be back."

Aleister nodded, but he wasn't looking at anything but Strange.

Strange brushed aside the shining beads, looked up and down the hall—hand up signaling Aleister to wait. There was still no sign of anyone. No sign that the theft of the diadem had yet been discovered. He nodded to Aleister and they made their way quietly down the hall to the great doors. Seeing their approach, the sentry dragged open the enormous doors.

Was it really going to be this easy? Every instant Strange waited for the outcry of discovery, an alarm to be raised at the revelation of his treachery.

Nothing.

The silence behind them echoed like with bell-like clarity.

Ahead of them the night was crisp and cold with distant snow—and the taste of approaching rain. In the atrium at the bottom of the empty steps stood Balestra and Caspar, saddled and waiting. Balestra tossed his head, whinnying softly. The pack pony stood placidly beside them, saddlebags bulging, Strange hoped with food.

They were mounted in seconds. Over each saddle was draped the blue cloak of a temple guard. They threw them over their shoulders. Aleister murmured greeting to Caspar in Parlance, stroking the gelding's neck.

The great carved doors were closing. There was the final swallow of wood on stone as they turned their horses' heads toward home.

Chapter Fifteen

The golden dome and minarets sank into the mist of the valley below like a lost city vanishing beneath black waves.

They'd made good time up the narrow trail for all that they had to go carefully and not risk the horse's legs in the darkness. Good time while the frosty stars crackled and scintillated overhead—and wild things watched, startled, from the rocks and bushes.

For a long time there was nothing but the clatter of hooves on rock, the creak of saddles, the jangle of bits, and their own hard breathing in the thin mountain air.

Relief at finding himself free again when he had all but given up hope, to be homeward bound at last, occupied Aleister for some miles, but then he began to notice how preoccupied Strange was. How carefully he was watching for pursuit. His heart plummeted.

"She didn't really let us go, did she?"

Though he spoke quietly, his voice sounded loud in the silence around them, and Strange couldn't have looked more startled if Caspar or Balestra had posed the question. "Of course she let us go. How would I have arranged to have the horses waiting for us?"

"Who are we running from then?"

"Your jilted bridegroom?" Aleister could just make out Strange's grim smile in the night. He was beginning to know all Strange's smiles.

"Something else, I think." It came into his mind what the something else was. "You have the diadem."

"Got it in one, Grimshaw. The diadem. The thing we came for."

Did Strange think he objected to retrieving the diadem? *Did* Aleister object? He wasn't quite sure. The diadem worried him, but not as much as the thought of being without it should the time of reckoning come. "You stole it?"

"She professed an unwillingness to part with it voluntarily."

Aleister considered this. "Did you…?"

"Did I?"

"Did you…" he steadied his voice, "murder her?"

Strange chuckled, startling him. "No. Didn't touch a hair on her gray head. Though it might interest you to know she had no such qualms about dispatching *you*. Told me to get rid of you before we reached Harappu, as a matter of fact."

Strange's eyes gleamed in the darkness. He was smiling but there was a hardness in his voice.

Hearing it, a queer feeling crept over Aleister…a sense of unbearable hollowness as though he were something thin and empty for the wind to blow through. And yet what was there to fear in what Strange said? Death came for them all in the end. Sometimes he wondered why anyone bothered to delay it.

He was all at once very tired. He wished he could read Strange's face, see what was in his eyes.

He felt a very long way from home….and no strength for the journey.

⌒

How long before the alarm had gone up? Hours? Minutes more like. The theft must surely have been discovered before they had gone many miles—probably before they reached the crest. But they were making good time, and Strange felt confident that Cholai and his men would have little stomach for a real fight.

So...a hot and furious chase and perhaps a token effort to take back the diadem, and then the retreat home to lick their wounds.

He kept one eye on the trail behind them and the other on Aleister, uncertain how well he was after weeks of white spice and trancing. Each glance back showed him calm and alert, but Strange knew he would have to pace this part of the journey carefully. Once they had outrun this immediate pursuit, they could relax a little. He would allow Aleister time to rest then.

As the horses jogged along he could feel the diadem resting over his heart, the metal strangely cold despite its proximity to his skin. He could feel the little prongs digging against him.

Kill him before you reach Harappu, Major Strange.

What could the old hag have meant? Insurance against Aleister returning to the temple in the mountains, surely? Nothing else made sense, did it?

"What about this god Dakshi?" he asked suddenly, turning in the saddle. "What finally happened to him?"

Aleister's voice floated emptily back, "I've told you. He wasn't a god. He was just a man. A magician. He had to choose between someone he loved and..."

"And what?"

"And everyone else."

"*Everyone* else?"

"Yes."

Just once couldn't he give a straightforward answer? Why did everything have to be a riddle? Why did there always have to be one of those cryptic utterances? Strange opened his mouth to say so when he felt the sting of something brush past his cheek.

At the same instant he heard an all too familiar buzz—and Aleister swearing. This was followed by the faraway crack of rifles.

"Ride!" Strange called back, spurring Balestra forward. He could hear the pound of Aleister's gelding close on his tail as they plunged down the trail. Bullets whined and hummed through the darkness.

He pulled his rifle out, reining to the side so that Aleister could pass him. "Looks like they've discovered we're gone!"

Aleister gasped out, "Those aren't monks or temple guards!"

Strange fired back at the muzzle flashes lighting the darkness behind them, then turned to follow Aleister as he kicked his mount forward. The horses' hooves slithered on the loose rock, but Aleister kept tight rein and Strange followed close behind.

They risked a canter down the dip in the trail and then started back up the uneven hillside. As they reached the saddleback, Strange looked behind and saw more flashes of gunfire on the hills to the side of them as riders moved in to cut them off.

Aleister was right. These were not the tactical maneuverings of Cholai and his temple guard. Bandits perhaps? He'd expected that, but not so soon.

"We'll have to ride hard," he threw to Aleister, drawing even with him.

Aleister needed no further encouragement. Caspar lengthened his neck and arrowed down the trail that was hardly a trail. Strange pulled up long enough to fire another shot at the hoof beats coming up fastest behind them. He heard the screech of the wounded horse, and a racket that could only mean man and horse crashing down the hillside. Then Strange was bounding down the hillside in pursuit of Aleister.

He caught him up, gesturing sharply, and they cut off across the rocky plateau in a suicidal bid to out flank their hunters. Aleister could indeed ride, and Strange adjusted his strategy accordingly, leading them over one hill and then quietly, cautiously doubling back nearly under the nose of their more cautious enemies.

That won them a brief reprieve, but when they regained the main trail they saw their pursuers ahead of them stark outlines against the paling sky, and shots rang out once again.

They urged their tiring horses into another galloping retreat, half-sliding half-riding down to the sandy river bottom of a canyon. A waterfall that was mostly magnified noise, tripped and trickled down the rocky wall and spilled into a shallow basin. When the rainy season came the bottom of the canyon would be a raging river bed, but at this time of year it was a sliver of winding pathway leading them through a maze of stone and greenery.

Once again they had bought themselves breathing room, but as near as Strange could make out they were headed in the wrong direction, running out of time—and luck.

They dismounted, walking to give the horses a chance to recover. Every sound seemed magnified in this stone chasm: boots and hooves, the creak of saddles, even the noisy breathing of the horses seemed to reverberate eerily.

Aleister stopped suddenly. "Up there." He pointed skyward, and Strange stared up—and then stared harder.

At first he saw nothing but jutting rock formations. Then a black silhouette against the fading stars resolved itself into a broken shelf thrusting into open space. Something too smooth, too symmetrical to be anything but manmade. A parapet,

"It's a shrine," Aleister said.

An ancient shrine teetering on the lip of the canyon, and Aleister must have eyes like a hawk to have spotted it.

"I don't see a way up," Strange said. He was listening hard for the sound of pursuit behind them, but so far the only sound bouncing off the stones of the canyon was that of their own muffled voices.

"There has to be one." Aleister was already tugging on Caspar's reins, leading him back the way they had come. "It'll be back this way."

"What do you mean, it'll be back this way? Why would it be?"

"It will be behind the waterfall."

"What the devil are you talking about, Grimshaw?"

He didn't answer but Strange thought he heard something else. He listened tensely, but now he could only pick out the strange whispery sound of wind through the lush jungle of the canyon cliffs and the feeble splash and tinkle of the dry-season waterfall.

Aleister loped back the way they had come, pulling his horse behind. Strange swore and went after him. By now he was, admittedly, lost himself, but he didn't like this. He'd had enough of old temples to last a lifetime, and he'd have preferred almost any hiding place to the one Aleister seemed to be proposing.

"We're going to run right back into our mates with the rifles," Strange warned him.

He got an impatient shake of Aleister's head in answer. Right, then. Sheer pig-headedness or witchery? Hard to say which might be their best bet now.

As they reached the waterfall, Strange heard the pound of swift approaching hooves, and this time there was no mistaking it for anything else.

He reached again for his rifle in the saddle scabbard.

"No," Aleister commanded. "Give me your helmet."

Strange pulled his helmet off, tossing it to him. "Whatever it is you're planning, you'd better do it quick. You've about seventy seconds."

Not answering, Aleister knelt beside the pool and scooped up a helmet full of water. He grabbed a hasty handful of pebbles.

Strange leveled his rifle on Balestra's saddle, while the black, sides still heaving, blew heavily into the chill dawn air. Aleister ran a few yards down the canyon toward the sound of approaching horses. Strange watched the bend in the canyon, ready to provide what cover for him he could.

Aleister said a few words in Parlance, then let the handful of pebbles slide through his fist into the helmet of water. More words in Parlance and then—just as the first riders appeared around the bend in the canyon, Aleister slung the rocks and water in their direction.

As the muddy soup flew it grew into a great wall of water and rock, a flash flood thundering up the channel of the canyon toward the horses and riders who tried in panic to turn and run from the wave crashing down upon them. The roar of water drowned the cries of the men and frantic whinnies of the horses and left in its wake a stark dripping silence.

Aleister turned and ran back to Strange who belatedly lowered his rifle.

"Now that's the kind of magic, I like to see," Strange said. And he did—as long as he didn't have to think of himself on the receiving end of it.

"Behind the waterfall!" Aleister caught Caspar's reins and drew the gelding forward to the shallow pool of water.

Strange followed suit. They led the horses, splashing, into the water, passing through the veil of water and clambering onto the sandy floor of a deep cave. Aleister reached into the pocket of his breeches his tunic and drew out a small round globe. He murmured words in Parlance and faint blue light issued from the orb—a surprising amount of light in fact.

"There," he said holding the globe high.

At the back of the cave Strange saw a rough-hewn staircase leading upwards into the mountain.

"How did you know this was here?"

"I didn't. At least…I've read about places like this. It's my field of study after all." Aleister cocked his head. "What's wrong?"

Strange shook his head.

Aleister studied him. "Are you…is it because I used the Craft to get rid of them? I know you don't like —"

"Don't be daft. That's why you're here," Strange said, clipped. "And you didn't get rid of all of them, you know. Just the riders who followed us into the wash. The others will still be searching for us."

"I know, but we've bought ourselves a little time at least. Time for the horses to rest perhaps." He turned away using his small globe lantern to explore the back of the cave.

Strange went to the horses. He slipped the diadem out of his shirt—and felt as though a great weight had been removed from his chest for all it was such a flimsy fashioning of gold and gemstones, His skin felt bruised and tender to touch. He put the diadem in his pack. When he next looked for Aleister he saw him vanishing up the stone staircase.

He shouldered his pack, leaving the horses standing quietly, and followed Aleister through the darkness. He could see the faint blue glow ahead of him as he started up the steps. The first steps were nature's handiwork, rough shelves of stone that gave way to a staircase that nature never created.

Strange climbed slowly, feeling his way. Aleister was moving much more swiftly, and he felt another twinge of unease. Why? Aleister was behaving no differently than he ever had.

He continued to feel his way, watching the swift ascent of the blue light, listening to Aleister's quick scramble up the steps that had been carved right into the mountain's fissures. Strange had to wonder at the marvel of architecture that had created this passageway of zigzagging ledges and broken rocks.

"How old is this place?" he asked, but if Aleister heard him, he didn't answer.

A small brass lantern was perched on a flat stone and Strange stopped long enough to light it.

The flickering light threw pointed tongues of shadow as he continued to climb until at last he felt cool air against his flushed perspiring face. He walked up the last two steps and found himself in an overgrown and crumbling courtyard. A dying fountain of opalescent stone spilled poisonous water in mossy basin. Beyond crystal paving stones was the toothless mouth of the temple itself.

"What is this place?" The waning starlight reflected off the glassy courtyard. It looked as though stars were trapped within the clear blocks of pavers. Aleister stood beside one of the milky, iridescent columns peering into the shadowy recess of the shrine. He shook his head. "I don't know. It's... old. Very."

"How old is very old?"

"As old as Nagara perhaps," Aleister said softly. "Perhaps older. I've never seen stone like this. Nor architecture."

A vulture roosting on the crumbling stone wall hissed, flapped its broad wings and took flight into the fading night. Dawn was coming, a cold, clammy gray daybreak.

Strange joined Aleister at the entrance of the shrine. Aleister glanced at him and smiled uncertainly. Strange followed his gaze and saw that he was staring at the creamy pillars which seemed to glow in the gloom.

"What's wrong?"

Aleister said slowly, "There are no designs, no symbols, no art. Nothing to indicate whose temple this is."

"So? They've worn away, that's all. You said yourself this place is older than Nagara."

"But mere age couldn't remove every sign and symbol. There isn't a single carving or piece of scrollwork or ornament of any kind to say whose seat this is. Nor is there any damage or defacement."

"Perhaps in those days people didn't carve the names of their deities where anyone could read them. Maybe it's not a temple at all. Maybe it's a...maybe it's this hunting lodge you mentioned earlier?"

Aleister was shaking his head as though Strange had suggested something utterly preposterous, and perhaps it was. Strange shrugged. The study of the past was the province of witches. He had his own problems—and at the moment they were prowling the surrounding hills, searching for him and Aleister.

"Does it matter? We're not setting up camp here. In fact, I don't know what we *are* doing up here."

Almost to himself, Aleister persisted, "There's nothing. No image. No carving or sculpture or painting." Despite the blue wool cloak he wore, he was shivering.

"You said that," Strange said brusquely because against his will he was concerned for the younger man. "Look, perhaps this god was the retiring type. Didn't like to advertise."

No smile out of Aleister. He walked the rest of the way into the shrine, the cloak unfurling gently, and Strange followed. They paused in front of a large stone throne in the center of the main part of the shrine. It was made of the same creamy opalescent stone as the columns and fountain—and it too was naked of any markings or emblems.

Aleister said slowly, "This would have been his sanctum. The crystals are arranged to amplify Power."

"Whose sanctum?"

Aleister put a hand to his forehead as though his head were aching—a feeling Strange could sympathize with. He reached out as the younger man swayed.

"Here," Strange said, wrapping his hand around Aleister's bicep. "Come and rest while you can." He guided him away from the stone throne. "We'll have to run again soon enough."

"Yes. I should like to rest…"

"We can both use a few minutes to catch our breath."

"I don't think they'll find this place, do you?" Aleister allowed himself to be led away from the throne although his gaze seemed locked on its stark majesty.

"Don't you?" Strange stopped dead staring at the fire pit in the floor. There were charred pieces of wood still piled in the center.

Puzzled, Aleister looked from Strange's face to the spent coals. "Oh," he said. "Someone's had a fire."

"Recently." Strange bent to pick up one of the blackened pieces of wood. "No more than a few days ago. Certainly not more than a week." He tossed the brand back.

Aleister was still standing there gazing at the fire pit as though mesmerized, and Strange took his arm again. "Come on. I think on second thought we'd do better to keep moving."

Aleister didn't try to free himself, but he didn't budge either, so Strange stood there with his hand wrapped around the younger man's arm, feeling the tiny tremors of cold and nerves shaking him.

"We aren't being chased by bandits," Aleister said.

"Who are we being chased by?"

A funny smile touched Aleister's mouth. "Don't you know? Truly?"

Strange's dark brows drew together. "How should I know?"

"They're the same men who followed us in the desert. They're the riders sent by your employer."

"My…employer?"

Aleister was gazing at him with those wide, light eyes as though he could see into the most private corners of Strange's heart. "The woman you met with the night before we left Harappu." He added kindly, as though Strange might have forgotten, "Lady Isabella Hyde. She to whom you promised Dakshi's diadem."

Chapter Sixteen

It took Strange a few seconds to find words. "What are you talking about?" The voice did not sound like his own.

"I saw you," Aleister said in that same calm, almost dreamy voice. "I saw her send for you, saw you go to the old palace by the river, heard her promise to forgive your debt of three hundred thousand rupees if you brought the diadem to her."

Strange's hand tightened on Aleister's arm. "When did you see this? When you looked into the past in the Chamber of Reverie?"

"No. I *Saw* it the night we met." He nodded at Strange's pack which held the diadem. He added calmly, "I saw what you did; I couldn't see what was in your heart. Nor can she—which is why she sent these hirelings after you."

"You don't know what you're saying."

But Strange couldn't stop staring at him. He hadn't permitted himself to think of the bargain Isabella had offered him lest Aleister pick up some hint. Some witches could do that: read another's thoughts—it seemed just the sort of trick that would appeal to Aleister. Strange was certain he had given nothing away, yet all this time Aleister had known? From the time they left Harappu. Known and said nothing.

She will betray you…

Those were Aleister's words to him in the mountain temple, words spoken under the influence of white spice. He had gazed into Strange's eyes and whispered it with conviction. And now it seemed he had been right.

Strange let go of Aleister's arm, though neither man moved away. "It's not what you think." At least…not entirely. On that point Strange was not sure himself.

Aleister rubbed his arm where Strange had gripped it. "No point arguing it now. Neither of us may live through the coming day and Dakshi's diadem may end as the headdress of a *devadasis*."

"Mind your tongue. Lady Hyde is no *devadasis*." Strange added grimly, "Anyway, you don't give a damn about the diadem. You never have—except as a historical artifact."

"I didn't, that's true. At first I didn't believe it could hold true Power."

But now he did believe. That was obvious—and Strange didn't want to hear it. He said, "Power to view the past. And what good is the past?"

Aleister's laugh was unexpected. "I'm the wrong person to ask. I've spent my life studying the past." His amusement faded. "It's more than that, though. It's…" His eyes gazed into Strange's and his pupils looked huge and dark, as they did when he was flying high on the magic carpet of white spice. He put his hand on Strange's shoulder, and Strange could feel the chill of the long fingers.

"I'm afraid I can't control it," Aleister whispered. "I'm afraid —"

"Stop it."

Aleister blinked. His face cleared and he said prosaically, "At the very least it's a powerful symbol."

"Exactly. A symbol. And there are plenty of other symbols more powerful than the diadem of a minor god or a sorcerer or whatever he was supposed to be that no one remembers."

"Is that how you'll justify it? Why does she want it so badly? That's what you should ask yourself."

Strange had no answer. He could feel the light weight of Aleister's hand on his shoulder, and the warmth of Aleister's breath against his face. It was difficult to think of Isabella when Aleister was around. Difficult to think of anything when Aleister was around. When exactly had that happened?

Or had it happened? Was it perhaps just more witchery?

Aleister said calmly, "She's planning another mutiny, did you know that?"

"Isabelle Hyde? *Lady* Isabelle Hyde?"

"She's a half-blood."

"What of it? Plenty of true bloods took part in the Inborn Mutiny." Strange added bitterly, "You have all the prejudices of class and caste, don't you? For all your family's disgrace."

"It's not disgrace to act on your conscience—even if you die for it."

"The devil it's not."

"Nor is it prejudice to imagine that a woman who is half Hidushi should wish more freedom for the Hidushi people. If you ever thought about anyone but yourself, I should think her sympathies would have been obvious."

Strange knocked Aleister's hand from his shoulder, pushing him back. "It's a disgrace to betray crown and country. It's a disgrace to break your oath —"

Aleister said simply, "I'm not plotting mutiny, she is." He added quite coolly, "But I hope she succeeds."

Rage surged through Strange, the desire to strike Aleister and keep striking him, to shut his mouth forever, shut the eyes that kept staring at Strange with that unwelcome emotion.

Kill him before you reach Harappu, Major Strange.

How the fuck dare Aleister look at him like that? With both a stubborn courage and...as though he felt *sorry* for Strange.

Instinctively, he moved forward—unsure of what he would do—when to his astonishment Aleister closed his eyes and put one hand to his forehead.

He whispered, "Valentine...will you help me?"

Strange's anger vanished in the face of alarm. "What is it?" He took the hand Aleister blindly reached out—as though he teetered on some edge—put an arm around him and Aleister leaned into him. The trust of that nearly unmanned Strange. He had been ready to throttle him a few seconds earlier; he was still shaking with the surge of adrenaline. Now he couldn't remember why.

"Are you ill? What's wrong?"

Aleister mumbled, "I...am...destroyed..."

Hair rose on the back of Strange's neck. Merely a turn of phrase, surely? He peered down at the head resting against his shoulder, but Aleister didn't finish the thought.

"You're all right. You need sleep, that's all." Strange spoke bracingly as he looked around but there were no comforts to be had in this place. Cold stone floors and walls open to the damp and chill dawn. "We can spare a little time to rest. They won't find this ruin easily."

Aleister didn't answer although he still seemed to be conscious. His eyelashes flickered against his colorless cheeks, his lips moved soundlessly. Strange half-walked, half-carried him to a sheltered area, settling him on the floor, braced against his own pack. He took off his cloak, shaking out the dark blue folds and covering Aleister with it. He seemed to be sleeping even before Strange rose to his feet.

He stared down at him, at the gold bristle on Aleister's jaw and the delicate design of long lashes and winged brows. Some unreasonable and unwanted emotion twisted through him, threading its way through his heart and mind. No. He could not afford to feel like this. Certainly not about Master Aleister Grimshaw. That would not fit in with his plans at all.

And yet he could not bring himself to move away, staring down, watching with hard, unwilling anxiety as Aleister's fingers twitched and his eye lashes quivered in restless sleep. Surely he was all right? Just weary. They were both weary. And Aleister most likely was starting to feel the withdrawal of white spice.

At last Strange turned and went down the mountain staircase to tend to the horses. He found them nibbling at the clumps of scrubby grass near the water's edge. All was quiet. He considered unsaddling them, but decided against it. They might have to leave in a hurry if their hiding place were discovered.

He checked the packs on the pony, and discovered that the Crux had given them sufficient provisions to see them to the bottom of the mountains. The extra rifles and pistols were there. Strange's brandy flask had been refilled with some unfamiliar native liqueur. He sniffed and sampled; liquid heat ran down his throat and pooled comfortingly in his belly. He pocketed the flask to give Aleister a swig when he woke.

He wished they might risk a fire, but that was out of the question. Sleep was the main thing Aleister needed and he would have as long as Strange could give him. In any case, he found that he was in no hurry to face the other man. Although Strange was no longer angry, he was still shaken by the rage that Aleister should say to *his* face that he hoped there would be another insurrection! And that Isabelle was a mutineer!

And yet…though the thought had never occurred to Strange before, now that it did, well…it was not beyond belief. The people who came to her parties—Hidushi society, yes, but also artists and writers and philosophers, the poor but pampered creative elite. Recalling now some of those conversations…audacious, clever, intellectualizing that no one took seriously. Or that *he* had not taken seriously. Perhaps he hadn't wanted to know.

It pained him now to remember how amused and, yes, a little charmed he'd been by the attentions of a certain handsome, effeminate writer who had questioned him in detail about military tactics, ostensibly as background for an illicit and racy novel about the adventurous life of a Benhali Lancer. All those flatteringly intelligent questions about military strategy and tactics. Strange winced recalling a fanciful quiz about how a soldier of Strange's experience might take a city such as Harappu were it defended by the likes of the Alban army? Strange had laid out several schemes. And the writer had taken careful notes.

He hoped the young man wasn't a mutineer. He'd been rather looking forward to reading that book.

As for Isabella wanting the diadem…well, there were any number of reasons for that. She was a woman who liked rare and exotic things. She possessed a fine and valuable collection of Inborn art. Invitations to her parties were always in demand, and her annual masquerade ball was one of the great events of the season. There were harmless enough reasons for Isabella asking him to fetch the thing, for offering to clear his debt.

He was relieved now that he had not given her an answer; that he had pretended to believe she was joking. At the same time it wasn't as though there were anything pure and noble in the Holy Orders intent to buy the diadem. The church had been snapping up religious relics for years now, and not merely for historical study. Brahman Warrick had made no pretense the diadem was wanted for anything but its possible political significance as a symbol of the state.

At least Isabella wanted it for… But he didn't finish the thought. Instead, he closed his eyes remembering the creamy satin of her skin, the perfume of her raven hair, the extraordinary brown-gold of her eyes—eyes that seemed to smile all the time. Lovely woman, she was. Beautiful and intelligent and charming. The perfect companion, the perfect lover he'd have said before this trip.

But now as Strange thought of her, he felt oddly little. Once he had been quite mad for her…it was almost troubling the way he'd seemed to fall back on his old tastes on this journey. It had not been so long an expedition after all. A few weeks.

It had been years since he had wanted a man, but in recent days when he tried to summon the memory of Isabelle's lovely face, the image that came to mind was Aleister's angular and sardonic expression, and instead of soft breasts and smooth shoulders, the body he imagined pressing itself to his own was Aleister's hard, wiry one. Even the memory of Isabella's coaxing, flattering ways faded, as though punctured by Aleister's sharp tongue and brusque comments.

Had Grimshaw done something to him? Bewitched him somehow? To what end? Simple amusement? That seemed unlikely. Aleister was nothing if not sincere. Too sincere, in fact. Too transparent.

Strange checked his pocket watch. They needed to be on the move again. Tempting though it was to hole up in the shrine until nightfall, he was uneasy about those signs of recent bonfire.

He started back up the stairs, moving quickly now that he was more familiar with the eccentricities of the architecture. He had just spotted the watery daylight at the top level when he heard a scream of such desperate pain and terror it sounded inhuman.

Strange ran, taking the steps two at a time, reaching the top in time to see twin, grappling hooks sail over the broken wall of the shrine. The talon-shaped hooks scraped along the paving stones and then anchored on the chunks of broken masonry. The ropes went taut.

Racing to the wall, Strange leaned over and shot the man attempting to scale the height from his horse. As the horse bolted, taking the body with him, Strange fired at the second rider, but this one had dropped the rope and ducked under the precipice. Strange's bullet missed. He kicked loose the grappling hook and hurled it back over the side.

He sprinted into the shrine. It took his eyes a moment to adjust to the gloom, to pick out the outline of pillar and throne and altar. Aleister was sitting bolt upright on the stone throne, his hands clutching the stone arms. He wore the diadem upon his head and the stones winked dully in the wan light. Aleister's eyes were fixed and open and his face was so white and blank that for a flash Strange that he must have been struck dead as he sat there. But there were no visible wounds, no mark on him, and as Strange bent over him, he saw that Aleister's chest rose and fell. He was still alive.

The relief was nearly as weakening as the first, still un-examined, dread.

"Aleister? Grimshaw?" Aleister's gray eyes were empty of any thought or feeling. His skin was ice cold to the touch as Strange felt his throat, seeking a pulse. He found it, found the beat too fast and too hard as though Aleister were in mortal terror. "What is it? Aleister?"

Aleister stayed stiff and straight, staring into the abyss.

Strange bit back his exclamation, pulling him out of the stone seat where he would not be such an appealing target. Aleister continued to breathe in terrified gasps, his eyes focused on something only he could see.

Magic. Witchcraft. A perfect example, this, of why it was always such a very bad idea outside the controlled environ-ment of a temple.

There was the scrape of boot on stone and Strange turned in time to see a tall, bearded Hidushi striding toward the shrine entrance. He wore a blue turban, brown kurta, and carried one of the newer pistols. Aleister had been right. Not bandits. Mercenaries. Men like Strange himself. Professionals—and possibly better armed.

Behind the foremost man he saw another grappling hook snake over the wall—and another kurta-clad figure wriggle over the escarpment and drop to the courtyard.

Strange fired but the Hidushi had spotted him and dodged behind the nearest pillar.

Strange used that distraction to drag Aleister behind the throne, leaving him sprawled behind the sparse concealment. With the tall stone arm for cover, he drew his service revolver and fired at the second Hidushi in the courtyard. He clipped him in the shoulder, fired again but missed. The man ducked down behind the fountain.

The big Hidushi fired from behind the pillar, the blast from the big pistol taking a chunk off the top of the throne.

Another mercenary was coming over the wall. Strange aimed, fired, and the woman gave a squawk and fell from her perch like a big ungainly bird.

The man behind the pillar fired twice in quick succession. Strange ducked back, reloading fast. He heard the Hidushi race for the next pillar. He couldn't let him get to third pillar or they'd be sitting ducks, caught between this one and the mercenary in the courtyard.

The man in the courtyard opened fire, perhaps in an attempt to give his compatriot cover. The bullets whined past the throne, plowing into the stone walls, gouging the pillars and the thick stone of the throne Strangle huddled behind. He let the man shoot, let him empty his revolver harmlessly, while he waited and waited for the man behind the pillar to move again.

Come on, you bastard. I haven't got all day...

The revolver of the man behind the fountain clicked to silence, and in that abrupt silence Strange could hear Aleister panting his fear and distress. What did he see in that waking dream? He reached behind, squeezing Aleister's shoulder, trying to offer some comfort, some reassurance that he was not alone, though his own gaze never veered from the place where his quarry hid.

The waxen sun flexed fingers of sunlight, reaching the threshold of the courtyard, and Strange could now see the shadow of the man behind the pillar. He watched, saw when the shadow gathered itself to move, and fired.

He hit him squarely in the chest. The tall man fell with a yell, throwing his arms out. His cry was echoed by his comrade in the courtyard who, having reloaded, began to fire with reckless fury.

Perhaps they had been more than comrades. Brothers. Or lovers. Either way, they would soon be reunited. This skirmish had to end swiftly. No more mercenaries were scaling the walls, but there had been two bands of riders, and Strange could not rely on Aleister's water spell having completely wiped out the men in the canyon.

Resting his arm on the arm of the throne, he steadied his aim, waiting. The mercenary behind the fountain ran out of ammunition again, and Strange was up and over to the nearest pillar. A few feet away, the man in the blue turban lay motionless, the pool of blood spreading beneath him, seeping through the crystal stones and forming attenuated characters across the shining surface.

Encouraged by the lack of return fire, the man behind the fountain jumped up, laying down a steady barrage at the throne where he apparently believed Strange still sheltered. He ran forward and Strange stepped out behind the pillar and drilled him through the throat. The mercenary went down coughing blood. He lifted his revolver with a heavy hand, trying to center it on Strange, who shot him through the head.

In the sudden silence Strange could hear the gurgle of the dying fountain. The smell of gunsmoke and death was on the breeze. He reloaded automatically, fingers blindly shoving brass cartridges in the chambers, and glanced up as a shadow, like a dark wing, fell across him. The sun had already retreated and the clouds were growing heavier and darker. Rain moving in from the north.

Going to the courtyard wall, Strange stared down. The dead woman lay in the dust. The trail beyond was empty but for one riderless pony trotting in the distance.

He turned and went to check the body of the body in the middle of the courtyard.

The mercenary had been young, and would not be getting older now. Strange searched him quickly and efficiently, finding nothing but a religious medal—Brigantia. He liberated the pistol from the hand still clutching it, rose and went to the other body, the bearded man who had died in the temple.

No identification of any kind on him either. Certainly nothing to prove he had been sent by Isabella Hyde. Strange pocketed that pistol as well and then went to retrieve the diadem from where it had fallen near the throne. He wrapped it and placed it in his pack.

Aleister was lying as he had left him, eyes wide and staring, chest rising and falling. It was as though he'd been struck been lightning; every speck of life and intelligence blown out of him and nothing left but this breathing, staring shell.

Strange knelt, pulled the flask from his pocket and put it to Aleister's lips, tipping a few drops in. The plum-colored liquid spilled out the corner of Aleister's mouth.

Strange swore, tried again, massaging Aleister's throat, and this time the younger man swallowed convulsively. Strange watched for any change of expression, but there was none.

"Come on," he muttered. "We're running out of time."

He put the flask away, found his canteen, unscrewed the cap, and splashed a few drops—and then more—over the still, white face. Whatever this was, it had nothing to do with White Spice. He'd seen enough of that in the army to recognize it.

"Aleister?" The sightless gray eyes didn't blink. "You'd better bloody wake up if you don't want to be left."

No response.

Strange struck the younger man's face a hard, stinging blow. Nothing.

"Wake the fuck *up*." Strange slapped Aleister again, harder.

The mark of his hand stood out on the colorless cheek. Aleister's mouth parted slightly, but he said nothing; it might have been the force of the blow. At some point he had stopped panting, but the eerie silence wasn't much improvement. Quite the opposite, really, since the struggle to waken seemed to have ended in defeat.

Strange grabbed his pack, slung it across his back and rose. He stared down at Aleister.

"Listen to me, if you're in there."

Not so much as the flick of an eyelash.

"I can't take you with me like this. I'll be lucky to get myself down the mountain. If I try to drag you along, we won't either of us make it." He watched fiercely for any sign of consciousness, alertness.

There was nothing. The gray eyes continued to stare blindly up, the breath moving softly, almost imperceptibly.

"Oddrot you, Grimshaw. What the devil's the *matter* with you?" He bent over, grabbed Aleister by the shoulders and shook him. It was like shaking a dead thing except that Aleister's breathing changed, got choky. Strange dropped him.

He straightened, raking an impatient hand through his sweaty hair.

He had to go. He couldn't waste any more time, couldn't afford to lose any more precious daylight. The rain would start soon and the mountain trails would turn to mud and rockslides. The mercenaries would come back. The temple guards would catch them up. Bandits...

A dozen excellent reasons why he could not—should not—do this. But he'd given his oath, and—well. He'd given his oath. That was all. Had Aleister anticipated something like this when he'd requested that Strange kill him rather than leave him at the monastery?

Strange swore, squatted down. Grabbing Aleister's arm, he rose, heaving him up onto his own shoulder. Aleister draped there, head dangling, a dead weight. And, despite his light and sinewy build, no featherweight.

Strange strode across the courtyard. A vulture perched on the broken wall, spreading its great black wings at the sight of him, but not taking flight. It watched fearlessly as Strange passed close by on his way to the curved doorway that led to the staircase down.

Halfway down the precarious steps he saw a fuzzy white light coming toward him. The sound of the waterfall below had muted the approach of boots or puttees until nearly too late.

He paused, shifting the unconscious weight over his shoulder, and drew his pistol. As the face loomed up, a slash of shadows and white planes in the lantern light, Strange fired into it.

The man fell back without even a cry, his lantern bowling down the staircase in a bouncing arc of light—and the body plummeting after.

Pistol at ready, hanging tight to his burden, Strange continued down the staircase. But as he rounded the stairwell he could see to the floor of the cave below and no one lay in wait. The fallen lantern was burning itself out in the damp earth. The horses tossed their heads, sidestepping nervously at the corpse that had landed near them.

Strange slung his pack over the pony, got Aleister into Caspar's saddle, using his webbed belt to tie him there. He eyed the slumped figure doubtfully. If the chestnut fell or decided he'd had enough of the inert weight on his back, that would be the end of Aleister, but…one bloody thing at a time.

Strange led the horses out through the waterfall. The dead mercenary's pony grazed untroubled beside the pool. Strange caught its reins and tied it to his own pack pony. He set off down the narrow canyon as the rain began to fall.

CHAPTER SEVENTEEN

"There's nothing to be afraid of, you know," the voice said gently. "Open your eyes."

Aleister opened his eyes.

The first thing he saw was a painted ceiling but the forms didn't seem to mean anything to him. There were shapes and colors but he...couldn't recognize them. He no longer remembered the names of these things. Numb horror spread through him as he recognized the truth: he had slipped back into madness. Somewhere on the physical plane his helpless body lay foaming and gibbering while his mind—what remained of it—wandered lost through the maze of memory and delusion. He had rejected the aid of the temple healers and now it was too late. He could only pray that Strange kept his oath and did not abandon him to his fate. What would death feel like? Would it simply be another phantasm?

"You're not mad. You never have been."

If he wasn't mad, where was that voice coming from? How could it know his thoughts? Wasn't this what all madmen believed—that they were sane? At least he had never been *that* arrogant. Arrogant enough—and foolish—in rejecting the help Ehimay had urged. He had wronged Ehimay...

Aleister gathered courage and looked about himself. He seemed to be standing in an old palace...very old. Ancient. Fifth century? Maybe even older. In fact, maybe even not Hidushi. Alban? No...but lovely. Truly lovely. He put a hand out to a graceful green pillar shaped like a lotus and touched cool marble. Real. It always felt so real.

The floors too were a swirl of green and white marble. As he looked down, the pattern in the marble seemed to shift like weather patterns seen from high above. He closed his eyes, momentarily dizzied, and voice chuckled—a sound as deep and soft as warm velvet.

"You're not mad and you're not dreaming. You can smell the flowers, can't you?"

And he could. A sweet, intense perfume of the mingled scents of roses and jasmine and champa. Beyond the green marble pillars was a vast garden with ornamental pools and ancient, primitive statues.

"Why am I here?" he asked.

"Because you want to be."

Aleister shook his head. "No."

"You do, you know. That's why you always return." The voice grew mocking, "After *they've* worked so hard to heal you, too."

"I never want to be here," Aleister said intractably.

"Very well," the voice was amused, easy. "You're here because I want you to be. I've been waiting for you for so long…"

Aleister began to walk, following that lazy, alluring voice down the row of green and white pillars, past oblong meditation pools filled with golden water. Blue water lilies floated on their shining surface.

He came to a long room with rich rugs and tapestries and heavy, ornately-gilded furniture shaped like animals. A blue flame burned in a marble fireplace. On a long divan that resembled a cheetah reclined a tall, beautiful man. He was smiling welcome at Aleister, holding his hand out.

Aleister approached him slowly. The man's eyes were the same shade of red-bronze as his long hair. His skin was the palest and most delicate shade of green. His teeth were very white as his smile widened.

As he took Aleister's hand, he drew him down to the divan and held him. His cool cheek pressed against Aleister's, his arms were warm and reassuring.

"Here you are at last," he murmured, rubbing his cheek against Aleister's.

Aleister whispered—or perhaps the words were only in his mind, "You're not real."

"I'm not? I will be soon. I promise you."

He smelled...comfortingly familiar. Like flower tea and seaweed and...tobacco. He smelled like Aleister's father. He smelled...safe. Emotion rose in a tight knot closing Aleister's throat, making it hard to draw a breath. A sob tore out of his chest. Ashamed, he tried to bury it in the shoulder pressed against his face.

The arms closed still tighter against him. His father's voice said, "I miss you too."

Aleister struggled not to cry, but it was a losing battle. He'd held the grief in for years and now it was clawing its way out of him, destroying him.

The other voice soothed, "Don't cry. You don't have to be alone any more. I've come back for you."

Lips pressed to his temple and he could feel the smile behind the kiss.

"Everything is all right now," the voice told him. "You're home now."

"Am I?" He felt tentative and uncertain. If this was true—he hoped it was—it solved everything. He needn't worry or struggle anymore. It was like...the white spice. Only better. For a time Aleister rested against that strong, broad chest, allowed himself to be comforted as though he were a child again.

Another voice, unpleasantly familiar said suddenly, "Oddrot you, Grimshaw!"

Aleister sat up, pushing his hair from his face. He was being addressed by one of the horse head andirons in the giant marble fireplace. He rose, absently loosing the hand of the green man, and walked over to the fireplace. There was something familiar about that black wrought iron horse head. He bent down and the andiron horse drew its muzzle back and spat out, "What the devil's the *matter* with you?"

⌐

It was after midnight on the second night following their escape from the temple in the mountains that Aleister raised his head and began to speak. At first it was the softest of whispers, but Strange heard him and dismounted, squeezing along the narrow trail to the chestnut gelding.

"Aleister?"

The whisper had gained in strength and Strange could now make out words, but they were not in any language he'd ever heard.

He'd put a hand on Aleister's thigh, jostling him. "Aleister?"

Aleister spoke his gibberish more loudly, but his eyes by moonlight were still dull and vacant.

Still, a promising sign. Strange had to believe that. Had to believe their luck had turned as they picked their way down the sheer mountainside and Aleister shouted his garbled message to the black crags.

Strange was chilled, wet to the skin. They both were, but he didn't dare stop to find shelter. The horses' breath smoked in the cold night. They were nearly as miserable as the humans. Human. It was unlikely Aleister knew how miserable he was. Luckily for him.

The black-edged clouds parted, and the moon appeared, a gold scythe in the purple night. A jackal cried out on the left... another answered. No lonelier sound in the world, in Strange's opinion. They hunted in pairs, jackals, but it was unlikely they'd pose a threat to Strange's small train.

The last time Strange had been this tired and miserable he'd been in the Lancers fighting Bazgals along the frontier.

Well, at least no one was shooting poisoned arrows at him this evening, and that was something to be grateful for. He'd been tired, cold, and hungry before. Probably would be again.

And look on the bright side. At least he wasn't thirsty. It hadn't stopped raining for more than thirty minutes since they'd started across the mountains.

A day and a night and no sign of further pursuit and yet the eyes of the hills seemed upon them all the time. Aleister continued to rail at the stars. What was going on in that rattled brain of his?

Reluctantly Strange was forced to concede it was remarkably lonely without the often annoying but generally amusing Master Grimshaw.

Strange glanced back. Aleister's chestnut was close on the heels of his black. The pack pony had come up lame and he'd had to stop to shift supplies to the dead mercenary's pony. No easy task on the narrow ledge of trail. Thinking about it made sweat break out on his back. And all the while Aleister had sat there like a statue, like a blasted out shell. Strange had been wishing he would say something—anything.

He'd got his wish. Now he wished Aleister would shut up.

His ragged voice echoed off the rocks and rang down the canyon in strange, arcane words. Could he cast a spell in this state? That's all they needed. Aleister wishing a rockfall down on them.

The moon sliced its way through the shroud of night and disappeared. The night grew darker and colder.

Balestra plodded down the twisting turns of a track that lay along the continuation of a shelf running along the steep mountainside. To their right, the side of the pass sloped in a precipitous drop to a river foaming far, far below—a river that had not been there even two days earlier. Above them, boulders rose like battlements. A fine place to stage an ambush. But there had been no sign of pursuit since they'd left the weird shrine in the wilderness.

Strange was taking pains to keep it that way. He kept them moving, and during the brief rest periods resisted the comforts of lantern and fire. He was trying to get them through the pass as quickly and quietly as possible—or had been until Aleister had begun raving.

It was a relief when at long last his hoarse voice fell silent again.

So silent was he, that when they reached a place in the trail wide enough to dismount, Strange swung his aching carcass from the saddle and carefully felt his way back to make sure Aleister was still there. Still breathing.

He was there. Marble cold and motionless. The pulse in his wrist—when Strange clasped it in his own—was frantically beating away as though Aleister were under some terrible strain or putting forth some great sustained effort.

The gelding blew out, and bumped Strange's hip with his long face. A good horse and well-trained; Strange thought the animal was missing Aleister too. Well, if there was a plus side to all this Aleister was most likely breaking whatever hold the white spice had on him without having to go through the pangs of withdrawal.

"Come back," he said, squeezing the chilly hand hard. "Come back, my friend."

For a moment he had the impression that the icy fingers flexed, closing fleetingly around his own. But then the long, lax hand was motionless again.

It was unlike anything Strange had ever seen, and he had seen many horrific illnesses and wounds during his years of military service. Aleister seemed capable of following simple physical directions, but emptied of all thought and emotion.

Had using the diadem outside of the protected environment of the temple done this? Or was it something entirely different? Strange recalled something Aleister had said when they first reached the temple and he had been given the diadem to wear—something about only the true descendant of the god being able to wear the diadem and live.

Was Aleister now paying the price of their charade?

Strange returned to Balestra and remounted, nudging the weary horse forward, their little caravan set in motion once more.

On they went, and Strange, who hadn't slept since they'd left the shrine was occasionally overtaken with drowsiness, with the uncertainty of whether he was still in the saddle or whether he was dreaming and safe in his comfortable own bed. Each time his eyes drifted shut, he would jerk back to alertness, listening for Aleister.

The third time it happened, he didn't have to listen, for it was Aleister's voice that recalled him. Strange turned, and Aleister was a straight silhouette in the saddle, ranting angrily in that queer tongue. His indignant voice seemed to ring off the distant snow-capped mountains and bounce back in answer.

There was something about it—something so intrinsically Aleister having this last word even in this tranced state—that Strange had to bite his lips to keep from bursting out laughing. But then he was himself nearly hallucinating with exhaustion.

At last they rounded a shoulder of the hill and came out on flat, bare top. The trail dipped apically and dangerously from there, the ground slick with mud. Strange reined in, considering how best to handle it. He couldn't see far ahead in the darkness, but what he did see was ominous. Retracing their way, however, was not an option.

He swung down from the saddle, knotting Balestra's reins over the horse's neck, and went to Caspar. Aleister was going through another quiet spell have shouted himself to silence. The gelding was calm, but drooping with weariness. Strange stroked his neck, then holding tight to bit and bridle, walked him slowly and carefully down the knife-edge trail. He stayed as close as he could to the uphill side, gorse catching at his collar and cloak.

If he'd been more awake he might have thought twice about it, might have considered waiting for daylight which wasn't too many hours away now, but all his focus was getting down the trail and across the ridge before any pursuit caught up with them here in the open where they'd be unable to take shelter.

He had no fear of Balestra following, and the lead of the pack pony was fastened by a breakaway link to horse in front—Caspar in this case. Slowly, painstakingly, Strange guided Caspar down the slimy slope. Darkness on either side, darkness below, darkness above…he had the unnerving sensation of losing his balance, losing track of which way was up, floating in black nothingness…

Strange's dizzy exhaustion shattered at the sudden clatter of hooves. Caspar balked, nearly jerking the bridle from Strange's hand. There was a scrabbling noise followed by the crash of something heavy slamming into the hillside brush, the rattle of metal, and then a peculiar animal scream. This was followed by an eerie and absolute hush.

Far, far below Strange could hear the roar of the river over the rocks.

He grabbed the gelding hard, one hand going to steady Aleister who seemed to balance instinctively, keeping his seat by some miracle of horsemanship.

Caspar stood unmoving, sides heaving, trembling. Strange soothed him, resting his face against the sweaty hide for a few seconds before he had the strength to drop the reins and edge past down the trail. He could just make out the shape of the lame pony standing a few yards further down—and Balestra standing behind, ears twitching curiously. Between the lame pony and Aleister's shaking chestnut was an empty stretch of ledge.

The pack pony was gone.

Even understanding this, it took Strange a few seconds to put it all together. The pack pony had gone over the side. The pack pony had gone off the cliff into the river below.

The pack pony carrying all their supplies. Carrying their food and blankets and medical supplies and extra weapons—and his own kit bag. His kit bag in which he had stowed the diadem.

Gone. All of it.

The diadem was lost.

Strange leaned back against the rock face of the mountainside and began to laugh. All at once it seemed the funniest thing on earth. He laughed and his voice rang down the chasm. He laughed till he cried—though that might have been the rain, which had started again.

When he had his breath back, he made his way forward to Caspar again, stroking and sweet talking—praying all the while that Aleister would stay silent and still. And finally, at last, the gelding stepped forward with near-human hesitancy and they continued down the ridge.

Foot by foot.

Hoof by hoof.

Somehow they managed it, managed to cross the steep backbone of muddy rock, and then the trail grew a little wider. The sun was just raising its cautious head when at last the sheer drop on the right began to fill with trees and grass. There was gravel beneath Strange's boots again and he saw that they had reached a long meadow with a thermal spring.

He recognized the valley they had passed on their trip up the mountains, and with relief he saw that they had somehow found their way back approaching from the opposite direction.

He helped Aleister out of the saddle and left him reclining in the grass while he unsaddled the horses and let them graze. There were red gazelle in the meadow, and Strange was tempted to use his rifle, but although they seemed to have outrun their pursuers for the time being, he was conscious of the fact that the mountains were home to many bandits and outlaws, and that he was in no shape to hold off any serious assault. He couldn't risk drawing the wrong attention either by building a fire or firing shots.

He drank water and ate some mushrooms and wild berries while studying Aleister who lay motionless in the grass, a graceful sprawl of long limbs, face turned unseeing toward the moody sky.

"Speak up if you want something to eat," Strange advised.

Apparently Aleister was not hungry.

Eying him, Strange felt an unusual sense of helplessness. Various ideas occurred to him but he wasn't sure they wouldn't make matters worse.

He finished his rough meal, wiped his hands on the wet grass and watched the horses grazing.

Bone weary though he was, his natural optimism began to reassert itself. After all, he was still alive, still in one piece, and he knew where he was now. It wasn't raining. That was something.

And Aleister...

Well, he was alive. It was just a matter of snapping him out of this shocked state or trance or whatever it was. And there were healers of body and spirit in Harappu. All Strange had to do was get him back safely, and the odds of doing that were improving.

Strange sat for a few minutes more watching the heron at the edge of the spring and the hypnotic motion of the wind moving through the winter grass.

He fought the desire to close his eyes and sleep. He recalled that during the journey up the mountain Aleister had grown enthusiastic—enthusiastic for Aleister—about the grass growing in this meadow. Something to do with winter grass and summer worm...he'd pointed out scarlet and green mushrooms growing in this meadow, claiming that they had remarkable medicinal properties. In fact, he'd said he wished to stop on the journey back and dig up a few of them. Strange hadn't paid a good deal of attention because the mushrooms were apparently inextricably linked to caterpillar fungus making them—in his opinion—inedible.

But perhaps he could collect some of those medicinal mushrooms for Aleister so he'd have something to cheer him up when they reached Harappu. He'd need a little cheering up when he learned that their mission had ended in failure.

What would that delectable little liar Brahman Warrick say about their lack of success? Nothing good.

Strange did not dwell on why he should care whether Aleister needed cheering up.

He rested his weary bones—weary everything—for a time longer, but he was conscious all the time that they should be moving again. Delays were dangerous.

"Time to mount up," he informed Aleister. "No arguments."

Aleister made no objection.

Strange sighed.

His bleary gaze rested on spring and an idea occurred to him. The Harappun elite were always raving about the benefits of mineral baths. Perhaps a bath in the mineral spring might help bring Aleister around? If nothing else it would warm him up—warm them both up. It seemed a very long time since Strange had been warm; two days of being soaked and chilled to the skin.

He rose and walked across to the spring, pausing long enough to use his knife to dig up a handful of the mushrooms Aleister had wanted. He dropped them in his pocket and continued to the spring edge noting how muddy the ground was near the water.

Steam rose in a white mist from the wind-ruffled surface of the spring. Strange gazed down into the surprisingly clear water and made out the outline of what…after a few seconds of swirling motion…resolved itself into a skeleton. Two skeletons.

A horse and a rider. The bones had been mostly picked clean but he recognized the scraps of Paisley shirt and the disintegrating rifle scabbard.

Perhaps in the end Nanak would have been better taking his chances with the Crux and Stork.

Chapter Eighteen

"You still haven't called me by my name."

Aleister looked up from the shapely green hand holding his own. "I don't want to call you that."

"It's only a name." The voice was gently teasing.

"There's power in names."

"True. Shall I say your name first, then? Aleister son of Grimshaw."

Aleister shot an uneasy look at the horse andiron, but it had said nothing since the green man angrily commanded it to silence. He said carefully, "Last son."

"Yes. It doesn't matter much, does it? We're done with all that."

Was he done with all that? What exactly was 'all that?' He closed his eyes and focused on the comfort of being held in strong arms, his head against a broad shoulder, the hand holding his own. He felt his hand raised and lips brushed the back of his fingers.

"Surely you're not afraid of me?" The voice ordered gently, "Say my name."

"Venavir."

"Yes. Not so difficult was it?"

Aleister moved his head in slight negation.

"Of course not. You're not afraid of musty old legends. You're a scholar and a witch. A very powerful witch. Don't believe the lies these fools have tried to make you swallow. *They're* the ones who are mad."

Aleister swallowed. He wished they would not speak of this. It reminded him of things he had thought safely forgotten. "Ehimay says…"

Venavir said shortly, "What is Ehimay but a frigid old maid in priest's clothing? He's jealous of you, my dearest. And always has been. He hates himself for still wanting what you gave so freely. He spurned your love yet still craves your body. Don't let him frighten you with his nonsense. All that is behind you now. Behind us."

Venavir's head bent and his mouth found Aleister's in the sweetest and most tender of kisses. Aleister's heart seemed to melt. And yet…

He opened his eyes, looking uneasily to the fireplace. The mouth of the black horse andiron was moving again.

"Come back," it said passionately. "Come back, my friend."

‹⌒›

The cave was about six feet deep and ten feet wide. Large enough to protect them from the wind and rain that had started up again not long after they left the mountain meadow. Inside it was dry and fortunately empty of other inhabitants, animal or human, which saved Strange having to kill them. One way or the other he and Aleister were going to have shelter that afternoon.

Finding Nanak's body had refocused Strange remarkably, and that burst of adrenaline had seen them miles down the trail until he had reached this clearing and spotted the cave. Initial investigation had proved promising. The cave was uninhabited and the tall trees surrounding the clearing provided a natural screen. If he had to make some kind of stand, this was about as good a position as he was likely to get.

Strange untied Aleister and pulled him off the gelding. He unsaddled the horses, hobbling them and leaving them to graze outside the cave while he collected dry pine branches from beneath the wet fallen ones—shaking them well to dislodge any scorpions and beetles. He dragged them back to the cave where the horses were sheltering from the rain, and made up a bed of branches and saddle blankets.

Aleister continued biddable as a zombie. He obediently got to his feet when urged and walked over to the bed where he stretched out as guided, staring at the roof of the cave with that maddeningly immobile expression.

Strange left him there and spent a little while making a fire to take the chill off, for the cave was very cold. He'd have given a great deal for a cup of hot tea or coffee, but all that had gone with the pack pony into the river. He was also very hungry but it was too wet to start hunting berries—let alone the things that could run from him. He sat at the fire looking past the horses to the mouth of the cave, which offered a splendid view of the snowcapped mountains and the green valley below.

Well, it could all be worse. They could be dead. As it was, they would sleep here through the night and make an early start tomorrow morning. By evening they would reach the foothills. From there they could make their way easily to a village or outpost and...

And...?

He smiled a sour smile thinking of how truly disastrous this quest had ended up. The bearers all dead, the diadem lost, the witch tranced...

Yet, once again the soldier in him could only rejoice that against the odds they were still alive. And that they had stopped moving, could close their eyes for a few minutes. And were finally getting warm.

From across the cave he heard Aleister's stomach rumbling. No wonder. He'd had nothing but water and the plum-colored liqueur the Crux had given them. Strange considered what he could do to feed him, and he thought of the mushrooms he had pocketed in the meadow. He could make Aleister some kind of soup perhaps, or mushroom tea. He wasn't convinced he wouldn't rather starve himself.

He rose, got his metal canteen cup, filled it with water, and cut up some of the mushroom—which looked more like a deformed root. He cooked it over the fire, let it cool and then sampled a sip of it himself. He managed not to spit it out, but he decided it was selfish not to let Aleister have it all.

He went over to the bedding, propping Aleister against his shoulder, and held the cup of mushroom broth to his lips. By now Strange was getting this down to a science. He tipped the broth in, massaged Aleister's throat and Aleister swallowed. Strange thought—though he was not certain—that Aleister's face quivered at the first taste of that ghastly brew, but that was the only sign of consciousness.

Strange got two cups of the broth down Aleister, and then he lay down in the bedding, pulling Aleister to him, settling his head on his shoulder. He told himself he was acting to preserve body heat, but in fact it was comforting to hold Aleister. He could feel his heart still pounding in apparent panic against his own. He wondered how long the human body could hold out in such a state of silent panic. Surely Aleister would die if it continued much longer.

With dismay he realized exactly how he would feel about that.

When the devil had *that* happened?

Impractical. Illogical. Impossible. And yet...it seemed to be true. It felt true. It felt true all the way to his bones. "Don't do this to me," he murmured, and he was not quite sure what exactly it was he didn't want Aleister to do. He seemed to have done his worst. Barring dying.

Strange stroked the damp, pale hair, kissed Aleister's forehead and bristly cheek. "You're safe now. Wake up."

But Aleister did not wake. He breathed those soft warm gusts against Strange's throat, while his eyes looked past Strange's chin.

Strange sighed and kissed him lightly one final time, settling them more comfortably. He closed his eyes. He could still feel the rolling gait of Balestra beneath him, hear the steady, slow, clop, clop of hooves, see the black void of the chasm yawning before him.

He let himself fall.

⏤

"If you won't eat, you must drink at least, my dearest. Else you will fade out of this world and return to the half-life of the next."

Aleister looked down at the goblet. The liquid was dark and rich looking, and he was very hungry. He looked at Venavir who was gazing at him with both love and concern in his glowing red-bronze eyes.

"Drink, dearest. Save yourself. In that world you are ill and mad and alone. In this world you are a prince—and my beloved. Drink."

Aleister brought the goblet to his lips but the smell of blood nearly gagged him.

Venavir's hand covered his shaking one and steadied the cup for him. He raised the cup to his lips once more.

"Drink and grow strong. And when you are well and yourself again, we'll make love in the garden with only the flowers and the stars to care."

"Our bodies will join," Aleister said slowly.

"Yes, my beautiful one. Our bodies will be one. All will be exactly as you've so long desired." Venavir slowly stroked his hair, tucked a strand behind his ear. "*Exactly* as you've long desired." He bent his head to Aleister's ear and whispered the delightful things he would do to him—dark, illicit things Aleister had secretly longed for though he had not desired Venavir to do them to him. His face grew warm. He had not thought of Venavir like that at all…it puzzled him now.

He had been afraid of Venavir. Terrified of the madness that possessed him—a great brutal hand reaching into the

fragile shell of his brain and crushing his reason and will…
He had fought it. Each time he had fought it.

He said slowly, "You'll possess my body and use it for your own."

"Of course, my dearest. But it's what you want, isn't it? For us to be one."

Aleister shook his head. "I don't —"

"But you do," Venavir insisted gently. "That's your wish. Your secret wish. I know all your secret wishes…"

Once again he softly reminded Aleister of the things they would do together; tender things—and things that Aleister had to pay whores to do. Things that Venavir would do willingly, lovingly.

Love.

"Drink," Venavir urged. "Drink from the cup and then I shall drink from you." His breath sent little chills of delighted alarm across Aleister's bare throat. The cup pressed against his mouth, the metal seemed to bite into his lip and the warm scent of blood clogged his nostrils. Aleister's gorge rose.

He could not do this. Not for all the pleasures in the world. Not even to save himself. Not for anything. He pushed away, rising to his feet and tossing the contents of the goblet into the fireplace, splashing the burning wood.

Venavir leaped up as well, crying out. "What have you done, little fool?"

The eyes of the andiron horse flew open. Valentine Strange's voice said, "You're safe now. Wake up."

Aleister dropped to his knees, stroking the sharp ears, the smooth iron of the horse's thick neck. Blue flames leapt around his hands, setting his silk robe alight, consuming him. Venavir reached out, but recoiled as the flame spread throughout the room, catching the rich carpets and gossamer drapes. Even the golden water burned. Flames crept up into the backdrop of starry sky revealing the void beyond. Yet Aleister felt no pain. Only freedom.

"Take me home." He leaned forward pressing his lips to the cold-hot metal.

"Climb upon my back," the andiron horse said, and its neck thickened and arched. Aleister clutched tight as the iron horse found its legs and rose beneath him. He could feel hard metal giving way to warm silky muscle and flesh pressing against him, moving against him as they took flight. He could feel the beat of wings and the beat of the pulse between his legs, and he began to push back against it, pushing, thrusting, fighting to fly still higher.

⌒

Strange slept and dreamed of the sun: of baking rocks and the shimmering haze of heat, the scarlet blaze of cactus flowers, the dry taste of the wind and the smell of hot horse and hot leather, the jingle of bits and the dry suck of sand.

He woke to a surprisingly urgent prodding for attention. Fuzzily, he became aware of the not unwelcome sensation of lean, living warmth plying itself to his body, of a flat muscular chest pressed to his own, of bony hips rocking against his in small pleasurable movements. It dawned on him what that poking in his groin meant.

Cautiously, doubtfully, Strange pried open his eyes and in the dull and rainy afternoon light saw Aleister's face closed in pained concentration a few inches from his own.

The bright wide eyes were closed at last and Aleister's breathing, while uneven, was no longer frantic. There was a stain of color in his white face and he was thrusting his fierce erection against Strange's.

There were far too many clothes between them.

Strange woke up fully and reached down to deal with all the fastenings and openings in a couple of quick moves. His mouth found Aleister's. He kissed him, hungrily—starving actually—and Aleister's mouth opened to him.

Strange muttered, "Are you awake?" He was not sure he cared.

Aleister tasted extraordinary. Smoky and sweet. Like blue shadows on snow and the glistening amber heart of fire. It was intoxicating and Strange remembered wives tales and warnings about the temptations of witches—and their voracious carnal appetites.

One could but hope.

He deepened his kiss and Aleister made a soft sound. Strange lifted his head thinking it might be a protest, though the body rocking against his did not appear to be anything but aroused and longing for release. The black lashes flickered against Aleister's thin cheeks. Strange relaxed, pulling Aleister more tightly to him, and there was nothing lovelier than the feel of warm naked skin on warm naked skin.

By instinct they found a quick, relentless rhythm and in a matter of moments blissful blood-hot relief spilled between them.

Strange fell back into the pine branches, gulping. Now *there* was magic. Nothing made a man feel more exalted—or vulnerable—than that rushing release. He took Aleister in his arms, stroking the bony body, trying to soothe his trembling.

"It's all right. You're all right now."

To his shock Aleister mumbled something in his neck. Strange's arms closed more tightly around the lean frame as though afraid Aleister would slip away from him again.

"Aleister? You're back?"

More incoherency. Strange rolled back to try and read Aleister's face, and Aleister's arm locked around him, holding him fast. Strange tried to recall if anyone in his entire history had ever relied on him to supply such comfort. He drew a blank.

Awkwardly, he patted Aleister's back. He still could not make out what Aleister was snuffling into his neck. He probably did not *want* to know, but he bent his head closer and muttered, "You're all right now. We're both all right. Nothing to —"

He broke off as he felt wet slip down his neck. Strange swallowed hard and patted the thin, muscular back some more. "There's a lad," he said for lack of anything better.

The next moment, Aleister was pushing away from him. He sat up, wiping his eyes on his arm, gazing at Strange. "It's true. It *is* you."

"Who'd you think it was?" Strange felt obliged to inquire.

"How did we—how did you?" He looked around the cave. "But I *am* free."

"That's one word for it. Do you remember what happened?" Aleister's gaze fell on him, and Strange added, "Er...earlier. You took a fit in the shrine in the hills and have been insensible for nearly two days. I'd nearly given you up for lost."

Aleister's eyes were dark and seemed to look inward. "He... found me. He found me in the temple in the mountains and followed me to the shrine. Or perhaps he was waiting for me. Perhaps he—it—has been waiting all the time."

Not what Strange had hoped to hear. He propped himself on one elbow. "*What* found you?" He wasn't sure he wanted to know. If Aleister wasn't ill he'd been ensorcelled. Or possessed. That was worse than any fever or fit. "What are you talking about?"

Aleister face was somber, his eyes dark with dread. "The ghost of Venavir. He tried to possess me."

"The ghost of..." He didn't bother to finish it. Wasn't sure he wanted to hear.

"The sorcerer king."

Strange was shaking his head. "That means nothing to me."

"*Venavir*," Aleister repeated as though perhaps Strange hadn't heard properly.

"Got that. Never heard of him."

Aleister's jaw dropped, then he said, "But of course you wouldn't know. It's a Hidushi story. Hidushi history." He swallowed. "In ancient times there was a sorcerer king by the name of Venavir."

"Witch or magician?"

"I —"

"Never mind. Go on. There was a king named Venavir who dabbled in sorcery."

"Yes. Venavir was a good king but his true interest was in magic. One day one of his enemies summoned a skaith against him."

Aleister fell silent, staring at nothing.

"What's a skaith?" Strange asked, and Aleister started, seemingly recalled to himself.

"A skaith is the spirit of a woman who dies violently while pregnant. They're very beautiful but very angry."

"Known a lady or two like that."

Aleister smiled faintly, but it faded almost at once. "Skaith exist only to wreak vengeance but…first they charm and beguile their victims. As this skaith did with King Venavir. He fell in love with her and then she turned him into a rubaipurish." He rubbed his forehead tiredly. "It was so real."

Strange watched him. He said finally, briskly, "Go on then. What's a rubaipurish?"

Aleister made an effort to shake off his preoccupation. "A blood-drinker. The more it drinks, the thirstier it grows. It's caught forever in the cycle of drinking blood and craving more."

"Bit like the cycle of white spice," Strange observed.

Aleister ignored him. "Because Venavir was both a king and a powerful sorcerer his thirst went unchecked. There was no stopping him, and his hunger for souls and blood grew greater and greater. He killed hundreds of people, and then thousands. Any who stood before him were destroyed by his demon army."

"This is a legend," Strange objected.

"No."

"Of course it's a legend. If it was history, we'd know the story in Marikelan."

Aleister seemed not to know how to respond to that. He managed at last, "But it's not just a legend. They called him the Extinguisher of Light because the sun itself turned red."

Ah. The Extinguisher of Light. Now it began to make sense. Or at least as much as these things ever did.

"So what happened to this Extinguisher of Light? Why have I never heard of him before?"

"There are different accounts of his death."

"Myths, you mean."

Aleister ignored that. "One story is that all the gods banded together to stop him. Another story is that he drank the blood of the only child of the cobra king and the venom killed him. And then there's the ridiculous story that Warrick told us about Purya vanquishing him in battle."

Strange repeated tersely, "What do *you* think happened to Venavir?"

Aleister said slowly, "Venavir's greatest friend was another powerful sorcerer by the name of Dakshi. When Dakshi saw what had become of Venavir and that there was no reclaiming him, he gathered his own forces and went into battle against him."

"And he slew him."

"I…yes. I suppose so."

Strange frowned. "Did he slay him or not?"

"First he killed the demons Venavir had summoned and he formed a diadem from their eyes to focus his Power. He did destroy Venavir by trapping him inside a sacred chamber…"

"And?"

"After that he…went mad with grief."

Always some catch wasn't there? Strange took a few seconds to absorb this before saying, "He went mad?"

Aleister nodded, seeming to avoid his gaze. "Because he was becoming a danger to the world himself, he…in a moment of sanity he had himself walled into the same sacred chamber where he'd trapped his friend—the tomb."

Silence.

Strange said briskly, finally, "Well, mission accomplished then, right?"

Aleister's face was haggard. He was staring at his hands. He said almost inaudibly, "You don't believe me."

"I believe there was a sorcerer king named Venavir. I don't know about demons. I've never seen a demon. I've never met anyone who saw a demon, but then I've never met anyone who saw a god or a goddess, and I dare say I believe in gods and goddesses. As far as they go."

"As far as they go?" Aleister repeated weakly.

"That's right. I think of them as something belonging to the past. Plenty of old stories about demons and gods, but not many new ones. Their day is done."

"Perhaps their day has come again."

"Why should it?"

Aleister seemed at a loss. "I don't understand you."

"No. I can see you don't. And I know enough to know that there's usually some grain of truth in every legend." Strange reached from beneath his cloak and squeezed the hand clenched on Aleister's knee. "Something happened to you in the shrine. I know that much. But this is ancient history. Even if it were true —"

"The past is repeating itself. Venavir has returned."

Strange opened his mouth, but the fact was he had no idea what to say.

Aleister said desperately, "Valentine, his mortal body was destroyed, but his spirit could only be entombed. That portal was opened…decades ago…and every year he grows stronger. I believe he's…going to return to this world." His hand turned beneath Strange's and his fingers gripped Strange's tightly. His eyes were haunted. "I believe he's waited only to find a…mortal host."

Strange loosed his hand and sat up. "Stop it."

"He overtook me in the shrine."

"Shut up."

"Even before I put the diadem on I could feel it—him. He's been waiting for me. He's coming back to destroy the world. The Crux knew that Venavir was stalking me. That's why she gave you that…instruction."

Kill him before you reach Harappu, Major Strange.

"Shut the fuck up," Strange said, and he got to his feet, fastening his breeches. "Let me tell you what your problem is, Grimshaw. Too much time spent studying the past and too much white spice."

He was irritated to find his hands were shaking. Well, why not? He hadn't found Aleister again only to lose him to this insanity.

Aleister was saying with a kind of eerie calm, "You asked me about Gomar. About the excavation of the tomb. My grandfather led the expedition."

"Yes, I know, Nanak told me all about your grandfather's doomed expedition."

Aleister ignored his interruption. "My grandfather was an experienced antiquarian and a powerful witch." He swallowed sounding unexpectedly young. "It was my first dig, right after my first initiation."

"How old were you then? Ten?" A fledging witch on a tomb excavation. Apparently madness ran through the entire Grimshaw line.

Aleister was still talking in that unnaturally calm voice. "Part of every excavation is to exorcise those spirits that are not at rest. But we didn't exorcise the spirit at Gomar. We woke it. Time hadn't faded this spirit. It was—it reached out"

"Stop thinking about it."

"I can't. Not thinking about it won't stop it."

"It might. One thing's for sure, brooding is unhealthy."

"I'm not brooding. I'm trying to—can't you see that I need to face this? I've spent most of my life trying to pretend it didn't happen and it's driven me half mad."

Strange exercised supreme will and managed to resist asking *What* didn't happen?

"Why don't you ask me who was buried in the tomb at Gomar?"

Strange shook his head.

Aleister said with a sort of bitter triumph. "I'll tell you anyway. The sorcerer-king Venavir is buried at Gomar."

Strange rocked back on his heels, absorbing the full implication of this information. Everyone spoke as though the Great Temple of Harappu and the Tombs of Gomar were two separate places. In fact, they were one and the same.

And that being the case, what the devil was Warrick and the Holy Orders doing having Grimshaw of all people working in that ruin? And what the devil was Grimshaw doing agreeing to such a thing? Frankly, he was beginning to think the whole lot of them mad—himself included for getting involved with them.

"Right," He said shortly, "Well, if it's true what you say about this damned ghost – he's going to have to go through me the next time he wants you. Got that?"

Aleister was blinking at him in that bemused way, and discomfited at his outburst, Strange rose.

"Going to water the horses," he growled, and stalked out.

⁓

The rain spilled down like shining needles outside the mouth of the cave. Aleister was careful not to watch that glinting, shimmering fall too closely—the real world still showed a tendency to waver, and he would have preferred not to be on his own.

It seemed a very long time before Valentine returned.

"I didn't tell you before," he said crisply, "but you might as well hear it now. The diadem is lost."

Aleister stared. "Lost?" he repeated faintly. Whatever he had expected to hear, it was not this.

"That's right. It went over a cliff with one of the pack horses."

"*Lost.*" Aleister repeated faintly. It seemed too much to take in at once.

"Nothing wrong with your hearing," Valentine observed. "Look, it was bucketing down and the trail had turned to mud. I'd stowed my kit bag on the pack horse when I was dealing with you at the shrine. The pack horse went over the side when we were coming down the mountain. We're lucky the lot of us go with it."

Aleister heard all this vaguely. He had been steeling himself to face his demon—to face literally his personal demon—knowing that he was probably doomed to failure given how quickly he had succumbed at the shrine to a will so much stronger than his own.

All that unnecessary anguish. Because if the diadem were truly lost…

Yes, perhaps this was the answer. The unlooked-for reprieve. If he only better understood how the diadem figured into it all. It's disappearance from the excavation site twenty years before was much more than coincidence. It was part of a pattern. A pattern he had believed irreversible, but if the diadem was unexpectedly removed from circulation?

Truly lost.

Strange continued in that hard, brisk way that brooked no discussion. "You see, it's over. Venavir. Dakshi. It's all over. The diadem is at the bottom of the river. So I don't want to hear anything more about it. About the Extinguisher of Light or any of the rest of it."

Lost.

It could not be mere coincidence. So it must be part of the pattern? The hand of fate at work again—and this convenient accident the result of divine intervention. But which divinity had intervened? Valentine would probably say none, but Aleister didn't believe it.

At last he shook off his preoccupation. Valentine was right. His part in all of this was over, even if Aleister suspected his own had just begun.

"I'm sorry," he said, putting his own concerns aside for the moment. "You were counting on that money, Val. What will you do?"

"I'll manage," Valentine replied. "Something will turn up. It always does."

Proof of what a fool he was, even now Aleister couldn't help asking, "Are you going to marry her, then? Lady Isabella?"

Valentine said irascibly, "Just how much did you see when you were scrying on me?"

A small smile tugged at the corners of Aleister's mouth. He tried to conceal it, but not well enough. Valentine's eyes narrowed. "Right. If you don't want that bony nose of yours broken, keep it out of my affairs."

Aleister noticed that Valentine hadn't answered his question. Not that he had really expected an answer—or at least not the answer he'd have liked. Valentine was a survivor. He would do what he needed to, and he would do it well. In any case, it was a question Aleister shouldn't have asked.

Diadem or no diadem.

He said mildly, "My apologies. I didn't mean to pry. I was uneasy about the journey to the White Mountains. I wished to know who I'd be traveling with."

Valentine grunted. "You found out quick enough."

"Yes."

Valentine's eyes narrowed at that demure response, but he said evenly, "What will you do? Brahman Warrick seemed set on getting his relic."

Aleister's smile was twisted. "He did. But then I've disappointed him before." He felt suddenly relieved—almost lighthearted. Perhaps Valentine was right about the diadem. Something had broken the spell that had ensnarled him. Perhaps this was the answer. The diadem was destroyed and with it...

Did it make sense? He wasn't quite sure. The diadem had belonged to Dakshi; that was indisputably true. The diadem had provided Dakshi the focus with which to vanquish Venavir. But it had provided the instrument of Aleister's defeat.

So surely losing the diadem for good was the best possible thing for all. That had to be why he'd been able to break free of the will that had possessed him in the shrine; separation from the diadem had given him the strength to throw off the influence of Venavir in his dream state. What else could it have been?

The growing fear that had gripped him in the mountain temple could at last be forgotten. The diadem was gone. The cycle was ended. When he returned to Harappu and the Great Temple he would see that all was well, the evil influence that had haunted him for weeks—years, had he but known it—would be gone.

"How long before we're back in Harappu?" He looked around the cave, only then becoming aware of their rugged surroundings. "Where exactly *are* we?"

"All the way down to the pine forest." Valentine was still crisp, still businesslike. Still not meeting his eyes. "We'll rest up today and continue traveling at first light. We should reach the foothills by noon tomorrow. From there we'll head for the eastern border. We can get pick up supplies there for the trip back to Harappu."

That couldn't have been easy, getting them all down this far. In particular, getting *him* down this far. Aleister wondered how Valentine had done it—and why.

He nodded. "As you think best."

Valentine raised his brows at this—just as though Aleister were not usually perfectly cooperative. He turned away, saying, "I've fed the horses. I may as well see what I can find for us to eat." He hesitated. "There's something else you should know."

Aleister stared at him with apprehension.

"I found what remained of Nanak in the mountains. It looked to me like he fell afoul of bandits."

Aleister found his voice at last, "An unlucky expedition all around."

"Yes," agreed Valentine.

CHAPTER NINETEEN

Y ou will have to go back for it." Brahman Warrick sat in his study at the rectory. He had plied Strange with brandy and cigars and they'd had a pleasant enough visit but the priest was getting down to brass tacks now. "There is nothing for it. You must go back."

Strange pretended to consider, studying the tip of his cigar— an expensive cigar at that—and expelled a long stream of blue smoke through his nostrils. He shook his head. "Not possible."

"With the Goddess all things are possible."

That was the sort of smug things priests always said, wasn't it? And why not, sitting in this orderly, comfortable room looking out over the lovely old garden with its rose arbors and gentle fountains? What could Warrick know about slogging your cold and hungry and exhausted way through rain and mud—hired killers at your back and a bottomless chasm before you?

Strange said mildly, "Even if I knew the exact place the pony went over the side—and I don't by a long shot—it would be impossible to retrieve from the river whatever might be left."

"You don't know that. If it was too dark to know where the pony went over, it was too dark for you to know that the packs could not be retrieved." Warrick offered an appealing smile. Strange smiled back. He found it interesting that although he'd found Warrick a startlingly attractive young man before his trip to the White Mountains, he was utterly unmoved by the charms the priest was so obviously exerting now.

"Forgive my bluntness, Holiness, but I was there, you weren't."

"You *were* there, Major Strange," Warrick said pointedly. "The Holy Order paid you two hundred thousand rupees to be there."

"I'm well aware that I failed to fulfill my end of our bargain. I told you at the outset it mightn't —"

"And Lady Hyde paid you three hundred thousand rupees to be there. Did you perhaps decide to take the higher offer?" Warrick's tawny gaze glittered.

Strange said evenly, "The pony went over the ledge." He added, "I didn't take Isabella Hyde's money, regardless of what he told you."

"He?" Warrick's silky brows drew together. "Oddsblood. Do you mean Master Grimshaw? No. Grimshaw said nothing. He resigned his temple post, you know."

Strange did not know. He had not seen Aleister since their return to Harappu. He'd meant to call on him, of course, once things quieted down again. But it was awkward. Failure was always awkward, and Aleister knew things about him that he would prefer not to be reminded of.

In any case, it had only been two weeks. And a complicated two weeks at that. No need to look overeager.

"Why did Grimshaw resign?"

Strange did not like the expression that fleeted across Warrick's face. It gave him that funny prickle between his shoulder blades—the one that often signaled someone was about to start shooting at him. The priest said staring at the blotter on his desk, "Health reasons. He has been unwell for some time. We had all hoped that the trip—the break from routine and new things to occupy his mind—might help. Unfortunately, it proved quite the opposite."

"You discharged him."

"Certainly not. He chose to resign. We were all greatly distressed. Especially as —" Brahman Warrick stopped as though realizing he was being indiscreet.

Something that had never worried Strange.

"Especially as what?"

"Especially as he refused to place himself in the care of our church healers."

Strange snorted.

Warrick's cheeks flushed attractively. He said tartly, "Forgive me for being blunt, but yours is an ignorant attitude, Major Strange. Aleister is very ill and has been for most of his life. You see, he suffers periodic bouts of madness, the result of the tragic experiences of his youth. The fact that he has spent the last few years in a period of relatively calm productivity is solely due to the diligent care he has received from our healers."

Strange had heard the rumors before they'd ever left Harappu, but he said flatly, "Exactly what do you mean by 'mad'?"

"Unable to tell the difference between what is so and what is not, Major Strange. Unable to read or write or even speak coherently. Unable to understand the simplest of commands. No more able to care for himself than a small child. Mad." He added succinctly, "As a hatter."

"And so you sent him with me into the Benhali Mountains?"

Warrick rang a gong and a small, sleek young novitiate silently appeared bearing fresh brandies on a silver tray. "As I said, we hoped to stave off this latest crisis with a change of scenery and new challenges. Sadly, we were wrong."

Strange considered this. "What makes you think so?"

Warrick made an impatient gesture, as though waving foolish questions away. "No sooner did he resume his duties than he began babbling about the temple monkeys and then about fountains of blood. The delusions grew daily worse. He claimed that the temple was built on a mass grave and that the great altar is filled with skulls. When we tried to reason with him, tried to remind him that this was the old and familiar pattern of his illness, he grew hysterical and claimed that the ancient sorcerer king Venavir had tried to seduce him, tried to possess his body but because of a talking andiron he had been able to escape the king's magical pleasure garden." Warrick stopped and pinched the bridge of his nose. He seemed for one instant truly discomposed.

The young novitiate eyed him with solemn sympathy. Warrick lowered his hand and said heavily, "I blame myself."

Strange pondered this then said, "What altar do you suppose he was talking about?"

Warrick's eyes narrowed at this tangent. "We have just uncovered the temple's original altar."

"Did you check it for skulls?"

Warrick began to sputter. "No, we didn't check it for skulls! Destroy a valuable antiquity because of the ravings of a madman? You will be interested to hear, by the way, that the andiron that rescued Aleister looked like your horse and spoke with your voice." Warrick shook his head. "I've heard the whole story. Twice."

The novitiate snickered.

Strange was surprised at the rush of angry blood beating in his temples. It was quite likely Grimshaw's decision to resign had been his own. He had not been happy at the temple. And he was...highly strung, to put it politely. And smart and loyal and courageous. Qualities Strange valued. He was a friend. Yes, a friend. And Strange had few enough real friends left in the world. Plenty of good companions, a few lovers, but very few real friends left, now that he thought about it.

And while on the subject of friends, Aleister—mad or not—deserved better than Warrick.

"Anyway, this is neither here nor there. Aleister is lost," Warrick was saying, "And so, according to you, is Purya's diadem."

"It wasn't Purya's diadem. It was Dakshi's diadem."

Warrick's face stilled. He said slowly, "Dakshi... Where did you hear that name? Why should you say the diadem belonged to Dakshi?"

"The priests of the mountain temple said so." Well, perhaps not in so many words. But they had been clear enough that it wasn't Purya's diadem.

"That's a fairytale. Dakshi! Did Grimshaw —?"

Strange decided that perhaps he had volunteered enough information. He preserved a granite silence and Warrick said, "It's nonsense. Utter nonsense. And beside the point. Perhaps you thought to play one side against the other? Though I am not a man of the world, I know how the world works. Perhaps you —"

Strange cut in, "I haven't sold your precious relic to Isabella Hyde. It happened exactly as I told you. The horse and the pack went hundreds of feet down the canyon." He was startled to hear himself add, "If you want me to go back and look for it, I will. But it will cost you."

Brahman Warrick's eyes lit with hope. Before he could speak, Strange continued, "And I'll need Grimshaw."

"*Aleister*? Why? Have you heard nothing I've said?"

Strange leaned forward and carefully—so as not to disturb the burn ring—set his cigar in the fine 5th dynasty enamel ashtray. "I've heard all you've said, Holiness. And all you haven't said. I need Grimshaw because I need a witch and he's the only witch I know. Or trust."

Warrick was smiling again. "The temple has many witches in its employ. Witches with nearly the same level of training and experience as Master Grimshaw, and none of the problems."

"Grimshaw knows the terrain and is familiar with the diadem."

"Familiarity with the diadem is not needed."

"It is, given the fact that it's probably beneath about six feet of water right now. Grimshaw used the diadem for scrying in the mountain temple."

"He *used* the diadem?"

There was no disguising the shock there. Warrick actually lost color. Interesting that Grimshaw not shared that bit of information with his colleague, but felt free to speak of talking andirons.

"Wasn't his choice. In fact, our survival might have relied on it."

Warrick's gaze seemed peculiarly intense. "You should know that even before this final unfortunate incident triggered his collapse, Master Grimshaw was becoming increasingly unreliable. His work had suffered and the general opinion was he was no longer capable of meeting the rigorous standards of temple witch. I suppose I kept him on out of —"

Strange interrupted, "Which unfortunate incident are you referring to?"

Warrick worked to preserve his smile. "But I've already told you. Grimshaw hasn't been well for some time, and not unexpectedly, his nerves were shattered after his recent experiences."

One thing Grimshaw had never seemed was particularly nervous. "What unfortunate incident?"

Warrick made a dismissing noise. "As you're well aware, for the last sixty years the Holy Orders have been involved in excavating the temple at Gomar. Inevitably in such an old place of Power there will be irregularities."

"Irregularities. Right. Go on."

"Things that might be mistaken for…manifestations."

"Such as?"

"Any number of things. Crumbling architecture. A nest of vipers at the foot of a statue. Minerals in the water."

"Minerals in the water?"

Warrick stared at Strange for a moment. He said testily, "Minerals have turned the water in the fountain of the main hall, red. As I told you, Grimshaw became quite hysterical. He ranted about a spring of blood. Between that and the monkeys…you can see why it was better for all concerned that, choosing to forgo the care of the church healers, Aleister agreed to resign his commission."

"Did it never occur to you that he might simply be telling the truth?"

"No," Warrick said crushingly. "It did not. What is the truth as perceived by a lunatic? But because of this, because of the minerals and the old stories, it's all the more important that the diadem be retrieved. Thanks to Grimshaw's latest outburst rumors have spread and are now flying through the capital."

Strange said nothing, studying Warrick as he watched the graceful retreat of the handsome novitiate. As though feeling his stare, Warrick returned his gaze to Strange. He said, "A loyal soldier would do as I asked without debate, Major Strange. This is a very delicate time in the history of our nation."

When was it not?

"You're quite right," Strange said briskly. He reached forward and stubbed out his cigar. "Very well, Holiness. All you need to concern yourself with is finding the funds to finance another expedition and this loyal soldier will go."

Warrick studied him warily. "Is that the truth? If these funds can be procured, you'll return to the Benhali Mountains and find the diadem?"

Strange picked up his silver-topped walking stick, and rose. "I'll do my best."

"And you'll—I hope we may rely on you not to disturb Master Grimshaw any further?"

"No need to concern yourself, Holiness," Strange returned. "I appreciate your honesty. I didn't fully understand the situation before. Now I do."

⌒

The Grimshaw estate turned out to be a large, secluded bungalow in the oldest section of the Alban cantonment. It would have been a beautiful old place once upon a time though the villa was in obvious disrepair and the gardens were overgrown. Blue jacaranda blossoms drifted gently down while Strange waited on the long veranda. A koel bird sang melodiously from the leafy branches above. He studied the starry sky above thinking that once those sparkling constellations had seemed foreign to him.

Given the chary attitude of the elderly family retainer who came to the door, Strange was prepared to have to force his way in, however after a brief disappearance, the little man returned and Strange was led through long rooms furnished in the fashions of the past. There were oil paintings of Alban landscapes on the white walls and crystal chandeliers. Bone china cups and saucers and silver tea things sat on a silver tray on a fine old table.

Everything had been chosen with an eye to comfortable elegance, and although the furniture was old and well-used, unlike the outside of the villa, all within was clean and polished to the highest degree.

Strange was not sure what he had expected, but it had not been this snug, well-organized household. If Aleister were indeed ill and requiring care, this looked like the place to receive it.

However, when Aleister came in from the evening garden he did not appear ill. A little thin, a little tired perhaps. He wore only soft, loose cotton trousers of a pale blue. Torso and feet were bare and honey-brown. The rings in his ear, nipple and belly caught the light in little flashes as he moved across the room. He looked cool and composed—especially for someone who had been painted as barking mad by his erstwhile employer.

Until he saw him smiling in the warm amber glow of the lamps, Strange had not realized how much he had missed Aleister. In fact, his own rush of elation took him aback. He had been careful not to permit himself to dwell on any feelings he might have for the witch. At best they were awkward, at worst, they were liable to disrupt his plans. He did not like disruptions to his plans.

"Hullo. What brings you to this wilderness outpost?"

"Happened to be in the neighborhood."

"Oh yes?" Aleister was still smiling—and what an engaging smile he had. He went straight up to Strange offering both his hands, and Strange took them automatically. Aleister's grip was strong and warm. His eyes shone like silver and his skin gleamed smooth and golden. Strange wanted to touch it. Very much.

It dawned on him what was going on here. "You're bewitching me!" he exclaimed. He wanted to drop Aleister's hands, but somehow couldn't seem to.

Aleister laughed. "Am I?"

"You know you are."

"Well, perhaps I am." He seemed amused by it, not guilty at being caught out. He gave Strange's hands a little squeeze and let go.

Strange was sorry for that—further proof that Aleister was exercising his Craft.

A little wizened woman appeared and Aleister requested more tea.

"Not for me, thanks," Strange said. "I've plans for dinner."

But Aleister ignored this, leading the way to the comfortable silk-covered chairs and dropping gracefully down.

"I expect the truth is you've been to see Ehimay again?"

Ehimay. Yes, Strange had wondered about that connection. After today's visit to Brahman Warrick he had the priest pegged for the ambitious lover of Aleister's boyhood—the one who had dropped him because of Aleister's family background. It would be interesting to know for sure, but it was not really his affair.

"You're right," Strange said. "I have. But I was coming to see you anyway."

"Were you? Did Lady Hyde have a prior engagement this evening?" Aleister was still smiling that wickedly charming smile.

"After all," Strange pointed out, "you could've always called on me."

With unexpected seriousness Aleister inquired, "And had I called, would you have been at home?"

Would he? Strange wasn't sure. He wasn't easy with his feelings for Aleister. Had yet to sort out what those feelings were exactly.

When he didn't answer, Aleister's smile twisted. But instead of answering, he said, "So I suppose I owe this visit to the fact that his Holiness has convinced you to return to the Benhali Mountains?"

This direct approach—though generally his own—took Strange off-guard. "I came to see you because he told me you were ill."

"Oh." Aleister's smile faded a little. Then it brightened. "Were you concerned?"

"I suppose so." Strange considered and then admitted, "Damned worried, if you want the truth. He said…"

Aleister did not let the awkward pause stretch. "That I was mad? I might be. I don't think I am, but I'd be the last to know, I imagine." He bit his lip looking oddly young and unguarded. "Did he tell you…everything?" He added quickly, "Well, he would, wouldn't he?"

"He gave me some cock and bull story, yes."

"Oh. The thing is, it's…er…true, unfortunately." He cast a quick look at Strange from beneath his lashes. "I've had these…lapses most of my life."

"Why?"

"*Why?*" Aleister blinked and then grinned, seeming truly entertained by the question. "That's a new one. I'm not sure anyone's ever asked before."

Strange said brusquely, "Something must trigger these bouts, after all. You seem sane enough most of the time. All things being relative."

Aleister's grin widened, but then faded. "You know what triggered it in the mountains. A ghost tried to possess me."

"And you went into a trance. Even I can tell the difference between madness and a trance."

Aleister's gaze fell. "Yes. It is—it feels different this time. Sometimes it's worse. Sometimes *I'm* worse."

Strange didn't quite know what to say to that. It was not a particularly comfortable thing to realize he might be starting to care very much for someone who suffered periodic bouts of madness. Periodic bouts of demonic or ghostly possession wasn't much improvement.

Aleister said earnestly, "But I'm not making it up, Val. Whatever Ehimay told you. Even if I am ill again, I'm not wrong about these things. I'd hoped it would be over. That when the diadem was lost, everything would return to normal. But there's still something wrong at the Great Temple."

"Blood pumping from the underground spring to the fountain in the main hall."

"Minerals in the water." Aleister's tone was mocking.

Strange said slowly, "I noticed the first afternoon I went to the temple there were no monkeys. That's a first. I've never known deep jungle without monkeys."

The little wizened woman returned with a silver tea tray so enormous, Strange expected to see her overbalance. However she deposited it with practiced dexterity on the table between them and silently served frosted cakes and small sandwiches—it had been many years since he'd seen such dainties.

Neither man spoke while tea was poured and sandwiches served. The old woman withdrew unspeaking but Strange caught the doting look she threw her master as he ignored the piles of triangle sandwiches and went straight for the cream-filled cakes.

The cakes *were* excellent, but so were the sandwiches. Strange tucked in, surprised to find he was hungrier than he'd realized.

When he'd eaten an uncivilized amount, he asked, "Where does the diadem fit into all this now?"

Aleister licked a bit of icing from his finger, and Strange felt an uncomfortable corresponding stirring in his belly that had nothing to do with a liking for sweets. "I don't know," he admitted. "I'd hoped that when the diadem was lost, it would stop...it."

"But the diadem does fit in? It must."

Aleister said vaguely, "That's for the priests to determine, I suppose."

"Well, they've determined that I need to go back to the hills and find it. I want you to come with me."

Apparently Aleister was ready for this. He didn't flinch, didn't even look up. "No."

"What do you mean, *no*?"

"I mean no. I'm not going. Nor should you." He did look up then, and Strange knew that expression.

"It'll be different this time," Strange told him. "I've already told Warrick that this trip I'll need to go armed—a real expeditionary force with plenty of men and supplies. There's no point trying to hide what we're up to anymore. Rumors are going through the countryside like wildfire."

Aleister was still shaking his head.

"I'm not sure I can succeed without you."

Aleister made that small sound that was neither laugh nor snort. "I wasn't even conscious when the horse went over. I've no idea where the diadem is. And even if I did..."

He would not want it found. That was clear enough.

"I don't understand your attitude. Especially with the things happening in the Great Temple. If it's true, the thing you're not saying but that you obviously believe, then —"

"That's *why*," Aleister said, and abruptly he was on his feet, moving around the long room with barely controlled energy. "Don't you see? My being anywhere near that thing is a danger to all. He—it—followed me into the mountains and took me over when I wore the diadem. I can't go back.

It's waiting for me. And if it takes me over again…don't you understand what that means?"

"Say it," Strange said coolly. "The Extinguisher of Light, that's what you believe, right? That's what you fear. You think the ghost of Venavir is waiting to take you over and…what? Use you to destroy the world?"

"*It's not a joke!*"

"Am I laughing?" Strange inquired into the silence that followed that howl of pained outrage. "Nor do I think you're mad. Although I could be wrong about that."

Aleister threw himself in his chair once more and buried his face in his hands.

"You academic types," Strange said wearily. "You've got it all wrong, don't you see that? The diadem was used to defeat Venavir. That's the bloody legend, isn't it? His mate Dakshi used the diadem to defeat him. That's why we've got to go back and get it."

Aleister was shaking his head without raising his head. "You don't know what you're talking about. Venavir possessed me and it wasn't until the diadem was lost that I had the strength to throw him off."

"It wasn't the diadem. The diadem went over the edge more than a day before you came back," Strange said. "It was the mushrooms."

Aleister did look up at that. Granted, not the most intelligent expression he'd worn. "The…?"

"Mushrooms," Strange informed him. "The ones you went on and on about having such magical properties. I picked a few of them in one of the meadows and made you broth. That's how you were able to break the trance."

"You're joking."

"No. The diadem was lost the day before. It wasn't until I made you soup out of those mushrooms that you had the strength to break free."

Aleister's brows drew together, considering this. "That can't be right."

Strange shrugged. "It's the way it happened."

"But that doesn't make any sense."

"Makes as much sense as you thinking the diadem could turn you into the tool—the pawn—of the Extinguisher of Light. If that's what's been triggering your madness, this Venavir bloke has been after you since you were ten years old. Long before you'd ever even heard of the diadem."

Aleister seemed to be considering, weighing, remembering. Slowly he shook his head. "Perhaps you're right. Even so, I can't do it, Val. I can't face it again. I'll lose. I'll be lost forever. And perhaps the world with me."

"If I'm willing to take that chance—and if you're right, I've got as much to lose as you—then you should be willing to. Isn't that so? I need you with me. We made a good team, you and I. And I'm not sure I can do it without you."

Another long moment, during which Aleister seemed to consider and discard various responses. Finally he asked, "Why?"

"Told you, didn't I?"

Aleister shook his head. "Not really, no."

Strange said slowly, "All right. Maybe I don't know myself why. But I can tell you this much…you're the only person who didn't question my story about the diadem going over the cliff with the rest of the supplies."

"I don't follow."

"Don't you think it's strange I stowed that damned thing in my bag and left it on the pack pony? A valuable object like that? Our sole reason for journeying into the White Mountains?"

Aleister seemed to relax. He said, faintly amused, "I know you didn't steal the diadem."

"How could you know? You were senseless most of that ride. Or did you see it in your trance?"

Aleister's amusement disappeared. "I didn't see it in trance." He said slowly, as if only now reasoning it out, "You had your hands full at the shrine. And afterwards. And I expect you didn't trust the diadem. You don't like artifacts of Power. Valuable or not. That's why you stowed it with the supplies with the pack pony."

Strange's smile was caustic. "Close enough. But this is the first you've stopped to work it out."

"You're not a thief."

"No? But you thought I might have agreed to hand the diadem over to Isabella Hyde, didn't you?"

"At first, yes." Aleister met his gaze. "Later, no. You don't go back on your word."

"Don't be so sure of that."

Aleister was smiling crookedly. "You don't go back on your word when you've meant it."

It wasn't exactly the conclusion of a strictly logical mind but that loyalty of Aleister's meant something to Strange. Not that it mattered. Aleister was shaking his head again. "I'm sorry. I can't do it, Val. I can't go back."

Strange was hard pressed to understand his disappointment. After all, everything Grimshaw had said was true. He was unlikely to be of help finding the diadem and the mountains had nearly killed him. Probably the wisest thing he could do was steer clear of them. And Strange himself wasn't exactly sure why he himself was going back after the diadem. For the money, certainly, to put right his failure, definitely, but did he honestly believe the ghost of the Extinguisher of Light was hanging around the Great Temple?

He said neutrally, "Is that your final word?"

"Yes."

Strange rose. "All right. Fair enough. Perhaps when I get back...?" He let it trail as he wasn't sure what he was asking. Perhaps they would dine together? Perhaps they would sleep together? What did he want from Aleister? He had no idea.

Aleister rose too. He was staring at Strange. "Yes," he said in answer to whatever it was Strange had not asked.

But it was there in his expression: he did not expect to see Strange alive again.

Neither spoke as they went to the front door. Aleister opened the door and the sweet evening scents of the wild garden reached them, Strange hesitated. He realized he wanted to kiss Aleister. It might be the last time, after all.

It was probably witchery, but…nonetheless, he wanted to press his mouth to Aleister's and taste him. He couldn't think how to manage it.

Easy enough if Aleister had been a woman, but he wasn't.

He turned away and Aleister put a hand on his arm. "Stay," he said huskily.

CHAPTER TWENTY

For the first time in two weeks, Aleister felt at peace. Which was probably conclusive proof that he really *was* mad.

Still...whatever the future brought, he would not have traded those few hours of moonlit intimacy, and when he opened his eyes in the morning, feeling pleasantly battered and stretched and sated, wrapped tight in Valentine Strange's powerful arms, Valentine's genitals soft against his own warm skin, he felt well and whole in a way he couldn't remember experiencing ever before.

He rested for a time listening to the comforting sounds from the early morning kitchen, to the rain beating against the roof. It would be raining harder in the mountains, and the trails would be treacherous. He closed his eyes.

Stay.

He smiled faintly remembering how Valentine had interpreted that plea last night. Or perhaps Valentine had better understood him than he had understood himself. Anyway, no regrets there, but it made it all the more difficult to let him go now. Not that he could stop him. Not that he *should* stop him.

But difficult. If he were stronger, braver, saner he would go with him. And if they died—and they almost certainly would—at least it would be together.

"Can hear the gears turning from here," Valentine murmured, his breath warm against Aleister's neck. He shivered pleasurably, and Valentine said, "Chilly? I can warm you up."

He proceeded to ably demonstrate.

Afterwards it was Aleister's turn to hold Valentine close to his heart, kiss the dark curls, the stubborn jaw.

He asked lazily, "Did you tell me you won your commission to the Lancers in a card game?"

Valentine grunted acknowledgement.

Aleister studied the normally haughty profile—now curiously young and relaxed. "Aren't there rules about the qualifications of the candidates—and serving a minimum number of years at each rank? Can commissions be bought and sold like that?"

"Sometimes." A smiled played about Valentine's mouth. "This commission was in the name of Valentine Strange."

"Valentine Strange is your name."

Valentine's eyes opened, bluer than the Lancer's uniform he'd once worn. "It is now."

After an astonished moment, Aleister burst out laughing.

⸙

It was the most pleasant morning Aleister had spent in many years. They slept late and breakfasted in the garden beneath moody clouds. It was tempting to think what it might be like to make a regular occurrence of such mornings, but of course there was no chance of that. Even if Valentine came back from the mountains with the diadem—what would he be coming home to? That was the question that haunted Aleister these days.

He wasn't sure if he was relieved or disappointed when Valentine did not try again to persuade him to join the next expedition to the Benhali Mountains.

"When will you leave?" he asked as they were finishing up their tea and date nut bread.

"Soon. It'll take no more than a few days to prepare."

He wanted to ask Valentine if he would see him again before he left, but if he asked he was liable to ensure that he didn't. Aleister didn't have a great deal of experience in these things, but that much he knew. Valentine was uncomfortable with his feelings for him—he much preferred to think that Aleister had somehow bewitched him.

It would have been funny if they had more time.

"Anything you can tell me that might make the trip easier?" Valentine asked.

"Don't go."

Valentine laughed. "Besides that."

Aleister shook his head. "It's the rainy season. There's word that the Phanisgars are attacking travelers and pilgrims right outside the city."

Valentine said easily, almost gently, "You stick to the Craft, Master Grimshaw. Let me worry about road conditions."

Aleister shrugged. "Who is Warrick sending with you?"

"A Master Scrivener."

"Scrivener!"

"You know him?"

"I know him." At Valentine's inquiring look, he admitted with reluctant fairness, "He's learned enough. Very much one for following the Great Grimoire to the last letter." He could imagine what Valentine would make of fussy Master Scrivener—and vice versa. He didn't think Scrivener would be much help on the journey, but as he was unable to risk it, well, there were worse choices than Scrivener.

When the time came for leave taking, Valentine was brisk. "Take care of yourself, my friend."

Aleister nodded. There were many things he wished to say, but none of them were likely to help matters.

Strange turned away, throwing casually over his shoulder, "Perhaps I'll see you one last time before we leave Harappu."

Aleister watched him until he vanished down the street.

⌒

Strange was approached by a man in a rickshaw not far from Grimshaw's estate.

He'd been in the mood to walk, his thoughts preoccupied with both Aleister and the upcoming expedition, and upon being hailed, he waved the man away.

Then he recognized the man as one of Isabella Hyde's servants, and he got in the little cart and let himself be carried off to the old Hidushi palace by the river.

Isabella was in her sitting room having a dress fitting.

He had forgotten how very beautiful she was. She waved off the seamstress kneeling at her feet and came to greet him in a gown of flame-red satin trimmed with gold beads—the kind of thing that no Alban woman could wear without looking cheap and tawdry—or merely anemic.

"Two weeks, you cad!" She was laughing though as she kissed him lightly. "I was beginning to despair of you. Truly."

He felt again the power of her considerable charm again, yet was unmoved by it. Perhaps because he'd just spent about as energetic and satisfying a night as a man could hope. Or perhaps it was something else.

He kissed her back with every appearance of enthusiasm, however, and let himself be led off to sit next to her on the claret-red sofa with the tiger skin draped across the back.

"Sadly, there's nothing like scandal and failure to keep a man occupied," he apologized to her. "In any case I wasn't sure I was still welcome—given how hard your men worked to kill me in the mountains."

Isabella laughed. She had an enchanting laugh and used it frequently. Rapping his knee with the small painted fan she held, she said, "*My* men? And you told me you never indulged in soma in the morning! Don't tell me you were attacked by bandits and thought that I'd sent them!"

"These were no bandits."

She arched her eyebrows. "I assure you they were no servants in my employ. What, by the dust from the four corners, would make you think they were mine? Did they wear my crest?"

"No."

"Of course not." Her smile never faltered, yet he sensed an infinitesimal relaxing and knew he was correct. Or rather that Aleister had been correct.

She had betrayed him.

He was not precisely shocked, though he was more than mildly surprised. He had imagined she was quite in love with him, and while he didn't place undue importance on such things, he supposed himself to be a fairly good judge of women. Or maybe he was a little more sentimental than he realized. He'd been genuinely fond of her.

Either way, his feelings for her died there and then.

He was still exploring how he felt about that as she questioned casually, "So the diadem really did exist?"

"Yes."

"Yes. The stories are rife as to how you cheated the Holy Orders and brought the diadem of Dakshi to me. Except...you didn't."

She cocked her head, scrutinizing him with those extraordinary gold-brown eyes.

"The diadem is at the bottom of a river gorge."

"So the story goes. But it sounds so unlike you, my dear. If there's one thing you are, it's terribly efficient. And losing ancient crown jewels just isn't you."

"So I've been given to understand. Still, it's the truth. I swear on Suri's sari."

Her smile grew wry. "The only problem with that is you don't believe in Suri. Or Purya. Or Brigantia. You don't believe in any deity that I know of. You're even remarkably free of the soldier's superstitions."

Strange stroked the silky tiger skin across the sofa, saying impassively, "I believe in honor, courage, and loyalty. And in maintaining my arms and equipment."

She gurgled a delightful little laugh. "The soldier's code." She purred, "Do you believe in love?"

He examined her smiling face thoughtfully. "I've never thought much about it."

Looking mildly pained, she changed the subject. "Now the rumor is that you're going back to the White Mountains to retrieve the diadem."

"Where did you hear that?"

"Oh, my spies are everywhere. Well, not in the White Mountains trying to kill you. But everywhere else." She offered a coquette's smile but her eyes were hard. Funny that he'd never noticed how hard her eyes could be. The eyes of a fanatic or merely a seasoned officer? "Are you going to try to convince me it's not true?"

"No. It's true enough. I'm leading an expedition back into the hills as soon as I can put one together."

"And who is financing this expedition?"

"I'm still in the employ of the Holy Orders."

"Those words sound so odd coming from your lips." She snapped open and closed the fan, apparently thinking rapidly. "The Holy Orders are financing a rescue operation? Throwing good money after bad? They must want this trinket very badly."

Why not? You do. He didn't say it, though.

She treated to him to another of her smiles. "I'm wounded that you could possibly think that I'd want to harm a hair on your head." She spread and closed the yellow fan again, little green fishes appearing and disappearing with each snap. "I know that you're a hard man, Valentine, but I imagined that between us..."

He smiled. "I assure you, Isabella, you're quite alone in my affections." As he unconsciously stroked the tiger skin hanging over the back of the sofa, his fingers picked out a flaw in the hide...a hole.

Isabella tapped her painted fan in a tattoo against the sofa arm. She seemed to be trying to reach some kind of decision. Strange's fingers continued to stroke the hole in the skin draped over the sofa back. That particular size and shape…like a bullet hole.

He went very still.

She said, "Suppose I were to expunge your debt to me and pay you an additional two hundred thousand rupees to bring me this trinket? That would make it an offer of five hundred thousand rupees in all—in addition to undertaking outfitting this second expedition."

Still trying to make sense of the bullet hole in the tiger skin over the sofa, it took Strange a few seconds to make sense of her cool words.

She continued lightly, "After all, what is it but a treasure hunt really? Dakshi is a fairytale for children. A folktale for superstitious peasants."

"Where did you hear that name? According to the church, the diadem belongs to Purya."

"Purya?" She laughed. "A minor goddess of hearth and home resurrected by the church? What would Purya have been doing fighting demons? Dust demons perhaps. Either way, what does it matter? The entire thing is a hoax."

"A hoax?"

"Of course, Surely you don't think—well, perhaps you do. We've all heard the rumors. The temple witch went mad. The last of the Grimshaws, wasn't he? Well, they were all born mad." Her eyes were curious, and surely it wasn't his imagination that he recognized that look as one he had seen too many times down the barrel of a rifle?

When he didn't confirm or deny her words, she continued, "It's so simple, really. The Holy Orders arranged to plant this diadem in some godforsaken temple in the middle of the wilderness so that it might be discovered and retrieved and offered as a symbol of national hope and unity."

His scattered thoughts seemed to re-form and crystallize with wonderful speed. What she said made only too much sense.

Brahman Warrick had been remarkably vague about how he had learned of this mysterious diadem. *A hoax.* Yes. He could easily believe it. Hadn't Warrick rattled on about the need for this national symbol of unity? He had certainly never doubted the diadem existed. And what about that odd insistence that a male statue was female? Because Purya was a state approved deity and Dakshi belonged to Hidushi's colorful, violent—and pre-Alban—past.

Warrick might never have realized the diadem was actually an artifact of Power. Or perhaps he had known....

Granted, that didn't explain why the Crux had changed her mind about letting them leave with the diadem, but it had clearly been a change of heart. The original plan had obviously been to let them cart the thing back to Harappu. He wondered whether it was true that her decision had been based on her belief that the Holy Orders were corrupt—or her fear that Aleister would lose the battle with the spirit attempting to possess him.

Belatedly, Strange noticed that Isabella was observing him rather closely. Watching to see if he bought into this theory? He asked genially, "If you don't believe this diadem is genuine, why do you want it?"

Her eyes widened like a cat spotting movement inside the mousehole. "Why, I suppose the idea of wearing the headdress of a god does appeal to my vanity. Imagine the sensation it would make at my annual masquerade ball?" She rallied, "They say godhead goes with everything."

"You're suggesting spending a great deal of money on a tiara."

"Well, I *have* a great deal of money." Her lip curled a fraction. "Something that we both know you need rather urgently."

"Yes. Unfortunately, my dear, having first accepted the offer of the church, I can hardly drop that commitment because a better comes along."

"A debt of honor."

"Precisely."

"And yet...do you not have other debts of honor that require discharge?"

He reddened. She was right, of course. It was a damnable thing that he had borrowed money from her—worse now, knowing that whatever he had imagined was between them had been exactly that: his imagination.

Seeing his discomfiture, she continued, "Oh, you mustn't think I would make things awkward for you. Surely we're too dear of friends for that. But...shouldn't old debts take new—first—priority? And with five hundred thousand rupees you might discharge *all* your debts and still have a tidy sum left over."

He said shortly, "Isabella, I've given my word. I can't help you."

"How much is the church paying you?"

"It doesn't matter —"

"Six hundred thousand rupees," she replied, unabashed. "A doubling of my first offer."

He raised his brows. "You do want it badly."

"I've told you."

He shook his head. "I can't do it. Not even if I understood why you want it so urgently."

The charming mask slipped. "It's doesn't matter why I want it. The bottom line is that I can and am willing to pay for it. Seven hundred thousand rupees."

"You said it was a hoax by the church."

"I believe it is a hoax."

"Then it makes no sense —"

"Eight hundred thousand rupees. That's my final offer."

He shook his head and rose from the sofa. "You could offer me a million rupees. It's my duty to go back and recover the thing—fake or not—for the Holy Orders."

She swallowed. "A million rupees..."

He stared at her. Meeting his eyes, her own gaze sharpened.

"A million rupees," she repeated more confidently.

CHAPTER TWENTY-ONE

The morning before Strange was set to leave Harappu he met with Brahman Warrick one last time. As on the previous occasion Warrick chose to meet in Harappu at the rectory of the old Alban cathedral rather than at the excavation site at Gomar.

"How are you and Master Scrivener faring?" he asked cheerfully coming to greet Strange in the neatly tended rose garden with its marble statues of Brigantia—or perhaps they were supposed to be Purya now. "He tells me preparations are complete and you leave tomorrow at dawn."

Master Scrivener was, in Strange's opinion, a wet sock. He said bluntly, "If he's the best you've got to offer, I suppose he'll have to do. I can't say that I'm impressed so far. Has he ever been outside church walls?"

Warrick continued to be in good humor, rubbing his long, beautiful hands together in unconscious pleasure. "Master Scrivener is a very capable man. You'll see. He's very well trained. I think you'll find him a great help."

Translation: Master Scrivener would kick up a ruckus if all did not go according to his interpretation of what the church wanted and expected from this expedition. It was already clear to Strange that Master Scrivener was a stickler for rules and regulations. A kind of spiritual quartermaster.

"So long as he sticks to his own business and doesn't tell me how to mind my own, we'll do fine."

Warrick chuckled. "You'll find him a little less disinterested than Master Grimshaw. Master Scrivener takes his responsibility to the church very seriously."

"How is Grimshaw?"

"Grimshaw?" Warrick looked vague. "Sadly he continues to resist all efforts to help him. I believe the Guild is moving to have him placed under protective care."

The Guild was the officiating body over all practicing witches. It worked in conjunction with the Holy Orders. While the Holy Orders had no control over Grimshaw except as regarded his employment as a temple witch, the Guild did indeed have authority over him both personally and professionally.

Strange said narrowly, "What do you mean 'place him under protective care'?"

"Provide asylum and ministration until such time as he is deemed recovered enough to resume his duties and responsibilities. Or at least care for himself."

"You're having him locked up?" Strange eyed Warrick in disbelief. "Are you that afraid of him?"

"I'm afraid *for* him," Warrick said. "We all are. Sadly, this relapse is nothing new, nothing, in fact, that could not be predicted. You don't know him, Major Strange. Allow those of us who do, to see that Aleister receives the care he desperately requires—before there is a tragedy we would all greatly regret."

Strange bit back saying the things that would help neither Aleister nor himself. Instead, he asked, "How goes the excavation? Found any skulls yet?"

Warrick said coolly, "There are delays. It's the rainy season. That's to be expected."

"I heard that the fountain of blood in the main hall overflowed and flooded the entire ground level—and that you've been unable to find marl to work the site."

Warrick bit out, "It's not a fountain of blood. The water is red due to the mineral content of the spring beneath. If Aleister had not gone around saying wild and ridiculous things, these vicious rumors would not be circulating the city. And, for your information, we have workmen on the site even as we speak."

Yes, Strange had heard that. Untouchables, the lowest caste of all, were now working to excavate the site—for the first time in history. He supposed that could be considered progress of a kind.

He asked, "Holiness, have you ever heard of the Extinguisher of Light?"

Warrick groaned and actually put his face in his hands. "Aleister, what have you *done*?" he demanded. He raised his head and said, "As I'm sure you're well aware by now, Major Strange, the Extinguisher of Light is an ancient Hidushi legend. One of the earliest. First Dynasty. It's not history, it's the silliest and most primitive of mythologies. And it is tied dangerously to Hidushi nationalism. The fact that Aleister is spouting such monstrous calumny is proof that he's seriously deranged, or worse, that he's following in the footsteps of his traitorous patriarchs. Or both!"

"I see." Strange preserved a grave expression. "No wonder you're concerned for him. I'll leave you now, Holiness, as I've still a number of things to attend to before tomorrow."

Warrick recovered some of his usual smoothness. "How long do you suppose it will take you to reach the White Mountains now that it is the rainy season?"

"Two weeks if all goes smoothly." Rarely did all go smoothly, but no doubt Master Scrivener would make sure to keep the Brahman posted.

Warrick offered his hand. "Then I don't suppose we shall meet again before you leave. I wish you the best of Alban luck, Major Strange. I pray that your journey will be successful—for all our sakes."

Strange said goodbye briskly and departed. From the cathedral it was a short ride to the Alban cantonment where he found Aleister at home enjoying a late breakfast of buttermilk blackberry shortcakes.

Aleister looked up at Strange's entrance, eyes lighting, although he said prosaically enough, "To what do I owe this honor?"

Strange had firmly told himself on the ride over that it would be best to keep matters platonic between them for now, but Aleister once again exerted his witchery and Strange was drawn straight to the table. He leaned down kissing Aleister's startled mouth, tasting the sweet tartness of blackberries—and Aleister himself.

"You underestimate your charms."

Faint color rose in Aleister's face though he said calmly, "Ah. And my charms have dragged you back here, have they?"

"Actually, it was the possibility of a decent breakfast."

Aleister snorted and summoned one of the elderly retainers. Shortly thereafter Strange found himself with a plate of blackberry shortcakes and a cup of hot coffee.

"I've been to see your old mate Brahman Warrick," he said, sectioning the shortcakes into triangles. "He's planning to have you locked up so you can't go around telling people that the Extinguisher of Light is coming."

Aleister grimaced. "It's not as bad as all that. It's true that I have to face a Guild examination in two days, but it will be all right. I'm not mad." He added thoughtfully, "At least, I don't think so."

"Do tell them just that. It ought to reassure them no end."

"It's just a formality. The Holy Orders —"

"You really are quite touchingly naïve," Strange said through a mouthful of shortcake. "They're going to lock you up, my lad, to keep you from blabbing anything else about the Extinguisher of Light or the fact that the diadem belonged to Dakshi."

He could see from Aleister's expression that this was not the first time the idea had presented itself. "I shall have to convince them not to."

Strange sighed and shook his head. "I can imagine only too clearly how you think you'll do that. Perhaps when you're released from asylum and ministering in about ten years, we can have dinner."

Aleister scowled and devoted himself to his plate. "Assuming you get back from the Benhali Mountains alive," he muttered.

Observing him for a few moments, Strange asked, "Is there a possibility that Dakshi's diadem is a fake?"

Aleister looked up, his brows knitting. "You know it's not."

"No, I don't. I'm going solely by what you've told me. Is it possible that Warrick and the church elders might have concocted an elaborate hoax—something that might even fool you for a time?"

"No. Why should they try?"

"An effort to come up with a supreme unifying symbol for the state while the government is so precariously balanced?"

Aleister drank a mouthful of coffee and replaced the cup in its china saucer. "The only way such a hoax could work is if I was in on it. Is that what you're asking me?"

"No. No, in fact, to be successful it would be necessary that you *not* be in on it. Your unwillingness to go, your disbelief would all be vital to the verifying of it."

Aleister seemed to consider this dispassionately. "It was not a fake."

"Perhaps it was a very good fake."

Aleister shook his head. "My particular field is First Dynasty art and antiquities. I tell you, I would have detected a forgery."

Strange, watching him closely, detected a certain reserve. "But...?"

"But what?"

"I know you, Aleister. Something troubles you about the diadem."

"You *know* me?" Aleister's smile was derisive.

Strange repeated, "Something about the diadem troubles you. If it's not a fake, what is it?"

Reluctantly, Aleister said, "I believe it's First Dynasty, and I believe it belonged to Dakshi, but...I don't understand—I can't believe that it was the tool with which he defeated Venavir."

"I don't follow."

"I wore the diadem but was unable to resist Venavir taking me over. It's supposed to work as an apex of focused Power—the jewels are all focus stones—but though I could use the diadem to see into the past and even the future, none of it was clear—and even with the diadem I hadn't power to resist —" He broke off, swallowing hard.

"You were weakened from the white spice."

Aleister remained uncomforted. "I don't think it was that."

"Well, it was missing one of the largest stones," Strange pointed out.

"That's true." Still Aleister didn't sound convinced or reassured. "My fear is that rather than serving as a weapon against him, the diadem might provide Venavir with a instrument."

"Hmm." Strange weighed this, then said, "More likely you're not the witch this Dakshi was."

Aleister's face tightened. "I'm aware of that. Thanks for pointing it out, though."

"Look," Strange said reasonably, "What's the point of me telling you comforting lies? Your skills lie in other directions, that's all." He forked in a bite of shortcake, chewed, swallowed, and said, "Not to change the subject, but is it possible Isabella Hyde is a shapeshifter?"

Aleister's jaw dropped. An expression Strange sincerely hoped he did not wear when he was facing the Guild examiners. "The bloodline on her dam's side is very old and rather murky. I suppose it's not *im*possible. Why do you suggest it?"

"Partly instinct. Partly —"

"You have an instinct for shapeshifting?"

"I have an instinct for trouble," Strange said bluntly. "And she has a tiger skin in her sitting room with a bullet hole in its shoulder. I hit the tiger that followed us into the hills in the shoulder, and that hide looks to me to belong to a young, smallish tiger."

"Were you not able to examine her for new scars?" Aleister's tone was mocking, but it did not mislead Strange.

"I haven't been with Isabella since I came back." He added, "Too busy."

"Ah. Well, if there's a tiger skin in Lady Hyde's parlor, it sounds to me that rather than shapeshifting, she's using some kind of tribal or primitive magic to alter her form."

Strange mulled this over before asking, "Let me ask you this. Why d'you suppose she offered me a million rupees to bring the diadem to her?"

Aleister's eyes widened. "A…million…rupees…"

"That's right."

"I don't understand. Unless…"

"You're getting more cryptic by the second. Unless what?"

"She wishes to publicly reveal the diadem as a hoax."

"But it's not, according to you."

"It's a First Dynasty artifact. There's no proof it belonged to Purya—in fact, we know it didn't, although Dakshi might actually be better…" He narrowed his eyes in that way he had when he was concentrating. "Either way there's nothing to support it being anything more than an ancient trinket—beyond my word."

"And you're supposed to be mad."

"Oh." Aleister swallowed. "Yes. I see what you mean."

"I think if you don't want to spend the next year or so being bathed in elephant urine and getting oiled, sweated, and purged on a regular basis —""

Aleister laughed, although his humor seemed forced. "Witches don't subject the mad to such cures. No one does excerpt the most ignorant peasants."

"Again, I think you miss my point. If you don't want to be locked up, I think you should return with me to the Benhali Mountains. Post haste."

Aleister shook his head. "I'm not going and neither should you. You don't even believe it *is* an artifact of Power."

"I didn't in the beginning, that's true. No more did you. I went because they paid me. This time it's different."

"You warned him—Warrick—that it might be an impossible task and it was."

"It wasn't, actually."

"But it is now," Aleister said earnestly. "You fulfilled your obligation, Val. There's no need for you to risk your life again. If it was dangerous before, it's tenfold the danger now. Not only do the previous dangers exist, now half the countryside knows what you're attempting to do—and more than half the countryside would like to stop you from doing it."

"Shut it." Strange said. "That's sedition, Aleister. And if anyone should know it, it's you."

"I know exactly what it is. And whether I say it out loud or not, we both know it's the truth. And furthermore, if you think I'm going to risk my life to bring back that artifact so that it can be used as a symbol by a bunch of corrupt Alban refugees who simply want to hang onto their power for a few years, you can bloody well think again."

"Don't say another word." Strange felt obliged to speak, and yet…he felt oddly dispassionate hearing these things from Aleister.

He liked Aleister, perhaps that was part of the trouble. Knowing Aleister had changed his ideas about such things in ways he had never expected—or wanted.

"Why don't you wake up?" Aleister said. "You can't tell me that these thoughts have never occurred to you. You've spent your life protecting and serving the men who've enslaved your country as well as mine."

"You're an Alban true blood!"

"I'm *Hidushi*. I was born here. I've lived my entire life here. I'll die here. I never even saw Alba except in pictures. Before they destroyed themselves. My loyalty is to the land of my birth, and I hate —"

Affection or not, outright treason could not be permitted. Strange rose. "One more word and I'll shut your mouth for you."

"Will you?" Aleister rose too.

Strange smiled a slow, dangerous smile. "Magic against might? Is that it? That what you want to try?"

Aleister's shoulders slumped. "No, it isn't. Of course it isn't." He sounded merely tired now. But then he straightened. "Listen to me, Val. I'll give you a million rupees not to go."

Strange opened his mouth and closed it. At last he managed, "Do you have a million rupees?"

Aleister said grimly, "I can get it," and Strange believed him.

"Why would you do that?"

Aleister moved quickly and with an unusual awkwardness—banging against the table as he came around it, like a blind man in a strange room. "Why? Because that artifact is dangerous to all of us. And because I can't bear the idea of you throwing your life away on such a fool's errand. It's a waste. A stupid, pointless waste. And for what? To protect a government as bloated and corrupt as a-a spider bladder?"

Strange's anger faded, and he laughed. He pulled Aleister to him and found his mouth, kissing him with rough efficiency. "Shut up. I don't plan on throwing my life away."

Aleister kissed him back with unexpected ferocity. Then he sighed and rested his forehead against Strange's. "You're very sure, Val. Is there anything you're not confident of?" He opened his eyes, met Strange's gaze, and his smile grew wry. "You're confident of that too. You don't fool me."

"Come with me," Strange urged. "I want you. You can protect me from the evil powers of the diadem. How's that?"

Aleister muttered, "I can't even protect myself."

"Then I'll protect you. Come with me, Aleister. Come back with me to the White Mountains."

CHAPTER TWENTY-TWO

There was a saying. *A thousand men may live together in harmony, but never two women though they be sisters.* The same, in Major Strange's opinion, could have been justly said of witches. From the beginning Masters Grimshaw and Scrivener were like two cats in a bag.

To start with it affronted Master Scrivener that Grimshaw had unexpectedly joined them on this expedition. He seemed to see it as implied criticism of his abilities—confirming that some witches were indeed able to read minds. This triggered in him a desire to reaffirm his own position, which he did by insisting on regular prayer breaks and rest stops to augur from various signs and omens.

The fact that this irritated Strange and most of the company—and amused Aleister—made it all the worse. Perhaps there was previous history between Scrivener and Grimshaw. Both witches were silent on this score. In fact, they spoke to each other as little as possible.

Granted, Aleister was, even for Aleister, unusually uncommunicative this trip. Did he regret coming? Probably, but Strange was glad to have him all the same and glad to have kept him out of The Craft's asylum for a few more weeks, at least.

Akanhe, a former associate from the Lancers and his second-in-commad on this trip seemed to find the silent warfare between the witches mostly diverting—although after nearly a week of it even she was losing patience.

"I wish one of them would get it over with and turn the other into a stoat or a zebu," she muttered to Strange on the fifth day out of Harappu. Strange snorted and signaled her to quiet.

They had stopped for the daily prayer break beneath the great windmills that provided the city generators' with power. Scrivener was once again invoking…well, frankly Strange had no idea what he was invoking. Which was probably why Scrivener felt obliged to keep doing it. Strange kept a polite silence during these rituals out of respect for the three bearers and the cook who took it all seriously. Akanhe and the two other troopers followed his lead and minded their manners. Mostly.

As for Aleister, he demurely meditated on his own during these rest stops. Perhaps he had learned something the last time out.

"Witches apparently don't do that kind of thing these days," Strange informed Akanhe, removing his gaze from Aleister who sat on the edge of the camp facing the pinwheeling forest of windsails. Aleister's eyes were closed and his hands rested, palm up on his knees, but Strange knew him well enough to suspect that he was not in any state of elevated consciousness—though he clearly knew how to make it look good. "It's all history and hallmarks now. Strictly legislated and controlled."

Akanhe chuckled. Back when she had been Lieutenant Patel, she had served with him in the Lancers fighting Baz-gals on the Border. Akanhe had taken a poisoned arrow in the thigh and been invalided out. After recovering, she'd gone into mercenary work and built an excellent reputation for getting the job done. He'd hired the other two troopers—ex-soldiers both—on her recommendation. The bearers and the cook had been retained on the word of his old friend Captain Archibald Bracy, who was generally a better judge of character than his other old friend Captain Desmond.

Scrivener raised his hands, chanting, "May you rescue us from the hand of every foe, may you guide our footsteps, may you…"

"Be more chance of that if we actually kept moving," Akanhe observed, drawing Strange's attention back to the small circle around the temple witch. The troopers looked bored, even the bearers seemed a little pained at this additional early stop. Strange decided that he would have to curtail Master Scrivener's spiritual activities from here on out.

Yes, a very different journey this time. They had men and arms and supplies and they knew…roughly…where they were going.

"Major Strange!" Aleister called—he was generally careful to observe the proprieties in public.

Strange glanced around. Aleister was on his feet gazing out across the plains. Strange went to join him.

"What is it?

Aleister said tensely, "Riders."

There was no sign of them in the rainswept distance, but that didn't mean they weren't out there.

"An attack force?"

Aleister's worried gaze met his. "I…don't know."

"How large a band?"

Aleister shook his head. "I can't tell. They're cloaked—protected from me."

"By spell or incantation?"

Aleister nodded automatically, his eyes once more scanning the plains.

"But you're sure they're coming?"

"I'm sure." He did not sound sure. He sounded uneasy. "They're approaching fast."

Strange stared at Aleister's profile for one long moment more and then he whipped into action, breaking up Scrivener's prayer party, ignoring the witch's s squawks as he moved about the encampment giving the orders to set up their defense. The bearers took shelter behind the windmills. The troopers found strategic positions and pointed their rifles at the silver distance.

But the riders didn't come. Minutes passed. Then half an hour.

"I don't understand it," Aleister said, when at last Strange signaled the all clear.

Holstering his pistol, Strange studied the younger man's tired face. Aleister was not sleeping; Strange knew this as they were sharing his tent—though strictly platonically—at night. Over Aleister's shoulder he could see the smug if annoyed satisfaction on Master Scrivener's face. Scrivener also wanting a word with Strange.

"You're sure of what you saw?"

"Yes." Aleister seemed to speak more from stubbornness than confidence.

Strange was surprised to hear his own voice console, "Then they're out there somewhere and we're forearmed."

Aleister nodded with quick gratitude, but his eyes were troubled as he moved away. Strange summoned a polite expression for Master Scrivener and went to speak to him.

"Next time perhaps you will do me the courtesy of consulting me first," Scrivener said. "*I* am Temple Witch. *I* am in charge of all spiritual and magical matters on this expedition."

"You don't need to remind me."

"But apparently I do." Scrivener was about his own age. He was a tall, rawboned man with red hair and freckles, and there was the faintest Alban burr to his words when he was agitated—which he frequently was. "Grimshaw is no longer with the church. He shouldn't even be here. He has been remanded to the custody of the Guild pending his failure to appear them for examination."

"I've heard it all before, Master Scrivener," Strange interrupted. "Master Grimshaw is here because I want him here."

"He's *mad*," hissed Scrivener. "He's a danger to us all. Oddsblood, haven't you just seen proof of it? He jumps at every shadow."

"Because we haven't seen the riders so far, doesn't mean they're not there," Strange returned, moving away.

But later that evening when he and Grimshaw had retired to their tent, he asked softly, "Why do you suppose the riders didn't attack today?"

Grimshaw, settling down into the blankets next to him, said with equal softness, "We haven't found anything yet."

"Not raiders then, not bandits?"

"No." He added with that nerve wracking honesty, "I don't believe so."

"But you thought they were going to attack?"

"I did. I was wrong." He added as an afterthought. "Sorry."

Strange laid down and studied him. He thrust an arm out of his blankets and asked, "Sorry you came?"

Aleister gripped his hand hard. "Are you?"

"No."

"Still early days."

"I'm glad you're here, Aleister."

"Me too." Aleister withdrew his hand and tucked it back into the warmth of his blankets. "Pleasant dreams."

⤚

Aleister's own dreams were far from pleasant. More than once he opened his eyes to find Valentine shaking him awake. He never remembered what he dreamed—and that was a very bad indication. He was trained to remember his dreams. The fact that he could not—no matter how hard he tried—was another strong indicator that he was indeed under some kind of persistent spiritual attack.

That inability to remember and interpret his dreams had accompanied each of his other lapses into supposed insanity, and had he confessed that this was again the case during Guild examination, that alone would have been reason enough to confine him to care. Granted it was all moot now. By having failed to present himself to the examiners, he had in effect consigned himself indefinitely to the Guild's wardship. All the more reason why he and Val could not afford to fail in their mission—although, frankly, compassionate incarceration was the least of his worries.

Yet he did not regret his choice to accompany Valentine Strange. Not if it cost him several months of freedom—or even his life. Which was not to say he was not afraid. He was very much afraid. But...he was used to that. He had spent much of his life in fear, and he had learned to mostly work around it—as though he were blind in one eye or lame. He had many tricks for ignoring it, for hiding it—even from himself.

And the trip was difficult enough that he had plenty to occupy him. He could stand the cold better than the heat, but he hated being wet and they were wet a great deal as they traveled across the plains. In fact, if he hadn't been mad before, having cold water trickling constantly down the back of his neck would probably do the trick.

Still, if the end of the world was coming, he'd rather spend his remaining days in the company of Valentine Strange. And he fairly sure the end was near. And that he was probably going to be the instrument of destruction if he didn't come up with a very good plan when the hour arrived.

There didn't seem to be much he could do about it before the fact. The hand of fate appeared to be firmly wrapped around his neck and propelling him forward. Struggling against these things was always pointless. It had probably been his destiny since the ghost of Venavir had first reached out to him in the tomb of Gomar. All his life had merely been spent traveling to this time and place.

Wherever the time and place was.

That was the problem, of course, no one was exactly sure where they were headed—other than somewhere in the White Mountains. That left a lot of room for error. He and Valentine had managed to get themselves very lost escaping from the temple, and nothing that had happened after leaving the shrine had improved matters. Valentine admitted that he had not recognized his surroundings until he had found the mountain meadow where he'd discovered old Nanak's bones and picked the mushrooms that he still credited with breaking Aleister's trance.

"If your fears are correct," Valentine told Aleister privately, "we won't need to find the diadem, it will find us."

That didn't do a lot to cheer Aleister up, although he was aware that Val was at least partly teasing him. Valentine Strange, for reasons Aleister couldn't fathom, seemed very glad to have him along, and did his best to keep Master Scrivener from annoying him too much. Aleister would have understood the desire for his companionship if they'd had enough privacy to fuck, but Valentine ran a tight outfit and there was no fooling around of any kind. They rode together and slept in the same tent, but they rarely touched except casually.

Even so, Aleister found an odd kind of peace in these long, wet days riding beside Valentine, talking idly of this and that. Balestra and Caspar were old friends now and they moved alongside each other whether guided or not. The days slid past and because of the cool weather they made even better time than the first trip. The prairie fell to the tea bushes of the foothills and then they spent a night at Nagara.

"Do you ever sleep anymore?" Valentine muttered, coming awake while Aleister was scrying long after the rest of the camp was sleeping. He reached out and ran his hand down Aleister's sleeve. "You've been traveling again."

Aleister nodded. He crawled to the mouth of the tent, tipped the water from the scrying bowl outside, and spilled the stones back into the pouch, drawing it tight. Through chattering teeth, he said, "I th-think I know where to l-look for the diadem...."

He had been so close…if he closed his eyes he could see the knife edge of ledge, the tumbling silver of the water far below… everything that Valentine must have seen that fateful night.

"Good." In the faint blue light of the tent, Valentine's eyes looked black. "You're turning blue and it's not Power. Come here and get warm." He raised his blankets and Aleister stripped off his wet things and scrambled in beside him. Valentine sucked in a breath as cold flesh met, heated.

It was warm between the blankets, the air scented of Valentine and wool. A hard, muscular arm wrapped warmly around him, and pulled him close. Slowly, Aleister relaxed into the humid warmth of the blankets and male fug.

He wished his thoughts would quiet with his body, but they kept running over the hills and rocks, covering the same ground again and again.

"Val?"

He felt Valentine jerk awake. "Mmm?"

"If Venavir should possess me completely…promise you'll kill me."

"Not that again."

"Give me your word."

There was a long silence. Valentine said calmly, "You have my promise. And if you don't let me sleep, I promise I'll kill you sooner than you think."

Aleister gave an unwilling laugh and closed his eyes. But Valentine slept long before he did.

～

"Strange, isn't this your mark?" Akanhe called.

Strange dismounted and joined her at the rock face. There was a small V sharply cut into the lichen. He stared at it trying to remember carving that symbol, but drawing only a blank. There was no doubt it was his mark, however.

"It's mine."

She grinned. "Nice to know your pet witch is steering us true."

There had been some difference of opinion on that score that morning. Master Scrivener had insisted that they must not leave Nagara without performing a ritual for those who had died there the last trip, and Aleister had abruptly broken his cooperative silence regarding all things spiritual and insisted they needed to leave at once to find the diadem.

This had naturally made Scrivener dig in his heels and importune Strange that they not leave until he could work his Craft.

"Time is of the essence," Aleister insisted.

"You have no idea of what fell influences your actions may have brought upon us all," Scrivener had asserted seeing Strange watching Aleister.

Aleister said hotly, "I performed that ceremony in accordance with —"

"*You*? The man who slew one of them? That you could think an act of murder befitting a temple witch only goes to prove you've lost your mind."

"All right, all right," Strange said as Aleister drew himself up. "I'm happy with Master Grimshaw's efforts on behalf of the dead mutineers."

The word "mutineers" settled it for the troopers, but Scrivener could not let it rest, and the bearers had grown more and more uneasy as the witch insisted this disrespectful and callous treatment of the dead would bring disaster on them all.

"My suggestion, Master Scrivener, is that you stay here in Nagara and perform the ceremony," Strange said at last. "The rest of us will travel ahead into the mountains, retrieve the diadem, and rendezvous with you on our way back in a few days. That way we'll cover all contingencies."

Whatever outcome Scrivener had expected, it clearly wasn't this. "I can't possibly stay behind!" he protested.

And in the end, he didn't, though it was clear he was bitterly resentful that Aleister had—in his perception—won that round. He had treated Strange to a long dissertation on the role and authority of temple witches on expeditions such as this one as they rode up through the orchids and blue poppies. Strange had nodded at appropriate intervals and considered the best ways of scaling the canyon walls once they pinpointed the place the pony had gone over.

He had no doubt they would find it. He trusted Aleister's ability. Even before they'd found his mark cut into the rock, the terrain had begun to look familiar. He took out his spyglass and scanned the peaks and ridges around them.

There. There in the distance... silhouetted against the sullen sky was a rock formation that nature never put her hand to.

"This is the trail. The shrine is just over that ridge and the temple on the other side of the pass." Strange glanced back at Aleister who was staring at the ridge as well.

Feeling Strange's gaze, Aleister said, "It looks different in the daylight."

"Where did the horse fall?" Scrivener demanded, urging his mount forward between them. He looked from Strange to Aleister.

Akanhe said something under her breath, but Strange preserved his expression, pointing at the other end of the canyon. "Between here and there."

Odd to think how short a distance it looked in the dry daylight. Less than a mile. At the time it had seemed endless journey.

They continued up the narrow trail past barren hillside and the queerly-shaped rock formation until they reached the part of the trail that was too narrow for more than single file. The roar of the river drifted up from far below, and they could see it glinting and winding through the rocks like a blue snake.

They strung out then, traveling slowly and cautiously. Strange's spyglass lingered over every scrubby bush and cairn of rocks as he searched for the remains of the dead horse down the cliffside. In some places the cliff was less sheer than others, but even so it did not look promising. Given the weight of the pack, the horse would most likely have crashed all the way down to the river. Even if it had hung up, scavengers would have been tearing at the carcass within hours and the pack might still have gone plummeting into the water.

What if the priests from the temple had tracked their escape route and found the dead horse and pack? Strange considered and then rejected this. No. They would rescue the pack, but it was unlikely they would go to the effort of retrieving the dead horse. If pony and pack had not gone straight into the drink, then somewhere along this mountainside should be the carcass or a dead horse—or at least its skeleton.

Feeling an odd prickle between his shoulder blades, Strange turned away from the edge and scanned the hillside behind him. There seemed to be nothing to see but miles of stone and scrub. He glanced down the trail and Aleister was still trotting Caspar along the rim, scanning the slopes. A trooper followed slowly, gingerly. And behind—Strange glanced around—Akanhe and the others followed at a cautious pace.

As he watched, something glinted in the hills beyond. Strange brought the spyglass up, searching, but not seeing the tell tale gleam again. An optical illusion?

"Here!" Aleister shouted.

His unease forgotten, Strange swung out of the saddle, squeezing past the next rider, and jogging along the path until he reached Aleister who was off Caspar and pointing to a precipice below the long ledge that formed a grassy shelf from the side of the mountain.

"Where?"

"It's here. I can feel it."

"I don't see anything!" That was Master Scrivener, and how he'd managed to catch them up so quickly was anyone's guess. He must have crawled over the troopers between them. "What's he raving about now?"

Strange turned away in time to see Aleister climb nimbly down the ledge and head across the grassy pocket to where a shoulder of rock jutted out, barring their view of the next turn.

Strange was down the slope and after him, catching him up in couple of half-running strides. "Whoa. Where d'you think you're off to?"

Aleister shook him off. It was doubtful he even knew who grabbed his arm. He moved with definite purpose toward the razor-sharp bend in the trail. And watching him, Strange felt an odd conviction—a sudden recognition. He turned, calling back to the watching men and woman, "This way. Bring the ropes and grappling hooks. We'll go down the mountainside."

Scrivener began to splutter, "Go down? Go down *where*? It would take a monkey to climb down there."

Strange wasn't listening, moving quickly to rejoin Aleister as he strode fearlessly down the uneven path toward more ledge, more precipice—unseen and unexpected because of the grassy dip that Strange had missed in the night and the rain.

Aleister's boots slipped on gravel, his feet shooting out from under him. Strange caught him. "Slow down. If it's really here, it'll wait five more minutes."

"Oh, it's here," Aleister said, freeing himself again. "But wait it won't."

Strange let him go reluctantly. What could he mean? Strange studied the landscape around him. The grassy berm had thrown him, he'd thought the ledge was sheer all the way. No wonder the journey across the canyon had seemed so much shorter today. He considered that crest of the trail and was glad he had not tried to make it in the daylight. It seemed sheer luck that he had managed it by night.

Aleister stopped. "Val," he said, his voice sounded hoarse.

Strange reached him and stared down the hillside—no spyglass necessary—at the bundle of canvas and bleaching bones lodged against a gnarled and knotted tree growing crookedly out of the ledge.

The dying sapling had bought purchase in the shelf of land thrusting from the cliffside. Below this lip of land, the earth fell away into nothingness, a long, sickening drop to the glint of the seasonal river five hundred or so feet down. The pony's fall had been broken by the sapling that speared it, the impact nearly dislodging the tree so that its roots stuck like claws into the naked sky.

Absently, Strange was aware of Aleister's fingers digging into his forearm. Neither found words in the face of that vast emptiness of sky and silence.

Then Strange said lightly, "And to think I believed you were sleeping all that time."

He wasn't sure Aleister even heard him as he started down the slope, pebbles sliding beneath his boots, and Strange beckoned to one of the bearers to throw him a rope.

"Wait!" Scrivener protested. "He mustn't! He's liable to bring the whole ledge down and then the crown *will* be lost!"

The crown.

He was still raising objections as Strange followed Aleister. Strange thought that Akanhe was calling out to him as well, but his attention was on Aleister who was as ever oblivious to the extreme danger.

The slope angled steeply, but Strange was careful—much more careful than Aleister—and he managed to keep his balance and footing. Aleister was nimble as a mountain goat, but a couple of yards from the crumbling edge, his foot slid out from under him. He pitched forward and began to slide toward the edge of the cliff.

Chapter Twenty-Three

Watching Aleister's swift remorseless slide toward the gaping fall beyond, Strange had the curious sensation of time standing absolutely still. He could see every detail in perfect clarity: A bush with small yellow flowers pulling out by its roots as Aleister clutched at it, the pebbles skittering out from beneath Aleister's dusty boots as he tried to dig in and stop his slide, the black dilated pupils of Aleister's eyes as his gaze found Strange's.

He was not sure how he managed it—an impossible burst of speed, a superhuman wrench of muscles—but as Strange dove forward, he managed to clamp down on one of Aleister's wrists, gripping it hard and fast. He heard Aleister's grunt of pain, and his own echoed it. They slid another few feet before Strange was able to halt their descent.

Aleister was halfway over the edge, his free hand, fingernails torn and bleeding, clawed at the ragged soil held together by grass and wildflowers, his legs swung out into the rushing air of the void. Strange could hear his jerky gasps over the echo of rocks banging down the cliff and the thunder of the water below. His own lungs were going like a pair of bellows.

"I've got you," he grated. It was slightly overstating the case. Aleister's wrist felt absurdly fragile in his grip. Strange's other hand was locked into a handful of rotting reins and dying pine needles. Astonishingly, the whole edifice of tree and skeleton did not instantly give way and send them all crashing to earth. It did shift, however, the trunk cracking hollowly, and more dirt raining down on the cliff below.

"Val." Aleister's eyes, enormous in his white, face held his own.

"Don't move."

Aleister choked out, "I'm going to pull you over too."

"Don't move."

Behind him he could hear the pound of footsteps and the yells of those running to their rescue. It was only a matter of seconds. All he had to do was hold on.

Out of the corner of his eye Strange saw motion. A flash of color and serpentine slither. Olive green, pale yellow, black...a swaying motion. He froze. Didn't even dare draw breath.

Aleister had been attempting to get his fingers around Strange's wrist, but they stilled, ice cold. His voice was almost inaudible. "Val..."

Strange tried to speak without moving his lips. "Don't move. Don't let go."

Without turning his head he could just make out the hypnotic sway, the bronze eyes watching beneath the wide cobra hood, the flick of the tiny tongue, he could hear the terrifying hiss peculiarly like a dog's growl, feel the brush of sinuous, shining coils against his hand.

His mind was quite cool as he reasoned his position. Perhaps the cobra would not strike. Most likely it would. He could not get to his pistol without letting go of Aleister. Aleister could not get to his pistol without letting go of the slope. If either of them moved, the snake would likely strike Strange—in which case Aleister would fall. But he could not hold Aleister much longer anyway; his arm muscles were silently shrieking protest. Any way he argued it, Aleister seemed doom to fall. His only chance was to let go of Aleister and pull his pistol.

And that he could not do. He stopped trying to reason it. He would hold Aleister as long as humanly possible. That was all.

His gaze found Aleister's—and Aleister's eyes were calm. No. More than calm. Tranquil.

More.

Mesmerizing.

"It's all right. Let me go, Val. It's your only chance."

He could feel...the weight of Aleister's will pressing down on him, pushing him inexorably toward...making it difficult to remember what it was he had to do...wanting only to do what the voice in his mind was telling him...

Let go.

With an inward start he realized what was happening and his fingers bit hard into Aleister's flesh.

Shut it. He didn't say it aloud, but he thought it. It was all he could manage for the cool slide of the snake's skin across his own paralyzed his thoughts. He had never pictured himself dying in his bed, but this was not the death he'd have chosen. He waited every second for the snake to strike.

He was dimly astonished to hear Aleister speak in normal tones. It took a second or two to realize that the failure to understand was not his; the words were in Parlance. The snake continued to sway languidly back and then it dropped. Strange flinched, expecting to feel the puncture of fangs in his arm but though the heft of the snake was resting on his forearm, the creature seemed to be sliding over him, uncoiling in gleaming glints of green, black and cream as it glided right over his arm, passing in front of his face—Strange shut his eyes—and then felt it slithering over his other arm.

Aleister was still speaking in Parlance although he sounded faint. The fingers clutching Strange's wrist were trembling.

The cool weight glided swiftly across his arm, slipped beneath his wrist, an alarming caress of silken scales, and then wound around the top of his hand. The snake's head slid beneath Strange's palm and streamed over Aleister's fingers.

The cobra coiled around their joined arms, binding them together in a living lanyard.

The pound of footsteps halted, the voices shouting for them to hold on, dying as their predicament was absorbed. Aleister's voice faltered as the dying pine tree began to vibrate, its remaining roots tearing loose. Rocks bounded away, clacking against the face of the mountain, and hurtling down.

Everything seemed to happen at once. The tree gave way, Strange slid forward, grabbing with his suddenly free hand at nothing but air. His other arm was bound tightly to Aleister's, and though Aleister dropped down, Strange was able to hang onto him despite the terrible strain on his shoulders. His feet and legs and jacket were caught by rough, desperate hands and he was being yanked back to safety—and Aleister with him.

They were dragged back from the chasm, and as Aleister's knees cleared the edge, the snake seemed to uncoil and drop off like a cut rope. It bounced, coiling and uncoiling, down the rocky slope.

Hands were everywhere, voices gabbling, and Strange hauled Aleister the last few feet just as the tree's roots finally tore away, the sapling following the snake down the hillside—and taking the speared cage of horse bones and rotting canvas with it.

Still clutching Aleister, Strange watched it go. With shock he realized he had made his choice without thinking once of the diadem. Aleister sat up, looking after the tree and skeleton, his expression stunned.

"Got it!" Master Scrivener exclaimed.

He stood a few feet away, Strange's kit bag with its weathered writing dangling from one hand. With the other he held the diadem aloft to the light. The red and gold stones winked and blinked like cold fire in the chilly air.

The marl and the troopers murmured, awed, as Scrivener cried, "Behold the Crown of Purya!"

Having absorbed the fact that while everyone else was rushing to save himself and Aleister, Scrivener had gone for the diadem, Strange was not disposed to the warmest feelings toward the temple witch—not that he could argue with the decision, it had been a practical one—he was still startled when Aleister snarled and leapt up, grabbing the diadem out of Scrivener's hands.

Scrivener shrieked, "What do you think you're doing? That's church property!" He lunged for Aleister, who gracefully sidestepped.

Scrivener lurched toward the edge, and it was for Strange, moving to get between the two witches, to keep him from falling over. He jerked him back by the collar and Scrivener tried to reach past him, clawing at the diadem which Aleister held out of his reach.

The others moved hastily back. Master Scrivener, quivering with rage—and fright at his near fall—looked in outrage from Aleister to Strange. "That's a valuable artifact of Power. A holy relic. It can't be left in his charge. He's no longer with the church."

Strange said calmly, "It was in his charge before,"

"And the goddess was so offended she took it from his keeping and struck him mad."

Aleister rejoined with a particularly vulgar phrase Strange had never before heard from him.

To Scrivener Strange said, "I believe Master Grimshaw views the matter somewhat differently."

Scrivener controlled his voice with palpable effort. "Brahman Warrick will hear of this blasphemous action, Major Strange. When he does you can be sure you will never work for the Holy Orders again." Scrivener looked around the watchful circle of faces and said a little wildly, "None of you shall!"

"And a great disappointment to all of us, you may be sure," Strange said equably, turning away. "Mount up," he ordered, and the others hastened to obey.

Behind him Scrivener said with shaking voice, "He has bewitched you, can you not see that? He has played you for a *fool*."

"It's not true, Val," Aleister said quickly, hands still clutching the diadem in a white-knuckled grip.

Strange turned back to Scrivener. "Shut it now or you'll be riding back to Harappu in a sack. Now get on your horse." His eyes met Aleister's. "You as well. Mount up. We're going home."

CHAPTER TWENTY-FOUR

Long before they could see Harappu they could smell the burning.

"What could have happened, do you think?" Akanhe asked Strange quietly as they rode through the overturned windmills that lay like the bleached and broken bones of giants. "Smells like a funeral pyre."

In the train behind them the troopers and marl were eerily silent. The whispers had stopped when they saw the wreckage-dotted plains. Even Master Scrivener had nothing to say these days.

Strange grunted noncommittally, glancing at Aleister who rode silently at his side. Aleister's face was blanched of any color as his eyes slanted toward Strange's.

"Whatever it is, it's manmade," Strange said—mostly for Aleister's benefit. Not that it was much solace. He was not even sure it was entirely true.

Aleister said tonelessly, "The second Inborn Revolution has begun."

Strange had no answer to that. No one did.

Strange no longer had to drive his little band. They drove themselves harder and faster to reach whatever lay ahead— though it was clear to all that whatever lay ahead was trouble of the worst kind.

Less than a day's ride from the city the sky turned a sickly green hue, and over Harappu itself the clouds seemed to glow fiercely red. On the edges of the jungle, Strange called for the midday halt—although no one had any appetite for tea and rice soup.

Aleister sat beside him on a fallen log sipping his tea. He stuck close to Strange now. No going off on his own to meditate. No trancing at night. He carried the diadem against his heart at all times, but he never wore it. Never even spoke of it. But then he spoke very little.

"What do you think happened to our friends?" Strange asked him, spooning up the last of his rice soup. "The ones who followed us out of Harappu."

Aleister held his tin cup in both hands as though to warm himself against the chill and gloomy day.

"I think they were recalled home when the revolution began."

Assuming they had ever been there at all.

"You're convinced there's a mutiny in progress?"

Aleister raised his head. "Revolution. Aren't you?"

"We haven't met anyone to confirm it one way or the other. We should have by now. Should have run into refugees fleeing the city or Hidushi regiments riding to its aid."

"Nonetheless." Aleister gazed down at the murky hot liquid in his cup.

What would they do when they reached the city? Strange was still undecided. He had yet to hear Aleister's ideas on the subject—and that was no little source of unease. Before recovering the diadem it had not occurred to him that he and Aleister might be on opposing sides of what to do with it should they manage to succeed.

He opened his mouth to say something—of which he later had no recollection— when one of the troopers suddenly stumbled forward with a choking sound. Blood spurted from his breast, his knees gave way, and he fell to the ground as shots rang out in the jungle around them.

"Take cover," Strange shouted, He grabbed Aleister, tumbling him backwards behind the fallen tree they had been sitting on seconds before. Bullets ploughed through the dried bark as soldiers—ex-soldiers?—dressed in the navy uniform of the Natal guard advanced through the trees firing on them.

"Bandits!" Master Scrivener cried, waving his arms in panic. He seemed rooted to the ground while the others took cover around him.

"All right?" Strange spared a quick glance for Aleister, who had already drawn his pistol.

Aleister nodded tightly.

"Get down, you fool," Strange shouted at Scrivener who was still frozen in place—so far unharmed. Either the emblem of the Holy Orders still held some weight or their foes were particularly bad shots.

Strange whistled for Balestra, who cocked his ears alertly, and trotted forward unperturbed by the buzz of bullets around him. As the horse reached him, Strange jumped up, grabbing his rifle from Balestra's scabbard. He signaled the big stallion to lie down, and Balestra obeyed, front legs folding, then rolling onto his side, providing a partial bulwark for Strange who flattened himself once more in the depression behind the fallen tree trunk. He proceeded to give Akanhe and the remaining trooper cover as they scrambled for safety behind rocks and trees.

"Last time the Natal Guard stayed loyal," he commented to Aleister.

"They may be loyal now," Aleister pointed out. "They may have been sent to guard the city's periphery. They may believe that *we* are mutineers."

Strange considered this grimly. Bullets tore through the foliage overhead. "Then they should have asked," he said at last and briskly returned fire.

Aleister added, "Or they could have massacred the Natal Guard and stolen their uniforms."

A rough laugh escaped Strange. "That's what I like about you, Grimshaw. You keep an open-mind."

For a few seconds there was nothing but the retort of gunfire. Aleister said suddenly, "They've got a sorceress with them."

"Bully for them."

"She just tried to spellbind me." He sounded more surprised than alarmed. "She's very young. Still…" Aleister drew bead on a fast-approaching blue-clad rider.

"You're not going to hit anything with that at this distance." Strange put the rifle to his shoulder and fired at the soldier who fell like a stone. "What can you do about her?"

"If I can get close to her, I can try to kill her."

"Or she could kill you?"

"I suppose she might get lucky."

Strange considered this as he reloaded. For personal reasons he would prefer that Aleister not be killed. That went without saying. The main consideration remained the diadem. His own survival was also of some interest.

"Can Scrivener deal with her?"

Aleister threw a contemptuous look at the other witch who was currently huddled behind a spindly bush. "Possibly. If he doesn't die of fright in the next five minutes."

Akanhe brought down the next rider. She signaled to Strange that she was moving to higher ground. Strange acknowledged and told Aleister, "Take the diadem and make for the temple at Gomar. We'll meet you there when we can."

Aleister turned quickly. "But why?" he protested. "You need me here, Val. There are too many of them."

"Listen to me. That thing —" he nodded at Aleister's chest where they both knew the diadem rested inside his shirt, "cannot fall into the wrong hands, and well you know it."

"*I* might be the wrong hands."

Strange shook his head. "The legend is that only a descendant of Dakshi can wear the diadem and live, isn't that right?"

"I'm not descended from Dakshi's line. I'm Alban."

"I hesitate to tell you your business, Master Grimshaw—" Strange paused to aim and fire. His face tightened in annoyance as he missed. He reloaded quickly, but Akanhe brought the rider down. "There are spiritual descendants as well as physical, right?"

Aleister was silent.

"I've no idea why you seem to be at the center of all this. But one thing I do know is that one of the rules of your Craft is that there are no coincidences."

"That doesn't mean that I'm not the instrument of destruction!"

"The diadem is the tool with which Dakshi defeated Venavir, correct? That's the other part of the legend. It doesn't matter whether you think the legend is right or not, *that's* the legend. And even I know enough to know that there's no arguing with legend."

Aleister's voice shook a little as he said, "Don't you understand? If Venavir takes possession of me again, takes possession while I have the diadem in my possession —"

"Don't *you* understand?" Strange interrupted. "You must do after the cobra. It wasn't losing the diadem or drinking mushroom soup that allowed you to break free of Venavir. *You freed yourself.*"

Aleister was shaking his head, rejecting this.

"Yes. *Yes.* Look, we're a bit pressed for time, so let's stop debating it. There's a reason for all of this, and it's time you figured it out. You'll have a better chance of that if you don't have your head blown off, so mount up."

Aleister swallowed hard. "I'm not leaving you, Val."

Strange scowled. "You bloody are. I didn't bring you along for your sparkling conversation, you know." He spared Aleister a brief grin. "Well, not entirely. If I can rejoin you at Gomar I will. If I can't…then you make damn well sure this hasn't all been for nothing." Strange nodded at the black stallion lying patiently, playing dead on the ground a few feet away. "Take Balestra. He won't spook under fire."

"Val —"

"Go." Strange's eyes were on the newly arrived riders who were now dismounting and running to take shelter in the deep, green undergrowth.

Aleister swore bitterly.

Strange ignored him, but as the younger man started to inch past, Strange caught his shoulder, giving him a hasty, hard kiss. "Take care of yourself, Master Grimshaw."

Aleister kissed him back, fingers biting fiercely into Strange's biceps, holding on as though for dear life. Holding far more tightly than when he'd nearly plunged off the cliffside. An awkward, desperate kiss—and then he was gone. He grabbed Balestra's reins, the horse rolled upright, and Aleister jumped into the saddle.

The next moment he had spurred Balestra forward and was galloping through the bullets flying his way, ducked low on the horse's neck as tree limbs slapped at his head and back. Strange spent a few lively seconds making it extremely unhealthy to fire at the black stallion charging down the uneven trail.

When he had the next chance to look, horse and rider had vanished in the wet green silence.

⌒

Aleister expected to be followed, expected to have to fight for his freedom—at the very least to have to lose valuable time escaping pursuit. But there was no pursuit as he weaved and wound his way down the muddy narrow trails. The rolling echo of gunshots from the jungle road behind him faded into the leafy hush and before long there was only the pound of Balestra's hooves on the soft earth and the uncanny calls of unseen creatures that lived in this place.

Beyond the grieved certainty that he would never see Valentine Strange alive again was anger and dismay that Strange should have left this final leg of their quest to him. It was all very well to say that Aleister was at the center of the mystery surrounding the diadem, but Aleister had no idea how to proceed. And surely the wrong action was worse than inaction now?

Yet he rode on, rode like the madman he was reputed to be, taking Balestra over fallen trees and streams with ruthless disregard for the horse's knees or his own neck.

If he could reach Ehimay—Brahman Warrick—and finally make him understand the true nature of the artifact Aleister carried, then there was still a chance he might succeed. Ehimay had all the knowledge and mystical resources of the Holy Orders behind him if he could only be persuaded to see the situation clearly, without his previous bias. He was Aleister's best hope for an ally now for—despite his ambition and impatience for weakness—Ehimay was smart and strong and the sanest person Aleister knew.

But when Aleister at last reached the outer perimeter of the city walls, he discovered his way cut off by blockades of towering flames. He realized that he would have to circle round and find one of the many side gates or hidden entrances and then work his way through the heart of the city to the Cathedral.

An impossible task. Even if he managed to find an undefended gate, he would surely be killed before he made it past the flower markets. But what was the alternative? If he could not reach Ehimay, he would have to go to the Great Temple himself.

At the thought of it he felt a sick and unreasoning panic rising within himself.

Impossible. He couldn't do it—deliberately place himself in Venavir's grasp? Never. Dangerous enough to try it with Ehimay's help. Without it? It was tantamount to suicide. And if he failed, if he died, what would become of the world?

He tried to picture himself explaining this to Ehimay who already believed he was once more in the grip of madness.

Even if he did manage to safely reach Ehimay, what if Aleister couldn't convince him that he was sane?

The more he considered his position, the more hopeless he felt. Didn't Valentine realize how impossible the whole thing was? How could he have asked this? Didn't he realize what they were all risking by sending Aleister on his own?

And yet he had to try. Not for Valentine. Not even for himself. He had to because—

Whatever conclusions Aleister might have reached were cut short as the ground beneath him shuddered. Balestra suddenly reared up. Aleister nearly lost his seat, but somehow contrived to stay in the saddle.

His first thought was earthquake as the road rucked and and twisted beneath him, and Balestra scrambled to retain his footing. But the ancient trees around him began to moan and howl as though in the force of a great wind.

Yet there was no wind. Only a vast and echoing stillness.

When the earth's rumble subsided, Aleister wheeled Balestra heading for the oldest part of the city and the Hangman's Gate.

～

Bullets struck the wall over his head with a pat, pat, pat, and white lime dust and stone showered down. Heart pounding, Aleister ducked behind a bronze monument dedicated to the courage and sacrifice of the empire's soldiers in the Inborn Mutiny. It had been apparent to him within seconds of his arrival in Harappu that if anything he had underestimated the dangers of trying to travel through the city—and matters had not improved in the last few minutes.

Despite the fact that his sympathies were, at least philosophically, with the mutineers, his skin color and caste made him a target and he reluctantly recognized that no dialog would be possible.

He had left Balestra safely tethered outside the city gates—the stallion was too appealing a prize for the thieves and cut-throats now prowling the city and made Aleister conspicuous. But traveling on foot left him feeling more than a little vulnerable.

So far he had managed to avoid being trampled by the terrified horses galloping madly through the streets as he ran down the winding alleyways and criss-cross of mazy back-bazaars, past the burning military barracks—managed thus far to avoid the howling mob flooding the labyrinth of narrow passages and deep sided back streets overhung by trellised windows and loopholed walls and guarded stairways.

Harappu had become a charnel house. The sky above the city glowed red with the fires raging through gilded palace and rat-infested slum alike, and the very ground seemed to shake with the remorseless pound of the sacred war drums, the volleys of gunfire, the screams and cries of mutineers—and their former masters.

And as intensely as Aleister had believed this day must— and should—come, the fact that once again it was coming with bloodstained footprints struck him with horror. Had nothing been learned from the failure of the first mutiny?

He had to fight his first instinct which had been to head for the safety of Alban cantonment and protect the nearest thing he had to home and family. In the end he'd resisted. If he failed in his mission, the battle in Harappu would be the least of the world's problems.

So he had made his way through the city, past temples, storehouses, shops and hotels, avoiding flame and looting and pitched battles—and the occasional rampaging elephant or crazed camel.

He flinched as more bullets dug into the walls behind him, pinged off the Emperor's broad breast. Drawing his pistol, he fired at a soldier in the yellow uniform of the Imperial House Guard. Presumably Aleister was being shot at merely because he was Alban true blood. Another failed lesson from the first mutiny.

The guard fell to his knees, and Aleister scrambled up, fleeing down the street.

The smoke was thick on High Street and he lost time trying to find his way through the panicked crowds.

He could see the towers of the Alban cathedral in the distance and for the first time it occurred to him to wondered if Ehimay was still safe. Like Valentine Strange, Brahman Warrick had always seemed to Aleister about as indestructible as a man could be, but Aleister had left Valentine to die on the jungle road, and Ehimay might have met a violent end at the hands of the worshippers he had so ably served for years.

Granted, last time the churches and temples had been left untouched. Most of the damage had come from the Empire's own troops searching for those trying to claim sanctuary. This time might be different. Would almost certainly be different.

Aleister ran down a crooked side street, footsteps echoing hollowly, and then raced down a narrow passageway of steps that seemed eerily empty.

He halted at the bottom, hand to his side, trying to catch his breath. His eyes watered, his nose and throat felt raw from inhaling gunpowder-laced smoke.

Last time he had hidden with his mother for two days at the bottom of a dry cistern in the Alban Cantonment. He recalled how thirsty—but no. He could not afford these memories. Not now.

Hearing a whisper of sound behind him, he whirled. It took his tearing eyes a second or two to focus—and his brain another instant to make sense of what he saw. A tiger stood at the end of the alley, its golden-brown gaze pinning him in place. Its upper lip curled up and the long whiskers moved in a soundless snarl.

Reality shuddered then arranged itself in a recognizable pattern.

Aleister spread his hands and spoke Parlance.

The tiger didn't move, didn't twitch a whisker.

Aleister lowered his hands. "Good evening, Lady Hyde."

The tiger seemed to shimmer. Fleetingly, he saw a tall dark woman in men's breeches and overcoat, but it was the tiger that stood before him again. It raised its muzzle and said, "Is it evening, True Blood?"

"Evening for the Alban Empire, I think."

Her laugh was a sandy, raspy thing—her amber gaze never wavered.

"True. And will you try to tell me you're a friend of the revolution, True Blood?"

"The Grimshaws have ever been loyal to the revolution."

In the silence that followed his words he could hear the distant bells of the Cathedral ringing out in alarm and the din of the mob growing closer.

"Grimshaw," she repeated at last. "Yes, that is a name that loves Hidush. Then you are the last of the Mad Grimshaws?"

"The maddest of the lot," Aleister admitted, and she uttered that growling laugh again.

"A sad thing were the Grimshaws to die out the very day of Hidush's rebirth." She reached up and tore a piece of her skin, handing it to Aleister who automatically tied it high around his arm.

"That should buy you safe passage."

Aleister, with childhood memories of mobs once they had the bloodscent, doubted it, though he appreciated the thought.

"Thank you," he said gravely.

"Don't thank me. Hidush no longer loves the Grimshaws. You're an exile now, True Blood. Good fortune in farewell."

She was gone with a whisk of her orange and black tail, and there was nothing in the alley to show she had ever been there.

Aleister turned the opposite way.

Near Empire Park, not far from the Alban cathedral, he

spotted a dappled gray trotting, reins loose, from a blood-drenched beggar. At the sight of Aleister, the "beggar" pulled out a kukri machete and advanced on him.

So much for safe passage. Aleister grabbed the reins of the horse, swinging into the saddle, he wheeled the animal and shot the saffron-clothed man as he charged forward.

Kicking the gray into a canter he cut across the park's flowerbeds and hedges riding for the cathedral. As he watched he saw the great blue flowered stain glass windows of the tower explode.

CHAPTER TWENTY-FIVE

After Aleister's escape the mutineers—for Valentine had determined that was the only way to think of the Natal Guards firing at them—moved up the trail to try and cut the rest of them off from retreat. One of the bearers broke and ran for it and was mowed down before he made it two yards down the lushly overgrown slope.

Akanhe tried to work her way back to a sheltering outcrop of rock, but was quickly pinned down behind a clump of banana trees. The cook, who turned out to be a surprisingly good shot with his old black powder musket, tried to come to her rescue but was prevented by the sudden appearance of a small cyclone that came whipping down the slope above them sending rocks and wood hurtling like shrapnel at everything in its path.

Strange took advantage of this distraction to call for Master Scrivener to join him behind the fallen tree trunk. Scrivener declined to move, apparently under the impression that he was cowering behind something more substantial than a half-dead shrub.

"It's not a request, Master Scribbles," Strange returned, one eye on the cyclone that was bounding along the ground toward his remaining bearers like a hunting hound picking up scent.

Scrivener quivered some reply Strange couldn't make out.

"Shift your arse now or I'll shoot you myself," Strange yelled, losing patience.

Scrivener lumbered across the bare stretch, howling his panic as bullets kicked up the moss behind him. He flopped into the trench with Strange.

"I need you to take care of that for me," Strange said, talking over Scrivener's objections to being subjected to this kind of peril. Strange pointed out the cyclone and Scrivener shut up.

He appeared to rack his brains for a few crucial seconds—apparently out of practice with practical magic—and then he grabbed a handful of mud and threw it at the cyclone. He rattled out a few lines of Parlance. The cyclone promptly split into two cyclones, one of which changed direction veering for Strange and Scrivener's position.

Scrivener gave a groan of dismay and grabbed another fistful of dirt. This time the cyclone broke into five large dust devils. Strange ducked down, burying his head in the crook of his arm and the dust devils flew across them blasting them with dirt and gravel.

He raised his head as Scrivener spat out a mouthful of grass and a few more words of Parlance. The large cyclone dissipated before it reached the bearers.

"Very good," Strange said with what he felt to be remarkable restraint. "Now figure out how to get rid of that bloody sorceress."

This however seemed to be beyond Master Scrivener's ken. In fact, his efforts over the next hour fell so short that the young sorceress was emboldened—or exasperated—into showing herself and challenging Scrivener to a duel of magic—whereupon Akanhe shot her dead.

This brought roars of outrage from her compatriots who had apparently believed her invincible, and a reckless barrage of gunfire. The entire mountain shook and a rockslide came crashing down the mountainside in front of them. Far above the canopy of glistening green, the sun turned a sullen blood-red.

"Did she do that?" Strange asked, turning to the temple witch.

Scrivener's stricken expression silenced him.

"What is it?" he demanded then. "What's happened?"

"He's free," whispered Scrivener. "The Extinguisher of Light is free."

As ominous as these signs were, the mutineers did not flee. Even when one of the large boulders on the mountainside tipped loose and came smashing down through the greenery to land like an anvil in the trail, they did not flee. Strange had to give them credit. They held their position and kept firing, doing their damnedest to keep Strange and his band pinned down.

Strange counted twenty. His own outfit was sorely outnumbered, but he'd stake himself and Akanhe against most comers. And nightfall would turn the advantage their way.

But nightfall was a long time to wait and the extra ammunition was with the horses up on the trail.

And meantime there was Aleister to worry about.

Strange didn't pretend to know how these things worked, but unleashing the violent ghost of mad sorcerer with a quenchless thirst for blood was bound to be a miscalculation on someone's part. Hopefully not his own.

The long afternoon hours passed in stalemate.

Strange fell back on his favorite strategy and let the mutineers expend their ammunition, signaling his own men to hold their fire. Eventually their foes realized their mistake and stopped firing, and for a long time things were very dull.

The rain started again but it was a weird warm shower that sizzled and smoked, drifting out over the jungle like a black pall.

"Can't you think of anything useful to do?" Strange inquired of Scrivener who brooded quietly at the other end of the log.

"I'm continuing to pray for guidance," Scrivener replied.

There was activity on the trail and Strange took out his spyglass. It looked like the mutineers were mounting up. He'd have liked to think they were getting tired and heading home, but he feared it far more likely they were planning to rush what remained of his own scattered and stranded force.

Strange whistled. Akanhe turned a weary face. He signaled warning and she nodded understanding.

"What did you mean 'crown'," he asked Scrivener absently, while counting his remaining cartridges.

When Scrivener didn't respond, Strange glanced at him. "When you pulled the diadem out of my kit bag, you called it a crown. Everyone else has called it a diadem."

"It's the same thing."

"'Crown' has a different connotation, hasn't it?"

"No."

"Who called it a crown? Or did you come up with that on your own?"

In the failing light, Scrivener's expression seemed to indicate he believed Aleister wasn't the only lunatic prowling the jungle. "How should I recall?" he snapped irritably. "I suppose it must have been Brahman Warrick."

It was night—pitch-dark red-tinged night—by the time Aleister reached Gomar.

It had been no easy task to fight his way out of the city, and it was mostly stubbornness that kept him in the saddle now. Witnessing the destruction of the Alban cathedral had left him numb—and without a plan. Not that he'd originally had much of a plan; essentially he'd hoped to drop the problem of the diadem in Ehimay's lap. But even if Ehimay still lived, Aleister had no idea how to find him. Where the cathedral had once stood was now a blasted out crater.

Only one choice seemed to remain—though it wasn't much of a choice—and Aleister had retrieved Balestra and headed for the jungle and the ancient tombs. Back to the beginning.

He found the site deserted, the wooden scaffolds and ladders and framework of the excavation site looking skeletal in the smoky darkness. Rain pattered softly on leaves and somewhere a frog was croaking. The moist heavy air smelled of sulfur.

The chaos of Harappu had not yet reached here, although it was probably only a matter of time—unless the recent stories of the site being haunted acted to protect it now.

The pale blue light of Aleister's globe guided his footsteps down the rickety wooden staircase. No one hailed him as he crossed the rain-dark paving stones of Purya's moonface, his footsteps sharp and brisk in the smothering night. He went inside the temple unchallenged.

Once inside he was struck by the abandoned feeling of the place. Could he be wrong? Was this not the appointed hour? Had he confused a massacre and seismic activity with prophecy? No, the one glimpse he'd had of the moon's twisted and terrifying countenance before it slipped back into the cloud cover had confirmed his worst fears. The time had come—and the fact that he was not ready was immaterial.

The diadem felt like a rope of ice about his heavily pounding heart as Aleister went quickly down the winding, steep stairway, his footsteps echoing loudly—or so it seemed to his overstrung nerves. The wall torches were blackened and burnt out, but the small globe threw sufficient illumination, the carvings of stars and moons gleaming in sharp relief. They seemed to be smiling in the blue light—he could see the sharp teeth of the stars.

Before he reached the bottom of the staircase he could hear the murmur of the fountain. It sounded odd to him…rather like the sound a baby made suckling a breast. As he neared the main level he saw that it was indeed flooded.

He reached out to steady himself as his stomach roiled, The stench of blood made him dizzy and sick. How could anyone pretend that this jet black wet was just water?

He…couldn't. Could not face this on his own. No one could.

He turned and stumbled back up the staircase, the fanged stars and planets blurred and harmless through the tears stinging his eyes.

No one could ask this of him.

Valentine had asked it of him.

He reached the top level and walked blindly out to the courtyard, mopping his wet face with his sleeve. The sulfurous stink of the humid air was fresh and sweet compared to the blood-drenched cavern below. He walked across the broken paving stones—he had no direction, no plan. He could not leave; he knew that—yet he didn't have the courage to proceed.

He walked blindly, impatiently wiping his eyes again, afraid to look up at the sky—afraid to see the ghastly face of the moon. Uncaring, unknowing he walked down a short flight of steps and went through the broken remnants of a cloister to a smaller courtyard. He dropped down, exhausted and despairing, on the dusty green marble bench and buried his head in his hands.

He could not do it. If Valentine were here—or even Ehimay—but they were not. It wasn't that he was afraid of dying—or at least that fear seemed near trivial compared to the dread of the fate that awaited him if he pitted himself against Venavir and failed. And how could he *not* fail?

He had already failed. The fact that he sat here doing nothing while The Extinguisher of Light devoured the world proved that.

There was a tiny scrape of sound in one of the shadowy corners. Heartsick, Aleister raised his head, probing the darkness with dull eyes.

Nothing moved.

But as he sat there, he began to take note of his surroundings. Twisted, dead rose bushes lined the walls of a small and private courtyard that had belonged to the ancient tombs rather than the later temple. No effort had been made to salvage this courtyard making it an ideal place for meditation and prayer—or just a few minutes peace and quiet. How many times had he sought refuge in this small forgotten corner of the excavation site when Ehimay's criticisms and disapproval grew too painful?

Often enough that he had come to take his sanctuary for granted. Aleister blinked at his obtuseness as he registered the long unbroken slab of silver set like a door in the dusty green marble.

A tomb.

An unmarked tomb.

He had always known that this was the resting place of some ancient and long forgotten king, but strangely it had never occurred to him to wonder just *who* this king might have been.

No one very important, was the consensus opinion of the previous witches and scholars in the employ of the Holy Orders. Now Aleister wondered. The courtyard was deliberately set apart, deliberately left unmarked and unadorned. He was reminded suddenly of the lost shrine in the Benhali Mountains. The hair stood up on the back of his neck.

But it could not be Venavir's tomb. Assuming the legends were correct, his bones lay beneath the great warren of catacombs that formed the foundation of the later temple.

So who slept in this lonely grave? Whose was this mournful and secluded corner of Hidush history?

It seemed to Aleister now that there was only one possibility. And as the thought dawned, he realized that another man had once faced what he faced now. That another man had surely risked everything he did—had battled fears as great as his own. Maybe greater—because Dakshi had loved Venavir.

Rising, Aleister went to the tomb and knelt, resting one hand on the smooth silver surface. He whispered a long overdue prayer for the lost sorcerer king Dakshi.

Here was proof of a courage he could barely imagine. Dakshi who had slain his beloved friend and lover to spare the world—and then walled himself within this silver tomb when he felt the madness possessing him.

Was it strange to be comforted by the thought of Dakshi's fate? Yet he was. Aleister prayed and then rose, resolute, walking back through the small courtyard, up the stairs to the deathly still larger court, and entering the temple.

Despite his determination, when he reached the bottom of the staircase and viewed the lake of blood—when he heard the furtive lapping sound—he had to battle his revulsion.

When he stepped into the liquid purling at the bottom of the staircase, he found it only a few inches deep. Not that that was much comfort. He sloshed through the arched doorway into the main hall. Starlight glimmered through the holes in the roof forming glimmering lily pads on the shining surface.

He stared at the wine-dark blood spilling over the edge of the fountain, stared up at the ten foot tall golden statue. The moss that had once obscured its features was gone and the beautiful purity of the golden face and body robbed him of breath.

Yes. This was the hour. He had no doubt now. On that score at least.

He forced himself on.

The tools of his craft were on Caspar's back somewhere in the jungle outside of Harappu, but Aleister had in his possession a tool more powerful than any he had ever commanded—if he could manage to use it without losing himself to it. And what better place than Dakshi's own temple?

Did he dare try?

Did he dare *not* try?

He cupped his hand using the rest of his canteen to anoint his forehead, lips, and the place over his heart, then he took a deep breath, took the diadem out of his tunic and placed it on his head.

If he was wrong…if he failed, it would be to Valentine to stop him, stop the thing that he would become. And Valentine might well be dead even now.

He continued across the hall, listening for any sign of life, but there was nothing. He went down to the next level, stepping carefully for the steps were slick with blood and moss.

When he arrived at the bottom he paused, thinking he heard voices.

There.

A murmur like running water—like trickling blood? Voices or one voice? Aleister wasn't sure but he followed the sound down the short hallway that led to the spell chamber. A lantern burned from within and, as he watched, he saw a shadow flicker across the wall, shading the marble features of the statue of Dakshi.

Seeing the statue bolstered his courage. He'd forgotten about it. Forgotten all about what had first incited the quest for the diadem. He stared at the broken face, the breastplate emblazoned with its fanged cobra, the raised sword—and, in the statue's other hand, a small red glass globe.

The red globe seemed to pulse and glitter in the hazy light like a living heart. It seemed queerly hypnotic…

The murmuring voice from within the tomb broke his abstraction.

"The skull is the altar and the thought is the prayer. My prayer is the will of gods."

Ehimay—Brahman Warrick—stood in the chamber reading aloud from a scroll that Aleister recognized from the First Dynasty collection at the Holy Orders Library.

He felt a surge of relief. Ehimay was safe and unhurt after all! Here was a strong ally if Aleister could only convince him of the approaching danger.

But his relief vanished as swiftly as it rose because the voice that came from Ehimay's throat was much deeper than his own, and the accent was unfamiliar and archaic.

Dread held Aleister motionless. This was the voice of his childhood nightmares. The dulcet tones of Venavir.

"Mine is the kingdom of the roaring tempest, of the setting sun, of the eternity that is everlasting. My day dawns like the talons of a falcon —"

Ehimay broke off and turned to the doorway, saying in perfectly ordinary tones, "There you are. I knew you were near."

He sounded so normal, so like his old himself that Aleister was momentarily at a loss for words. Was he allowing weird accoustics and his own insecurities to drive his actions, to justify decisions he had barely paused to reason out?

"What are you doing here?" he asked uncertainly.

"I've been waiting for you, Ali." There was rueful affection in Ehimay's eyes, the warmth that Aleister had longed to see for so long. "I knew you'd come to me for help once you understood what had happened to you."

"What's happened to me?"

"You've gone mad again." Ehimay said it gently as though it were a perfectly ordinary occurrence and nothing to be worried about. "That's why you ran from the Guild. You knew—we all knew—that you couldn't pass the examination."

"That's not why I left. I went with Strange to find this." Aleister touched fingers to the diadem, reassuring himself that it was still there. That he wasn't imagining this.

Ehimay's gaze sharpened as though only noticing what Aleister wore. "But you musn't wear that. It's a sacred relic. And very dangerous to you. To you above all, Ali."

Aleister was shaking his head, but Ehimay overrode him with that almost tender ruthlessness, "Don't you see? Even now? Using it is what's driven you insane."

"But I'm *not*."

"If you *weren't* mad, you'd see the truth. As it is, you *must* trust me on this. Using the diadem was an act of terrible sacrilege."

As Aleister drew back, Ehimay smiled quickly. An expression Aleister remembered on the faces of his keepers during his previous fits of insanity. Ehimay's voice was soothing. "Don't be afraid. I'm not angry. It's not your fault. You can't help it. You've been ill and confused for so long."

"I have to make you understand," Aleister said. "The madness comes when Venavir posesses me. I've managed to fight him off each time but he's growing stronger."

He stopped at the pity on Ehimay's handsome face.

"I'm not mad! Will you listen to me for once? I came back because I need your help to fight —"

Ehimay said pacifyingly, "Of course, my dearest. But you must *let* me help you." He stretched his hand out. "Here. I'll take care of the crown now."

Aleister stood very still. In all their years of friendship Ehimay had never called him "my dearest." He held his breath as Ehimay reached but his fingers did not touch the diadem although his fingertips were close enough that Aleister's hair crackled with static electricity.

"Take it off, Aleister," he urged. "Before it's too late for you."

"Take it from me," Aleister said through stiff lips.

Ehimay shook his head. "You must relinquish it yourself, my dearest. No one can do that for you."

Aleister shook his head.

"Aleister," Ehimay was patient, chiding. "Can't you see that this is part of your illness? You're forgetting things again. You're forgetting that you went to find the diadem for me. You're forgetting that you came here to give it to me."

Aleister said slowly, with difficulty, "I haven't brought it to you."

The smile faded from Ehimay's face. "Why are you here?"

"To stop you."

After a pause, Ehimay laughed, but the laugh was not his own and as he laughed a great wind seemed to rise and roar through the underground tunnels of the temple. The light of Aleister's globe went out. In the darkness he could feel a thousand pinpricks like shattered glass burning his skin or insects stinging him.

"Avert," he cried, but the wind blew the word away.

"Give me the crown!" howled a deep and booming voice.

Aleister bent his head and felt his way forward, his hand brushing the wall as he felt along the room. His globe was dead and dark in his hand. The wind pushed him hard against the empty stone shelves, but he stumbled along and his outstretched hand brushed cold stiff fingers. The statue. He groped and felt the globe. It was welded fast to the marble palm, but he recited the spell for finding lost articles and yanked with all his strength and it broke off in his hand.

"Stop me then," Ehimay invited from across the room. "But I shouldn't leave it too long if I were you."

"Ehimay, can't you hear me? This isn't you," Aleister cried. "The ghost of Venavir has posessed you as he did me. But you can fight him. More easily than I did. You're stronger than me."

"I *am* stronger than you," Ehimay agreed. "And with Venavir I'm stronger still. Stronger than any creature alive."

"That means nothing to you in your right mind! You're a priest. Your life has been devoted to the Holy Orders."

"It means I have the power to crush this rebellion and restore order to our lands. It means I have the power to destroy all enemies of the crown, and under my protection Alba's empire will achieve the true pinnacle of greatness."

Aleister stopped listening. The truth was too painful to contemplate. He closed his eyes more tightly and focused. As a boy he had read stories about duels between sorcerers, witches, battles between forces of Power, and like all witches had been taught the basics of self-defense, but this…this was completely out of his ken.

From the mists of his boyhood reading he recollected half-forgotten phrases, whispering, "May I unharmed stand under the mantle of the Sun, the Moon, the Stars. May the Lady raise sword and the Lord raise shield. I know your name."

The wind died. The voice that was not Ehimay's inquired curiously, "What is my name?"

"Venavir Unas, King of men when you lived in the mortal realm. Now you are demon and ghost and memory."

"Memory?" Warrick laughed. "I'm no memory. I'm flesh and blood as you are for these last moments. I know your name, too. Aleister Styrling Grimshaw."

Aleister heard his name with a sense of fatality. Not exactly a surprise that he was named and known by the spirit of the tombs at Gomar. Chance did not enter into these things.

But perhaps there was a brighter and better reason than he had previously dared believe in his being chosen to find the diadem. He recollected the many hours he had spent unknowing beside Dakshi's tomb, the hours spent using the diadem in the mountain monastery's Chamber of Reverie, and the the cobra that had saved him from plunging to his death on the cliff. Valentine was right. Somehow it had fallen to him to wear Dakshi's diadem—even if it meant his death.

Not that he wouldn't prefer to live.

There was time for that thought and nothing more. He felt the blow that struck him right through his chest and there was a great rushing in his ears.

And then utter silence.

He became aware that he was lying back against something hard and cold and that he felt very ill—and bruised. As though he had fallen on rocks from a great height. He hurt in more places than he could name; it was hard to draw a full breath.

But he *was* still breathing—which was something of a surprise.

He opened his eyes and found himself surrounded by a horseshoe of men holding torches. He blinked again. The men grouped around him wore white dhotis and white turbans like priests. But the expression on their weathered faces was anything but holy.

"What have you *done*?" he demanded, bewildered. How had they broken the magical conflict between himself and Ehimay—or Venavir as he truly was?

Ehimay stepped into the light of the torches. He was smiling, "But, my dearest, I thought you were such an expert on the needs and desires of priests. These are *my* priests. Those who have remained loyal to Venavir all these long centuries. The Phansigars."

One of the white-clad priests reached forward and plucked the diadem from his head. Aleister snatched for it instinctively and another man grabbed his wrist. It took him a few seconds to place that particular face. Then he remembered. The slim, gentle-eyed pilgrim Strange had left to make his own way through Phansigar territory.

Chapter Twenty-Six

They lost another bearer in the surge, but between Strange, Akanhe, and the remaining trooper, they managed to make it a very costly enterprise and at last the mutineers began to fall back leaving their dead in the wet ground. With a total of twelve dead mutineers the odds were much more even, and with this evening of the ratio of probability, their attackers seemed abruptly to lose taste for the fight.

Which was lucky indeed because Strange was down to nine cartridges. It was time to make their bid for freedom under the cover of the rainy, moonless night. Strange imitated a bulbul and Akanhe answered.

"Can you create a distraction?" Strange asked Scrivener.

Scrivener lifted his head from his hands. "What kind of distraction?"

"I'm not particular at this stage. Something to get them watching the north."

Strange could just make out the movement of bushes as Akanhe skirted along the bottom of the sloping hillside to the clearing where their horses were wandering further and further from the gun battle. There was more motion in the darkness as the cook and remaining bearer followed her at a leery distance.

Scrivener groped around in the grass, squeaking as his hand came in contact with something unpleasant. He took a deep breath, pulled out two sticks and began to rub them briskly together, muttering a spell.

There was a single blue spark and then tongues of flame sprang up in the lush greenery lighting the position of the mutineers. There were cries of dismay as the blue fire caught, racing through the jungle eating brush and leaf despite the dampness.

"Don't burn the entire damned forest down," Strange hissed over his shoulder as he crawled out from beneath the log. "We're in here too."

"You should have thought of that before," Scrivener hissed back.

Far ahead of him, illuminated by the fire, Strange saw Akanhe and the others reach the horses. She began to lay down a covering fire.

Followed by the huffing and puffing witch, Strange crawled salamander style through the smoldering tangle of undergrowth. When they reached the now badly spooked horses, Strange jumped up, catching Caspar's reins and jumping into the saddle.

Return shots rang out but they had a half-hearted quality as the mutineers ran shouting to their own mounts in an effort to escape the increasingly erratic pattern of the magical fire.

Strange kicked Caspar into a gallop, aware of Scrivener wailing his alarm as his own mount crashed through the greenery in pursuit.

After a time Strange knew that their pursuers had either given up or they had managed to lose them. As they cleared the deep jungle and started down the wide road toward Harappu he heard the gasps of his companions and looked up to see the enormous face of the moon appear briefly from behind the red-tinged rafters of cloud.

Shockingly, the moon's normally benign aspect seemed to be a twisted, tortured parody of a human expression.

Akanhe drew even with him. She asked breathlessly, "What by the dust of the four corners is *that*?"

He could only shake his head.

"It has to be a trick of the light." He could hear the effort it took her to keep her voice steady. "The sky is so red. The city can't be—I don't believe —"

He could understand only too well the reluctance to believe and she was too young to remember. Only a few years younger than him, true enough, but young enough to have missed fighting in the Inborn Mutiny. The first Inborn Mutiny.

His throat felt rough as though he hadn't used his voice in a long time. "What don't you believe?"

"It looks like…" She half-swallowed on the words. "It looks as though the world is burning."

"The old world is burning."

Strange turned in the saddle, looking for Scrivener. The temple witch was staring into the red distance. Feeling Strange's gaze, he said bleakly, "He did this. Grimshaw. I tried to warn you."

"How could he do this?"

"Purya's diadem is a powerful —"

Strange cut across, "I don't believe even you still think that diadem belonged to Purya. What do you know about the Extinguisher of Light?"

Scrivener began to shake his head.

"What do you know?" Strange demanded.

Scrivener stopped shaking his head and yelled,"He brings the end of the world!"

"How?" When Scrivener stared as though he did not understand the question, Strange repeated harshly, "How will the end of the world come?"

"*How?* How should I know? What does it matter how it comes? It's coming, that's all. *He's* coming drenched in blood and fire. People have been whispering of it for weeks. And now —"

Strange reined Caspar in. "For your information, Master Scribbles, what you're seeing is not the work of the Extinguisher of Light. Not yet. What you see is the work of man—and woman."

He was speaking to Scrivener's back as the witch continued to ride slowly toward the main gates of the capital. He started to call after him, but then let him go.

To the others he said, "We'll circumvent the city and make for the Great Temple."

Akanhe said, "Strange, my home—my family—is in that city."

"I know. I need you with me."

She stared at him uncomprehending.

He had never been known for eloquence, and he was too tired to try. He said, "If Aleister is still alive, he'll be at the ruins of Gomar fighting to stop what's coming."

"The Extinguisher of Light?" Her laugh wavered. "And I always thought that was just a legend. Something to scare naughty children."

"It seems not. And if Aleister fails…there may be nothing left for any of us but ashes."

"Do you know what you're asking me?" She looked at the remaining men. "Asking all of us? If it's true, what you say, what can we do? That's the province of witches and magicians. We're just soldiers. And our families need us now."

"Listen to me. By now whatever was going to happen in Harappu has happened. The only thing left to us to do is ensure that Aleister succeeds."

"And how do we do that?"

"We ride for Gomar."

She said nothing.

Strange turned Caspar's head and left the cobbled road heading away from the city.

He did not look around, but he knew the moment when she slowly moved to follow. One by the one, the others fell in behind her.

⌒

The rain had stopped again by the time they reached the excavation site. They found the temple bright with light as though it lived again. Every window was lit and radiant. A crowd had gathered in the central courtyard and in the blaze of torchlight Strange could make out Aleister standing within a ring of white-clad priests—apparently giving them a piece of his mind.

Crouched with his little band atop the ledge looking down on the excavation site, Strange, for once, couldn't think of a single word to say.

"Purya's knuckles," Akanhe whispered at last. "Are those *Phansigars*?"

"Yes." It sounded more like a growl than a word as he watched a large man with a scimitar approach the circle surrounding Aleister.

"What is he saying to them?" Akanhe asked uncertainly as Aleister continued to snarl his objections to his captors.

Strange shook his head. They were too far away to make out the words, but Aleister's tone was clear—and unpleasant. No one likes to have his plans for saving the world disrupted.

"He really *is* mad."

Strange said grimly, "I'm beginning to think so." He counted twenty-three members of the murder cult. Just enough to make life interesting—if it hadn't been Aleister's head on the block. On the bright side, Aleister's upbraiding seemed to hold the fanatics surrounding him spellbound.

Another figure crossed the courtyard—slim, elegant, and only too familiar. Brahman Warrick. He snapped out his orders and two of the Phansigars moved forward to grab Aleister's arms and force him to his knees.

Aleister's tone changed and grew desperate. Strange rose, drew his cavalry saber, and said to Akanhe, "You're a better shot with a rifle. You cover us." To the trooper he said, "Swords."

The wide-eyed trooper drew his sword and the bearer drew his machete.

They crept quietly down the stairs, the wood creaking beneath their surreptitious footsteps. Halfway down the staircase, Aleister's voice fell abruptly silent. Strange saw the Phansigar swing his scimitar up, saw Aleister's face in the torchlight, defiant and cold as he faced his death.

And then Akanhe's rifle cracked and the executioner staggered back and fell like a tree beneath the ax. It was pandemonium in the courtyard, white clad figures crying out and pointing at the ledge where Akanhe, backed by the little cook with his black powder musket, laid down a steady and deadly barrage.

A handful of Phansigars ran for the staircase, not yet spotting the men climbing down through the shadows of the overgrown hillside. Strange greeted the first to reach the stairs with a sword through his belly.

The bearer cut the throat of the next man. But the trooper's victim cried out as he died, and they lost the small advantage of surprise. Strange slashed his way through the wall of bodies blocking him from Aleister, white dhotis turning scarlet as he ran his saber through first one man then a second. After that it was too close to maneuver and he had to resort to crude slashing and slicing, using the sword hilt to bash heads and faces and buy himself a little room to move.

The Phansigars were not swordsmen; their weapon of choice was the garrote, but a tall, lean man with the bearing of a warrior separated himself from the milling crowd and launched himself at Strange, using both hands to hack at him with a double-edged straight khanda sword.

Strange blocked him, raising his sword overhead. The blades clanged against each other. The Phansigar swung from the left, then from the right. He fought with skill and a contained fury that Strange had rarely met—and never from a non-professional.

He felt a burning pain down his right shoulder and cursed his own carelessness—fatigue was making him clumsy. But he still knew a trick or two learned in the backwoods of Marikelan and perfected on the Borders of Hidush. He tossed his saber, switching hands from right to left, swinging the weapon around and neatly skewering his astonished opponent.

From above the courtyard the rifle fired with unhurried and fatal accuracy, Akanhe reloading with the speed of long practice. Strange scanned the crowd of white for Aleister's khaki-clad form. He couldn't find him although he spotted Warrick disappearing into the temple doorway. More than that Strange had no time to see, moving to the aid of the remaining trooper. He was too late and the soldier fell beneath the curved, flashing knives. Akanhe fired at the mound of white but then the rifle went silent, and Strange knew that she must be out of ammo.

Ignoring the pain of his injured shoulder, he hewed his way through gleaming steel and fierce faces—and at last found Aleister wrestling for his holster and pistol with a lithe young priest. Aleister managed to wrench the pistol free, aimed—but the pistol jammed.

The priest laughed as the hammer clicked harmlessly.

Strange pulled his own pistol and used his final cartridge— distantly aware that he had wasted his chance for a quick, kind death in order to give Aleister a few more seconds of life.

The young Phansigar crumpled.

Aleister dropped his pistol, raising his hands. He was speaking, and at first Strange thought he was too far away to hear the words, then he realized they were in a foreign language reminding him of the birdlike trills of the green people at the mountain monastery.

The remaining Phansigars dropped their knives and garrotes and began to back away.

Aleister continued in that fierce singsong.

In disbelief, Strange turned to watch the white-clad figures melt in the darkness. He tensed, raising his saber again at the sound of footsteps behind him. Akanhe appeared, her sword stained scarlet.

"Why did they run?"

Strange, hand clapped to his shoulder, nodded at Aleister.

He stood unharmed before them, still speaking in that odd, ancient tongue, but meeting Strange's eyes, he lowered his arms, falling silent. For a time there was only the sound of the guttering torches dying out on the damp paving stones— and the final breaths of one of the white mounds littering the moonfaced courtyard.

"I thought you must be dead." Aleister sounded weary past words. "I thought —"

"I'm not that easy to kill."

"No. Fortunately." He started to smile, but it faded. "Where's Brahman Warrick?"

"He went into the temple."

Aleister's face changed—looked stricken—and then he was gone, racing to the brightly blazing temple entrance and vanishing inside.

Strange followed only vaguely aware that Akanhe was on his heels. Ahead he could hear the reckless echo of Aleister's racing footsteps.

"What is that *smell*?" she muttered as they wound their way down the staircase.

Death, Strange thought. Death was the smell wafting down from the courtyard. Gunsmoke and blood and death.

They reached the bottom of the staircase and he saw that the floor of the main hall was flooded with water black as ink. Aleister knelt at the edge of the fountain fishing his hand in the foul water. He turned at the splash of their footsteps and said despairingly, "Help me!"

Strange reached him in two strides. "What is it?"

"The diadem is lost."

"What makes you think it's in the fountain?"

"Because I threw it in there! After the Phansigars captured me, I managed to break free and snatch the diadem. I threw it in the fountain to hide it before they chased me out to the courtyard."

"Where did you —?"

"I don't know!" Aleister grabbed him with a fierceness that verged on desperation. "We have to find it. Val —"

"All right. Keep your head." Strange knelt beside him, thrusting his arm in the gelatinous liquid. "We'll find it."

"We have to hurry. He's transfiguring himself. It may already be too late."

"*Strange!*"

A note in Akanhe's voice caught Strange's attention. He raised his head and saw that she was pointing at the tall golden statue in the center of the fountain. Dark liquid poured from its mouth and eyes.

Her voice shook as she said, "The fountain is pumping blood."

⮌

"Of course it's too late," Ehimay said. "It was too late twenty years ago."

He stood at the far end of the hall still wearing the robes and earrings of his station, but he was changed. His dark hair was lighter, red-bronze—his eyes too looked red. In the bright light that flooded the hall Aleister could see that his skin had a green tint. But his smile was his old smile, kind and teasing.

He put out his hand. "The diadem belongs to me, Major Strange."

Aleister looked down and saw that Strange had indeed, with his usual efficiency, retrieved the diadem. He was holding it out to him. It dripped in soft plops.

"Take it, Aleister," Strange said.

"What is this? You took my money in good faith, Major," Ehimay objected. He sounded a little hurt. "You gave me your word. Now complete the deal and you have *my* word I'll leave you here unharmed. Both of you."

"No offense, Holiness, but I didn't trust you even before your eyes turned red." Under his breath, Strange said, "Take the damned thing, Aleister."

Aleister made one last plea. "Ehimay…"

"Yes, Ehimay. *You* trusted me once, my dearest. Trust me again. For the sake of Alban Hidush. For the sake of the country we both love." He stepped toward Aleister and Strange moved to intercept. Ehimay—Venavir—raised a hand, and Strange froze in place.

Aleister took the diadem dangling from Strange's motionless hand.

Venavir said gently, "You're not thinking very clearly, are you? Give me the diadem and I'll let your soldier laddie live. It's not a bad trade. The diadem did you no good before."

Aleister ignored him. He reached in his pocket and pulled the red stone he had taken from the statue of Dakshi. He pushed it into the open setting in the diadem. It snapped into place and all the stones seemed to brighten as though lit from within.

"Oh, Ali," Ehimay's voice said regretfully. "Why must you make everything so difficult for yourself?"

Aleister placed the diadem on his head. The metal felt unexpectedly warm and seemed to tingle against his skin in a way it had never done before. He said—and hoped it was true, "I cast you out once. I can defeat you again."

"But there's nothing to cast out," Veniver said in that pitying way. "You're a mad, weak thing, Aleister, and I chose another as host. One much stronger and surer than you, one who welcomed the gifts I bring."

"He didn't bloody welcome you! You took him over just as you did me."

Venavir laughed. "Of course he did. Only a madman would refuse infinite power and eternal life. There was no struggle. He told you himself. Ehimay embraced what I offered—he embraces it yet."

Aleister closed his eyes, calling upon his anger, feeling the buzz of it building inside him like the hiss of a cobra, crackling through his nerves, his blood, his bones, feeling the tingling heat and energy of it. He focused, pointed at Venavir, and a lightning bolt struck the carved wall behind him, sending bits of marble stars flying.

"Very good!" Venavir laughed. "You just learned that, didn't you? Your aim is a little off though. Is it the form I wear that distracts you?" He raised his own arm and a crimson wave rose from the fountain as tall as the golden statue itself. It curled like an open jaw and lunged for Aleister.

"Avert," he gasped.

The wave hit him, knocking him to the wet floor. It was a shock, but he was not badly hurt. Surprisingly, the childhood charm had worked. Gore dripped from every part of him, invading his nostrils. He blew out, wiped away the moisture careful not to swallow any of the sanguine liquid.

He scrambled up again, muttering incantations, concentrating on the puff of breath leaving his lips. The small warm gust blued as it wafted, then began to spin, picking up speed, rolling faster and faster, forming itself into a cyclone. Aleister hurled it at Venavir who took a hasty step back as the blue funnel enclosed him. He made a chopping motion and the cyclone broke apart.

"*Avert!*" mimicked Venavir. "This is child's play. I could have killed you a dozen times by now if that's what I wished."

"Then do it."

Venavir's ruby eyes narrowed. "It's not my patience for fools for which I'm remembered. Don't try me too far, Aleister."

But that was exactly what Aleister wished to do. Push and prod until he irritated Venavir into some careless mistake. It was already obvious too him he didn't have the experience or skill to fight Venavir on his own terms; that kind of magic was a lost art. No one used Power like that anymore.

He began another spell and Venavir said, "Enough. Give me the diadem or Strange dies." He added in a kind of silky purr, "In fact, perhaps it's time for a salutary lesson —"

He held out his palm and a ball of blue fire appeared. He hurled it at Strange who continued spellbound and stone still. Aleister leaped between them, and a ball of fire hit him squarely. It was like being stabbed through the chest with a red-hot poker. He felt to his knees, feeling the blistering heat from heart to guts.

"Avert," he gasped out, belatedly. Though the pain had been terrifying, it died swiftly away. Crouched on his hands and knees, gasping for breath, he could hear Ehimay—Venavir—reasoning with him.

"Why are you fighting me when I'm offering you everything you've ever longed for? Is this the judgment of a sound mind? You've trusted Ehimay all your life; why will you not trust that his is the right decision now?"

He closed his mind to it. He was now certain that if Venavir could simply kill him, he'd have done it. He was not sure if it was the diadem preserving his life or his own instinctive skill, but either way it was clear that he couldn't keep this up for much longer. He shuddered with the memory of that last blow.

Focusing inwardly, he called to the spirit that had crafted the diadem.

"Dakshi, warrior and sorcerer, I call upon thee…"

Another blow struck him from the side and he felt that his bones were peeling beneath that searing pain. He whimpered, pain robbing him of the power of speech, but in his mind he continued to appeal for aid, and as he did he felt something stir in the air around him—and then wash through him.

Or was that shimmering brush a hallucination born of the pain of his burned chest and belly—the feverish delusion of a dazed mind? There was a breathless tension coiling through him, tingling, twinkling, spangling against the inner walls of his body and mind. Starfire pouring through him. The world receded, darkened, and he panicked at the recognition that he was slipping back into gibbering madness, his reason tearing loose once more beneath Venavir's onslaught.

Instinctively he fought for control. He could not let this happen. Not until he had accomplished what he had set out to do.

The glitter inside him crackled and stung like flying ice, like shattered glass. It was hard to catch his breath. It hurt. It had never hurt before.

All at once with ice cold clarity Aleister recognized his mistake. Understood that this madness was not the old madness; that he had called this upon himself. He had sought a weapon, but the weapon was himself. The answer to his prayer was the hand that would wield the weapon he had become.

Painfully, deliberately, he surrendered himself to the force of the other's will.

His last thought was that losing himself was—in the end—a small price to pay for saving the land of his birth and the life of the one he loved best. Then he felt the wellspring of steely sorrow rise within him, felt himself drowning in a swell of cold resolve. He let go...

When he saw Aleister fall in flames, Strange determined that he would kill this fucking demon bastard Venavir if it was the last thing he did. But despite an effort that should have moved a mountain, he could not budge. Could not lift a hand or foot, could not do more than watch in rage as Aleister fell.

He willed him to rise, and at last Aleister managed to get to his knees, but then he had no strength to go on. The night air was sickening with the scent of burned flesh and blood.

He could see Aleister's mouth moving but he could not hear the words, could not tell if Aleister was crying for help or reciting an incantation. Strange tried again to move, focused all his will, and could have wept himself when he failed to crook even a finger.

But then, to his astonishment, Aleister rose in a quick, lithe movement, took two steps toward the former Brahman Warrick, and rattled out a string of gibberish that sounded like the language of birds.

Venavir cried out, and there was no mistaking the shock in his face or voice. He looked like he had seen a ghost.

But he recovered quickly, answering in that same whistling tongue—it sounded to Strange like he was pleading.

Out of the corner of his eye, Strange saw a geyser of pure water burst from the head of the golden statue in the fountain. The bloody tide at his feet began a swift retreat as though sucked right through the cracks in the marble floor.

Venavir's voice grew shrill.

A bolt of blue lightning flew from Aleister's fingertips—and this time it did not miss its mark. It speared through the human form of Brahman Warrick as clean as any sword thrust. Warrick screamed and fell forward.

Strange staggered forward, suddenly freed from the invisible vise that had held him prisoner. He caught his shins against the rim of the fountain, recovered, hearing Akanhe exclaim as she too was freed; his attention was all for Aleister as, breath sobbing, Aleister swayed and then dropped to his knees.

The diadem fell from his head and chimed on the marble floor like the final toll of a bell. Slowly, slowly Aleister slid forward and slumped onto his side.

He lay there, sides rising and falling, panting in exhausted wheezes.

"Is it over?" Akanhe asked muffledly. "Was that it?"

"Grimshaw? Aleister?" Strange knelt, dragging him into his arms, mindful of his injuries. Aleister smelled queerly scorched though the charnel house stench of burned flesh was gone from the temple. The rain dripping through the holes in the roof no longer smelled like sulfur.

There was movement across the courtyard and Strange looked up in time to see Brahman Warrick—restored to his own self—slowly picking himself up. He was muttering to himself.

Aleister's eyelids fluttered. He opened his eyes. They looked black and enormous as they had when he used the white spice. He said in a faraway, faint voice, "Val?"

"I'm right here," Strange said roughly over the tightness in his throat. The burns had faded from Aleister's body; there were no marks on him at all, but he seemed so hurt and tenuous. Had he been mortally injured in the duel of Power? Strange had no notion beyond the fact that the newly saved world would be an empty place for him without Aleister.

Behind them Warrick's voice rose in a chant, rose in desperation. Aleister stiffened in Strange's arms. His hand clutched Strange's tunic.

Strange lowered his head to hear Aleister whisper frantically, "He's calling Venavir back! Don't let him. Don't let him complete the summoning..."

Strange's head jerked up and he stared at Warrick who had raised his hands above his head in supplication and was crying out to the heavens—or possibly the hells.

"Strange?" Akanhe called uneasily.

Very carefully Strange lowered Aleister to the eerily shining floor, and rose, drawing his sword. It slid from the scabbard with a hiss.

He was across the hall in a couple of steps. As he reached Warrick, the priest looked up and snarled the final words of his spell. His eyes took on the red-bronze glow. Strange brought his saber up and then down in a single clean, swift stroke.

Warrick's head tipped and dropped. It fell to the floor in a wet slop. An instant later the weaving, headless body followed.

Aleister moaned and the eyes in the depacitated head seemed to roll in his direction. The red glow went from the fixed gaze.

Breathing hard, Strange stared down at the maimed body. When he was sure it wasn't going to rise again, he returned to Aleister and Akanhe beside the fountain. Aleister was trying to sit up. Strange put a supporting arm around his shoulders, and Aleister leaned into him.

"Are you alright?"

Aleister nodded. "I am now."

Over his bent head, Strange's gaze met Akanhe's. She said grimly, "Something tells me the Holy Orders are not going to pay us for our time and trouble."

⌒

It was nearly daylight when they finished burying Brahman Warrick beneath a cairn of stones in the jungle overlooking the excavation site of the Great Temple.

"Hopefully, assuming anyone finds him, they'll put it down to the mutiny," Akanhe said, wiping her sweaty forehead.

Strange answered something noncommittal. He watched Aleister all the time. Aleister looked ill and his voice dragged with weariness as he delivered the invocation for the dead, but he seemed sane and mostly unhurt.

He knelt and drew Suri's sigil at the foot of the grave and whispered the incantation to prevent ghosts from pursuing the living.

"You stand behind the gate of time. Your heart is still, your hand is stayed, your tongue is mute. All those that you hate are forgotten. All those you love. You cannot cross the threshold. You cannot find your way back. That which was your life is but a dream now. You are banished from the realm of the living."

The sigil flared red and died almost instantly. Aleister wiped his eyes and then reached his hand to Strange, who pulled him to his feet.

Akanhe said, "I'm going back to the city to find my family now. What will you two do?"

Strange looked at Aleister—and found Aleister waiting for his answer. "We haven't decided," he said, and saw the imperceptible relaxing of Aleister's tall figure.

"The war drums have stopped," Akanhe said. "Maybe it's over."

And if it was over? If the revolution had succeeded there was no place in Harappu—maybe in Hidush—for Aleister or Strange. And if the revolution had failed? Either way Strange still wasn't convinced there was a place for him or Aleister. Full circle had somehow left them in an entirely different place.

Aleister's mouth parted and he exclaimed, "Do you hear that?"

Both Strange and Akanhe stared at him, and he said, "The monkeys. Can't you hear them?"

Sure enough the towering trees overhead seemed alive with the chatter and screeching of monkeys.

"They're back," Strange said and Aleister smiled for the first time since Ehimay had died.

Not long after that, Akanhe left them with promises to find Jishu and Priti for Aleister. Then Aleister led Strange back to the private walled court which housed Dakshi's tomb.

They stood for a time in silence gazing at the silver slab in the marble. Strange put his arm around Aleister, and Aleister leaned back against him.

"Are you all right?" Strange asked gruffly.

Aleister smiled faintly. "Yes. You can stop asking. I'm as sane as you are. Of course, that might not be saying much."

"The problem, Master Sticks and Stones," Strange said, "is this is the first time my happiness has depended on someone else's welfare. It's an uneasy feeling."

"You get used to it."

"I doubt it, though a decade or two of you underfoot will probably help."

Aleister sniffed in a ghostly echo of himself. "I suppose you realize the world's in utter chaos?"

"Well, whose fault is that? Anyway, when is it not? Besides, it's just our corner of it. There are other corners of the world we might like just as well."

"Possibly."

"Settled then, is it? Going to throw your lot in with me?" He broke off at the scrape of footsteps outside the court, and drew his pistol.

A moment later the tiny, bent figure of the mountain monastery abbess—The Crux—appeared at the top of the stone stairway. She made her way—clinging to Cholai's arm—down to the stairs to them.

Strange hoped he didn't look quite as confounded as Aleister, but he wouldn't have liked to wager on it.

"Greetings, Grandmother," Aleister said politely, recovering himself. "You're a long way from home."

The yellow eyes stared out from behind the wooden mask. The Crux said to Strange, "Thou did not take my advice, Major Strange."

"No. Lucky thing, eh?"

"Perhaps." She turned to Aleister. "Thou did well, child. Better than any could have foretold."

Out of the corner of his mouth, Strange said, "I think that's an apology for asking me to slay you."

Aleister reached into his tunic and pulled out the diadem. "You've saved us a trip, Grandmother."

Strange could feel the old woman's surprise although the dark, wooden features gave nothing away. "Thou are returning it to us of thy own free will?"

"As you see."

"The gods work in strange ways," she pronounced at last.

Aleister made that little sound that was neither laugh nor cough. His gaze slid to Strange's.

"Indeed they do."

She took the diadem, turning it over and over in her gnarled hands.

"Thou art right. This will be better in our safe keeping—till the next time it is needed."

That shut them up effectively. She gave a final curt nod, leaning on Cholai's arm as she turned toward the stairs. She threw back, "Good fortune in farewell, Major Strange."

Cholai gave Strange a long, level, look which Strange met with a grin.

When the shuffling sound of their footsteps departed, Aleister knelt and said a final prayer over Dakshi's tomb. This time there was no incantation to prevent the return of ghosts.

When Aleister rose again, he said without looking at Strange, "Since you mention it, I've always wondered what lies on the other side of those White Mountains."

Strange said casually, "We could take a look. We've seen the lost city and the flying monkeys. Might as well try for the armies of giants. That what you want?"

"Part of it." He gave Strange the look that never failed to stop his breath in his chest. No point trying to fight that kind of bewitchment, was there?

Aleister added, "There's the chance that we might be headed into worse trouble than we've left."

"We might at that." He was smiling as he pulled Aleister into his arms. He wasn't worried. Strange was a man who liked to gamble.

ACKNOWLEDGMENTS

The author would like to sincerely thank both Dawn and Nikki Kimberling without whose faith and encouragement—and wild imagination— this book would never have been written. Thank you for your friendship. And the raspberry chocolate jam.

Thanks also to Lisa B. who had to listen to more whining and second-guessing than should be required of any pal.

Special thanks to Kevin. For too many reasons to count.

Also, sincere thanks to Alex Beecroft for an early— and much appreciated—read-through of the manuscript.

Finally, the author wishes to acknowledge the following sources of inspiration for this work of fiction: Maud Diver, G.A. Henty, Ruyard Kipling, Talbot Mundy, Elswyth Thane, Louis Tracy, and Percival Christopher Wren.

Sources

Arms & Armour, Fredrick Wilkinson, The Military Book Club, 1978

The Encyclopedia of Witches & Witchcraft, Rosemary Ellen Guiley, Checkmark Books, 1999

The Last Home of Mystery, Alexander Powell, Garden City Publishing Company, 1929

Murray's Handbook for Madras, John Murray, 1879

The Romance of the Indian Frontiers, LT.-GEN. Sir George MacMunn, Jonathan Cape, 1931

Vignettes From the Indian Wars, LT.-GEN. Sir George MacMunn, 1932

Weapons of the British Soldier, Colonel H.C.B. Rogers, OBE, Seely, Service & Co., Ltd. 1960

Josh Lanyon is the author of numerous short stories, novellas, and novels including the Adrien English mystery series.

Novels
Fatal Shadows
A Dangerous Thing
The Hell You Say
Death of a Pirate King
The Ghost Wore Yellow Socks
Somebody Killed His Editor

Mexican Heat (with Laura Baumbach)

Novellas
The Dark Horse
Cards on the Table
Dangerous Ground
Don't Look Back
Ghost of a Chance
I Spy Something Bloody
Lovers and Other Strangers
Out of the Blue
Old Poison
Snowball in Hell
The White Knight

Short Stories
A Limited Engagement
In a Dark Wood
In Sunshine and In Shadow
Until We Meet Once More

Non-Fiction
Man, Oh Man: Writing M/M Fiction for Kinks & Ca$h

Other Titles Avalable from Blind Eye Books

The Archers Heart by Astrid Amara
In the ancient kingdom of Marhavad, noblemen dominate the lower castes, weilding mystic weapons. But now, as whispers of revolution are heard in even the royal palace, three men of passion, ambition and power must choose where their allegiances lie and what they will sacrifice in their hearts and on the battlefield.
$16.95 ISBN 978-0-9789861-3-1

Turnskin by Nicole Kimberling
Suspected of murder, Tom Fletcher seeks refuge in the Turnskin Theatre, where his shape-changing skills can be put to good use on and off the stage. Here, at last, he has the chance to fufill his dreams of stardom and romance—just so long as he can stay one step ahead of the cops, criminals and theater critics.
$14.95 ISBN 978-0-9789861-2-4

Wicked Gentlemen by Ginn Hale
When faced with a series of grisly murders, Captain William Harper turns to Belimai Sykes, a prodigal descended from ancient demons, to aid in his investigations of the steaming slums of Hells Below.
$12.95 ISBN 978-0-9789861-1-7

Tangle edited by Nicole Kimberling
Eleven stories, featuring extraordinary heroes, fill this anthology with adventure, humor and passion.
$15.95 ISBN 978-09789861-0-0

Tangle Girls edited by Nicole Kimberling
Six stories, featuring astounding heroines, fill this anthology with action, adventure and wonder.
$12.95 ISBN 978-0-9789861-4-8

Blind Eye Books
Look for them, because they can't see you.

blindeyebooks.com